Liam's Story

A Novel

by

Tommy Coletti

Published in the United States by HW Publishing, a subsidiary of House of Walker Publishing, LLC, New Jersey.
Library of Congress Control Number: 2012942102
Copyright © 2012 by Tommy Coletti
Liam's Story by Tommy Coletti
Cover design by: Tommy Coletti
ISBN: 978-0-9834762-3-8

Dedication

To my soon to be 90 year young Mother

Dorothy Strong Coletti.

With thanks for being the source for most of the

Stories incorporated into this novel.

To my wife, Donna and close friend, T. Fred Thompson

Thanks for listening, editing and suggesting.

To Michelle Nelson of HWP,

Your contributions were limitless

Introduction

Centenarian Liam Corcoran tells his family story. He is the son of an Irish immigrant who travels with his mother and sister from Quincy, Massachusetts to Norwich, Connecticut after the death of his father in 1914. His mother arranges for them to board with a large Italian family while she searches for employment. His life changes quickly only days after arriving at the boarding house when his mother and sister die from pneumonia. He becomes a fourteen year old orphan. The kindness and generosity of the man, woman and their family at the boarding house, changes his life forever when they welcome him in as a member. With much gratitude, he accepts their love and guidance. He expresses his love for them in this story.

During his journey through life, he serves in two world wars, celebrates marriage and the births of his children, many nieces and nephews and mourns their deaths one by one as he outlives them and the friends he held close.

Liam tells his story to his great-granddaughter and her aspiring author boyfriend from the bed of his convalescent home as he slowly recovers from a stroke that has afflicted his body, but not his mind. The story telling is therapeutic. He finishes the telling after leaving the hospital and living in an assisted living center.

His religious beliefs, values, patriotism and crass personality exposes the reader to Liam's mind. This is Liam's Story.

Tommy Coletti
June 2012

Contents

Chapter One   Remembering

Chapter Two   Coming of Age

Chapter Three   The Runner

Chapter Four   Going Home

Chapter Five   Prohibition

Chapter Six   Prosperity

Chapter Seven   The Good Life

Chapter Eight   The Depression Begins

Chapter Nine   Hard Times

Chapter Ten -   Happier Days

Chapter Eleven   The Gathering Storm

Chapter Twelve 6th Naval Construction
Battalion

Chapter Thirteen   Seven Letters

Chapter Fourteen   Better Days

Chapter Fifteen   The Quick Years

Chapter Sixteen   Decades of Good- Byes

Chapter Seventeen   Jack and Jill Party

Chapter Eighteen   The Wedding

Epilogue

The Family Tree

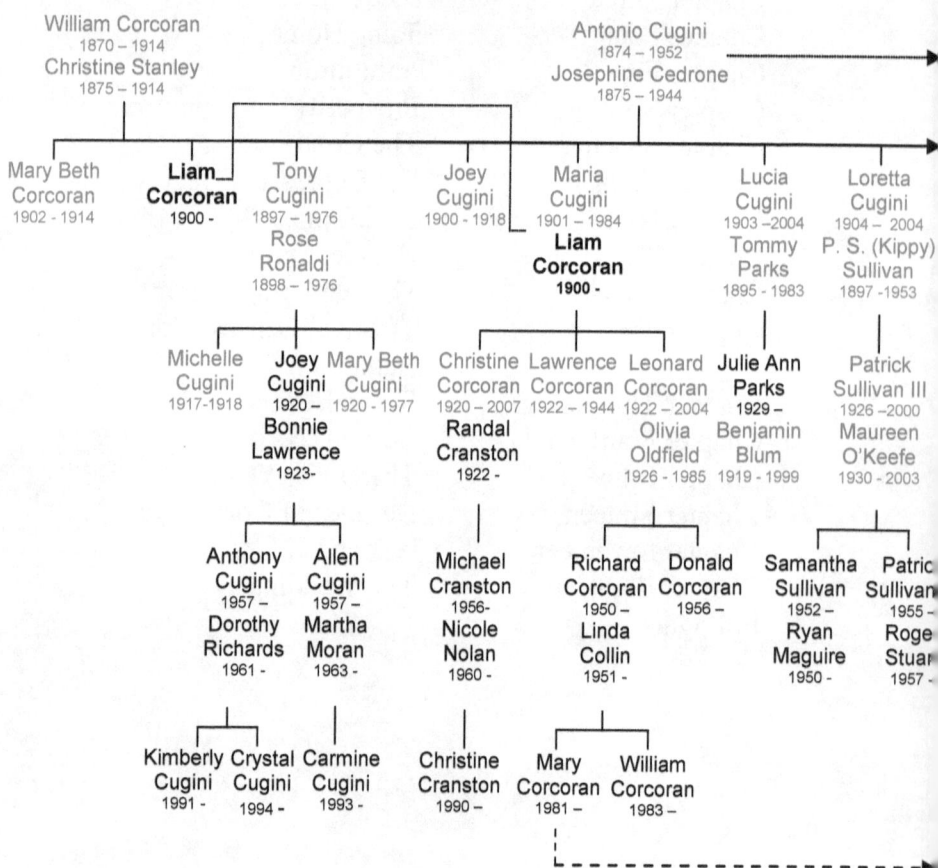

The Family Tree

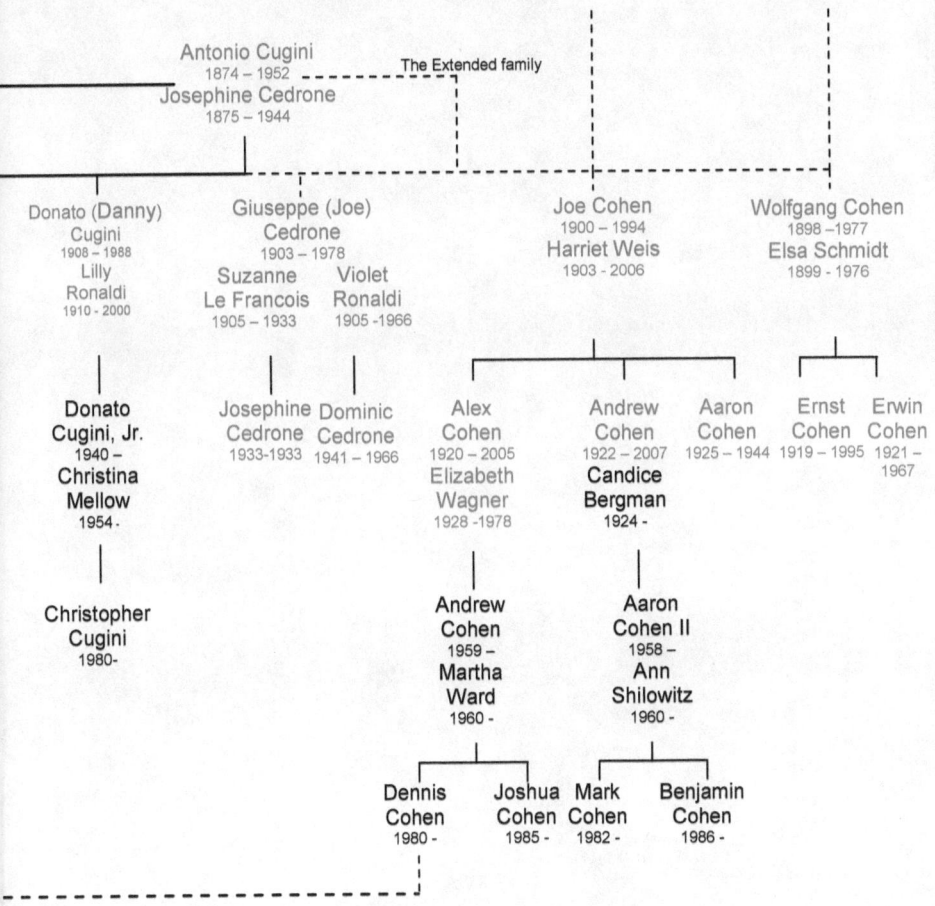

Antonio Cugini
1874 – 1952
Josephine Cedrone
1875 – 1944

The Extended family

Donato (Danny)
Cugini
1908 – 1988
Lilly
Ronaldi
1910 - 2000

Giuseppe (Joe)
Cedrone
1903 – 1978
Suzanne
Le Francois
1905 – 1933
Violet
Ronaldi
1905 -1966

Joe Cohen
1900 – 1994
Harriet Weis
1903 - 2006

Wolfgang Cohen
1898 –1977
Elsa Schmidt
1899 - 1976

Donato
Cugini, Jr.
1940 –
Christina
Mellow
1954 -

Josephine
Cedrone
1933-1933

Dominic
Cedrone
1941 – 1966

Alex
Cohen
1920 – 2005
Elizabeth
Wagner
1928 -1978

Andrew
Cohen
1922 – 2007
Candice
Bergman
1924 -

Aaron
Cohen
1925 – 1944

Ernst
Cohen
1919 – 1995

Erwin
Cohen
1921 –
1967

Christopher
Cugini
1980-

Andrew
Cohen
1959 –
Martha
Ward
1960 -

Aaron
Cohen II
1958 –
Ann
Shilowitz
1960 -

Dennis
Cohen
1980 -

Joshua
Cohen
1985 -

Mark
Cohen
1982 -

Benjamin
Cohen
1986 -

Chapter One – Remembering

The Convalescent Home

The light was very bright in the room as I opened my eyes. The breathing machine's swooshing noise continued its steady rhythm with the other monitoring devices that measured my blood pressure and heart beats. Being one hundred and six years old and going in and out of consciousness, didn't increase my odds of recovering from what happened to me. I didn't know the amount of time that had passed since remembering the pain in my head and then fainting. It was difficult to open my eyes, but I managed to get them open and looked around. The bright lights forced me to close them almost immediately because of the burning. I decided to only open them if someone spoke to me. I could hear the doctors whispering to my family. Much of the quick conversations consisted mostly of, "…it won't be much longer until he passes away."
Great, I thought. *They have a lot of faith in me.*

My great granddaughter, Mary, sat by the side of my bed reading and periodically talking with the nurses and attendants that came into the room to monitor the machines that were keeping me alive. When they had finished their tasks, I could see Mary in my peripheral vision. When she saw my eyes open, she hoped for some sign to indicate that I knew she was there. She had faith in me, but seeing no changes, she would just resume-reading.

The physician that checked me once a day continued to reinforce his original diagnosis that the stroke had been massive and that I had very little time left.
Every time I heard that, I would think, *what did he know? I*

just need to get out of this frozen state. I heard him again repeat his suggestion that they should consider removing all the artificial life support and let me go naturally. I was a little pissed at this guy. *The son of a bitch wants to pull the plug!* It was pleasing to know that my family chose to give me, their patriarch, more time to assure themselves that there was still some hope of communicating with me. I just had to concentrate and free myself from this paralyzed state I was in. My sweet Mary had convinced most of the family that I was semi-conscious and that when she talked to me, I seemed to respond by opening my eyes. She continually tried to convince them that it was a sure sign. She hoped that my eyes would be a way I could communicate. She saw my eyes open again and decided to talk to me.

"Liam. Liam Corcoran. Can you tell me the story of when you came here as a young boy with your mother and sister? Tell me the story again, please."
My eyes closed again. I was thinking,
Liam, keep your damned eyes open and communicate with her. She's your only chance.
"Open your eyes and try to talk Liam. I do love that story. Please try great-granddad."
I was able to force my eyes open for a few minutes which encouraged her. I quickly tired and closed them. The last thing I heard was "please." I had already begun to tell her, in my mind, my story, one more time, but she didn't know it.

The Story

The big house stood at the top of the hill for as long as anyone could remember. It was built by one of the founding city members who had long been deceased since the mid-eighteen hundreds. The present owners had bought it with all the money they saved in the first ten years they lived and worked in this country. They managed to save the minimum down payment for the one hundred year old home that the local Dime Bank of Norwich required for a thirty year mortgage. Antonio and Josephine Cugini had lived in the house for twelve years when I first arrived there with my mother and sister just after St. Patrick's Day in 1914.

It was a cold March day when we departed the train that had taken us from Quincy, Massachusetts. My sister asked my mother if the building in front of us was our new home. I remembered my mother smiling and explaining that the large building looked like a bank to her.
"We'll just follow the instructions Mr. Cugini gave us in his letter to get to his house," she said.

As we climbed a slight hill from the train station, a horse drawn trolley car had just arrived. My sister asked if we could take the trolley to our new home.
"No Mary Beth, we will walk. I'm sure it isn't very far," my mother explained.
Mary Beth complained that her suitcase was too heavy. I remember mother took it away from her. As we started up a street that I would later know as Franklin, the wind picked up and an occasional snowflake could be seen blowing around. It was getting late in the afternoon as the gray sky hindered any sun from shining through and began to darken the day. We walked about a mile through the bone chilling wind and frozen

3

streets of Norwich until we reached Boswell Avenue. The street was mostly hill and steep at the beginning. The three of us trudged on, counting the house numbers as we climbed. What we eventually found was a majestic house with white clapboards and a large porch.

My mother, holding the letter she received from our new landlord several weeks earlier, knocked on the door. She glanced at it one more time reassuring herself it stated that he had agreed to boarder us. The letter also stated that he agreed to take three months board in advance to stay there until she could find work and a place of her own.

It had been three months since my father, William Corcoran, was killed working for the railroad in the Quincy rail yard. The little money they had saved while he worked eighteen hours a day for the railroad, covered the first three months of rent we needed. Money given to us from the Knights of Columbus aided my mother in her time of need and allowed us train fare to Norwich. Some of the remaining money was used for food while we waited for Mr. Cugini's letter accepting us as boarders in his home. I remembered that we arrived there with less than ten dollars and three suitcases in our possession. The door opened.

The middle aged man smiled and invited us in as he saw the three of us standing on the porch shivering. In broken English, he invited us into the reception room. It was a welcome sound as we stood there in front of him and out of the cold March air. I still can remember the vaulted ceiling in the reception room of an era that passed. The dark oak doors and elaborate wood trim against the white plaster walls didn't add any warmth to it as we stood waiting for Mr. Cugini to show us to our room. He looked over my sister and me and shook his head at what he apparently saw. He asked my mother,

4

"When is last time you eat?"

"We've been traveling since the early morning. We had some bread on the train."

"Not enough," was all he said.

He turned and motioned for us to follow him as he opened up one of the several doors and lead us out of the reception room.

The smell of food cooking immediately filled our nostrils and excited our stomachs as we followed the gentleman into the kitchen. The room had served the original owners and staff for many years of entertaining and now served to support the many boarders the Cugini's had in the large old home. Mrs. Cugini looked up from the large coal burning stove and smiled as he instructed her, in Italian, that she was to feed their new boarders before we were shown to our room. It would be years before I could translate what the man said, but I understood when she motioned for us to sit at the large oak kitchen table. We sat as my mother made one last prideful attempt to explain that her children were fine and didn't need to be fed. She tried to explain that we could wait until the six o'clock sitting as it had been explained in the letter that she had almost memorized. The gently smiling man never responded to her one sided conversation until all three of us were sitting at the kitchen table. His soft blue eyes glistened as he looked at my sister and me shaking and probably looking pathetic as we sat in anticipation of receiving food.

"Mama, you feed them, yes, they cold" he said.

She smiled at me as she placed three bowls in front of us. She gently pinched my sister's pink cheek and looked at him and said, "Bella, bella."

The elderly man just smiled and nodded as he looked at my twelve year old sister. Within moments, our bowls were filled with hot chicken soup that the woman had been brewing on the stove to be part of the evening meal. Each one of us was given a warm piece of fresh bread to accompany it. The couple smiled and my mother finally quieted as my sister and I quickly began to devour the soup and bread. She soon followed and began to eat to the enjoyment of the hosts. As we ate our meal, the warmth of the kitchen stove thawed us until I was forced to remove my overcoat. My sister and mother soon followed suit.

She came into the kitchen unaware that three new boarders had been taken in and were being fed there. Her bright blue eyes, shiny dark brown hair and sparkling teeth were the first things I remembered seeing. In years to come, other attributes would accompany those I first saw at fourteen. I later found out that she was the third child of Antonio and Josephine Cugini. She looked to be about my age. She stopped in her tracks when she saw us. She was the prettiest thing I had ever seen. She never looked at me as she noticed my sister and mother. Her father and mother only glanced at Maria, but never made any attempt to introduce her to the new boarders. She said something in Italian in which her mother responded and pointed at my mother.

"My mother has asked me to show you to your room when you have finished your meal," she said. "I will return in a few minutes."

As she left the kitchen, she smiled again at my sister, but ignored me completely.

When we all had finished, Mr. Cugini asked, "You full? You want more?"

My immediate reaction was to ask for a second helping, but I looked at my mother. Her cold Irish green eyes cut through me like a knife indicating that it was time to leave. The elderly man noticed my mother's stern look, but allowed some of her pride to stay intact. He yelled for Maria who appeared and motioned for us to follow her.

Maria did not say anything until we climbed the second set of stairs leading to the third floor. The temperature in the house became warmer as we ascended the several flights of stairs carrying our suitcases. We came to the end of the hall where our new, temporary home was to be. Maria unlocked the door, opened it, and handed my mother several keys.

"I hope you will like it here. My name is Maria"

"I'm Mary Beth, but you can call me Mary," my sister replied. "I'm twelve."

Maria smiled and said, "I'm going to be thirteen this month."

I spoke up and told her I was fourteen. She just smiled and explained to my mother that the bathroom was at the opposite end of the hall. She said that all the boarders on this floor used that bathroom. My mother's expression was enough for my sister and me to realize she wasn't very excited about that accommodation.

Maria left as we entered the room. Two beds had been placed on opposite sides of the fairly large room.

"Liam, the single bed will be yours. Mary Beth, you will sleep in the double bed with me," my mother said.

I noticed that there was a chamber pot under the double bed. My mother also saw it and pointed, as she sat on the edge of my bed and looked around, "That will never be used unless it is an absolute emergency."

The two windows in the bedroom allowed us a bird's eye view of the street below. The faint ring from the horse drawn trolley car could be heard as it passed, up from the center of the city.

"Mother, how come we didn't use the trolley car when we got off the train to come here?" my sister Mary Beth asked.

"It wasn't that far and we really don't have the money," she said as she began to unpack the suitcases. I think about it now and how that small amount of change would have been well spent to keep the three of us from catching the chill that would soon blossom into something that would change my life forever.

I woke my mother at 5:45 p.m. as I had been instructed to do. I had to shake her several times until she awoke from her deep sleep. She coughed several times and looked at my sister still sleeping on the bed. She gently woke her and said,
"Both of you go and wash your hands and faces in preparation for dinner. We must arrive at the dinner table several minutes before 6 o'clock."
She gave other instructions, but then noticed that my sister had fallen back to sleep and never heard the specifics as to how we were to mind our manners and speak only when spoken to. She gently shook her again, but the look on my mother's face showed some concern when she placed her hand on her forehead. She realized she had a fever, but coaxed the complaining youth to get up, wash her face and hands.
"Mary Beth, you will feel much better once you have some food in your stomach. You can return to the room directly after dinner and get back in bed if you like."
I asked if she was alright.
"I think she has a fever, Liam," was all she said.
I noticed that my mother coughed and that her face was rosy too. She never indicated that she felt ill. We arrived at the large dining room on the first floor exactly as mother had planned to find twenty other people sitting in their assigned seats at the large dining table.
Mrs. Cugini smiled and pointed to three empty seats that had been reserved for us. She waited until my mother was seated before she gave orders to her three daughters to begin serving. One of those servers was Maria who had been assigned to our section of the table. As she filled each of her guest's bowls with the hot chicken soup that we had tasted on our arrival, conversations among the guests began on how their day was,

8

how the evening weather had turned bitter cold and that some sleet and snow had accumulated on the sidewalks and roads. The boarders also discussed some of the newspaper articles of the day. A few conversations were directed at my mother who explained where we were from and her intent of finding work at some of the affluent homes, or the local laundry or with a seamstress in Norwich. She also mentioned she had experience with the Church. She asked if anyone knew if the good monsignor at St. Patrick's needed additional help in the rectory, church or even the school because she had a very good recommendation from her parish priest. She didn't receive any information because I was sure that if anything of that nature had been available, someone at that table would have already taken it or passed the information onto one of their family or friends to pursue the job. But everyone seemed polite and said that they would let her know if they heard that anything like that was available.

As soon as I finished my soup, the bowl was immediately taken away by a young boy about my age. The boy was the Cugini's second son, Joseph. He and his oldest brother Antonio, Jr. were assigned to clean up each course as it was consumed by the boarders. Joey and Tony, Jr., as I would nickname them later, worked quickly under the watchful eyes of their mother who stood against the wall of the dining room and supervised the event. I later found out Joey was only a month older than me and Tony, Jr. was almost eighteen. Five of the six Cugini children worked serving two meals a day to their boarders at the big house. The youngest child, Donato, was only six and he occasionally came into the dining room, but was immediately directed back to the kitchen by his mother. He stayed in the kitchen pestering the five other siblings as they came in and out of the kitchen performing their tasks.

9

The second course of the meal arrived to my delight. It was baked chicken and potatoes seasoned with onion, garlic, oregano, salt, olive oil and pepper. The two younger daughters, Lucia and Loretta, placed several platters of the second course in strategic places on the table so that all of us could serve ourselves. I began to take my portion when the glare of my mother's eyes alerted me that I should let the adults serve themselves first. But to my rescue came a voice, "Come on son, dig in and get your fair share before it's all gone."

To my delight Mr. Gregory, a cobbler by trade and in his mid-twenties, handed me several potatoes and a drumstick. My mother's glare had diminished and I was free to consume the best meal I had had in months. I felt my stomach filling as I finished the chicken and potatoes with several pieces of homemade bread.

To my surprise and delight, Maria and her sisters arrived with steaming hot platters of spaghetti, meatballs and sauce as Tony, Jr. and Joey removed the dishes and untouched chicken and potatoes of the second course. The feast continued until almost 7:30 p.m. when coffee and homemade Italian cookies were served. I overfilled my plate and had to force myself to finish the third course. I had to decline the cookies which I would never again refuse once I learned to pace myself at the Cugini's dinner table.

My sister had not eaten very well and it was noticed by Mrs. Cugini. She asked Maria to translate for her as she inquired about Mary Beth's lack of an appetite. My mother explained, "She's probably getting a cold and is just tired from the exhausting ride."

Mrs. Cugini listened to Maria's translation, but didn't buy my mother's explanation. She walked over and touched Mary Beth's head, turned to Maria and spoke in Italian.

"My mother says that she feels warm and that she could have a

10

fever. We have a physician only two houses down from the here and that Dr. Moore could come if my mother requests it," Maria said politely.

"Oh no child. You tell Mrs. Cugini that Mary Beth will be just fine. But thank her for her concern," my slightly embarrassed mother stated.

She paused as she looked at the facial expression of Mrs. Cugini. She then attempted to reinforce her earlier statement.

"I'm sure that Mary Beth will recover from her cold. It should pass in a few days," my mother emphasized.

Her explanation didn't convince Mrs. Cugini, who too emphasized through Maria,

"If the child worsens, I will call Dr. Moore for you."

My mother thanked her new landlady again and excused us from the table to return to our room.

The next morning was our first experience with the community bathroom. Luckily for us, it was Sunday and the bathroom wasn't occupied at 5:00 a.m. My mother and sister used the facilities first and were in and out in a matter of ten minutes as I stood outside with my legs crossed thinking of anything other than relieving my bladder and bowels. Finally my five minute turn came just in time. As we dressed, my mother checked my sister's forehead.

"Is she cooler?" I asked.

"Yes, her fever has lessened and I feel a little better too," she replied.

We arrived for breakfast promptly before 6:00 a.m. Mrs. Cugini, her three daughters and two sons were busy placing platters of sausages, eggs and bread on the table for those guests that had risen early for Sunday breakfast. We all ate in relative quiet as some murmuring of conversations could be heard amongst a few of the other boarders.

With the encouragement of my mother, my sister ate a little

11

portion of the eggs and sausage she had prepared for her. Mrs. Cugini was pleased to see this. I couldn't get enough of the sausage, but paced myself in case there was a second course. There wasn't. We were about to be given the directions and approximate time it would take to walk to mass at St. Patrick's when Maria and Lucia volunteered to walk with us to the church. The March wind was still biting at us as we headed up Boswell Avenue, then Broad Street to Broadway and St. Patrick's church. The cold air helped to cool the heat flushed faces my mother and sister had from their low grade fevers.

We arrived to see a multitude of patrons entering the church to attend the eight o'clock Mass. It was at this point that Maria and Lucia asked to be excused. My sister asked,
"Where are you going?"
"The Italian Mass is in the basement," Maria said.
My sister began to ask questions when my mother silenced her.
"We don't understand Italian, Mary Beth. We will attend the Mass on the main floor that is said in English."
It wasn't the language barrier I would later understand that separated the two Masses; it was just immigration protocol that all new nationalities would endure until they assimilated into the community. It would be almost twenty more years until first generation Italians heard Mass on the main floor.

We returned to the house almost two hours later. Maria, Lucia and Loretta were already working in the kitchen preparing the afternoon meal. We were informed that Sunday afternoon meals were provided only for the immediate Cugini family and their guests in the kitchen. Our dinner would be available at six o'clock in the main dining room. Thus the schedule had been set. We ate twice a day at the big house. Lunch was not available for the tenants and it was only for the immediate family on Sunday. It wouldn't be long before I was invited to attend those Sunday afternoon meals. My sister and mother returned to the room and the comfort of the double bed. They laid down to ease the weariness they had developed from the long walk back from attending mass. I spent the remaining afternoon exploring the area outside of the big house.

I returned to our room and found my mother and Mary Beth still asleep in bed. I looked at the alarm clock that my mother had brought with us. We only had fifteen minutes until it was dinnertime. I gently shook my mother. She didn't respond. I felt her forehead. It was very warm and her face was flush. She continued to be unresponsive when I shook her. I felt Mary Beth, who stirred and attempted to roll over in bed. She too felt very warm. I shook my mother one more time. She did not respond. I knew I needed to get help and quickly ran downstairs to find Mrs. Cugini. For a few moments, the busy woman was annoyed that I had interfered with her busy schedule preparing dinner until Maria explained my concerns. She listened as Maria translated and then hastily followed me upstairs.

When we reached the bedroom, she touched the foreheads of my mother and sister. With concern, she immediately yelled to Maria in Italian. Later, I realized that she had summoned Dr. Moore. It seemed like an eternity for the old doctor to arrive, ascend the stairs and examine them. I heard him speak to Maria after his examination.
"Explain to your mother that they have pneumonia. The woman is in more danger than the child."
He explained to Maria what he wanted her mother and her to do for their immediate care.

Dr. Moore left the house shortly after watching Mrs. Cugini and Maria caring for my mother and Mary. I watched from the bed next to them. Mrs. Cugini, Maria and I were left to care for the two patients for the night. Every hour after midnight, Mrs.

Cugini would arrive at the room, change my mother's and sister's cooling cloths and smile at me as she attended to them.

I fell off to sleep only to be awakened as Mrs. Cugini spoke excitedly to Maria at my mother's side of the bed. The landlady seemed to be very upset as she instructed her daughter in Italian. I later realized that she had summoned the doctor again. It was almost an hour before he arrived to check them. He shook his head as he examined my mother. He moved to my sister and checked her temperature and vital signs. He bowed his head before he looked back at Maria and Mrs. Cugini. I will never forget the look on his face as he then glanced over at me. The doctor never said a word as he began to care for the two patients in relief of Mrs. Cugini and Maria.

I remember waking once to see the old doctor applying cold compresses on both of them. He would alternate the cool compresses and occasionally prop up each one's head and administer water. I dozed back off to sleep, but the early morning street noises awoke me again. Dr. Moore was asleep on the chair next to my sister's side of the bed.
"Are they doing better?" I asked.
The old man did not respond at first.
"Excuse me doctor, are they getting better?"
He slightly tensed as he woke and said,
"I'm afraid not, my young man. They both have a very serious case of Pneumonia. I am very concerned for both of them," he paused as he recognized the apprehension on my face and continued,
"I will stay with them until they respond to the treatment I am giving them, son."
He stopped any further explanation as Mrs. Cugini arrived with a hot cup of coffee for him.

I remembered a short while later Mr. Cugini was summoned

to our room. He entered and listened to the doctor and his wife while they conveyed information about the two boarders. He shook his head and then addressed the doctor.

"I return from work in three days. You take care and I pay."

Dr. Moore reassured him that he wasn't concerned about his fee, but he was about his two patients. I remembered him looking at me and whispering instructions to Mr. and Mrs. Cugini which I couldn't hear. Several minutes later, I was taken to Tony and Joey's room by Mrs. Cugini and instructed by hand gestures as she spoke to me in Italian. I surmised that I was to stay with them until my mother and sister recovered. Joey was surprised and Tony grumbled until Mrs. Cugini corrected his attitude and instructed both of them to move my bed into their room.

After moving my bed, I followed the boys down for breakfast. I watched Mr. Cugini leave for work through the front door. He carried several bags of goods and tools as he walked to catch the trolley at the top of the hill.

"What does he do for a job?" I asked Joey.

"He's a stonemason. He works for the railroad repairing stone bridges and tunnels. He'll be back in a few days."

I would learn later that he also cooked in the evenings for the rail workers at their campsites to earn extra money.

As often as possible, I would look in on my mother and sister. Each time I appeared, I would always ask their condition. The doctor would never respond, but only motioned for me to leave. After every meal, I would return to the room to visit them. I will always remember the look on Mrs. Cugini's face as she and the doctor saw me approaching on the third day. Dr. Moore closed the bedroom door behind them and stood in the hallway to face me. The three of us stood there for several moments before he spoke.

15

"Son, I'm sorry to have to tell you that your mother has just died of complications from pneumonia. I am very sorry. I did all I could to save her."

I was shocked. Then numbness engulfed my body. My ears rang and I could just about hear what Dr. Moore said to me next about my sister.

"I do not expect your sister to live much longer, so you should pay your last respects to your mother and visit with your sister for as long as you can." I could remember thinking, *It had taken less than seventy-two hours for me to experience another tragic event in my new life.*

I entered the room and stayed only minutes as Mrs. Cugini accompanied me and held my hand. Dr. Moore checked my sister as I knelt near the double bed my mother had died in. He shook his head as he removed his stethoscope from my sister's chest and said,

"I'm sorry son. She has gone as well."

My two fair skinned relatives were already beginning to turn gray as I glanced back at them while I was led from the room several minutes later. I couldn't understand how this could have happened and began to ask why. Without receiving the explanation I wanted, I remember becoming upset with the doctor and screaming. I don't remember much after that as I went hoarse and was lead back to the boy's room by Mrs. Cugini.

The Convalescent Home

Mary stood over me in amazement as she watched the tears streaming down my eyes. They had begun to soak the pillowcase. She bent down close to me and said,

"Great-granddad, try to show me what is wrong. Why are you crying? Please talk to me."

16

She didn't know how much I wanted to be able to tell her, but my condition wouldn't allow it. After she wiped my eyes, she left and fetched the nurse. I saw them standing next to my bed and heard the nurse try to explain that maybe my eyes were irritated and that's why they had begun to tear. She told Mary that she would request the doctor to order eye drops.

What a bitch this woman was. Christ, couldn't she see I was upset, I thought. Thank God Mary wasn't convinced. I heard her say that she thought I was trying to communicate with her.

"Could he be in pain, Nurse?"

"He's just a very old man who has suffered a massive stroke. He's not the same man you knew."

Bullshit! I thought to myself. *I'm not dead yet, you fool, and if I have anything to do with it I'll find a way to communicate with her. I know if I have enough time, she'll see it too.*

The nurse left a note on my chart to ask the doctor to order some type of eyedrops. Mary came back and sat down. She smiled as she looked at the few remaining tears she had missed. "Please great-granddad, try to tell me a story like you use to. Come on Liam, give me a sign that you are in there. I love you."

I blinked my eye once which was the first time I had managed to do that. She didn't notice it.

Shit Mary! I need you to watch me again, I thought as she looked away. I tried again, but was unsuccessful. Exhausted, I and thought about the day my mother and sister died.

The Story

I laid on my bed most of the afternoon as Joey and Tony, Jr. came in and out checking on me. It was almost 6 p.m. when I heard a knock on the door. I didn't respond until I felt a large hand resting on my shoulder. The power in the hand turned me over. It was Mr. Cugini. He'd returned from work. I later found out that Mrs. Cugini sent one of the boarders to inform him of the deaths. He saw my tears and state of sadness and shook his head. He grabbed me and pulled me to his chest never saying a word. The warmth and strength of him reminded me of my father and only worsened my condition. I remember crying while he held and rocked me. He said some words in Italian as he tried to comfort me. We stayed in that embrace for several minutes until I was only sobbing. Between my sobs, I can remember telling him a little of my family history. How my mother had been an only child and her parents had been deceased before I was born. My father came here from Ireland alone. His brothers never followed him. The look on my face must have convinced the gentle man to make the most important decision in my life up to that point. He pushed me gently away and said,

"You stay with us. You live in big house with family. Antonio, Joseph and Donato are now you brothers. The girls be you sisters. Mama and me take care of you. You now my son."

I remember that day as if it was yesterday. Even though I was a Corcoran, I became a member of the Cugini family. He accompanied me down to the kitchen where all the Cugini family was waiting to eat dinner. The boarders had finished their dinner and left the dining room. It was time for the family to eat in the large kitchen. Mrs. Cugini and the children never spoke a word until I'd been seated next to Joey and Maria. Mr. Cugini said the evening prayer of thanks. I didn't understand a word he spoke at that time except Jesus. We finished praying and then he spoke in English. He announced that I would be staying with them. Everyone remained silent for a brief moment, but one by one, they smiled. Mr. Cugini looked at Mrs. Cugini and spoke in Italian. She smiled and nodded her approval. Mr. Cugini looked at me and said,

"Good. Then it is done. We have one more in family. We eat

18

now."

That was the signal for the family to commence their various conversations. Even though Mrs. Cugini had smiled and nodded, I'm sure they talked later about his announcement. I was now the ninth member of the family.

After dinner, the other children immediately began doing their assigned chores. I wasn't given chores to perform yet, so I sat there watching until Mr. Cugini took me aside, sat me down, and told me what would be happening in the next few days. He explained, in his broken English, that I would have to be brave and act like a man now that my mother and sister were gone. He said that he made all the arrangements to bury them in St. Mary's cemetery in Greenville. I didn't know where Greenville was, but realized after I had gathered all my thoughts and control over my emotions months later, that he had also paid for their interment.

There was no formal Irish wake for Christine and Mary Beth Corcoran. There wasn't anyone to pay their respects except the Cugini family members and their boarders. The funeral director opened the funeral parlor for several hours to allow the boarders who could attend and the Cugini family, to view the bodies. They said a few personal prayers and recited the Rosary. I can still remember looking at both of them lying in the wood coffins. Their gray pallor had left due to the undertaker's cosmetic attempt to make them look alive. He failed, in my opinion, to make them look like they were just sleeping. I never remembered the prayers that were said or the condolences I received. It was, and still is, a part of my memory that is clouded.

Their funeral Mass followed immediately at St. Patrick's. Except for standing, kneeling, sitting and participating in an occasional prayer, I didn't remember much more than that. I do

19

remember leaving with my adopted parents, each holding one of my arms when Mass ended as we followed the coffins out.

Mr. Cugini arranged for a small floral arrangement for each of them to be placed on their coffin in the horse drawn hearse. The full window hearse offered the flowers to brighten the overcast and cold day. He had also rented an enclosed carriage for the whole family to ride in and follow the hearse to the cemetery. The gentle man knew he didn't want another repeat of a case of pneumonia with anyone else in his family, including me. I knew he still worried about me because I had been sniffling and coughing for the past several days since their deaths. The ride over Boswell Avenue to the Greenville section of Norwich is also a blur. What I clearly remembered was the wind still bit at our faces and nipped at our ears.

A priest waited patiently as the two coffins were unloaded from the hearse by four men that the funeral director employed. They were placed near the open door of a crypt that had been used to temporarily house the deceased when the ground was frozen. The priest that the Monsignor had assigned to say the Mass and perform the prayer service at the gravesite was Italian. I don't know whether the Monsignor had made a mistake or he thought that it was an Italian service because Mr. Cugini had paid for everything. Anyway, I never understood a word the man said at the gravesite. I did notice that when he said my family name of Corcoran, at the end, he looked a little perplexed. We left the crypt and returned home. It would be six more weeks until the funeral director and his crew would return to break ground and bury my two family members. I would return with Mr. and Mrs. Cugini on that day to observe the final resting place of Christine and Mary Beth Corcoran.

The six weeks gave Mr. Cugini time to make two small headstones in the basement of the big house. I watched him pour concrete into two wooden forms he made. He made small letters from wood and imbedded the letters into the partially set concrete. He removed them gently and let the entire form harden. Several days later, he returned to the basement, stripped off the forms and exposed the stones. He rubbed them every night for a week with a special stone and water until they were smooth. They held up very well until I replaced them over thirty years later with gray Vermont marble.

Chapter Two – Coming of Age

The Convalescent Home

I realized it was dark outside when I opened my eyes and moved them a little to look at window in my room. The machines were swooshing and beeping as I continued my pathetic existence in this world.

They're the loudest damned things, I thought. Then reality set in. *They're keeping you alive old man.* With that in mind, I thought a little more clearly.

I looked for Mary, but couldn't find her. An attendant came in, but never looked at me as she checked the machines and recorded the data she'd been sent to gather. I tried to concentrate by moving my hands and feet. I couldn't tell if I had moved them until I realized the top sheet and blanket on my bed were moving by the action of my toes.

Look lady, see, I can move. I thought I was screaming to get her attention.

Where are my hands? I thought. I couldn't see them because they had been placed under the top sheet and blanket. I wasn't sure what I was feeling as I tried to move them again. The attendant never noticed any of my movements. I laid there for what must have been hours until I was exhausted trying to repeat the accomplishments I had been able to perform earlier. I fell back to sleep for a while and awoke seeing the room window had changed from black to a medium blue. I realized that I was able to see what the time was on the wall. It was 6:06 and I knew it was morning. I would have to try to show Mary today what I had managed to do. Satisfied with my accomplishments, I fell back to sleep again dreaming about growing up in the big house.

The Story

The first year I stayed with the Cugini family was a constant adjustment to the new customs, different foods, learning Italian and attending a large public school. Italian customs were interesting. The food was plentiful and delicious. I had all the Italian swear words down pat in the first few months I lived in the big house. I thanked Tony and Joey for those. Within a year, I could understand and communicate in Italian successfully. I had also managed to finish my first year of high school. My height changed considerably by the time I turned fifteen which helped me to make the Norwich Free Academy baseball team. I was now five feet ten inches and stood five inches over my closest brother Joey. Ma Cugini was beside herself having to buy longer pants every time she looked at me. I felt like the ugly duckling when I went to school or family events. I always remembered Ma Cugini telling me not to slouch.

"Stand straight Lam," she would say. She never did learn to pronounce Liam correctly, but her English was as good as my Italian. I loved her even more for the nickname she had created for me. My auburn hair and light complexion stood out to compliment my height. Not very many Italian Americans had freckles on their shoulders and back like I did. The shirts I had to wear when the family went to the beach didn't always block the sun either like Ma Cugini had hoped. While all the brothers and sisters got tanner, I got redder and blistered. Ma would have to rub salve on my burns to reduce the blistering and pain I had to endure during the summer nights when I tried to sleep. Despite my acceptance as an equal sibling in the family, my physical differences were noticed by everyone outside of it.

Lucia and Loretta treated me like they did their other brothers. Personal arguments, sarcasm, sibling rivalries and all the other associated problems existed amongst me and them. Joey and I competed on and off the baseball field and in school. I was a better athlete, but he was the better student. We learned to control our rivalry and offered help when the other faltered. Joey helped me to improve my math and science skills while I helped him improve his bunting and hitting skills. As time went by, we grew closer and formed a bond that would make us inseparable.

Tony, Jr. was not as close to neither of us during those years. It would take a marriage, a war and a family tragedy to pull him closer to me. Donato became Danny. The nickname came from me and it stuck. Ma and Pa Cugini even started calling him Danny within the first year I was at the big house. I realized at a young age that if you wanted to fit in at the playground, the ball field or even the school yard, you needed a name that fit in. Danny thanked me many times for his nickname for the rest of his life.

Maria was pleasant, but seemed distant. I would see her occasionally look in my direction at mealtimes, but that's all it was. It was just looks. No matter how I tried to impress her, she remained distant. I dared not tease her like I did the other girls who enjoyed the bantering and teased back.

Life at the big house didn't change much until 1917. Ma Cugini always insisted during the previous years that I pay respect to my mother and sister at the cemetery on special days. Their anniversary, Easter and Christmas had been deemed by her the days I should visit as a very minimum. I added in their birthdays as an occasion to visit. In March, on the anniversary of their deaths, after I attended Mass, I walked to the cemetery. The cement stones that Pa made had bleached out to white, but the names and dates could be clearly read. Everytime I went, Ma would see to it that I had two roses to place on the graves. Ma and Pa would sometimes accompany me.

Tony, Jr. was now engaged to be married to Rose Ronaldi. The wedding had been set for late May on his twenty-first birthday. I remember that Rose wouldn't be nineteen by the time of her wedding, but she already looked grown up to me. Many women at that time were married by that age. Some even had children by then. She began to attend Sunday lunch at the big house starting every Sunday since they announced their engagement. She came from a large family too so she had several sisters to fill the bridal party. Joey and I had been asked to stand up for the couple as ushers. Tony's best man was Kippy Sullivan who had been his best friend from the time anyone could remember. Danny was nine now and had been designated the ring bearer, a position he reminded us all was the most important task in the wedding party. He wasn't given the rings though until twenty minutes before the actual ceremony as I recall.

Ma Cugini had offered to have the wedding reception in the reception room of the big house. The Ronaldi family accepted. All of us had assignments to make sure the room was prepared for the wedding. My job was to paint the entire room with a new coat of cream paint for the festivities. Joey had completed the sanding, re-staining and waxing of the oak floors and Tony, Jr. had replaced all the old gas lights with electric ones. Pa Cugini inspected the work weekly and praised the results. I remember he commented as loudly as needed when he didn't like something.

Maria had blossomed into a beautiful woman. Her hair had developed an auburn highlight, her eyes had become a deeper blue and her shape was perfect. She was always polite, but continued her cool mannerisms towards me. I can remember only one time that she actually kissed my cheek. It was the day I finished painting the reception room. I helped her hang several curtains back up and she pecked me on the cheek in appreciation for my assistance. The arousal I felt was almost shameful and overshadowed my mixed feelings for her as my adopted sister. I was pleased that only a few boys attempted to court her. She hadn't accepted any dates which was fine with me. I was in love with her and I was the only one she should date in my mind. But I was afraid to tell her. Really, I think I was more afraid of what Pa and Ma would say if I told them I was in love with their daughter. Many times I thought of confessing my love for her, but my common sense overruled my religious guilt. The fact of me going into a confessional and telling a priest I was in love with my sister, who really wasn't my sister, but lived in the same house as me, would have been really hard to do. I fantasized that she was holding out just to date me. Her sisters, on the other hand, relished the attention and liked dating even though they weren't old enough by the Cugini standards. Many times they snuck out of the house unbeknown to their parents. Both sisters were pretty girls, but neither one was as beautiful as Maria.

I remembered the Norwich Bulletin was full of reports that year of the war carnage and deaths in Europe. The news had become worse as the war progressed for almost three years. The President had announced that he'd given the German Government an ultimatum of war if they continued unrestricted submarine warfare and sinking ships carrying American citizens. The Cugini's worried that three of their four sons could be involved in service to their country if America went to war. The couple was pleased when Tony, Jr. became engaged and planned to be married soon because they thought it would keep him out of the military. That thought only lasted a short time. On the other hand, our brother Joey had stopped by the Norwich Navy Recruitment Office several times. He inquired about joining the Navy and being on destroyers. He hoped to be chasing the German submarines in the Atlantic Ocean. At night, he would tell me how being in the Navy and hunting down submarines would be the best way to protect America

26

from the Huns. I just hoped that Mr. Wilson would keep us out of that war like he had promised five month earlier during his re-election.

To my disappointment, in April of 1917, the President asked Congress to declare war on Germany. His request was granted. Four days later, Joey returned home to inform his parents that he had joined the Navy. He would leave for basic training after we graduated. His announcement came at Sunday lunch. Ma and Pa were never the same after that announcement.

We graduated from high school that June. Joey managed to graduate in the top ten of the class of 1917 at the Norwich Free Academy. I think I was in the lower part of the class somewhere, but that didn't change the way our parents thought. Ma and Pa were very proud of both of us academically and athletically. Pa let both of us play baseball at the Academy despite the chores that needed to be completed at home. Danny and Tony, Jr. didn't appreciate taking up a few more chores, but Joey and I paid for it every weekend, repaying their efforts during the week to keep the big house running smoothly. On the week days when we had a home game, Pa would manage to leave work a little early to watch his boys play ball. I can remember he attended several games to watch me pitch and Joey catch. We made him very proud, even if it took him several years to figure out what we were doing on the field.

I remember the late June day when I accompanied Pa to the train station to see Joey off to the Norfolk Virginia Training Center. Pa and I talked all the way home about Joey's insistence on joining the Navy to protect the country. The gentle man asked me if I felt the same way about joining as Joey had. I think I disappointed him when I told him it was Mr. Wilson's war. He was satisfied though when I told him I would enlist if called upon. When Joey left for basic training, there seemed to be a void in the household. Every Monday evening after Joey left, Ma would attend a Novena at St. Patrick's church. Her prayers were for Joey and his quest to protect American shipping from the German submarines.

I started working for the Torrance Construction Company of Norwich. Pa worked for them after he left the railroad construction crew and was influential in getting me hired. I worked for several months with him as a mason hard carrier. I became pretty strong lifting stones and brick, mixing cement and building staging on the construction sites. I developed a deeper relationship with my foster father while we worked together in those months. We talked everyday on our one mile walk to the construction office to be trucked to the work sites by our employer. We talked just about everything on those walks. Our main topic of conversation was when Joey sent letters home from the training center. Our bonding strengthened during those walks. Those conversations and walks were numbered the day I received my notice to report for service.

I announced the receipt of my notice at a Sunday afternoon meal. A perfectly prepared three course dinner was ruined for Ma and Pa. Even Tony and Rose looked concerned after my announcement. Lucia and Loretta seemed excited that I was going off to see a new part of the country and possibly Europe during my call up. Maria left the table during my announcement. She never said a word until the day I left for the Army. I left with a group of men that I had been called up with. I said my goodbyes to my family members the night before. Pa instructed me with the same words he had given Joey,
"Keep safe and make us proud."

The group of us walked down Boswell Avenue that late

summer day on our way to the train station laughing and kidding like all young men do when they are nervous. Just before I boarded the eight o'clock train, Maria appeared. I spotted her immediately standing near the boarding platform. I ran to her and asked, "Who are you looking for?"

She looked surprised to see me standing in front of her, but then said, "You!"

I found out she had just planned to wave to me in the window of the train as it left. Now that I was standing in front of her, she kissed me gently on the lips for several seconds and then whispered, "Be careful and write as often as you can."

She turned and quickly left. As she walked away, she turned once, smiled and said,

"I will miss you."

I noticed she had tears running down her cheeks as her smile turned to concern. She then ran away. I stood there confused. My mind cleared when I heard the whistle blow and the calls from my buddies to quickly get on the departing train. It was then that I realized that Maria knew she was not my real sister anymore.

As we traveled, I thought about Maria, her gentle kiss, her parting words and the tears I was surprised to see running down her cheeks. I knew I loved her since the first day I saw her in the kitchen of the big house. I knew I wanted to spend the rest of my life with her. I just needed to finish this temporary separation. I knew I would date her when I returned. Reality set in when I thought about Pa and Ma. *What would they say about a relationship between Maria and me? What would they say about our ages? She was only sixteen. How long would this war last?* God only knew the answers to my questions. I realized I would have to wait and see what developed in the days, weeks and possibly years ahead. One thing that I knew now was that she cared for me. I hoped that

29

it was love. Maybe as much love as I had for her.

We had to switch trains several times until we reached a National Army cantonment called Gordon in Georgia on a hot September afternoon. It had taken two days to reach our destination. We exited the train to find several trucks waiting to take us to the camp. No one said a word the entire hour ride. It was the first time in my life that I ever saw black people in abundance, working the fields and ignoring the multitude of trucks that transported the white men to their destination at the new camp. We exited the truck and were lined up in front of a stocky individual I was told would be my mother and father for the next twelve weeks. He had the oddest accent I had ever heard. It was called a southern drawl, as I later found out. He seemed to slur one word into another. It was hard to understand him, especially when he was screaming at us. He seemed to scream at us for the remainder of the afternoon and evening until we were assigned to our new barracks. It wasn't until ten o'clock that evening when Staff Sergeant Mullinax ended his tirade and left us alone until five o'clock the next morning. I lay on the top of my bunk sweating as I tried to drift off to sleep thinking of Maria kissing me just before the train left.

The Convalescent Home

I awoke and realized I wasn't in boot camp. I was still in the hospital and Mary was sitting at the side of my bed. Her head was down as she read. I moved my toes. She didn't look up. *Shit. Come on girl, pay attention,* I thought.
I moved them again a little faster which made a scratching noise on the white sheets. She paused and looked up. She smiled and immediately called for the nurse. Within seconds the nurse arrived to be shown my moving toes.
"I think that is involuntary movement dear. Your great-

30

grandfather is not trying to communicate with you."

What the hell is wrong with this woman, I thought.

"How can you say that," Mary barked. "Look at his fingers. They are moving as well."

The nurse paused and smiled.

"I think it's all just involuntary, my dear," she said.

Mary wasn't convinced.

"Great-granddad, damn it, show her you are trying to communicate. Move your fingers three times for me," she demanded. I obliged and moved them three times.

"See, I told you he is communicating," she said.

The nurse bent over me and looked into my eyes. If I could have bitten her nose, I would have. She spoke directly to me and asked,

"Liam, if you can communicate with me, move your fingers three times and your toes three times."

Okay bitch, look closely, I screamed inside.

She waited as I moved my fingers and toes as she had requested.

"Oh my, I'm going to fetch the doctor. Mary, you keep communicating with him."

She left quickly, seeking the physician who had treated me since my arrival at the convalescent home. Mary stood over me and looked into my eyes. She saw my side to side eye motion and my occasional blink. She didn't realize that I was working my tail off trying to move my frozen body.

Come on sweetheart, pay attention, I tried to say.

"Great-granddad, I knew you were in there somewhere. I love you. Tell me you love me. Move your toes four times and tell me you love me. Come on Liam, I know you can do it."

Damn girl, you're killing me, I thought, but I managed to move my toes four distinct times. She hugged me as she cried openly. I could feel the pressure of her body leaning on me. I hadn't felt anything before, but now I could feel the touch of my

31

great- granddaughter.

The doctor arrived and observed my feeble attempt to communicate.
"Have the staff monitor him for the evening," he said.
"In the morning, I'll make a decision whether to remove the breathing tube."

Mary asked me to move my fingers and toes twice again if I liked that idea. She hugged me when they all saw my response. She called the family to report the great news and that evening when I awoke again, I had new visitors. I had to perform again until I was thoroughly exhausted. I could move my wrists a little this time. I was encouraged as I fell off to sleep and found myself reliving my youth again.

The Story

I finished boot camp one week before Thanksgiving. I managed to qualify as a marksman with a Springfield rifle and a Colt automatic pistol. We all waited several days for our orders. I received mine for a combat training camp in Whitney, England of all places. I was to report to Fort Devens in Massachusetts in two weeks on December 11th and then be shipped over for training at the beginning of the New Year. Most of us received the same orders I found out later. As I stood in the warm sun that Friday afternoon feeling numb, the reality set in that I was going off to war. I remembered Pa Cugini's parting words to me to keep safe and make them proud. I was brought back to reality when one of my buddies slapped me on the back and congratulated me for getting the same orders as he.

"We'll be one of the first Americans to kill some Huns,

Corcoran," he said.

I just looked at him not saying a word.

"And what else is good is that you get some time home to romance that girl you keep telling me about. You better make it good if you know what I mean. You might not come back, you know."

I thought about how I wanted to slap the ever living shit out of him for his comment, 'if you know what I mean,' but I asked, "What do you mean not coming back?"

"Oh you know. You might meet one of those frog girls and never want to come back." *Frog girls,* I thought.

"Oh, yeah, I hear those French girls are pretty," I said.

But I really thought about dying for the first time. I knew millions of men had already given lives on both sides of this war.

It finally hit me that I was being granted leave. I knew if the trains ran right I could be in Norwich the evening before Thanksgiving. My letters never indicated when I would be home again. I relished the thought of showing up at the big house and surprising my mother and father on the holiday. Most of all, I thought about the ten days or so that would follow and my being alone with Maria.

Our letters had begun as small notes, but eventually had grown to two and three pages long. I wrote two or three times a week, but Maria only wrote once a week. After a while, she no longer signed her letters simply "Maria", they were signed "love, Maria." I tingled inside as I thought about being with her soon. The tingling stopped when I thought about Ma and Pa and what their reaction would be. I decided I would pick the right moment and tell them; that was if I was sure Maria felt the same way about me.

I was the only soldier left on the train when it arrived at the Norwich station the evening before Thanksgiving. Several sailors and I talked on the train until it reached New London. I asked a few of them if they knew Joey Cugini. None of them did because they weren't from around the area. They asked if he was on a sub stationed at the base. They laughed when I told them he was on a destroyer. It was the first time I ever heard the phrase that anything on the surface was a target. That would stick with me for the rest of my life, but I didn't know it yet.

The trolley was just arriving at the station when I departed the train so I jumped on, paid the fee and waited to begin my ride through Franklin Square, up Franklin Street and towards McKinley Avenue. Where Boswell intersects McKinley was when I pulled the bell for the conductor to stop the trolley. I departed and began my fast pace up Boswell Avenue and to the big house. Despite my heavy duffle bag over my shoulder, I reached the big house in a very short time as dusk commenced and the cool November air began reminding me I was in New England again.

The entire house was lit up. I can remember thinking, *What the hell is going on? Could it be a party?* I could see shadows through the frosted lower glass of the reception room. *Ma and Pa had something going on,* I thought to myself, but still felt a little uneasy. Several men were smoking and talking outside and noticed me approaching. The first person to call my name was Kippy Sullivan.

"Corcoran, is that you?"
"Yes, it's me. What's going on in the house? Is everything alright?" I asked.
"Oh the commotion inside is a little party for Tony and Rose. They announced that they are going to have a baby in six months. So everyone got together to celebrate the good news. They'll be surprised as hell to see you walk in," he said.

Just then, the front door opened. I could see someone coming out. I recognized him. It was Joey in his navy uniform. We both froze as we quickly comprehended what each was seeing. Joey jumped off the porch and immediately grabbed and hugged me never saying a word. We stayed in the embrace until Kippy said,

"Are you guys alright?"

We broke the embrace and shook hands. Neither of us could say a word until the choked up feeling left our throats.

"Welcome home brother. Welcome home." I hugged him one more time and said,

"Let's go in and surprise Ma and Pa."

Joey opened the reception door and stepped in as I followed. He pointed in the direction of Ma and Pa. As Joey and I walked towards them, the room became silent as I dropped my duffle bag. I stopped, looked around and said.

"I didn't mean to disrupt the party. I just wanted to come home and see my family."

Ma put her hands to her mouth and froze at the sight of her two boys in uniform standing in front of her. A few guests began to clap until everyone followed and joined in as Ma and I hugged. I squeezed her and lifted her off the floor. She talked so fast in Italian that I missed half of what she had said. The part I did understand was that she was mad that I didn't tell her I was coming home so that she could have been prepared. I looked over at Pa. He stood looking at Joey and me while holding his wine glass, beaming. He walked slowly over to me and shook my hand firmly. His mason's grip actually hurt, but it was his way of controlling his emotions as his eyes glistened. He could only whisper that he was happy to see me. He then handed his glass to Joey and hugged me. The room began to become quiet again until Pa looked around and told everyone,

"My two sons home now. Everyone be happy."

He grabbed his glass and toasted the two of us. I hugged and kissed Lucia and Loretta. I asked Danny, after we embraced,

"Where is Maria?" He rolled his eyes and said,
"She was here, but she must have gone into the kitchen. Do you want me to go get her?"
"No, that's okay, I'll find her."
I shook a few more hands as I made my way to the kitchen. A few guests were filling trays with food and getting more wine, but she wasn't in there. I looked around and saw that the kitchen door leading to the back porch was ajar. I followed my instincts and found her on the porch with her arms crossed looking at the cold November sky. She turned when she heard me say,
"I came home to see you. I'm leaving before Christmas to go overseas."
She burst into tears as she flung herself at me. We hugged for several minutes until she removed her chin from my chest and looked into my eyes. Our lips met and we kissed until I could hardly breathe. I was beside myself as I tried to talk. She stopped me and kissed me again. She gently pushed away after the second kiss and said,
"I've missed you. I love you."
I asked,
"What about Ma and Pa? What will they say?" She smiled and said,
"You underestimate them. I have talked to Ma and then Pa while you have been away. They have known since a year after you came here that we were in love. You will have to ask them, but I know you will get their blessing."
We embraced until Pa found us. He smiled and said,
"You two nice together. Ma sent me. Come. Join the party."
I started to talk when Pa touched his finger to his lips and said,
"We talk later."

Thanksgiving Day was cold and overcast. I rose early in the morning and planned to skip breakfast. I tried to leave the house without anyone seeing me. I needed to catch the early morning trolley to St. Mary's cemetery. As I slipped downstairs and through the reception room, I saw Maria waiting. She was dressed in her coat, gloves and hat. She smiled and asked, "Can I come with you to the cemetery?"

"How did you know?"

"I just did. May I?"

I hugged her and we quietly slipped out of the big house and up the street to catch the trolley. Within a few minutes, we were heading up Boswell Avenue and out to Greenville.

Maria did not talk during our ride to the cemetery. She held my hand and looked out at the city passing by. Occasionally she would glance my way, smile and turn back to her sightseeing. I built up enough courage and asked her,

"What are you going to do while I am away?" She turned and nonchalantly said,

"I will finish school and then get a job right after graduation in June. Maybe you will be home by then."

She looked away and continued looking out at the passing houses.

"No, I mean what are we going to do about our situation?" I asked.

She laughed and said,

"Oh that. Well, you will ask Pa for my hand in marriage and we will become engaged before you leave for Europe. We will write to each other and you will tell me all about the things you did and the places you saw. You will return and we will get married and have, three, or maybe four kids and ...."

I stopped her mid-sentence.

"Are you telling me that we are getting engaged and then married?"

She looked directly at me with those beautiful deep blue eyes and simple said,

"Yes, I am."

Her face changed from an innocent smile to a slight frown

when she quickly added, "Unless you do not want me."

"Want you? I can't believe that you even asked that question. Want you? I want to marry you right now, today and be with you every waking minute until the day I die."

I grabbed and kissed her until she pushed me away and looked around. Five or six people started clapping for us. Apparently, I spoke loud enough for the trolley car riders to hear our conversation. We both turned red as they smiled to show us their approval.

I saw the approaching sign for the cemetery entrance and I pulled the bell line to stop the trolley. The riders smiled and made comments to us as we departed. We hugged again as we watched the trolley pull away. I still felt my embarrassment and Maria noted it.

"You're still beat red, Liam."

"It's just the cold air and my Irish complexion," I lied. Our mood changed a little as I approached the gravesites of my mother and sister. We knelt in front of the headstones and said some private prayers. Maria unbuttoned her coat briefly and took out two yellow roses and placed one in front of each stone. My eyes moistened as she placed them, looked at me and said,

"Ma told me that you would be visiting here today. She gave me these from the party floral we had for Tony and Rose last night. Pa and Ma always accompanied you here on special occasions. It will be my responsibility now to come with you."

I hugged her again as we knelt to pay our respects. I said,

"I told you she was a special one."

Maria looked at me and shook her head. She knew I was talking to my departed family. We knelt there for several minutes until she made the sign of the cross, rose and said that it was time to go back to the big house and eat breakfast because she was famished. I crossed myself and followed her out of the cemetery to the trolley stop.

That evening, I found the time and courage to corner Pa and ask him his feelings about Maria and me. The man looked me in the eyes and asked,

"Do you like Maria?"

It was a strange question I thought. He repeated the same question again. I answered, "Of course I like her. I like her a lot. Pa, I love her and I want your permission to marry her as soon as possible."

He smiled and said,

"You like her. That's nice. You love her that's good. You marry her when you return. That's better."

I was going to argue when it hit me that I was going off to who knows where and maybe into harm's way. He was right even though my loins and brain were in constant conflict.

"You and Maria get engaged. When you return, you marry. You have my blessing."

I smiled, shook his hand and then hugged him. He pulled away and reached for some glasses. He poured some of his best wine in each and toasted our happiness. I could hear some giggles from the kitchen as we made our toasts. A few moments later, Ma and Maria entered the room smiling. All three of them knew my intentions and enjoyed watching me act out asking for permission to marry Maria. We all celebrated together and announced to the others when they asked what the celebration was all about.

Two days later, Joey had to report back to his ship in Brooklyn, New York. He bid his goodbye in the reception room of the big house. There wasn't a dry eye when he left that day on the trolley for the train station. He didn't want anyone to see him off at the train except me. The short ride was quiet as he composed himself after a few minutes and looked at me and said, "I'm glad that is done with. You know how emotional they all can get, especially our sisters."

I just smiled and watched him straighten himself out. We

continued riding to the station very quietly until it came into sight.

"I need you to promise me something, okay?" he asked.

"Sure, what is it?"

"You stay safe over there and don't get yourself hurt or even worse, dead. You promise?"

I laughed out loud as the trolley pulled up in front of the train station.

"Me? What about you? You're the one who's going to be out in the middle of the ocean somewhere trying to sink submarines that are trying to sink you. You be careful."

Joey laughed and said, "Well, if you say it that way. I guess I will, brother."

We waited at the station. When the train whistle blew, Joey's face turned to concern. "Okay Liam, I'm off. God bless you. Write when you are able. You have my ship address."

We looked at each other and shook hands that turned into a bear hug. The whistle blew again and the train began to slowly move. He grabbed his duffle bag and jumped up on the car step. As the train slowly moved away he saluted me. I came to attention and returned the salute. He finished his salute, smiled and waved. I felt a cold shiver run down my back as I wondered if we would ever see each other again. I walked home slowly, taking in the sights of the city. People smiled at me in my uniform as I walked home.

I approached the big house to find Danny waiting for me in the foyer. I could tell he was still upset from Joey's departure. The nine year old asked me a question in which I had to lie.

"Joey will be pretty safe won't he, Liam?"

"Sure he will, Danny. He's got a good job patrolling the coast. He'll be safe. No German submarines would dare get too close to American shores. There are too many ships like Joey's out there."

I didn't need to tell him that he could be assigned duty on a destroyer seeking U-Boats attacking convoys in the North Atlantic. He'd know that when Joey returned to tell him his sea stories.

The night before I was scheduled to leave, Maria came to my bedroom after everyone was a sleep. She slipped into the room quietly and gently closed the door behind her. She put her finger to her lips as she approached the bed.
"Are you crazy?" I whispered.
"If Ma or especially Pa catches you in here after they know how we feel about each other there will be hell to pay."
She frowned as she put her finger to my lips for me to keep quiet. I obeyed and watched her standing in front of my bed. She whispered,
"I wanted to be with you on your last night. No, I should say I need to be with you on your last night home."
She stood there and smiled as I watched her disrobe. The dim light that came through my bedroom outlined the perfect shape of her body. She didn't attempt to cover any part as she smiled and waited for my reaction. It was too much. I pulled open the sheet and blankets and invited her to my side. Within seconds, we were in an embrace that lasted until the early morning hours when I awoke from my sleep to find her missing. The slight scent of her perfume was evident on my pillow and sheets. I buried my nose in the pillow and thought about the loving we had made. I fell off to sleep again until it was light outside.

I quickly washed, dressed and packed my duffle bag. I gathered my belongings and placed them downstairs in the reception room. As I entered the kitchen, I found Maria making breakfast. Everyone was busy preparing the six o'clock meal as I bent over and kissed her on the cheek as she busily stood in front of the stove cooking scrambled eggs for the boarders. I began to do chores when she asked me to stay in the kitchen

41

and talk to her. She called to Danny to begin delivering the platters of eggs she had prepared. We talked the whole time she worked in the kitchen. When the breakfast was completed in the dining room and the boarders had departed for the day, Ma, Pa, Danny and my sisters sat at the kitchen table to share my last breakfast, for a while, with them. When we finished, I moved around the table and hugged and kissed them all goodbye. It was like Joey's send off all over again, except for Maria. She would accompany me to the train station so we could privately say our goodbyes.

We waited for the train to arrive. I would have to head east and change trains in Providence before I could head north to Fort Devens. I began to say how much I loved her for the gift she had given me last night when she covered my mouth and stopped me. "Yes, it was a gift. It was my gift to you, but your gift to me as well. I worry about you and where you are going. I couldn't wait until your return. I needed your love to hold onto until you returned."

She kissed me again, hugged me and quickly turned and left. I stood there as I watched her disappear around the corner. She never turned as she walked away. I thought about that moment everyday until I returned home over a year later.

Chapter Three – The Runner

The Story

My arrival at Fort Devens on December 11th was uneventful. The barracks were built close together, but didn't fully protect us from the cold Massachusetts wind. The exterior walls allowed the wind to penetrate them enough to freeze the latrine pipes if the fire watch on duty didn't check the plumbing hourly, run water and stoke up the coal stoves and keep them hot without burning the wood structure down. The eighty man barracks had four coal stoves with one at each end on both levels. I was lucky enough to be on the second level, near the stairway above the lower coal stove that also served to keep the latrine warm. The heat from the stove below and the heat from the stove near the stairway on the second level, kept my bunk area warmer than most of the eighty soldiers bunking there.

Within the first week, I was able to work well with the guard duty corporal and managed to be assigned day guard duty and early morning fire watch. I appreciated the day guard duty even when it was a raw day. It was twice better than the same conditions at night. Fire watch in the early morning hours afforded me the luxury of completing my four hour watch from mid-night to four in the morning. Once relieved from that duty, I got a chance to use the latrine before most of the men awoke. Nobody would take that time of the night, but I enjoyed it. I only had to perform the tasks about once a week so I thought volunteering was the way to get ahead in the Army. I learned to volunteer early which got me the best times for guard duty and fire watch. Volunteering would be a big mistake when I got to France.

The morning of December 20th was a typical cold morning. At mail call, I relished the letter I had just received from Maria. I found a semi-private area next to the Post Exchange where I could read it in private. When I opened it up and began to read the first words, I realized that this was going to be one of the worst days of my life. She gently informed me that Ma, Pa and my family were holding up well under the most difficult circumstances. Joey had been lost at sea and listed officially as killed in action on December 7th.

My heart stopped, it seemed, and I found it difficult to breathe as I re-read the sentence several times. I slid down the side wall of the Post Exchange until I was sitting in several inches of snow. A few buddies noticed my posture and blank expression and knew there was something wrong. I forced myself to read the rest of the letter which said that his destroyer had been assigned to patrol English waters searching for U-boats. For some strange reason, my mind drifted to remembering the statement the New London sailors had said about everything on the surface being targets. Maria's letter detailed that Joey had been seen helping others in the water. He succumbed to the water's frigid temperature before the remainder of the crew could be rescued. Her letter detailed the visit the Navy paid to the house and how Pa stood shocked, but proud knowing his son had died trying to help others live. I don't remember much more about the letter after that. My sorrow was evident as some of my buddies came and pulled me up from the snow I was sitting in sobbing. One friend read part of the letter and realized what had occurred.

I couldn't have attended the memorial service anyway. It had been held three days before I received the letter. I did inquire if I could be given a seventy-two hour pass to go home and be with my adopted parents. The Army didn't view it that way despite my trying to reason with Sergeant Major Chauncey. As far as he was concerned, Corcoran and Cugini were not even remotely related. The man had no compassion even as I attempted in vain to explain the circumstances on how I became part of the Cugini family. I will always remember his statement to me.

"Corcoran, don't bullshit me. There is no way in hell that a Mick like you can be part of a Wop family."

I wanted to hit him right then, but there were two factors that kept me from doing that, his size and the consequences. I retuned back to the barracks and wrote the longest letter I had ever written to my family trying to express my grief and console all of them as well. Maria informed me in the next letter that I received that Joey's memorial headstone was placed next to my mother and sister's graves. I realized then that Pa had used the Cugini family plot to bury my mother and sister.

Christmas and New Years were the loneliest holidays that time. There would be more of those in the coming years, but I didn't know that yet. We left by train for New York City and our port of embarkation on January 10th, 1918. It took us the entire two days to arrive at the Port of New York. I was told that there were over 3,000 of us that made the trip on the train. I'd been assigned to the 26th Brigade, 121st Infantry Division. The conversations about our Division and the other Brigades assigned didn't mean anything to me. It was just an enormous amount of men and material en route to somewhere over there.

The arrival at the Port of New York was beyond words as I struggled to describe in my letter to Maria later on what I witnessed as we stepped off the train and were marched in formation to the ships that were to take us to Europe. The Navy Transport Ship Atlas was the one my Brigade was assigned to. Three days later, we watched the Statue of Liberty disappear in the sunset as we steamed out of the harbor and into the darkness of the night. A routine that was set on the ship for the brigade involved showers, physical exercise, eating and training schedules. The Sergeant Major managed to orchestrate other things for us to do besides the orders he received from our Colonel to keep us busy on the voyage.

During the evenings at different intervals, we were allowed on deck to breathe fresh air. The inside of the Atlas had become foul despite the attempts to keep it clean. Odors from vomit and bodies from the crowded conditions contributed to the foul smell. Despite the cold, the deck privileges helped everyone's morale and senses. Looking at the stars at night and the slow swaying of the ship relaxed most of us when we were topside. Below deck was a different story. The swaying only added to the sickness.

I thought about Joey's death at sea and wondered what his last thoughts were before he died. Knowing Joey, I realized that he was probably too busy saving crew members to have any last second thoughts before he lost his strength and simply succumbed to the elements. He was a hero in my eyes and I hoped and prayed that I could function in a difficult circumstance just like he had done. A few letters later, after I had arrived in England, Maria informed me that Joey had received the Silver Star posthumously. It was given to Ma and Pa on a visit from a naval military official for Joey's efforts to save crew members of his ship. I also learned that Tony had joined the Navy and had completed basic training. It would be several months later before I received another letter saying he had been assigned to a Navy Transport ship ferrying more troops across the Atlantic to Europe.

I reached Portsmouth, England on January 15th. No one was happier than me to reach land. My enjoyment lasted approximately twenty minutes as I stood in the cold rain and awaited the canvas covered trucks that would transport us to

Camp Whitney. Whitney was larger, but no different than Devens had been. We were given twenty-four hours of rest until out training would begin in earnest. The intense schedule was maintained for another twelve weeks until we were in top physical shape and better marksmen than we were when we left Camp Gordon and Fort Devens. Training to crawl under live machine gun fire and hand to hand combat under the watchful eyes of experience British Non-commissioned Officers sharpened our infantry skills. In the twelfth week, I was promoted to Private First Class. I was very proud of the chevrons I earned to wear on my uniform. The letters home to Maria were more frequent now that I landed in England. Despite the intensive training I still had time each night to write. I experienced uneasiness every time I received a letter since Maria had informed me of Joey's death. We agreed to begin marking each letter with, 'Everything is fine,' on the back before we opened them. All the letters I received from Maria from that time on had that written on them. I again enjoyed mail call especially when I learned that Tony was a father of a beautiful baby girl.

By June, I was in France. In my letters, I wrote mostly of the good things that I saw in France. Despite the constant training we still endured, we were relatively safe, far enough away from the front. Describing the countryside and the people were the majority of the contents of my letters home. The minority contents were written at the end of my letters or sometimes I would add an additional page just for her to read privately. Maria shared all the letters I sent with the family during mealtimes, but they all knew that there were special parts of them that were for her alone. No one ever dared to ask her questions of the content of those lines.

Our training continued until early August when we were transported to an area called the Argonne Forest. We dug in there and awaited our orders. The nights were different now. The noises and flashes from the heavy artillery kept us awake at first until we became accustomed and managed to sleep several hours at a time.

During breakfast one morning, we were assembled and given information that we were going into combat soon. Our company Captain asked for volunteers to currier letters and information between headquarters and various posts along the lines. Being sick of the mundane schedule we had endured for the past few months, I volunteered with several other men. An hour later, we were instructed to pack our backpacks and prepare to depart to headquarters. Our arrival was uneventful for several hours until a Staff Sergeant realized that we had arrived to fulfill the currier duties. We were instructed to leave our gear except for our gas masks and helmets. Our instructions were given by a First Lieutenant who stated that our job would be to move through the trenches to other units with information on movements, orders, or anything deemed important by HQ to the other outposts.

While the Lieutenant lectured us, the Sergeant distributed .45 Colt pistols and satchels to defend and carry our messages. He was emphatic that we were to protect the information we carried with our lives. I asked if we could keep our rifles while we moved through the trenches. The officer looked in bewilderment and asked,
"Why would you ask a question like that, private?"
I responded, "Sir for our protection."
"The .45's we just issued you should accomplish that."
The Sergeant then said,
"Private, that Springfield will become very heavy with the amount of running you will have to do to get through the trenches without getting killed. It will only slow you down."

I realized I had gotten myself into a situation that I shouldn't have volunteered for. We were instructed then to stay within shouting distance of HQ so we could be readily available to receive and transport our messages when ordered to do so. We had to be prepared to leave within a moment's notice. We were also informed that we had to stay at the HQ until we were properly relieved. Despite what the Lieutenant and Sergeant had said, I elected to keep my rifle. I figured the worse I could expect to do if the rifle got too heavy would be to leave it in a trench. Until then, we sat outside HQ and waited for messages and orders to be delivered. I soon learned that we were going to be the only curriers and any replacements would only come when one of us was injured, captured or killed.

I was asleep near the HQ tent when I was awoken by the First Sergeant and instructed to report immediately inside the HQ tent. I did, and was given several messages to be delivered to a location that was indicated on a map, showing our location and the locations where the enemy was reported as being. The Lieutenant that assigned me the task stated that he had not heard from the currier he sent several hours earlier. I was ordered to complete my mission first, but if I found him, I was to instruct him that he was needed back at HQ and I was to accompany him back. I estimated the task to be approximately one mile away and looked to be a relative short run compared to what I had seen during the evening when other men had been given currier assignments.

My assignment took me through a wooded area that turned out to be the outskirts of the Argonne Forest. The name would become etched in my head a month later when a large offensive would begin there. As I scurried through the trenches in route to my destination, the Lieutenant's words became reality. I was tired, hot and the Springfield felt twice as heavy as I had been accustomed to. I began to think about ditching it

49

until I came to an intersection in the maze of the trenches I tried to navigate through. I stopped to get my bearing when I heard the noise of someone coming in my direction.

I froze and strained to hear. I could hear someone walking quickly, not making any attempt to be quiet as he came closer. I fixed my bayonet and waited. My rifle was ready and the safety was off. The figure came towards me and I yelled, "Stop and identify yourself."
The figure tried to stop and in doing so, slid in the mud in the trench and fell backwards. "Don't shoot. I'm Private Richard St. George, Bravo Company, 26th Brigade, of the 121st Infantry Division. I'm a currier."
"Get up St. George. You almost got yourself killed,"
He stood in front of me and said,
"I couldn't get through. I think I saw German troops in the trenches up ahead. I have been hiding from them for several hours now. Once they moved out, I headed back to HQ," he explained.
"Where's your rifle, St. George?"
"I don't have one. It's back at HQ. It was too heavy to carry through the trenches."
"Do you have a side arm?"
"I did, but I fell so many times I lost it in the mud somewhere. It's goddamned dark in these trenches and I wanted to keep going away from the Germans."
"Do you still have your satchel and currier papers with you that you were to deliver?" I asked.
"No, they're back there somewhere," he said.

I looked at him with a little disgust, but it wasn't my place to say anything to him except to ask where he thought he saw the enemy troops.
"How far down before I reach where you saw the Germans?"
"There's an open field in the middle of these woods. You can't

miss it."

He turned and began to move past me.

"Report back to the Lieutenant at the HQ tent. He told me to tell you. Tell him I'm heading through."

He never acknowledged me and then I realized he never asked for my name. I knew he had panicked. He disappeared into the darkness.

I continued on cautiously listening for any sounds. The mud in the trenches sucked at my boots and made it difficult to walk. Every twenty yards or so, I would stop and listen. I eventually came to the open area St. George mentioned that he heard the Germans and it started to rain. I listened intently, but only could hear the distant thundering of artillery and occasional pops from rifle shots a good distance away. The rain increased and thunder and lightning could be heard and seen in the distance. I continued on until I came to the edge of the clearing and stumbled upon St. George's satchel. The only way I stumbled upon it was the lightning flashes occasionally illuminating my way. As I picked it up, I realized it had been opened. There were no currier papers inside. I realized St. George must have seen or heard something, dropped his satchel and ran away. Whoever spooked him now had the information contained in his satchel.

I continued on and began going through a section of trenches that had many connections intersecting them. I felt uneasy walking while trying to listen intently. The lightning flashes helped me to see any movement. I thought I was hearing things. I guess it was the paranoia I was developing. Stopping about every twenty feet to listen only added to it. Then I saw movement to my left as I approached a fairly large open section in the main trench as another flash of lightning illuminated the area for a brief second. The adrenalin in my body was as at its peak. With bayonet attached and the safety off, I slowly moved forward as quietly as possible. The sucking noises my boots made in the mud made it impossible to do that. I hoped the thunder and rain would deaden the sounds.

The lightning intensified and it began to rain heavily as I inched along and tried to focus on the movement I thought I had seen to my left. The thunder deafened out any other noises the artillery was making when it occurred. As I approached the area where I thought I had seen movement, I paused and waited. I wanted to make sure I was seeing real movement and not my eyes playing tricks on me from the lightning flashes. I stood still and alert. My stillness must have caused some confusion and then curiosity for my possible adversary. The German soldier, that had heard me coming, moved out from his ambush position against the wall of the intersecting trench. He made the mistake by exposing himself just as a flash of lightning occurred. I lunged forward with my rifle as soon as I saw the movement. That alertness saved my life as I ran my bayonet into the center of his chest. He dropped his rifle that he held in his left hand. He squeezed off a round from the pistol he had in his right. The bullet passed by me and lodged in the wall of the trench behind me. The look of surprise, and then pain, on his face, registered quickly. He dropped to his knees carrying my bayonet and the barrel of my rifle down with him. I was able to dislodge the bayonet from his chest as he fell backwards into the mud. He never made a sound and never closed his eyes. He stared up at the sky as the rained splashed on his face. I remember his eyes. They were blue. His smooth skin and blonde hair made him look like a choir boy.

I regained my senses and looked around for other enemy soldiers. Convincing myself that he was the only one in the area, I checked him over and found the currier papers he had taken from St. George's satchel. I placed the papers into mine. I found other papers on him written in German. I didn't understand what was written on them, but I knew that they were not personal letters. They seemed official military correspondence so I took them.

As I started to move, I felt nauseous. I eventually vomited thinking that I had killed my first human being. The cold rain brought me back to reality that I must concentrate and move on. It was my duty to complete my assignment. I continued towards my objective cautiously and found my way to friendly lines. Somebody directed me to the officer in charge so I could present him with the currier papers St. George and I had been instructed to deliver. After he reviewed them, he barked orders to the officers and noncoms in his command post. He turned to me and asked why two sets of orders had come at the same time. I explained what had happened and how I met up with the previous currier. I also handed him the German papers in which he immediately had one of his staff begin to translate.

I never knew what those German papers contained until weeks later. I waited for return instructions for several hours until one of the NCOs told me to tag along with his company as they moved towards where HQ was. I felt a little more secure returning with these soldiers. My currier duties continued for several more weeks and were uneventful to my satisfaction. I never ran into St. George again and I wondered what happened to him. I know he never made it back to the HQ tent that night.

Early one morning, several weeks later, I was ordered to report to the HQ tent. I entered to find the Lieutenant I usually carried for, his commander and several other NCOs waiting for me. The Lieutenant introduced me to the group of men who acknowledged me, but never spoke. They waited for our Colonel to arrive. The Lieutenant called the group to attention when he entered.

53

"Everyone at ease," he said.

"Private Corcoran, I have the pleasure to inform you that you have been promoted to Corporal. I am recommending you for a Bronze Star for capturing enemy papers and delivering them in time for the command center to take action."

I didn't say a word. I liked the promotion. It meant more money. The medal didn't register. I thought medals went to heroes like Joey and were given posthumously.

"Corporal Corcoran, what do you have to say for yourself?" he asked. I guess I didn't answer immediately.

"Corcoran, the Colonel asked you a question," the Lieutenant barked.

I suddenly realized I had been addressed and responded,

"I'm sorry Sir. I just didn't understand why you were giving me a medal."

"Well you deserve one son. Congratulations. The papers you took off that German detailed a surprise offensive that would have split our division in two causing considerable loss of life and territory."

Later, I would be informed at a small ceremony that was held for me and some others in front of our brigade, that the Germans must have discovered the repositioning of our troops and cancelled their offensive. In late September, I was relieved of my currier duties and reassigned back with my brigade.

The Meuse-Argonne offensive, as it was called, started on September 24th, three days after I returned to the brigade. For two days, we lay in our trenches. We witnessed and heard the most incredible artillery barrage. On September 26th we moved out of our trenches and across several miles of open ground in the early morning hours. I remembered that day because it would have been my mother's thirty-eighth birthday. I said my prayers that morning and hoped that her spirit would guide me to safety on the other side of the forest as we drove further into enemy territory. The Argonne Forest would be the biggest battle sight fought by the American Expeditionary Force during the war. The section of the forest we penetrated was south of a place called Reims. We had it easier than others who had to deal with the heavy forest and slow advance north and south of us as we headed east. We followed the Meuse River on the first day and ran into little resistance. I fired my rifle at distant figures as they scrambled away from our assault. There were very few casualties on either side as we moved forward until the Germans detected our quick advance by the river and began shelling us to stop our progress. The intense artillery cut our ranks in half during the afternoon and evening hours of that first day. I saw men who were twenty or thirty yards ahead of me completely disintegrate when artillery shells exploded on them. The earth shaking from the blasts almost broke my legs at times as the ground moved to give way from the force of the explosions. Some men broke from the river's edge for the protection of the forest. It was a bad decision. They were killed or wounded by the millions of wood splinters and projectiles that cut through them from the force of the explosions hitting the fur trees above. I yelled to those who were around me to keep to the river's edge and hoped that we would be better off. Some followed, but some panicked and ran from instinct to the protection of the trees.

I found a large artillery hole and jumped into it to look at my map I drew from the satchel I still carried. I needed to get my bearings in all the confusion that had started when the Germans began their artillery fire. The river up ahead bent around towards a place called Forges. By the looks of the buildings that were visible, the city had undergone extensive damage for the past several years. The other city I saw on the map, Verdun, was southeast of us. I remembered reading about Verdun a few years earlier. I wondered how the French could have endured the destruction and carnage that continued to happen there. The forest encompassed the cities and we were almost in the center of this offensive.

A brigade sergeant major screamed at me to keep moving with the men I had around me. By the look on his face, he was more mad than scared. I followed his lead as the artillery barrage began to lessen as we advanced past the city. We advanced for another mile, occasionally finding some small groups of Germans attempting to make a defensive stand. I shot, as others did, at those who stood and fought. I never really knew if I hit anyone. Too many American soldiers were firing at the same men I was. I saw men shooting at the dead Germans to make sure they were dead as we overran their positions. We continued this advance until we stopped well inside the forest at dark. The sergeant major found me and several other non-coms and explained that we faced another very difficult task. I thought that we had just survived a difficult task already. I listened as he explained that the German lines we were attempting to penetrate were up to twelve miles deep and had been under development since 1915. He also explained that we had managed to penetrate the first line that ran through Verdun and Forges. The second line was based on the hill of Montfaucon several miles ahead. The third line, called the Hindenburg, was on the hills at Romagne ten miles from there. He told us that the entire area was hilly and wooded, cut by steep sided valleys, many running across the proposed line of advance. As we broke from his informal briefing, he told me to get some attention for my face and forehead. I realized then that the stinging I had been feeling in my face was caused by some shrapnel that had cut me and required medical attention. The medic who eventually treated me noticed that I had also received wounds to my upper chest and left shoulder. He spent about twenty minutes removing pieces of metal from my wounds. To this day, I never could figure out why I didn't feel more pain. Years later I was told by other combat veterans that the pain had to have been masked by the adrenaline my body was producing from sheer fear.

That night, we lay in hastily dug fox holes, artillery holes and behind anything that would protect us from German sharpshooters. We ate cold food due to orders that no campfires could be lit. I thought about Maria and what she would be doing at the big house during Indian summer. That was the best time to live in New England. I remembered the warm days and comfortable, cool nights. My dream world broke into reality as the sergeant major woke me at 2300 hours and stated that we would advance at 0500 hours the next morning. I tried to get a little sleep, but the artillery noise from both sides was deafening at times and my shrapnel wounds burnt too much for me to get comfortable enough to sleep.

The next morning, through thick fog, we advanced slowly for about ten minutes until we reached the next line of defense. We attacked straight away with as much enthusiasm that I had ever witnessed. I killed several men as we overran one of the many trenches and logged barriers the Germans had dug or built. I witnessed hand to hand combat where men were clubbing and fist fighting when they lost their weapons. I shot as many Germans as I could who were fighting hand to hand with Americans. We advanced about a mile until we came under severe rifle and machine gunfire and had to seek cover. Despite all the enthusiasm, our advance wasn't well organized and we splintered into small pockets until we could regroup during darkness. This continued on for several more days until our advance ended about five miles from where we started. I only recognized a few men that started out with me. The others must have been injured, dead or splintered into other groups as we attempted to advance in the thickness of the forest. Along the Meuse, we were able to advance five miles, but in the Argonne forest, they were only able to move about two miles.

57

By the start of October, the divisions used in the initial assault were exhausted and our commanders were forced to order a halt while we received new replacements all along the line.

We were allowed to rest for several days. In that time, I was able to get issued clean socks and underwear. I remember peeling off the ones I was forced to wear since our initial advance. I had never been as filthy in my life as I was during that time. I stripped and walked into the Meuse River one early evening. To my amazement, several hundred other men had the same idea. I had a little bar of soap with me. The soap burnt me as I washed my private areas that had been irritated by the lack of hygiene. A whistle blew as I was dressing on the bank. Some officer was screaming at us to get out of the river and back into our assigned defensive areas. We moved as instructed, but it was a very slow noticeable movement from the men back to their positions. It was ordered, that in the future, no bathing was allowed in the river at any time.

A day later on October 4th, our commanders ordered a series of frontal assaults for two weeks that finally broke through the main German defenses. In those two weeks, I witnessed every conceivable way a man could die at the hands of his enemy. Every night I rested with men that I would probably not see by the end of the next day. Companies became non-existent by the end of October as we had advanced the ten miles and had finally cleared the Argonne Forest.

Our advance continued slowly during the first ten days of November. In all, since our initial movement on the 26th of September, we had advanced less than thirty miles. In the early morning hours of November 11th, our company was assigned to probe enemy defenses about four hundred yards directly ahead of us. We prepared to move out at 0600 hours when we were ordered to stand down only minutes before. We expected that an artillery barrage had been ordered to soften up the advance. We lay and waited for the barrage which never came. It was noon time when we heard cheering and other noises coming from our rear positions. A major informed our company commander that an armistice had been declared an hour before.

I thanked all that was holy that God had finally intervened on mankind's behalf and ended the carnage. I thought maybe my mother had convinced the Almighty to spare me as well. The war to end all wars ended at 11.00 a.m. on 11 November 1918. Later, I was informed that the 121st Infantry Division had sixteen hundred wounded and twelve hundred dead. There were over five hundred men still reported missing. From September 26th until the armistice, all this carnage took place in only forty eight days. I stood in the trench and yelled and screamed as the others were doing. Then, as I comprehended what it really meant, I knelt down on one knee and gave thanks. I realized the tears were streaming down my face as I made the sign of the cross. I was going home.

We remained at our position for a week until we were ordered to phase back. We were transported by canvas covered trucks about forty miles from our most forward position. We set up camp for another two weeks until we were transported back to the Port of Cherbourg, France. All of us assumed we would be in New York in ten days, but we were transported to Portsmouth, England instead where barracks had been assigned for the 121st Infantry. Our daily schedule consisted of physical training starting at 0500 hours and ended at 1600 hours. In between the eleven hour days, we endured formations, marching, and rifle range practice to maintain our readiness for something. That schedule was maintained for several weeks until we started noticing men reporting for sick call in an ever increasing number. The Spanish Influenza began to take its toll on the 121st and other brigades stationed in England at

Christmas time. Within a week, I caught it and spent two miserable weeks in the dispensary with the worst chills, aches, diarrhea and vomiting I had ever experienced in my life up to that point. It took three weeks before the flu ran its course in our area. By the time it had worked its way through the American Expeditionary Force both in Europe and America, 53,000 men had died which was more than our combat deaths.

During that time our regiment suffered from the flu, the letters I received from Maria never indicated that the flu had reach the United States. Only a few days back from the hospital, I received a letter that didn't have the note, 'Everything is alright' noted on the reverse side. I slowly opened it to be updated that Ma, Pa, Rose and Danny had caught the flu, but were on the mend. Lucia and Loretta had not caught it despite both of them working at the hospital in the food service and the laundry after school. Maria stated that she had caught it too, but she was alright now. The tragedy had been the little angel that Rose and Tony had created. Their baby girl, Michelle, had died from the influenza several weeks ago. Tony was notified by wire, but he could not attend the funeral because he was still at sea on the transport ship, Trident. I thought about my sister Mary Beth when I heard the news. I didn't cry for little Michelle because I never knew her. I felt sorrow for Rose and Tony. Maria explained that both of them had written to each other stating that they felt responsible. Rose anguished for passing the flu to her child and Tony was guilt ridden for not being able to see his daughter before she was buried. It took me two days to write and finish the letter addressing my sorrow for the death of that baby. I finished and mailed it the same day we were informed we were going home. It took two days for the transport ship to gather as many soldiers it could handle for the trip across the Atlantic. Two days later, we embarked from Portsmouth, England and headed for New York City on January 10th, 1919.

I stored my gear in the three foot by two foot steel locker box I was assigned. It was several hours before I realized I was on the Navy Transport Ship Trident. That was the ship that Tony had been assigned to.

What were the chances of that, I thought, as I excited myself thinking I would be able to see Tony on my trip back home. Then, the reality of the situation set in. My mind wondered, *How was he going to react when he saw me on the ship and we talked about little Michelle?*

I decided that we could deal with it. We were family and Pa would want us to deal with it no matter how painful it would be.

Chapter Four – Going Home
The Convalescent Home

I woke up and found several nurses and technicians standing by my bed as the doctor talked to Mary. I heard him tell her, "There's a possibility that he would not be able to breathe on his own once I remove the tube and machine."
He paused for a few moments and asked,
"Do you want the breathing tube and machine reattached if he fails to breathe on his own?"
I loved her answer. She was a chip off the old block.
"Hell yes doctor," she said. "I want him to have every chance in the world to try to make it through this stroke. If he fails, I want him to have more time to build up his health to breathe on his own. His mind is fine and we just need the rest of him to catch up."
That's my girl, I thought while laying there.
The doctor never rebutted or commented. I waited for the tube to be removed.

It took less than thirty seconds for the tube to come out and the machine to be turned off. I was breathing on my own and I signaled with my eyes, fingers and toes that I approved. Mary laughed and bent down and kissed me as she saw my communications skills and smooth breathing. As the hospital staff departed, Mary and I carried on a question and answer game until I was exhausted. I tried to speak, but could only make a little noise. I must have looked frustrated, so she tried to calm me by sitting next to the bed and running her fingers up and down on my arm. I could feel her touch and that was a good sign. My feelings were returning ever so slowly, but returning. I began to tire and tried to force myself to stay awake, but the fatigue from all the activity of the day caused me to slip off to sleep again.

The Story

I asked Sergeant Major Chauncey to grant me permission to see the brigade colonel the second day of our steaming out of Portsmouth, England. I explained the circumstances and the old guy treated me better this time than he had back at Fort Devens. He arranged for me to see the colonel on the third day. When I reported, I had to sit in his outer office for the better part of an hour until I was finally called in. I entered, smartly stood in front of his desk, saluted and waited for his return salute. For several uncomfortable moments, I stood there waiting for him to acknowledge my presence. Finally, he saluted and said,

"Stand at ease Corporal."

I complied as he continued to read some papers in front of him. He finished what he was reading and then called out for his staff assistant to enter the room. The man was a lieutenant so I jumped back to attention and was immediately told to stand at ease again.

The colonel looked at me, smiled and said, "Sergeant Corcoran, that's right sergeant, I would like to congratulate you on your promotion. You have been highly recommended by several NCOs that observed you in action in the Argonne Forest. Your service is exemplary and this promotion is effective today. While you are here, I am also awarding you the Purple Heart for the shrapnel wounds you received on the Meuse River. Your medical report stated that you received nineteen pieces of shrapnel in your body of which some are still embedded there. Along with the Bronze Star you already have earned, I'd say you performed your duties to the utmost expectation of the Army, Sergeant Corcoran. Congratulations."

I didn't know what to say except thank you.

"Thank you Sergeant," he said as he handed me the medal box

and the sergeant chevrons.

"Now what was the original matter your Sergeant Major had informed me that you needed to see me about?"

I explained that my brother Tony was onboard the Trident and that I wanted to ask his permission to able to find him because I knew the troops were separated and not allowed to roam the ship and interfere with the crew.

"Tony Corcoran, I'll ask the Executive Officer of the Trident to let you visit Sergeant," he said.

"No sir, his name is Tony Cugini," I quickly stated.

I knew I should have been more specific so I explained the situation of our relationship. He actually listened for a minute when he stopped me and said,

"Sergeant, whatever your relationship with Cugini is, you've earned my permission. Lieutenant, contact the Executive Officer and arrange for Sergeant Corcoran's request."

I responded and thanked the man. He looked at me and said,

"Corcoran, before you go anywhere, you sew on those sergeant chevrons."

"Yes, sir and I will do that immediately." I saluted and was dismissed.

I quickly returned with, and sewed on, my new stripes. Several of my closest companions kidded me for being a lifer now and telling me that I would be staying in the army now that I was a sergeant. A few shook my hand and congratulated me. I quickly sewed them on and waited for permission to see Tony. Chow came and as I finished my meal, I still hadn't heard anything. *Typical army bull shit,* I thought.

Someone had to screw up this simple request. It had to fail because two branches of the military were involved. Each branch probably had enough trouble coordinating things within their own never mind having to coordinate anything between them.

Sergeant Major Chauncey yelled over to me to come and see him. His calling me Sergeant caught me off guard and he had to repeat his call twice.

"Did you forget your name Corcoran?" he asked.

"No Sergeant Major I'm just not use to sergeant yet."

"Well get use to it," he said as he handed me a piece of paper. I looked it over as he said,

"You got written permission for two hours to find Cugini, bullshit, and get back to your area. You arrange with him where you guys can meet at other times when both of you are not on duty. Do you understand?"

"Yes Sergeant Major, I do."

I quickly moved out of the mess hall and headed for the upper decks and on my way to finding my brother. I received a few odd looks from some of the crew until I was stopped by some Navy chief who screamed at me to stop where I was. After several uncomfortable moments, he read my permission slip and directed me to the upper forward bunk room where most of the crew slept. Several minutes later, I found the large room and began asking the sailors I encountered if they knew Tony Cugini. I became a little discouraged until I asked one guy who said, "Who wants to know?"

"I do. I'm his brother."

He looked at me strangely and said, "You sure don't look like him."

"I know. I'm his foster brother. His ma and pa took me in when I was a kid."

"Oh, you're the hero he's been talking about since his last letters came in from his wife and sisters."

"Mister, I'm no hero. I just want to find my brother," I said.

He pointed to a bunk and told me, "Sit there. He'll be back in a few. He probably went to use the head." I thanked him and waited which seemed an eternity.

Then I saw him, walking and kidding with a few guys as he made his way towards me. He didn't notice me at first until he was almost at his bunk. He froze when he saw me. His eyes widened and he looked me up and down several times. He never spoke. He flung himself at me as we embraced in front of all the sailors in the bunk room who looked at us strangely at first, but then realized that we were related. The word got out fast from the sailors who had heard the original conversation I had with one of Tony's friends who told me to wait at his bunk until he returned. Several started to clap as we stayed clutched together and not saying a word. I knew we were both happy, but saddened at the same time as we thought about Joey and little Michelle. We parted with tears streaming down our faces as we both tried to comfort each other on the tragedies that had occurred since we last saw each other. Most of the sailors walked away as they witnessed our reactions. There were a few misty eyes among them as they left us in private.

Tony and I sat on his bunk and talked for an hour. We cried as each of us described the pain we had when we heard about the two deaths in our family. We laughed as we reminisced of the days we spent together in the big house. Tony assured me that the last letters he received from Rose and Maria indicated they were all relieved that I had made it back from the front. I explained to him where I had been in the Argonne Forest. He listened and shook his head along with a few sailors that bunked immediately next to him who could hear the entire conversation. I kept close watch on my time. I set up a time to meet Tony near one of the deck stairs that separated the troop decks from the crew decks. We met every night at 1800 hours until the day we reached the Port of New York. In those ten remaining days, we bonded closer than we had ever done before.

We arrived at the Port of New York on January 22nd, 1919. The entire brigade watched as the Statue of Liberty passed us on our way to dock the ship. It had been almost thirteen months since I had seen the welcoming lady. Several tugs sprayed water straight in the air which at first alarmed me until I was told that it was a salute to the troops who had returned from the war. It took forever for us to dock and then another half a day waiting for our brigade to depart the ship. I did get a few moments that day to see Tony. We talked about when we would see each other again at the big house. I hoped to be discharged in a month or so, but he had several more months before he would be discharged from the Navy. He explained that he would probably have to do one more trip to bring soldiers and Marines back from England before he would get discharged. We hugged at the crew's stairway and I departed several hours later. It would be a three day ride to reach Fort Devens by truck this time, for discharge.

At Devens, we turned in our rifles and side arms in the first week. We were allowed to keep several uniforms and boots. Anything else was considered Government Issue and was expected to be returned. Two weeks later, I was honorably discharged from the U.S. Army just before my nineteenth birthday. I had a month's pay in cash and a year's worth of pay in my savings bank account in Norwich. I hoped to use part of that money to buy Maria a nice ring to officially mark our engagement as I climbed aboard the Worchester and Providence railroad car for my return trip home. The train slowly moved away from the Fort to the cheers of the hundreds of soldiers that had been discharged and were going home. We finally settled down as the train gained speed and headed for Providence. We reached the city nine hours later. I changed trains and had to wait in a cold station until the next morning. I spent half the night taking to other men who I never knew that had been to the same places in England and France that I had. Some fought in the same offensives and I never knew any of them until now. The Norwich and New London Train arrived early that February morning as a light snow began to fall. By the time I reached Norwich, there were three inches of snow on the ground as I stepped off the train. I slipped and slid in it as I pushed to get to the trolley stop before the next one came.

As the trolley arrived, I drew out some change from my pocket for the fare. I handed the driver three cents. He informed me that the ride was a nickel now. I didn't care because I was cold, hungry, tired and homesick. I would have paid a dollar to get to Boswell Avenue and the big house. I guess the look on my perplexed face caused him to react when he said,
"You just come home from the front?" I nodded in acknowledgement.
"Where were you at?"
"The Argonne Forest from August to Armistice," I responded.
"Welcome home son. The fare is on me." He handed me my money back. I smiled and thanked the man and found a seat.

The trolley ride through the snow was relaxing. Everything seemed to move slowly as the snow continued to fall. I stayed on until it stopped at the intersection of Boswell Avenue and Broad Street. I planned that so I could walk down hill with my heavy duffle bag. The snow was falling faster as I began to step on the porch. I could see someone walking up the hill from the city. The walk was unmistakable. It was Pa carrying his tool bag coming home from work early. The weather must have caused the foremen to cancel work at their construction site. I put down my bag and stepped back onto the snow covered sidewalk in full view as he trudged up the street. He stopped in his tracks when he recognized me. He dropped his bag as I ran, slipping and sliding to him, bent down and wrapped my arms around his stocky torso. We didn't say a word for several minutes. We just stood there and hugged. Occasionally, I could hear him sniffle, but I held him tight until

68

I had enough control of my emotions to speak. I managed to get a short sentence out.

"I'm home Pa. I stayed safe and I hope I made you proud?"

He was speechless and only nodded as he grabbed me again for another hug.

He finally spoke and said, "Come, we tell everyone you home."

I began to talk about Joey and Michelle when he stopped me by putting his finger to my lips and said, "This now is good time. We no speak of bad time. We talk later. This is special day. Come, we see the family."

We both entered the big house as Pa yelled that he was home early. I could hear Ma yell back that she was in the kitchen. He motioned for me to wait as he opened the door and said,

"I got present for you. Come see."

She didn't react at first as she attended to something cooking on the stove. He called out again,

"Mama, come see. I got present for you."

She hesitated as she tried to figure out the grin he had from ear to ear. He stepped aside for her to be able to see me in my uniform with all my ribbons. She burst into tears as she ran and hugged me. Her tears were happy, but I'm sure some were sad as well as she probably thought of the son and granddaughter she had lost a year ago. Lucia and then Loretta came running in from school and screeched when they saw us hugging in the reception room. They screeched and carried on so much that Pa had to tell them they were giving him a headache. I hugged them both. Little Danny was not little anymore. He had grown quite a bit since I'd last seen him. His likeness to Joey was uncanny. He hugged me as Rose slowly approached. I hugged her and quickly told her I had seen Tony and he would be home in a few months. We agreed to talk later so I could give her as much details as I could about him and the transport ship he was on.

69

It was so great to be home again amongst almost all my family. I looked at Ma and asked,
"Where is Maria?" She smiled and informed me that she was still at work. I had known she got a job after graduation through her letters. She now worked in the Dime Bank as a teller. She glanced at the clock on the wall and in her broken English said,
"She home from work very soon."

Pa directed everyone out of the reception room to the kitchen so that Maria would see me as soon as she entered the house. While I waited in the kitchen, I was offered coffee, cheese and fruit until I succumbed to some Italian cookies Ma had just made. Lucia yelled that she had spotted Maria walking up the hill in the snow. Loretta squealed in her excitement only to be quieted by Pa. Everyone quietly stayed in the kitchen while I moved back into the reception room.

I checked myself in the large mirror in the room. I adjusted my cap, pulled at my uniform to make sure it looked neat and swallowed the remaining cookie I had jammed into my mouth when I heard she was walking up the hill. I heard her stepping onto the porch and pounding her boots to get the snow cleared off them before she entered the house. The large oak door slightly squeaked as she opened it. Her eyes widened and the blue color I remembered so well and had kept in my mind was the deepest it ever was now. Her face lit up and her eyes moistened as she slowly, but steadily walked and threw herself into my arms. We embraced, kissed and cried as we stood there in that reception room while Ma, Pa and the kids took periodic quick glances at us through the slightly ajar kitchen door. I remembered that it was over eighty-seven years ago as I awoke and realized that I was still in the convalescent home bed.

The Convalescent Home

Mary noticed my tears and asked if I was in any pain. The concern on her face was very evident so I attempted to smile to assure her that I wasn't in any. Her eyes widened as she saw the ever so slight smile I managed to give her.

"Great-granddad, you just smiled at me. Well it looked like a little one, but nevertheless, it was a smile," she said.

I moved my hands, wrists and toes to indicate to her it was my attempt to smile. I felt more encouraged now that I knew I could get better over time. I just didn't know how much time it would take and if I had that time left.

Mary called for the nurse and asked if the doctor could order a physical therapist to work with me now that I showed signs of improvement. The same nurse that explained I wasn't the same man anymore pulled the same bullshit and said it was too early to even think about performing physical therapy on me. I thought, *there she goes again. What a bitch.* Mary made her disagreement known.

"Nurse, I want you to make a note in my great-grandfather's records to inform the doctor to see me personally so that I can discuss the therapy I want for him. Do I make myself clear?"

The nurse never repudiated the request, but the look on her face indicated her complete disagreement.

Go girl, that's my Mary, I thought, while I listened to the one way verbal cat fight.

My great-granddaughter elevated my bed slightly so that I could see more of my surroundings now that I could span the room with my eyes. Mary continued to talk and encourage me to move my wrists, ankles or anything I could manage.

"Feel your body, Liam. Concentrate on moving anything you

put your mind to. I will move your arms and maybe you will be able to feel them moving. Come on concentrate," she said as she slowly moved my right arm up and down. I closed my eyes and tried to concentrate as she had asked. I could feel my fingers and wrist, but I couldn't get control of my arm muscles even though I could barely feel her grip on my arm. She continued alternating my two arms until I moved my feet and toes enough for her to ask me if I was tired. I communicated by rapidly blinking that I was. She bent down, kissed me and said, "Now, I never saw you blink that fast. That's good. Okay, you rest for now. We'll do some more this evening when I come back with Mom and Dad."

I looked forward to seeing my grandson and his wife. I thought that maybe they would come more regularly now that I had shown some promise that I wasn't ready for the grave yet. I watched Mary leave and thought how much she looked like Maria did at that age until I fell off to sleep again from sheer exhaustion.

The Story

My first evening back at the big house was memorable. The heavy snow fell and the cold wind blew outside, but I didn't care one bit as I stood in the warm kitchen helping my family with the evening meal preparation for the boarders and then a special one for the family. Nothing had seemed to change in the thirteen months that I had been away except for the noticeable absence of Joey. I'm sure they felt the absence of little Michelle. Ma asked me why I had taken off my uniform so soon because I looked so handsome in it. I quickly responded,
"I just want to forget about the uniform, the Army and the time I spent away from home." She glanced at Pa who asked me to

come with him for a few minutes. I followed him to the cellar door. He stopped and motioned for me to follow him down as he then disappeared into the dim light of the wine cellar. I paused as I watched him descend the old stairs. He noticed my hesitation when he reached the bottom of the stairs and looked up.

"Liam, please. You come down and sit."

Once in the wine cellar, he picked out three bottles of wine that had he had apparently put aside. He had marked them with a red, white and blue ribbon tied around the neck of each bottle. I looked at the three bottles as he handed two of them to me.

"What kind is this? Something special you made?" I asked.

He paused for several seconds, cleared his voice and said,

"I make wine for each of you when you return. You home now. We drink wine tonight and be happy." I smiled as I realized the man had kept them for the return of his three sons.

"Okay, but we drink to Joey tonight," I said while patting him on the shoulder.

"We drink two bottles. One for you and one to remember Joey. You wear Army clothes to Mass on Sunday. Ma and me be proud. You be proud all time. You show to children someday you in war. We drink the other bottle when Tony come home."

The message was clear. I told him that I would wear it to Mass and after, I would always keep my uniform so that someday my children would know that I served my country. His eyes moistened and them he smiled. He grabbed several more bottles of wine and said, "Next day is Saturday. We drink much tonight, yes?"

I nodded as I took a few more bottles and we headed back up from the cellar stairs to the kitchen.

We ate, talked and drank. A few times during our supper, our eyes filled with tears as I would bring up something funny that

I remembered that Joey had said or done. Maria sat close to me and kept touching my thigh under the table. When she rubbed it during my conversation, it indicated that it was approved, but when she grabbed my knee and squeezed, it was a signal for me not to pursue the conversation. Too many references or conversations about Joey or little Michelle were those that I received the warnings on. Later, Maria told me that she didn't want her parents or Rose to get too upset during my celebration dinner. She felt the celebration was a good thing for everyone right now. She explained there would be a time to ask more about Joey and little Michelle. I remembered that Pa had expressed that feeling when I first hugged him on the street that afternoon.

We finished dinner and then, as we all began the cleanup, Ma told both Maria and I that the others could finish up and dismissed us with a big smile. We left quickly to find somewhere in the big house to be alone. It was almost impossible because Lucia and Loretta had invited some boys over and they would occupy the living room when they arrived. Ma and Pa would be there as well to keep a watchful eye on the young gentlemen. Danny followed us everywhere and stuck to me like glue. He continued to ask questions about Europe and the war until Maria started to become impatient with him. Several of the boarders who needed to talk to Pa or Ma on other matters became curious as well as to what it was like in France and England. Needless to say, it was midnight before we had the living room to ourselves.

We sat there and looked at each other. We laughed knowing that we had not been left alone all night and now that we were alone, we knew exactly what we wanted to do, but couldn't. I asked her if she would like to spend an afternoon in the Wauregan Hotel to be alone. She looked at me and said, "No hotel. This is our house and I will come to you when I feel it is the right time. We must be very discreet."

She kissed me and said goodnight. It would be several weeks before I found her in my bed for several hours of early morning passion. That very conservative conjugal schedule continued on for a few more occasions until June. In June, Tony was discharged just in time for him and Rose to stand up for Maria and me when we married in St. Patrick's. The reception was held in the big house and it was the beginning of a better time for Ma and Pa.

I had started working for Torrance Construction again in March when contracts for several new buildings were awarded for the Norwich State Hospital. We hoped the projects the contracts produced would keep Pa and me very busy for a few years. I worked mostly on the staging and carpentry crew. The day before I started my new job, I visited the cemetery to see my mother and sister. The cement headstones had bleached almost completely white. I placed two roses Ma Cugini had given me several days before at Sunday lunch, as a reminder that it had been five years since they had departed this earth. I thanked my mother for the prayers she must have said to protect me during those terrible months in September, October and November in the Argonne Forest.

I was pretty good at building staging for the masons and other trades. The trade superintendent took notice of my skills those first six months working. In October, I was promoted to staging foreman. This meant more money for Maria and me. We had moved to a comfortable three story apartment house Pa rented to us cheap. He had bought the property while his boys were in the service in anticipation that when they returned, they would marry and need places of their own. Tony and Rose lived on the main floor. The third floor was eventually rented out to a Jewish couple named Cohen that Maria and I became very friendly with in the winter of that year. Joseph Cohen was a finish carpenter who had just opened up a wood working shop in the city. He was a Navy veteran and served on destroyers like Joey had. His wife, Harriet, and Maria knew each other while they attended high school. All was well in the summer of 1919 when Maria and Harriet both announced they were pregnant. Not to be outdone, Tony and Rose announced that she was carrying twins. Life was good in Norwich and Ma and Pa excitedly awaited the birth of their new grandchildren.

We all gathered for Sunday lunch in late October. Most of us knew that Ma had been feeling tired and run down for better part of a month now. She had also developed a cough that we found out had been keeping her up at night adding to her general malaise. She managed to eat a little lunch that day, but quickly retired to her room. Maria decided to take action and eventually convinced her to see a doctor the next week. Maria arranged to take part of the day off from the bank in order to take her to the doctor.

I returned home from work several days later after Ma's visit to the doctor to find Maria sitting in the living room on the sofa. She had been crying. Alarmed that something was wrong with our baby, I tensed and asked, "What's wrong?"
"I just received a call from Ma's doctor. He called me at the bank to inform me that the x-rays he had taken of Ma a few days ago revealed that she is suffering from the early stage of tuberculosis. Liam, she will need to be hospitalized at the sanatorium until she recovers. God only know how long that will be."
"Does she know yet?" I asked.
"Yes, but Ma would not let me tell anyone until the family gathered at Sunday lunch. I tried to convince her to inform everyone immediately, but she wants everyone to be present so we can explain the seriousness of and the treatment for the illness. Her reasoning is that everyone should be told at once,

in front of Pa where all the questions can be asked and explained. What will Pa say?"

"Maria, calm down. What else did the doctor say?"

"He scheduled her for treatment to begin next week. He said she needed to get help and that she could be contagious to us. My God Liam, she could infect any of us. Worst yet, the doctor wants no physical contact with me especially because I'm pregnant."

She burst into tears. I consoled her. I can't remember what I said, but I remember holding her for a long time. Maria and I both dreaded that Sunday mealtime when it arrived, but we respected Ma's wishes and carried out her request.

We waited until the dessert was finished. Before Pa could light up his pipe and the activities for the cleanup commenced, Ma asked everyone to sit because she had an announcement to make. Stillness evoked the family members as Ma turned to Maria and nodded to begin. Maria explained, "You all know of Ma's visit to the doctor."

Everyone listened intently,

"The doctor read Ma's x-rays and diagnosed her with having tuberculosis."

Maria never finished because the initial reaction from the girls was hysteria until Pa pounded on the table for quiet so that Maria could continue explaining what would be happening in the months ahead.

I stood by her side holding her hand as she explained for several minutes and then looked around as she finished. Some whimpering could be heard from Lucia and Loretta as Pa asked,

"How long in hospital?"

"Pa, she could be in the sanatorium for as long as a year," Maria said,

"The doctor will not know that until Ma begins to respond to the treatment he has ordered for her. Only then will he have some idea for a timetable for her recovery and release from the sanatorium."

Ma never said a word as she looked down and occasionally shifted her eyes to Pa as Maria finished. Tony asked,

"Will she be cured of the illness?"

"The chances are very, very good that she will and live out the rest of her life free of the illness. That is, if treatment is administered as soon as possible."

Pa nodded and then requested,

"Please, everyone leave kitchen."

We immediately exited as he got up and sat next to Ma while removing Danny from her side who had failed to follow Pa's request to leave the kitchen. We never knew what was said between the couple, but the following week, Pa and I took the day off to accompany her to the sanatorium to begin her treatment. It upset Maria terribly that she could not go with us which made it even worse for Ma to see her in that state.

On the day he left her at the sanatorium, Ma hugged and kissed Pa good-by. I saw her whisper something in Italian to him. It made him cry openly until she whispered something else in his ear. It calmed him and also made him smile. She whispered one more thing that I did hear.

"I get better and be home before babies are born."

It made Pa smile again. I noticed a look of confidence in her face that she would get better as she turned and left both of us standing at the entrance way.

Every week after Sunday Mass and before lunch, Pa visited Ma at the Sanatorium. Each time he visited, he would bring one of his children with him so that they would have a special moment with their mother. Danny was one of the most frequent visitors and everyone thought it was justifiably so. Being only

78

eleven now, it took its toll on him not having his mother around every day. Maria and Rose still could not visit, which hurt them both so deeply. I visited every few weeks and could see the improvement in her condition. Ma looked forward to hearing about Maria and Rose and their pregnancies. We were all sure that her need to be home at the time of the birth of these grandchildren was the driving force in her to accelerate her recovery.

By January, the doctor informed the family that Ma was progressing very well. He hoped to be able to dismiss her by the end of March. It upset her knowing that Rose would probably deliver before then due to her size and the strain of carrying twins full term. Maria was due at the end of March. This being her first child, and only nineteen, she figured she would carry full term and may actually be late and deliver in April. Ma was right. Rose delivered on the twentieth of March. Lucia and Loretta assisted the midwife for the twin's delivery. The event lasted all morning and ended with the announcement that Rose had delivered a son and a daughter. With all the excitement that evening, I realized it had been the sixth anniversary of the death of my mother and sister. I felt very guilty that I had forgotten to visit and made a promise to myself that I would visit the following morning, early, before I went to work. I realized that Ma would have reminded me if she had been home because she would have handed me the two roses to place near their stones. Maria made my guilt disappear when she informed me that Rose and Tony named their children Joey and Mary Beth. I broke down with more happiness than sorrow when I realized these two beautiful little babies would carry on the names of two very important people in my life that I had lost. It seemed to me, at that moment, they were reincarnated. My tears of joy were comforted by the hug Maria gave me until I composed myself.

Pa and I visited Ma the following Sunday and informed her of the birth of the twins. She was ecstatic on hearing the news, but disappointed that she had not been there to assist Rose in the delivery. She talked with us for only a few minutes. She smiled at me and then asked that I follow her to her room. Pa began to follow when she motioned for him to wait and said,

"Only him. Lam help. We come back."

Pa looked perplexed, but abided by her wishes. She led me to her room where she had packed the two cases that she'd been allowed to bring with her when she was first admitted. She handed me both cases and said,

"You carry for me. I well now. Doctor say go home."

I hugged her and whispered into her ear,

"Maria is going to have the baby right now when she sees you at home."

She laughed and said,

"No, Antonio will have baby now, you watch."

She led the way back to the reception room. I lagged behind to give her time to tell him that she could leave now. I stood back and just watched. Pa sat down and cried. It took Ma several minutes of holding him before he composed himself as she hugged him. I slowly headed for the exit while he gathered himself for the trolley ride back to the big house. Before we boarded the trolley Ma smiled and said,

"See, he almost had baby. I tell you."

Maria cried almost uncontrollably when she saw Ma come through the kitchen door. Ma worried that she would deliver that day, but she calmed her as she could always do. I caught some grief from Maria because I didn't inform her that mother was being released. But Ma came to my rescue and explained she wanted to surprise everyone and she wanted some time alone with her husband because she knew how he would react. The best part of the day was after the reunion and the Sunday lunch with the rest of the family.

Ma was updated on all that had happened and was pleased to hear that Kippy Sullivan and Loretta Cugini were going to be the Godparents when Tony and Rose had the twins christened a month later. The sight of Ma holding Joey and Mary Beth and gleaming just before the baptismal ceremony was forever etched into my mind.

The Convalescent Home

I woke up crying. It was happy tears thinking about Ma holding those two little babies in her arms all those years ago. I realized that I had visitors. Mary bent over me and said, "My Mom and Dad are here. They are waiting in the lounge. We were waiting for you to wake up, sleepy head. You want to see them before visiting hours are over don't you?"
I smiled and said my first word, "Yes."
Mary quickly left to get them. Upon her return she asked me, "Great-granddad, please say that word again. They don't believe me."
I hadn't seen my grandson and his wife for months before my stroke. Dick and Linda never found time to visit me like their daughter had. But they were here and I was pleased that they had come. I smiled in which they both noticed. I concentrated and said, "Yes."
Dick and Linda both smiled at each other and then at their daughter. They had witnessed the beginning of something positive. Little did they know what I really wanted to say, but only thought which was, *Yes, you doubting brats, I can speak. I am alive.*

81

Chapter Five – Prohibition

The Convalescent Home

My grandson's visit was nice, but he let Mary handle all the communications between us. I guess looking at me drooling and listening to my incoherent sounds was too much for his wife Linda to handle, so Dick cut their visit short. If he had any fortitude left in him, he would have asked her to step outside while Mary and he tried to communicate with me. It was obvious to me and Mary that he didn't. Neither of us was very upset when he made up the lame excuse that they had to leave, but would be back soon.
Yeah soon, what the hell did that mean? I asked myself.

Mary was sweet and covered for her parents as much as she could. I motioned to her, in my primitive way that I didn't care right now.
When I could speak, it would be the time to let Linda and Dick know that I was disappointed in them, I thought. I wondered how a beautiful and compassionate young woman like Mary could have been created from the loins of those two nincompoops.

Mary stayed with me until well past the visiting hours. The charge nurse had to warn her to leave or be escorted out. I was thankful for this young lady. I also hoped that she wasn't letting her visits to help with my personal physical therapy keep her away from some boyfriend she hadn't told me about. With her beautiful looks and outward personality, she was a catch for any young man. I figured I would approach the subject when I could talk better. I watched her leave and closed my eyes. In a few minutes, sleep overcame me.

The Story

Two weeks after Ma returned and everything seemed in order, I returned from work to find the house empty. A few lights were on, but there was no sign of any activity that supper was being prepared. We hadn't received our new phone that we ordered yet. It would be several more weeks until it would be installed, so I quickly went downstairs to Tony and Rose's to see if Maria was there. Their apartment door was locked and no lights were on. Alarmed, I ran upstairs to check with the Cohens. It took Harriet, what seemed a lifetime, to answer the door. The little lady was finding it very difficult to walk now that she had come to full term and was expecting her baby any day. I asked,

"Have you seen Maria?"

Her only reply was, "You don't know?"

"Know what?" I said as I raised my voice in a slight panic. By then, Joe Cohen had come to the entranceway and said,

"Maria left with Rose and the Twins about 4:00 p.m."

"Was Tony with them?" I asked.

Both of them shook their heads negatively as I turned and sprinted down the stairway and headed for the big house. It took me less than two minutes to cover the quarter mile from Division Street to Boswell Avenue. I arrived to find Tony and Rose attending to the twins in the kitchen with Pa.

"Is Maria here?" I blurted out.

Pa rose and said, "Yes, and you sit like we do."

I went to question him when he anticipated it and said, "You Ma, sisters and doctor are with her now."

"Is everything okay?" I asked as my pitch became louder. Rose immediately calmed me when she said,

"Dr. Moore has arrived because the mid-wife was busy with another patient." She pulled me down to sit at the kitchen table while Pa poured me a rather large glass of wine. I shook my

head and said,
"I don't want any right now." Pa looked and said,
"Drink. You need. Drink now."
I sipped a little. He gave me the look that I would always remember when he was not pleased with one of his children. He never said a word, but pushed the wine glass closer to me. I took several more gulps and his facial expression changed. I looked at the clock on the wall. It was 5:17 p.m. We all sat at the table and waited. Several hours later, and several more glasses of Pa's best, I heard the unmistaken sound of a baby crying. We all looked at each other and then at the kitchen door leading down to the room that Ma had chosen as the birthing room. We waited for Lucia, Loretta or Ma to bring us the news of the new baby that we all had heard only seconds earlier.

It seemed an eternity until Ma entered the kitchen smiling. I stood up and she said, "Come see your little girl."
Tony shook my hand, but Pa asked, "Baby and Maria Okay?"
Ma smiled and nodded her head. Pa smiled and said,
"Salute."
He took a large gulp of wine that made his nose glow a little redder. Ma gave him the look and said,
"You make coffee for everyone, yes?"
He understood, smiled, finished the rest of his wine and moved to make the coffee. Ma had been nervous about Pa's drinking and wine making in the cellar ever since prohibition was passed over a year ago.

I followed Ma to the berthing room. My child bride was sitting up and holding our little angel. Maria's face had, what looked to be, freckles all over it. She smiled with those bright blue eyes and said, "Come and meet your daughter."
My expression wasn't what Maria expected.
"Are you disappointed, Liam?" The look on her face drove a deep pain in my heart.

"No honey, I am so proud and happy. Your face was a surprise to me. That's all," I said.

I knelt beside the bed and kissed her and the baby each on the forehead. Dr. Moore picked up on the conversation and said, "Liam, that's what we call Mother's mask. Most of it will go away in a month or so and eventually all of it will disappear. It's a natural thing when mother's push as hard as your wife did to have this baby girl. Congratulations."

He gave a few instructions to Ma as he finished washing his hands and then left.

Maria's face returned to the beam she had first exhibited when I first came into the room.

"Oh, you worry about everything," she said and smiled.

"I'll always worry about both of you for my entire life," I said and kissed her again. She asked me if I thought about a name. I paused and said,

"You pick her name."

"Well, I thought about it for a while and I would like to name her Christine in honor of your mother. Would that please you?" she asked.

I was choked with emotion and only nodded while moisture collected in my eyes. She noticed it and knew immediately that it pleased me and said,

"Good. Everyone meet little Christine."

Ma asked me to take Christine to the kitchen so the rest of the family could see their newest addition. I walked into the kitchen carrying my little angel and announced her name. It was one of the proudest days of my life. Danny was the last member to arrive in the kitchen. When I saw him, I told him that he was going to be Christine's Godfather. I turned to Lucia and asked her to be her Godmother. She squealed as usual which made the baby jump. Pa shook his head, gritted his teeth and looked at her. Loretta patted me on the back and said I had made a good choice.

The next morning, I visited the cemetery before work. I brought two yellow roses Ma had given to me when she realized that with all the activity, she had forgotten as well. I placed them in front of the headstones of my mother and sister and announced the arrival of little Christine. I'm sure both of them were pleased.

On the following Sunday after Mass, Maria and I brought Christine over to the big house for Sunday lunch. As we proceeded from Division Street to Boswell Avenue for the five minute walk, I noticed several men parked in a black Packard Sedan. I didn't think too much of it until I entered the big house when Tony approached me and said,
"Did you see the two guys sitting in that expensive Packard across the street?"
"Yeah, that's a pretty nice car. Who are they? None of our neighbors around here can afford a car like that." I said.
"They're not neighbors and they are not from around here. They have been coming and going for several days now according to some of our neighbors I checked with. Pa noticed them and asked me to inquire around as to who they were," he said as he closed the reception room curtain.

Tony motioned for me to follow him as Maria took Christine into the kitchen with the rest of the family to prepare for Sunday lunch. We descended the cellar stairs and found Pa busy filling wine bottles from one of the aging barrels that he had tapped. I can still see him with his glasses set low on his nose as he carefully poured his latest batch. He never looked up at the two of us as we stood there, until he finished with one particular bottle. Tony spoke up first and said,
"Nobody in the neighborhood knows who they are, Pa"
I remained quiet as he pondered Tony's statement and said,

"Not policemen. They drive Fords. Not Revenuers, they break in by now. I think they want to buy. I no sell to anyone."

I asked, "Pa, what do we do if they are bootleggers? You know the kind we read in the papers every week."

The old man looked away from both of us as he contemplated what I had just asked.

"I no sell. I break up wine cellar and make no more."

The thought of him breaking up the best Italian wine center in all of Norwich brought mixed emotions from Tony and me. The Packard stayed parked on the street for the afternoon. We ate lunch and seemed to forget about the two men until I asked Danny to escort Maria, Rose and the three children home before it got dark. I explained to both women that I wanted to stay with Pa and Tony for a few more hours. My hunch was right. The two men knocked on the door as soon as it was dark.

Tony and I answered the door. The first gentleman asked if he could speak to Pa. I invited them into the reception room and asked them to wait until Tony fetched him. As soon as Pa entered, the first man, who never introduced himself, stated that he had an employer that was very interested in purchasing some of his wine barrels. He explained that the word on the street was that Tony Cugini made excellent wine. Pa smiled.

"Yes, I make good wine, but not for sale. I no wanna break the law."

Taken back at first, the man paused and then said,

"Mr. Cugini, I am prepared to pay well to convince you to sell the barrels my employer needs."

Pa looked him squarely in the eyes and said,

"I break all wine barrels so no can sell to anyone. You get out. Tell you boss what I say." The man smiled and looked at both Tony and me.

"I will tell him, but I don't think he will be very pleased."

Several days passed before I stopped off at the big house on my way home from work. I noticed the Packard again. This time, it was parked directly in front of the house with two men standing near the car. They watched me as I quickly entered to find Pa sitting in the kitchen with two men. The first one was the same guy I had seen before. The second one seemed to be talking directly at Pa. When they saw me enter the kitchen, Pa rose and said,

"You sit and listen."

The conversation continued and I was able to surmise that the man wanted to pay Pa by the barrel for his table wine and was detailing how the deliveries would be made as to not alert the Revenuers.

The old man listened and pondered the profit possibilities and also the consequences. The boss guy finally became impatient and asked Pa,

"Do we have a deal?"

Pa didn't respond at first, which made me feel very uncomfortable by the looks I was seeing coming from these two characters.

"Do you fight in war?" Pa asked.

The boss guy looked perplexed at first, but then said,

"Did I do what?"

"You fight in war?" Pa asked again.

"No, I didn't. Neither of us did,"

"Why?" Pa asked.

"What difference does that make, Cugini?" the boss guy said.

Pa's face changed and he gritted his teeth as he spoke,

"My name Mister Cugini. All my sons fight in wars. One no come home. He win medal, but rests with the fishes."

He then pointed to me and continued,

"This one fight in France and win more medals. My oldest was in Navy. Stayed on ocean many months. You two not good Americans because you beat system and you no earn it. Get out of my house, now."

Both guys stood up very quickly. I followed suit just as Tony entered the kitchen which made the second guy turn around quickly and stare at him. I could tell by the bulges in their coats that they were armed and I hoped that they would just leave without any further incident. The boss guy said,

"You will be losing a lot of money, Mr. Cugini. I warn you, do not sell to anyone else."

"Get out of house. I smash all my barrels before I sell to anyone. I no break law,"

he said as I could hear his teeth grinding again and see his face turning redder. Both men exited quickly. The second guy kept his hand close to where I suspected he had a pistol as he backed out of the kitchen, through the reception room and out to the Packard. All four entered the car and left down towards the city.

Pa kept mumbling to himself as he slowly got control of his temper. Tony and I didn't say a word until he spoke first.

"In daytime, I pay Kippy to watch house. At night, we take turns to make sure nobody comes."

I asked, "You are not going to destroy the barrels and bottles are you?"

"No. I like wine. You like wine. We drink here. Okay. Nothing change."

"What do we do if they come back?" Tony asked.

"I call cops last time. I talk with Chief today. He will know about this today."

Tony and I smiled knowing that the old man was up front about everything. He had already reported them even before their second visit. Tony pointed it out to me on our walk back to the apartment house that night that Chief Mahoney loved Pa's wine.

"Don't you remember the Chief always stopped by the big house when he was just a patrolman?"

"No, I hadn't come to live here yet. But I do remember him

89

coming as he made rank."

"Pa always offered a glass and sat him down just to keep on the good side of the local patrolman," Tony said.

"Yeah, I always wondered why he came by the house on his off days too."

"It wasn't so much for him because Mrs. Mahoney liked the wine more," Tony said.

"She still owns a seamstress shop, doesn't she? I think Maria goes there to buy cloth," I said.

"Why do you think she always gave Ma good deals on materials and clothing repairs?"

"Yeah, come to think of it, Maria won't go anywhere else to get clothes altered."

"So now you know some of the connections Pa makes."

No further incidents occurred with the guys in the Packard except their occasional night drive-bys to check on us. I guess there were too many people in the city that enjoyed Tony Cugini's wine and his bartering system which included the Norwich Police. Everyone Pa dealt with was accustomed to the bartering system and it worked. He received goods and services and provided people with good wine for home consumption without having to sell one drop of it. There were incidents we heard of and we read in the newspapers where a boat would be confiscated off Long Island Sound or a still or two were broken up by the Revenuers in the outlining towns. We were fortunate to be rid of those guys that came to us in that Packard that year.

Christine was walking by the summer of 1921 when Maria announced that we were expecting another child. Again, and not to be outdone, the Cohens announced that they were expecting their second as well. Maria and Harriet joked that they would exchange babies if each one was the same sex as their first. Harriet and Joe Cohen's son Alex was growing leaps and bounds. He towered over little Christine, but would cry every time she grabbed him while they played together. It was comical to watch Joe cringe when his so-called little football player would cry every time little Christine pushed or took a toy from him. Every time Maria and Harriet would bring up the subject about exchanging babies I would always kid Joe that his second son would have to be tougher before I would take him. We teased each other a lot, but we were very close friends. The friendship we developed would mature into a partnership that would last a lifetime.

The Convalescent Home

I woke up to find my room empty. It was 2:15 a.m. according to the clock on the wall. My bitchy evening nurse had left instructions that they were to check me every two hours to make sure I did not soil myself like I managed to do on her shift twice in the past week. I couldn't help it then. I couldn't feel the urge to have a bowel movement and when I did have one, it had been loose. I overheard the nurse say that the intravenous nutrition I was receiving was causing the loose movements. One sense that I did still possess was smell. I pitied the staff when they had changed me. I also dreaded the indignity that I had to endure while they did it. Luckily, the changing was accomplished, so far, when Mary was not visiting.

A few minutes passed when an aide came into the room to check on me. She saw that I was awake and asked if I had the urge to move my bowels. I said yes because I realized that I could sense the feeling that I had to go. She called out to one of the male attendants who came into the room, lifted my hips onto a bedpan and waited for me to finish. I was actually pleased that I managed to accomplish this very elementary task. Until a few days ago, it was a major chore. I was also able to say thanks when the dirty deed was completed.

The information of my accomplishment was duly noted in my records. The attending physician commented on them when he visited me a few hours later on his early morning rounds. He wrote orders for the staff to remove my catheter now that I told him I had some feelings. I truly felt like I was becoming a human being again. I felt good about myself for the first time since the stroke. I was pleased that Mary had been influential enough to get the convalescent home doctor to recommend a regular routine physical therapy program for me. Every day I felt a little more strength and feelings in my body and I was grateful that God had granted me this each day.

I had seen Mary every day for the last several, but she didn't show one morning. I was disappointed, but was sure she must have had another engagement that she told me about, but I failed to remember. Her absence was more significant because it was the first day of my physical therapy. The attendant assisted me to sit me up in bed. My first assignment was to move my arms over my head. I struggled for what seemed an eternity, but I managed to move my arms away from my torso. The attempt was to get them over my head. I'm sure the therapist realized it would be a long time before I would be able to accomplish that task. The first therapy session lasted only thirty minutes. It seemed like thirty hours. I was exhausted from it and immediately fell off to sleep within minutes of my completed session.

The Story

The autumn of 1921 was an exciting time for Lucia as well as for the rest of the family. Ma and Pa were proud that she was another member of the family to graduate from the Norwich

Free Academy that June, but were even more proud when she received notification in July, that she had been accepted into St. Francis Hospital Nursing School. She had shown a strong interest in nursing when she worked in the Backus Hospital cafeteria after school part-time and other jobs she was given there. She also assisted the local mid-wives delivering babies. During the first week of September, Pa, Ma, Lucia and I departed for the nursing school in Pa's 1921 Ford Model T Touring car he just purchased for $620. Tony and I were the only two family members who had driver's licenses, so we had flipped a coin to see who would have the pleasure to drive them to the school. We started out on that warm Saturday September morning and didn't reach our destination until mid-afternoon after having one flat and two refreshment stops. The return trip was less eventful, but lasted into the later evening hours. Although happy that her daughter was attending the school, Ma was very apprehensive that she would be away from home months at a time. For the next three years, Lucia would live at the nursing dorm except for a few holiday breaks and a one month vacation every year in the summer. I laugh about it today because the Nursing School was only sixty-five miles from Norwich. In 1921 that seemed far away.

Maria and I became very close to Harriet and Joe Cohen that year. The women bonded deeper as if they were sisters. I spent a few hours every week working in Joe's finish carpentry shop. I only picked up a few dollars, but gained a lot of knowledge on finished carpentry. Joe was a great teacher and I absorbed as much as he could teach me. On weekends when he requested my assistance, I would help him install finished cabinets, deliver specialty furniture pieces or anything that required help for deliveries. The work at the carpentry shop began to increase and Joe hired me full-time when I was laid off from Torrance Construction during the harsh winter months. With my assistance and ability to learn quickly, by March of 1922 when

93

Torrance Construction called back their carpenters, I stayed with Joe's carpentry shop and invested most of our savings to become his junior partner.

Mr. Torrance tried several times to convince me to return to his construction company, but I politely declined hoping that Joe and I could build a cabinet and furniture business that could survive and support Norwich and the surrounding area. Mr. Torrance even called Pa to have him try and convince me to return to the stage building foremen's job. Pa was truthful with the construction business owner that I preferred finished carpentry. I knew that Pa had left the door open for me in case I changed my mind or in case the business didn't pan out.

Within the first months I worked in the shop, I convinced Joe that I could handle the furniture building and repair portion of the business while he concentrated on the specialty item portion that he was very well known for. Orders for Grand Father Clock cabinets, corner hutches, dining sets and colonial and old English reproduction pieces were increasing so that Joe had to hire two more apprentice finish carpenters to assist him. I was able to hire one more experienced furniture maker to assist me and our business began to grow. We worked twelve hours a day and six days a week as Cohen and Corcoran Carpentry Company grew in size and reputation. We were nicknamed the Triple C by our customers. Our two delivery trucks displayed three painted red, white and blue C's locked together, on the sides of each truck.

I finished work one night at five o'clock. It had been a light day and I decided to leave early to spend a little more time with Christine and to comfort Maria who was now in her ninth month. The warm May days were taking their toll on her. I returned home and found her sitting in the kitchen with a cold towel placed on the back of her neck trying to feed Christine

94

who was being a very difficult two year old. She burst into tears as I walked through the kitchen door hoping to find my girls excited that I had returned home early from work on this day. What I found was a very pregnant woman with messed hair struggling with her two year old to eat.

I came to the rescue and took Christine into my arms and tickled her. I used that to lure her into finishing her supper while Maria fixed us a plate. We all ate. I volunteered to wash the dishes and clean up while Maria retreated to the bathroom to draw herself a much needed bath to relax. About a half hour later she returned to help me put Christine to bed. No sooner than we thought we would relax, Maria told me that she needed Harriet and Rose. I knew from the expression on her face that she was going into labor. I immediately fetched the two women and called Ma and Loretta to come over as soon as they could. I wished that Lucia would have been home from nursing school in time for this delivery, but that was several months away.

I stayed with Christine in her room while the women arrived and began setting up our bedroom into a berthing place. Several hours later, the mid-wife arrived. She had been summoned when the women thought it was time for her to be there for the delivery. I paced back and forth. I could hear the occasional cries coming from the berthing place. At ten minutes to twelve that night, Maria delivered. I waited to be summoned by one of the women to inform me of the arrival of our second child. No one came as I heard a second cry. I began to feel uncomfortable and was contemplating going in before I was summoned, but decided against it. A few minutes later, after the clock chiming in the living room struck midnight, I heard footsteps approaching Christine's bedroom. It was Loretta, who beamed as she opened the door.
"Come see your babies, Liam." She squealed which startled Christine who had been sleeping until that time. Christine cried

95

as I passed Loretta out the bedroom door. She knew immediately to pick up Christine and cuddle her. My heart pounded as I entered the berthing room. Maria laid there exhausted, but her deep blue eyes confirmed that everything was alright.

"Say hello to your sons, Liam" I stood there a little confused until Loretta's statement and now Maria's sunk in. We had twin boys.

"My God Maria, twins. Holy shit, twin boys."

It wasn't exactly what Maria wanted to hear, but she smiled and nodded as she held the two of them, one in each arm. Ma immediately shook her head on hearing the statement I had made hearing the news.

"Lam, use better words next time," she said with a little frown which turned into a smirk. Harriet laughed at my remark as she waddled around awaiting her turn any day and said, "I guess there will be no need to exchange babies now that you have two sons, Liam." Maria asked if I had considered any names for our sons.

"Honey," I said, "It hasn't registered yet that I have a son never mind that I have two of them."

Loretta came into the room holding Christine. I took her into my arms, paused for almost a minute and said, "Sweetheart, meet your brothers, Lawrence and Leonard."

I looked at Maria for her approval. She smiled and I knew she agreed. I realized that this was the second set of twins in the family. I wondered if there were more to come. I made a point to visit my mother and sister's graves that following Sunday. Ma Cugini had the yellow roses ready for me before I left for the cemetery.

We christened the twins a few weeks later. We asked Tony and Rose to be the God parents for both boys. It was a task for them to make church on time with Joey and Mary Beth. Both of them were at their height of the terrible twos. We actually had to have a few cousins keep them preoccupied while Tony and Rose participated in the ceremony. As I watched the festivities, I couldn't help but think that Joey and my sister Mary Beth could have been the God parents of the boys. Joey would have been twenty-two now and Mary Beth twenty.

Who knows, I thought. *They could have fallen in love and had children of their own. It could have happened. I'm sure my mother would have approved.*
Being in the church relaxed me as I pondered. I even thought about heaven. *Maybe Joey and Mary Beth were together up there.* I had to get the thought out of my mind.
Would Joey love Mary Beth as much as I loved Maria? And if he did, could he make love to her in heaven or not?
The thought quickly went away as I realized everyone was looking at me. Maria nudged me and reality set in. The priest had apparently asked me to light a candle to begin the ceremony, but I had missed it. After that, everything continued on smoothly until the end of the baptism. Harriet Cohen's water broke and she was quickly escorted out of the church. That night, she delivered her second son. They named him Andrew.

In June, Cohen and Corcoran Carpentry Company received its first large order. The Norwich State Hospital had contracted with us for two hundred chairs and desks for the teaching section of the hospital. The order had to be completed by August and prior to the start of the training classes. I set up a schedule for ten sets to be made a week in order to include delivery of all the furniture by the last week in August. Joe was a little apprehensive of my tight schedule, but he assisted with his resources when it was slow in the specialty section. We worked ten hours a day and six on Saturdays to get the order completed in time. Our hope was to be able to get contracts as the new buildings were being built. We also planned to invest some of our profit into some automated equipment to reduce our time and increase our productivity. Joe started to look for a larger building to rent or lease to accommodate our expansion. The summer of 1922 was an exciting time for our growing business and families.

On the last Sunday of August, we all picnicked at Spaulding Pond in Mohegan Park. It took Pa's Model T Touring car and the Company's two trucks to get everyone up to the park for the day. This was the first summer that the family had begun to use the park. The children were introduced to the water for the first time and Pa, Tony and I were tasked with teaching the children, and some of the adults, how to swim. We enjoyed the hot weather, but enjoyed swimming and cooling in the spring water that fed the pond even more. Joe and Harriet explained that when the pond froze over, many people cut holes in the ice and fished. I remember seeing that going on when I was a kid, but confessed that I had never had time to try ice fishing. Joe stated that he would show me how it was done one Sunday in January. Harriet also promised to teach us all how to ice skate. We laughed when Joe stated,
"That is if you're not pregnant again." The laugh was on him when she responded with,
"I already could be. Did you ever consider that, smart mouth?"
We all laughed even harder.

The weather had been excessively hot that week and it seemed almost every day we had a summer thunderstorm that only contributed more muggy nights for all of us to endure. The children found it difficult to sleep and Maria and I took turns with the fussing twin boys. It seemed when one finally went to sleep, the other one would wake and the process would repeat all over again. It was during one of those hot nights when Loretta called us to say that Ma was having difficulty breathing and Lucia had taken her to the hospital. Luckily for the family, Lucia was home and she immediately recognized the signs that Ma was having cardiac problems. Kippy Sullivan had been dating Lucia when she was home from nursing school and the couple had just returned from an evening movie when Loretta had met them at the door of the big house to explain that Ma wasn't feeling good. Maria and I woke Harriet and Joe up and had them babysit for our three children while I took Maria in the Triple C Carpentry truck to the Backus Hospital.

When we arrived, we were informed by Lucia that old Dr. Moore had brought in a heart specialist to attend to Ma. We waited several hours until the specialist and Dr. Moore informed us that Ma had a cardiac episode, but that she was resting comfortably and that we could see her in the morning. The doctors explained that Ma would need to rest for several weeks and that her activities would have to be at a minimum. That meant to all of us that she could not be maintaining the big house which meant no fussing and pampering us and her boarders. We all made a pact that we would watch her constantly and do as much as possible to relieve her of her chores and the stress of running it.

Pa never said a word the entire time of the emergency except when the doctors had finished their prognosis. He asked,
"Can she travel soon?"
The doctors looked at him and agreed that if she rested and followed their instructions, she could be healthy enough to travel in two to three months. Pa looked at all of us in the hospital waiting room and said,
"Good. We do as doctors say. I send Ma to Italy to visit brothers and sister when time." He looked at Loretta.
"You go too, yes? Loretta smiled and said, "Yes Pa, but only if she is strong again and the doctors say so."
"Good. Then it is done. I tell her when it is time."

Two weeks later, we brought Ma home. After several days of being pampered, Lucia had to inform the family to stay away. We did. We also stayed away from Sunday lunch the following week which caused Ma to become more irritated than ever. That Sunday evening, we were all summoned to the big house. Amongst crying babies and snippy siblings, she entered the kitchen. We all quieted down and listened to her speak in Italian about how she appreciated our extreme kindness in helping her and also our obedience in staying away for her benefit, but she wanted her family back to normal. She realized she had been sick, but she promised to recover as long as everyone acted normal. If she felt she needed help, she would ask for it. She also promised to listen to her daughter, the nurse, so that she would recover quickly. She then walked around the room and kissed every one of us individually and told us she loved us. Her departing words for that evening were,

"Now go home. Love your children. Good night."

Pa beamed as he escorted her out of the kitchen and into the privacy of their room. We all knew that Ma was going to be just fine.

As the fall approached, Ma seemed back to her old self again. She had slowed a little, but she took control of her health following Lucia's instructions and had almost made a full recovery. It was at one Sunday lunch that she and Pa announced that she would be traveling to Italy to see her three brothers and sister. She explained that it had been twenty eight years since she had seen any of them. Ma had left Italy with Pa for the shores of America when she was a nineteen year old bride in 1894. I asked Pa that day if he should have taken some time off to visit Italy with her. He laughed and said,

"You Mada's family not like me too good. I take Josephine to America. No need to see. No need for them to see me. They never see Loretta and will like to see her. Loretta good for Ma

100

on trip."

That was the extent of the conversation. In October of 1922, Loretta and Ma left New London for the New York City Pier and a voyage by steamship to Italy.

Kippy Sullivan had spent that summer courting Lucia. They had dated frequently and we all knew that Kippy was in love with the future nurse. One evening, Tony came upstairs to our apartment and asked me to come for a ride with him. Very clandestinely, we drove down to a speakeasy in Norwichtown. The owner of the speakeasy had called Tony to come and fetch Kippy. Apparently he had become so inebriated, that he wet himself and was unable to walk, never mind drive.

We arrived at the place and were quickly escorted to a back room where Kippy lay unconscious. We carried him into the company truck and drove to small cafe where we could begin to start pouring hot black coffee into him before we took him back to the big house and his small boarder's room. We both agreed that we did not want to have Pa see him in that condition.

During the sobering up process, we surmised, through Kippy's crying, slurring and dry heaves, that Lucia had turned down his proposal for marriage. We both realized how in love he was with her. We stayed up with him for most of the night and convinced him that he would have to be patient because she had almost two more years of nursing school to complete. We encouraged him to wait for her and approach the subject when she was reaching her graduation date. That seemed to soften the rejection he had so miserably endured. A few weeks later when Lucia would return for the Thanksgiving break, Kippy asked her on another date. This time she declined knowing that he had feelings for her. She hoped that her rejection of him would be clear that she was not interested in

101

marriage. Even though she thought of him as a friend, she never wanted to mislead him. He finally realized she was not in love with him when Lucia didn't come home for the Christmas break.

Two days before Christmas of 1922, Ma and Loretta returned from their visit to Italy. Ma brought back an extra luggage case of personal items that her siblings had given her from her parents. Ma and Loretta told many stories about their experience in Italy. The down side of the visit was the change that Italy was going through from the rise in power of Benito Mussolini and his Fascist government. After her visit, Ma asked Pa to sponsor any of her nieces and nephews that wanted to come to America. Pa agreed, but only one nephew took advantage of his charitable gesture a few months later.

During the Christmas week, Kippy Sullivan was reintroduced to my sister Loretta. The eighteen year old had blossomed into the spitting image of her one year older sister Lucia. Loretta's attention to Kippy that holiday season far exceeded any of Lucia's past interest in him and the tall Irishman turned a new leaf. Although cautious with his relationship with Loretta, their affection for each other grew.

Chapter Six – Prosperity

The Story

Kippy continued to court Loretta in the winter and spring of 1923. Even Lucia's return for Easter didn't upset the lover's apple cart. We all held our breath when Lucia came home and was told that Kippy had been dating Loretta. To our surprise, Lucia could have not reacted better. Tony and I realized that she really didn't see Kippy as her future husband. He was just a friend. But Loretta, on the other hand, saw Kippy in a much different light. It was to our relief that all went well.

Once Lucia accepted their relationship, everyone in the family was pleased that a good friend and tested comrade would be the next son-in-law to Antonio and Josephine Cugini. Kippy asked Pa for Loretta's hand in marriage that April. The next day, on her nineteenth birthday, he asked her and gave her a diamond. Kippy was the first to buy a half carat diamond ring. It was the biggest stone I had ever seen in our family up to that time. They set a date in October to marry. Tony and Rose were asked to be the best man and maid of honor.

That spring Cohen and Corcoran Carpentry Company expanded into a larger building in the city. The furniture section of the company had doubled with the State Hospital furniture contracts and the Norwich board of education had contracted with us to make several hundred pieces of furniture for their expanding school system. We now had two full-time finish carpenters and six full-time furniture makers. Maria and Harriet maintained the books and payroll for the ten employees and life was good.

103

The Convalescent Home

"Great-granddad, great-granddad, it's time to wake up."
I opened my eyes and saw Mary standing over me. I looked at the clock on the wall and realized that I had slept in this particular morning. It was already seven o'clock and I had almost missed breakfast and the physical therapist would be barking orders at me in a few minutes. I slowly spoke.
"I guess I was tired." Mary just looked at me in amazement and said, "Great-granddad, that's the first full clear sentence you have said since you became ill."
Her eyes were moistened and she bent down and hugged me. I realized that what I had actually thought was actually what I said.
"Can you ask the nurse if I can have my breakfast? Did you understand?"
"Loud and clear," she said and gleamed.

My speech was not perfect by any means, but my ability to communicate had greatly improved. I was able to go through the physical therapy session and I was able to raise my hands and arms above my head two consecutive times. My therapist, my great- granddaughter and I were all pleased. My most pleasurable moment came that evening when my charge nurse came in. In her irritating voice, she congratulated me and said, "I understand you spoke a clear sentence today. Congratulations, Mr. Corcoran, you have come a long way."
I smiled and thought how negative she had been all during my recovery and now she was standing there congratulating me on saying a complete sentence. So I slowly, but precisely replied, "Nurse, you are so full of shit."
The attendant that was assisting me with my dinner, almost choked and started to chuckle, which did not amuse the charge nurse. She quickly told him to finish up with me and

concentrate on some of the other patients he was assigned to. She then abruptly turned and exited the room. He winked at me and mumbled under his breath,

"You started something now, Liam. You better get better a lot quicker and get out of here soon."

The next day when Mary visited, I could see by the look on her face that she was concerned about something. She began her usual pleasantries until I stopped her and asked, "What's wrong, Honey?"

"Well Great-granddad, I understand you were rude to the night charge nurse according to her turnover notes to the day shift. What was that all about?" she asked.

I smiled which probably irritated the sweet girl even more.

"Great-granddad, if you are ever going to get out of this place you must be as pleasant as possible. You'll get a lot more attention and better care that way. You once told me that you get more with honey than you do with vinegar."

"You are right. I will be nice to her," I said. I didn't mean it, but I would try.

The therapist came in and started my thirty minute session. On this day, I had enough strength to sit up with little assistance. For the first time in many weeks, I was turned so that my legs hung over the edge of the bed. I sat up straight with the help of the therapist and Mary on each side. My greatest achievement for that session was the ability to move my legs as they dangled over the edge. Ten minutes of that tired the hell out of me. As I lay back in bed when the session completed, I asked the therapist,

"When would it be possible for someone to lift me out of bed so that I could use a wheelchair? Wouldn't that be good therapy for my arms and chest conditioning?"

Both the therapist and Mary looked at each other until the therapist said,

"Mr. Corcoran, that's a good idea. We'll try it in a few days."
Several hours later while I lay in bed trying to nap, I thought
about the day we bought our first automobile.

The Story

Triple C Company had two trucks that were constantly being
used to deliver finished goods, pick up lumber and hardware
used in the shop as well as support two growing families when
we needed to go somewhere as a group. Joe and I both felt a
little guilty when we had to use the business vehicles for
personal use, so Maria and I decided that we could afford a
vehicle if the price was right. A new automobile for $600 or
$700 was out of our price range, but I was sure I could pick up
a mechanically sound used one for half the price. For several
months, we looked around and eventually found a used 1920
Model T Touring, as advertised, from a woman on Laurel Hill.

Maria and the children accompanied me in the Triple C
delivery truck after Mass one Sunday morning to look at the
automobile. The woman who was selling the Ford was
pleasant, but also a little melancholy as she discussed how her
husband had maintained it and the places he liked to drive to
during his retirement years. As she talked, I looked the car over
and observed that it needed some tires and one seat had a little
field mouse damage to it, evidence the car had sat in an old
shed for better part of a year since the owner's death. She
explained that her husband died in the shed where the
automobile had been parked. She told us that a neighbor found
him. Apparently, he collapsed while he was tinkering with it.
Maria could see the sadness in her expressions as she described
how he took good care of the three year old Model T. Maria's
kindness seemed to bring out the best in people who seemed to
tell her their life story. No matter where Maria went, people

106

were attracted to her and supplied her with more information than she needed to hear. Maria had a beautiful heart and always politely listened.

Such was the case until the twins started to act up while I checked over the car and started it. The Ford turned over very quickly and purred like a kitten. The woman switched stories and told Maria,

"You are very fortunate to have such beautiful children. My husband and I were not able to have any in our forty-three years of marriage. I guess the car was my husband's baby."

With all this going on, I didn't have the heart to ask the woman how much she would take for the automobile. I hoped I would be able to offer her $400 maximum. No more that $425 which was our entire auto savings. I waited for my opportunity, but my beautiful wife beat me to it when she said,

"Madame, you have some very interesting stories and I would love to stay and listen to as many you would care to tell me, but my children are beginning to act up and I need to get them home for lunch. I'm sure you understand. My husband seems to like your husband's automobile very much. I'm impressed as well, so what are you asking for the vehicle?"

The woman smiled and said,

"You have such a nice family and I'm sure you will take care of Harold's baby very well. I'm sure I could let her go for, let's see, $350."

Maria looked at me and I nodded, but she wasn't finished.

"That's a fair price, but it should be a good price in honor of your husband and the way he took care of his baby as you called it. Liam, go to the truck and fetch $370 for this fine woman."

Never questioning, I retrieved the cash and handed it to Maria.

"Now, here is your money. My husband will return with his brother to pick up the car this afternoon. Please have the title and a receipt ready and thank you very much."

That was it. I picked up the car after Sunday lunch. Tony and I spent the afternoon cleaning up the 1920 Model T Touring while Maria and Rose found some leather to fix the seat. I used the money we had left over to purchase four new tires and I kept the old ones as spares.

The next evolution in the modern era was to teach Maria how to drive. I wasn't sure what to expect when I began her driving lessons. She learned very quickly because she was a modern woman who knew that her independence would be increased by her ability to get anywhere she needed by herself. But mostly she did it for our family. The several emergencies she had experienced reminded her of the need for personal and available transportation. She enjoyed the summer months when we were able to go to Spaulding Pond at our convenience and take small leisure drives through Norwichtown and the surrounding towns for the children to see the dairy farms and horse stables. Maria did most of the driving while I watched the children and occasionally the road during the summer months of 1923.

Maria and I had set the standard. Within several months, Tony and Rose bought a 1921 Model T Touring from a family in Taftville. The car had been in a minor accident, but Tony, Skippy and I worked on it for several weeks and fixed or replaced the parts that were damaged. Once he had the auto painted, it looked brand new. Joe and Harriet Cohen outdid us all. They purchased a brand new 1923 Packard. They never told us what they paid for it, but the two Packard trucks the company used were very reliable and I'm sure that the dealer gave him a good deal. Kippy Sullivan got in on the action and decided to buy a used 1922 Nash Roadster Model 42. It was the prettiest car I had ever seen. With its tan convertible top and dark green color, it was the envy of many of the automobile owners in our neck of the city. Kippy bought it because it matched Loretta's eyes. He was a ham, but a good one and Loretta loved him for it. I can still see the two of them sitting in that pretty two door car waving to all the family members as they left the reception hall for their honeymoon that October.

That same summer, as everyone was considering or buying automobiles, the family received its newest member. Giuseppe Cedrone arrived from Italy. He was Ma Cugini's great-nephew and he alone had taken up the offer to be sponsored by Antonio Cugini to come to America. The twenty year old had arrived to begin an apprenticeship as a stone and brick mason. Previous to his year in the apprenticeship in the old country, he'd been passed from one family member of Ma's to another since his parents died. His father was killed in the Austrian Alps fighting in 1916 and his mother had died from the 1918 pandemic. Giuseppe saw no reason to stay in Mussolini's Italy after meeting and listening to Ma and Loretta talk about the advantages he could have if he came to this country.

Pa worked out an arrangement with Mr. Torrance for Giuseppe to begin his apprenticeship under Pa's guidance. In the meantime, Joe Cohen and I hired the immigrant as a part-time helper in the shop. He worked hard, but it was difficult for him to communicate with the rest of our crew when he first started. I worked on his English while improving my Italian. He stayed to himself even though Loretta and Danny tried to get him to acclimate to the customs and ways of New England. The biggest adjustment for him was the climate. The fall, winter and spring months of 1923-24 were some of the harshest we had experienced in years. The ground stayed white until several weeks after St. Patrick's Day of 1924. It affected Giuseppe more than most. We could always find him closest to the coal or wood stoves when he was not working. He kept to himself which worried Ma who had promised her brother that

109

she would make sure he was happy in America. Loretta even tried to get him to go with her and Kippy to the movies. On one occasion, Kippy invited his female cousin to accompany them. Giuseppe never said one word to her the entire time which ended Kippy's participation in getting the man any more dates.

We all backed away from pushing him too much when Pa told everyone to let Giuseppe make his own choices as to who he wanted to date, what he wanted to do and whether he wanted to stay in Norwich or the United States for that matter. By the summer of 1924, he was doing very well in his apprenticeship and was respected and liked by the Torrance Construction workers. He opened up a little, but still kept to himself on his free time. Pa was pleased with his work ethic and he showed signs of becoming a very good stone and brick mason. It made Pa happy that he was the second member of the family to be introduced to the Torrance Construction Company that performed well. Every so often, Mr. Torrance would ask Pa if I ever thought about coming back to the construction company. Pa would always say no, but now he would joke with Mr. Torrance that he had replaced me with Giuseppe. In essence he had. Giuseppe was doing a fine job.

Maria asked me to teach Giuseppe to drive. Her excuse was that Pa and Ma needed someone to be available in case there was another emergency or they just needed someone to drive them at a spur of the moment. Even though Pa owned the first automobile in the family and one of the first on the street, he never wanted to learn to drive. Tony, Kippy or me did the duties. Danny was one year away from being able to drive legally even though he was an accomplished driver at fifteen. We had seen to it that he learned young. We trained him on the Mohegan Park Road leading to Spaulding Pond and on the farm roads of Preston, Sprague and Lisbon. In Giuseppe's case, it was a different story. It took several months, but we trained him well; only to see him fail the written test. Danny and Pa worked with him for several weeks and on the second try, he squeaked out a passing grade.

Giuseppe wasn't overjoyed that he had passed his driving test. He still did most of his traveling on foot except when Pa or Ma needed to go somewhere and none of us were available to take them. He kept to himself and really didn't seem happy living in America. Tony and I took an interest in him and would spend time talking to him about our experiences when we were in the service during the war. The war was a sore subject for him since the death of his father, but the traveling and the places we saw interested him. It was just a good way to have a conversation with him and get a feeling for what his interests were. On the Fourth of July in 1924, Giuseppe surprised us all when he announced that he had joined the Marine Corp and would report to duty the first week in August. Ma did not approve because she had vowed to look after him for her brother. She didn't know what she would say to her brother that his grandson was going off to join the United States Marines. Her worries were eased by Pa who convinced her that this was his choice and a good one at that. There was no war on and this would be a great opportunity for him to travel and see places. Before he left, Tony and I asked why he'd picked the Marines. He simply stated that he wanted a different branch of service to tell stories about seeing that Tony had been a sailor sailing across the Atlantic and I had been a soldier in France.

Giuseppe continued to work for Torrance Construction until two days before his departure for the Marines. Pa had expected him to leave his apprenticeship several weeks before his departure, but the young man wanted the extra money he saved to be sent to him once he was assigned to a permanent location. He settled all his small debts and paid Ma and Pa a little extra to cover his room and board when he would visit on military

111

leaves. Ma put the money in a small savings account to give to him when she thought he would need it. He would need it four months later.

Tony and I took a few hours off from work the Saturday Giuseppe left for basic training. Before we left, Pa took all of us down to the wine cellar. In the corner was a select case of bottles of wine Pa had been saving for special occasions. He opened a bottle without saying a word and poured us all a glass. He then spoke,
"Giuseppe you now patriot. You goin' to be Marine."
His eyes filled as he raised his glass in salute of the soon to be marine.
"Salute," we all said as we followed suit.

Giuseppe realized then how important becoming a marine meant to his great uncle and family. Before we departed the wine cellar, Pa reached up to one of the cellar beams that rested on the stone foundation and pulled out three red, white and blue ribbons. I realized they were the ones Pa had tied to the wine bottles he had decorated for Joey, Tony and me when we left for service. He tied all three ribbons around a bottle and looked at Giuseppe and said,
"We drink this one when you come home again."
He hugged him. We all hugged him. Pa insisted that we open another bottle before we left, but Tony convinced him that it would not be very proper for the three of us to deliver Giuseppe to the train station a little tipsy. We all laughed and went upstairs for Giuseppe to say goodbye to Ma and the rest of the family. We would not see him until Christmas when he returned from training and would stay with us for a week. He'd spend the next two weeks traveling to San Francisco to board the USS Albany which had orders to return to the orient a few weeks later.

Lucia graduated from St. Francis Nursing School with honors that June. Ma, Pa and Tony attended the graduation exercise and brought Lucia back to the big house for one of the biggest parties that our family had seen in a long time. It surpassed any of the christenings or wedding receptions that had been held at the big house up to that time that I could remember. The greatest benefit of her new degree was that she had been accepted for a nursing position at the Backus Hospital Emergency Room. It was a proud moment for our family, but especially for Ma and Pa. Lucia had grown into a very beautiful woman and it wouldn't be long before the many young men would seek to court her.

I noticed how Lucia had changed from her girlish shyness to an outspoken young professional woman. She informed Ma and Pa that she would be living in her own apartment as soon as she could find one she could afford. The three years in Hartford had made her a strong and independent woman at twenty-one. She moved into a third story apartment on Lafayette Street which was walking distance to the hospital. We would see her occasionally for Sunday lunch due to her rotating shift schedule. The stories she would tell of the excitement of the emergency room kept most of us intrigued. Lucia would only relate the funny and happy episodes in the emergency room. She protected us from the gory and sad ones. She was a true professional.

Several months went by until one day she called Ma in advance to ask if she could bring a guest over for Sunday lunch. We were pleased to see a handsome man appear at our family table. Dr. Thomas Parks was introduced to the family. The twenty-six year old physician was from Woodstock, Connecticut and had completed his residency at St. Francis Hospital in Hartford. Apparently, he met Lucia during the final phases of her nursing training. He had been an instructor for

113

treating trauma patients. We all figured that they must have been attracted to each other during those last six months of Lucia's training. Whether Dr. Parks, or Tommy, as he insisted we address him, had intentions of coming to Norwich before he met Lucia or came because of her, remained to be seen.

Tommy's background, education, family and interests were thoroughly gone over by various members of the family. There was one minor fact, his religion, which was brought to everyone's attention. Good old Rose asked the question.
"Dr. Parks, what do you think of St. Patrick's church?"
He nonchalantly stated,
"It is a very impressive stone structure compared to the brick and wood structures I am accustomed to in Woodstock where I grew up. And please, call me Tommy."
Rose, of course, had to meddle further and asked him,
"No, what I meant was, what do you think of the inside of the church?"
Both Lucia and Tommy looked at each other before he answered.
"Well I have never been inside the church. Maria has asked me and I will make the effort to go to one of the services and let you know, Rose."
Rose wouldn't let it go.
"So you are not a practicing Catholic, Dr. Parks?" she asked.
"No Rose, I am not a practicing Catholic. I am not Catholic. I am a baptized Episcopalian," he said and smiled at her.

Tony broke the ice and probably bruised Rose's leg under the table when he piped up and said, "That's nice, that's as close to Catholic as you can get Rose."
She grimaced from the apparent pain Tony had intentionally inflicted upon her for asking religious questions in front of Ma and Pa. I'm sure she had a few words for Tony when they left that afternoon.

Ma and Pa never reacted to the information Tommy had provided about his religion. Ma did invite him back for Sunday lunch when his schedule could support an open invitation. Both Lucia and Tommy were pleased as they left that afternoon in Tommy's brand new 1924 Packard. Maria and I talked about our first meeting with Tommy Parks that night.

"I like him, but I think Ma and Pa will never agree for Lucia to marry a man outside the Catholic Church."

Being a man of travel who had lived in the trenches with men of all faiths during war time, it was a mute point for me.

"I hate to think about it, but Lucia might have to possibly choose between her family and Tommy if they became more serious," Maria said as she prepared the children for bed. I looked at my wife and said,

"You don't know your parents very well, sweetheart. Your parents will never chance loosing anyone of their children based on the religious preference of their future spouses. You forget that your parents accepted Irish husbands for you and Loretta."

"You were both Catholic, Liam," she responded.

I didn't argue, but finished the exchange with,

"Maria, my beauty, figure on Tommy, the doctor, being the newest member of the family."

She smiled to my compliment and responded with,

"I hope you are right."

Several days later, I stopped and picked up Pa with the truck as he walked up Franklin Street towards home after work. He puffed on his pipe as I drove him up to the big house. Before he got out of the truck I asked him,

"Well what do you think about Lucia's doctor boyfriend?"

"I like him. He smart. He nice looking. He love Lucia I think?" he said as he shut the door.

"Pa, he's not a catholic," I said.

The old man looked at me through the window of the truck

115

door, puffed on his pipe one more time and said,
"So, I not such a good catholic too. I no go to church much.
Anyway, you Ma likes him. Dat only count."
"Good", I responded and left as the old man smiled and waved
me on. I explained my little talk with Pa to Maria at dinner
that night and the subject of Tommy's religion never came up
again.

Tommy would play a vital role in our family months later. Ma
had been very busy running the big house and the toll of doing
so much work was slowly wearing her down. She was also
upset that Giuseppe had been stationed onboard a ship that was
steaming in the Orient. She had received only one letter from
her great nephew which upset her. No other help was available
as Maria was tied up raising three children eighteen months
apart and Rose had almost the same responsibilities. Despite
Danny's help to do errands for her now that he had his license,
the chores were a constant grind on the forty-nine year old
woman. Lucia warned her mother that the cardiac incident she
had before could return because she was doing too much work.
On a cold February evening in 1925 Ma collapsed at dinner.
Danny and Pa immediately took her to the hospital. Tommy
Parks was on emergency room duty that night. He saw Ma
slowly walk into the emergency room with a pale and lifeless
expression on her face.

Tommy immediately took Ma into an examining room. His
skills as an emergency room treatment physician saved her life
by the time the rest of the family arrived. Lucia was able to see
her while Tommy was working on Ma. She updated the rest of
the family when she was sure Ma was stable and admitted into
the recovery ward. She stated,
"Ma has lost thirty to forty percent of her heart muscle function
from the attack. She is very critical and, hopefully, she will
stabilize and begin a recovery in a few days. The next twenty-

116

four hours will be very critical for her. Tommy will be monitoring her until a cardiac specialist relieves him in the morning."

We all stared at each other until Loretta spoke up and said, "How did we not see this coming?" Maria looked over and said,
"We are all too busy and forgot that we all helped in running the big house. Now she runs it with poor Danny who never gets time to do anything and occasionally you, Loretta, when you come and visit her on Saturday mornings while Kippy is working half days at the auto shop. It's everyone's fault."
I didn't say anything. Pa spoke up and said,
"I get people to come in and run the big house. I no listen to her no more. I pay people to work."
He broke down which was one of the few times I saw the man cry hard. I was not around when he received the news about Joey or when little Michelle died in the big house, but my brothers and sisters compared it to those two incidents. We all closed in around Pa and tried to comfort him. We even joked about how strong Ma was and that she would bounce back like she always did. It didn't seem to comfort him for he sobbed on Loretta's shoulder until I motioned for Danny to drive him home. We all agreed that we didn't need two parents in the hospital. Pa refused to go home until Lucia went and got Tommy to convince him that it would be the right thing to do. Tommy's bedside manner was impeccable and I knew now why Lucia was so in love with him.

The handsome physician, once he heard how devastated Pa had become, came back to the emergency waiting room and looked Pa square in the eyes,
"Mr. Cugini you need to go home and rest. I am here with your wife and I will stay here until I know she is out of any danger. You have my word on it. She will be fine. Please go

117

home and bring back some flowers for her to brighten up her room."

The old man stopped and looked him straight in the eye,

"You no lie to me Tommy. I be here if she get sicker."

Tommy smiled and put his hand on the old man's shoulder.

"Go home Mr. Cugini. She will be fine. I would not lie to you ever."

Pa looked into his eyes and smiled just a little and then nodded. "You good for this family. You join soon, I hope."

Lucia never said a word as she looked at Tommy and her father. Tommy nodded back and said one more nice thing.

"Mr. Cugini, you already have made me feel as a part of this family and I will do my best to keep this family whole and together. Now go home and rest.

The Convalescent Home

I awoke up in the middle of the night dreaming about that night in the hospital when Ma had her attack. I was sweating profusely and really needed a change of pajamas. It was 2:10 a.m. and I was wide awake. I tried several times to try to get back to sleep, but soon realized that I was just wasting my time. I wanted to get up, but knew I would need help. For several days now, I had been assisted out of bed and onto a wheelchair. I was allowed to move about my room only. My arms were getting stronger every day, but my legs would probably remain weak until I could be assisted in standing and working the muscles that were much too old and unused. As I lay in bed, I got the damndest idea. I'd get out of bed and onto the wheelchair all by myself. I stretched enough so that my fingers were able to grab the wheel of the chair. I slowly, and with much difficulty, positioned the wheelchair right next to my bed. I used the electric button to bring the bed down as far as it would go. My speed to accomplish all of this took me five times what it would have taken if someone had assisted me. I persisted and put my legs over the edge of the bed while keeping my left hand on the chair. I gambled and slid off the bed and was able to keep half my bottom on the seat of the wheelchair. With the most strength that I was able to muster, I kept myself from sliding off and onto the floor which would have been a most embarrassing predicament. I prevailed and ended up sitting in the chair, exhausted, but nevertheless, sitting in the chair and ready to independently move about. The charge nurse, whom I didn't particularly like, would be making her rounds soon so I decided to scout out the place. It would be the first time I had the chance to see anything except my room which I had been kept in since my arrival here. I decided to rest just a little more for maybe a few minutes and then begin my scouting. Apparently my success at getting out of bed completely exhausted me and I fell asleep in the wheelchair.

The Story

Ma had several more slight attacks the next day, but Dr. Tommy Parks stayed with her and assisted the cardiac specialist the entire time. He went without sleep for thirty some hours while he watched over her and worked in the hospital. The cardiac specialist agreed with the treatment Tommy had prescribed for the matriarch. Pa did bring in the flowers the next afternoon, but Ma was too sedated after suffering the two small bouts she had and never saw them until the following day. It would be a week before Ma was sitting up in bed and able to keep a conversation going about family news. By that time, Pa had hired two Canadian women to run the house and take care of the boarder's needs. The women had run a hunting lodge in Maine the previous year, but it had gone under for some reason. They stayed in Lucia's and Loretta's old rooms and maintained the big house almost as well as Ma would have

119

kept it. Pa vowed that Ma would never work again in her lifetime and he meant it. He instructed Miss Gagnon and Miss Fortin to make sure of that.

The Convalescent Home

I woke up a little while later. I realized that I was back in my bed. One of the attendants had found me and reported what I had done. My charge nurse didn't seem pleased of my accomplishment because if I had failed, she would have had to explain why I died trying to get out of bed. I also had to hear of Mary's displeasure when she was informed of what I did. For the next week, the wheelchair was removed from my room and the attendants checked on me more routinely during the night shift. The charge nurse made sure of that. My daily exercising was improving and I was able to get out of bed and stand with the help of the physical therapist and Mary. My goal was to be able to walk out of my room and grab that wheelchair anytime I wanted it. It would be another several weeks before I would attempt that phase in my physical therapy.

I found myself staying up later every evening and was able to watch television until ten o'clock at night. The night charge nurse made sure to remove my remote controls for the television every night after ten o'clock so that I didn't watch any of the late shows. I had made the mistake of informing her that I watched them quite often before my hideous stroke. With the remote taken away and the wheelchair outside my room door, I was determined to work harder to be able to get out of my bed, sneak into the wheelchair and find a television in another place to watch those late night shows.

As I made my plans, I inevitably ended up falling asleep and

120

dreaming. This would go on for several more weeks, but as I grew stronger and my plan to stage a sneak out developed, the chance never came.

One week after I was able to get out of bed without any assistance, I was released from the convalescent home. It was a complete surprise and a wonderful event in my life. When Mary informed me, I asked,

"Where am I going?"

"Great-granddad, you have been placed in an assisted senior living center where you will have your own living area and come and go as you like."

"Why is that so different than where I am right now?"

"Great-granddad, this is a recovery convalescent home. Where you are going is a place where you can live with minimal care. People will be able to visit you every day, the staff will make sure you take your medicine and eat three square meals a day. You get your own TV, privacy and can do what you want within the confines of the place. I'll pick you up and take you wherever you want during the week when I'm available. Mom and Dad will do the same when they are free. Any of your grand kids can do the same once they know you have been moved to this new place. How's that sound?"

I didn't answer her at first.

"When do I go?"

"You go the day after tomorrow. I'll pick you up with Dad and Mom. They want to help you get settled into the new place," she said.

It was set. That night, the evening charge nurse came in and congratulated me on the completion of my recovery. She even came over and shook my hand. I still didn't like her very much, but I acted civil and just smiled and said thank you. I was disappointed I couldn't commit one last act of disobedience on her shift. I guess I really won anyway. I was being discharged from her care.

That evening, Mary stayed a little later than I expected and I wondered why.

"Honey, you need to start dating more. You stay here almost twenty-four hours a day and watch over me. You need to be on a date with some young man somewhere. You're too pretty and too smart to be watching over theses old bones," I said.

She smiled and said,

"Great-granddad, I like being here and I need you to tell me more stories about what it was like living at the big house. I have been keeping notes of the things you have muttered, dreamed out loud and told me when you could, about the family and the big house. Someday soon, I am going to write a book about it."

I smiled and told her to sit down. I had an hour before I would watch some TV. I began the story. I spent some time answering questions about things she didn't understand that she had either been told or that I had alluded to either mumbling or dreaming about.

The Story

Ma returned home after one month in the hospital. She was still weak, but Tommy had strict instructions that she was to do nothing around the big house except boil water to make tea. That was hard on a woman who had gotten up everyday and worked for as much as eighteen hours a day keeping her tenants, children and husband provided for. Her meeting with the Canadian women, Miss Gagnon and Miss Fortin, went well. She learned to appreciate what the two women, although paid to work there, had done to keep up her home. The house seemed to be in good working order and the tenants and Pa had been taken care of. She seemed a little disturbed about how her kitchen utensils had been placed in different locations and that the laundry was done every other day instead of daily. She

122

approached Pa to talk to the women and have them change their ways. I was there that afternoon when I overheard that conversation. Pa smiled, looked at her and said, "Josephine, you no do anymore. Why you care? You my wife and lady of house. You no need to work anymore. You live and be healthy. You take care of me only."

When she didn't answer him and turned to leave the room, she noticed me coming towards her and said,

"Lam, get the two ladies and bring them to me."

I did as I was instructed and fetched them. I thought that maybe there would be a problem, but Ma congratulated them on their accomplishments and only told them that when they needed to change something, they needed to tell her so she would know where things had been placed. That was it. From that time on, Ma became the lady of the house and just oversaw the running of it by the two Canadian women.

Chapter Seven – The Good Life

The Story

Ma made a complete recovery from her heart attack during the late winter months of 1925. Dr. Tommy Parks asked Lucia for her hand in marriage and a July wedding date was set. Tommy continually encouraged Lucia to continue her education and was able to arrange for her to study under the chief anesthesiologist at Backus to become a trained and certified anesthetist. Her training began in earnest that January and we did not see much of Lucia or Tommy with their busy schedules. Despite those conflicting schedules, they managed to slip off occasionally to Palm Beach, Florida, some medical conventions in Chicago and New York and an occasional weekend to some hidden retreat where they could be together. Ma and Pa never knew the arrangements they had, but Lucia slipped information of her exciting ventures to Loretta and Maria. Kippy and I would get all the details and both of us couldn't have been more pleased for them. We decided to keep the information away from Danny and Tony. Danny was kept out of the information sharing for adolescent reasons and Tony for being married to Rose. If Rose knew something, then everyone knew it. Although we believed Ma and Pa wouldn't have said anything because Lucia was a grown woman, they still wouldn't have approved which could have caused problems between the couple and our parents.

Our children were growing up. Christine turned five that April. She was a replica of her mother down to the deep blue eyes, skin color and personality. Lawrence and Leonard had become Larry and Lenny the terribles. The two of them could always find trouble to get into and they were only three years old now. We thought that the terrible twos would never end for us. They didn't; they extended into the threes. Maria and I thought about having more children, but we decided to wait a few more years until the twins were more manageable. Joe and Harriet Cohen, on the other hand, produced their third child in November; another boy which they named Aaron. They had their hands full with the three boys, but Harriet talked about another child soon after Aaron was born. Maria and I thought that she was trying to have a girl, but we both agreed that we would not compete with the Cohens. We'd let them win hands down.

Tony and Rose seemed a happy couple despite Rose's tendency to be nosey and opinionated. Their twins, Joey and Mary Beth, were five as well and very well behaved. Several things Rose possessed were patience and attentiveness. It showed in the personality of her children. Kippy and Loretta didn't have any children yet. The discussion of their future family plans came up occasionally at Sunday lunch, but they were having too good of a time vacation traveling, buying nice clothes and planning to build a new home on a piece of land that Kippy's father had offered to them on the outskirts of the city.

Danny had almost completed his senior year at the Norwich Free Academy. He would be the sixth family member to graduate from NFA. The idea of six children of immigrants to graduate from high school was a rarity in those days. It was seven if you counted me, the foster son. Danny was the only son to play football. His size afforded him the opportunity because he had grown into a five feet, eleven inch, two hundred pound fullback for the high school team. We watched as many games as we could during his senior year of football in the fall of 1924. Danny also volunteered and eventually received a part-time job at the hospital that Lucia had been influential in getting him. This made him aware of the opportunities for a career in medicine. He had also applied to the University of Connecticut and was interested in the Pharmaceutical field. Plus, a good friend of Lucia's, a young pharmacist at the hospital, took Danny under his guidance and influenced the boy. Danny's academic marks in high school were very good and we all waited for confirmation that he would be accepted into the University and eventually into its pharmacy program.

The Cohen and Corcoran Carpentry Company grew as well. We now employed twenty carpenters and had over three months of backlog orders from the Norwich Board of Education and the Norwich State Hospital. Joe and I had expanded the specialty shop when we opened a small store in Franklin Square to showcase Joe's finer carpentry products. Maria and Harriet spent several hours a day alternating the supervision of the sales clerks they hired to sell the specialty headboards, accompanying bedroom furniture, grandfather clocks and other finished furniture items Joe had created. When either woman was supervising, the other was watching the children. It was a great arrangement and the books indicated that we were making a good profit.

We also received monthly letters from Giuseppe onboard the USS Albany about his travels in the Orient. He wrote that he had spent some time in Hawaii and the Philippines en route to Hong Kong and the Chinese mainland. His letters also announced that he had been promoted to Private First Class. Ma and Pa both relaxed a little knowing that he was onboard the Cruiser most of the time and not dodging bullets. Ma had written her brother, Giuseppe's grandfather, of his decision to join the Marine Corps, but he never responded back to her. Ma never knew whether her brother approved of his grandson's decision or not. Years later, we would find out that her brother's family never told of their ties to America during the

Mussolini era. They never mentioned that one of their own had joined the United States Marine Corps. It was a reasonable decision because when World War II started, too many of Ma and Pa's relatives either joined, or were forced into Italian military service.

Tommy Parks and Lucia Cugini were married in St. Patrick's Church that July. Tommy had promised the Monsignor at St. Patrick's that their children would be raised as Catholics. The wedding was very simple and a little uncomfortable for Ma and Pa due to two tight restrictions the Church had of Catholics marrying non-Catholics in those days. The young priest that married the couple was a little more liberal than most up to that time and orchestrated a nice ceremony, but the couple was barred from being married on the altar like all Catholic couples enjoyed. They were only allowed to stand at the communion rail in the church. The sight of Tommy receiving communion from his minister was the second sign that it was a so called mixed marriage. Mrs. Parks had insisted that an Episcopal Minister be present to bless the marriage. Pa and I both thought how stupid both religions had become. Pa always would say, "God in my church is same God in your church." Ma had a different opinion, but all went well. After we left the ceremony, we all attended the reception at the big house.

Wine and good food always changed the atmosphere. I do remember that Pa tried to get both clergymen a little tipsy and was succeeding until Ma got wind of his devious plan. I think Mrs. Parks, Tommy's mother, had tipped her off. Two things that Tony and I noticed while the wedding reception was being held was that the Parks side did not partake in any of the wines that Pa made. Tommy, on the other hand, drank well. We also observed that two Norwich Policemen were stationed outside and a few houses down from the big house. We surmised that they weren't there to watch the festivities, but were there because Chief Mahoney and his wife were invited guests to the wedding and reception. Both of them enjoyed Pa's wine. Mrs. Mahoney really enjoyed herself which caused Ma to occasionally give Pa the evil eyes to indicate that he had to slow her consumption. Pa did eventually obey and slowly encouraged her to eat more food to absorb some of the wine. Tony and I enjoyed just watching the woman get plowed. Pa did have a sense of humor, we thought. Ma didn't think so.

Towards the end of the reception, Tony and I noticed Ma sitting in the corner reading something Loretta had given her. She read the message very intently and we could see her expressions change from across the room. Both of us became curious as to what she was reading. On closer observance, we could see that it was a letter. Tony asked Loretta,
"Who sent Ma the letter and is everything alright?"
"Yes, Giuseppe sent Ma and Pa a letter and everything is just fine." We later found out that Loretta had retrieved it from the letter box in the front of the big house as the reception was getting under way.

We left Ma alone until she finished it. Tears streamed down her cheeks but she didn't seem upset. She handed the letter to Pa who had come away from the festivities to sit beside her once he also observed her sitting there reading. As he read the letter, Loretta became concerned and asked Ma again if everything was alright. She smiled and said, "You read after Pa."
After hearing her answer to Loretta, Tony and I moved away to let Pa, Ma and Loretta be alone. We realized that it was very personal and that we would find out soon enough what was contained in it. We watched Pa finish the letter, hand it to Loretta, get up and move to the table where the bottles of wine had been set up for the guests. He poured himself a rather large glass and drank it quickly. Loretta took longer to read the

128

letter because it had been written in Italian. She eventually finished it with tears running down her cheeks. It would be several hours before the rest of the family had a chance to read it.

Maria and I had some family members watch the kids as we read the curious letter together. I struggled to read it and needed the constant help of Maria. I read where Giuseppe had informed the family that he had been promoted again; this time to Corporal. He described the places he had visited while on duty and leave. The content of the letter was his appreciation for what Ma and Pa had done for him. He explained how in the brief time he had spent with them; they had given him the appreciation of belonging to a loving family. He explained that he had taken the values of what they and their family had given him that he had never experienced in his life before. He apologized for leaving so abruptly because he probably should have stayed to enjoy the family more. But he emphasized how grateful he was for the guidance and love they and all their children had exhibited to him in his brief stay at the big house. He also told them that he boasted about his family to the other Marines he was stationed with. Some of them, like he, had come from broken families and had moved about being taken care of by strange relatives. Some of the Marines were orphans and could not relate to anything the family Giuseppe described. I finished it with moisture building in my eyes. The man was describing everything that I had experienced over ten years ago when I was taken in by this loving family and became part of it. Giuseppe had reminded me of my roots. As far as I was concerned, I had another brother.

The only child of Antonio and Josephine Cugini remaining to be married was Danny. We were very excited to hear a few days after the wedding that Danny had been accepted into the University of Connecticut and would start in September of

1925. His curriculum would be pre-med in anticipation of entering the newly establish Pharmacy School. Tommy and Lucia were especially proud of Danny for his dedication and also his being accepted into college. It was a big responsibility for the seventeen year old, but all of us knew he had always set his goals high and would achieve them. With the marriage of Tommy and Lucia, the family had a physician, a nurse who would soon be an anesthetist and a prospective pharmacist. I thought of how much of an inspiration these family members would be as role models for all the Cugini, Sullivan, Parks and Corcoran grandchildren.

On Thanksgiving Day 1925, Kippy and Loretta announced that she was pregnant and would be expecting a baby in March of 1926. The family was growing and Ma and Pa couldn't have been any happier. Nobody counted the months from the wedding to the delivery day except Rose. She was about to bring that to everyone's attention until Maria took her aside and told her to forget about the math. I heard her say, "Who cares anyway Rose? We can all count."

That Thanksgiving was the first time that Miss Gagnon and Miss Fortin were asked to be present for a holiday meal. Ma had become very friendly with the two women who didn't have children or relatives close by. Their work ethic mirrored Ma's and the three became very close friends despite Ma and Pa being their employers. Many years later, we learned that these two women lived in secrecy for the love that they had for each other. But Pa knew it from almost the first year that he hired them. In those days, no one spoke of it and no one probed if there were suspicions.

Christmas morning 1925 came and Maria and I spent the early morning hours listening to Larry and Lenny waking Christine to go into the living room and check to see if Santa had come.

It was exciting and pleasurable for us to hear the little ones trying to talk softly, but actually getting louder in anticipation of what was waiting for them under the tree. By five a.m., we couldn't stand it anymore and quickly went to the living room and called all three of them from their rooms. It was almost bedlam as they came running and screeching into the living room. Nothing pleased us more than watching the excitement in our children as they looked in awe at the gifts we had wrapped for them and placed under the tree and then check to see how much Santa ate of the snacks they had put out for him. That Christmas eve, I made sure that I ate several of the cookies that each one had placed on the table in anticipation of Santa's visit.

Of course Christine made the comment that Santa hadn't eaten the entire cookie she had left for him so Maria, quickly thinking, exclaimed that he must have been full and pointed out to her the large present he left for her near the tree. Maria and I had paid Joe Cohen fifteen dollars to make her a wooden dollhouse complete with four rooms of furniture. As in everything he did, Joe was a perfectionist and the dollhouse would remain in our family for many years. We spent almost fifteen dollars a piece on the twins to give them the beginning of their first Lionel Corporation train set. I fell in love with model trains when Joe and I delivered a special furniture set that our carpentry company had completed for a wealthy gentleman in New Haven. Joe and I drove to New Haven to deliver the set of furniture and saw an extensive model train set that the man had collected for himself and his three sons. We were impressed with the set. We both vowed to save a little extra money so that our sons could have one. We started a set for our sons after that holiday season which would become a hobby that would span several generations.

"Great-granddad, great-granddad, It's time for you to go to bed," Mary said as she gently shook me.

"How long have I been sleeping on you, honey?" I asked.

"You only nodded out for a minute or so. You were starting to tell me about the train set you started setting up years ago, but you fell off to sleep almost mid-sentence."

"Yeah, I guess I did. You know, I was wondering if your father would consider taking all those trains out from storage and setting them up again in his basement. Maybe he doesn't have time to set up all of them, but some maybe? I would enjoy coming over and running them. I'd be willing to set up the scenery again. I think it would be good therapy. What do you think? Could you ask him for me, Mary? I haven't seen those trains run in many years."

"Sure great-granddad, I'll tell him to set them up again."

"No honey, please ask him. I don't want to cause any problems with Linda, I mean your mother, or him because the trains would take up a fair amount of room in the basement to set all of them up again," I emphasized.

"Okay, I'll ask him to consider that or even move part of the set to your place and set it up here. Would you like that?"

I just nodded while she helped me to my wheelchair. I looked at the clock. It was only eight o'clock. I looked at Mary and asked her if she had a date tonight. She smiled and said that she did have to meet with a friend that she hadn't seen since graduating from college for a few drinks. She explained that she had met him again a month ago and had been dating him on and off for a while now.

"Is it a serious friend?" I asked.

"He is just an old friend. I can tell you one thing that might interest you," she said.

I smiled and waited.

"He's a writer."
I didn't question her anymore and let it go at that. I was
hoping she would date more now. Coming and seeing me was
nice, but I was sure she had better things to do.

The Living Center

I was transferred to the assisted living center the next
morning. The ride was across town and I enjoyed seeing how
the city had changed in the last few years. I arrived there and
was greeted by several nurses and an administrator and shown
to my area they had prepared for me. I was pleased that I had
my own living room with a T.V. and phone. The furniture
could support several visitors and it had been tastefully
furnished with wall to wall carpeting and nice curtains. A good
sized bedroom and modern bathroom afforded me the comfort
that I was accustomed to until my stroke. Mary and her parents
had done a good job getting me into this place.

Mary spent most of the day with me to make sure I adjusted
to my new environment. As new nurses and residents slowly
came by to meet me, she asked that I should be polite to all
them to start off on the right foot. Several times, I told her she
didn't have to stay, but to no avail. She stayed until the
evening hours.

The night crew for the center had been assigned to check on
me as Mary made sure I was tucked in for the night. I took the
few pills I needed and kissed her good night. As she left, I
turned on the TV and started to watch one of the sitcoms I
looked forward to seeing. After that, I continued to watch a
late show and remembered seeing one o'clock before I must
have fallen asleep again thinking about the trains I had talked
to Mary about.

The Story

I remembered the first time I took the children and Mary to New Haven to see the Lionel Corporation display at their factory. We went with the Cohens and spent the entire day riding the train and seeing the large model train system that had been set up at the Lionel factory. We even picked up another passenger car and two new circus cars that had Barnum and Bailey painted on them. The only negative side to the adventure was Ma's comment that we should have gone on Saturday so not to miss Sunday lunch with the family. Pa only smiled and shook his head when he heard her complaint. We went many more times in the next ten years and always brought back something new to add to the train set.

Loretta had her baby son on St. Patrick's Day, 1926. Patrick Sean Sullivan, III came into the world that day. Kippy was so ecstatic that he almost got himself too drunk to go back to the hospital to see his wife and son. Tony and Rose sobered him up enough so they could drive him the two miles to the hospital. Ma and Pa never knew why he was late getting back to the hospital. Tony and Rose fabricated a story that he had passed out so many cigars he lost track of the time.

Present at the birth of little Patrick was Lucia who assisted in the new hospital delivery room. A few months later, Lucia would receive her certification and full title as an anesthetist and Tommy Parks had become one of the most respected and admired doctors at the hospital. One day later, while Ma and Pa visited Loretta and the baby in the hospital, Ma had another cardiac episode. She was given immediate emergency life-saving procedures and luckily for her, she had the best available medical help. Tommy Parks was on the scene when she first stated that she did not feel well and then collapsed.

She was taken directly to the cardiac ward where she remained in critical condition. It was the first time that Ma would receive the last rites from Father Flanagan who was the pastor of the Sacred Heart Church in Norwichtown. He happened to be visiting some of his parishioners when he was summoned by Tommy and given the state of her condition. The fifty-one year old woman was fighting for her life for the third time. Loretta and Kippy's celebration was put on hold as we all waited and prayed that Ma would make it through this critical time.

Our father could not bring himself to leave her side for the first day. Pa remained in the hospital with her until Tommy had to convince him to leave and get some rest at home. He stayed at home to wash and change his clothes only. Tommy made arrangements for him to stay in the Doctor's lounge to cat nap and take some nourishment during the next several days while Ma recovered. Ma had been diagnosed with having another heart attack. All of us could not understand why she had been struck again because she had obeyed the doctor's orders and had not overworked herself or had endured any further stress in her life. We were told that there was nothing that could be done for her except medication and rest and a slow progression to get her strength back

Loretta and Kippy waited until Ma was released from the hospital and brought home before they scheduled the baptism of little Patrick. The Monsignor at St. Patrick's allowed them to have the child baptized in the big house so Ma could witness the event. By Easter Sunday, Ma was almost back to her old self again. We had to appreciate the work that Miss Gagnon and Miss Fortin did to keep the big house with all the boarder needs running smoothly while they looked in on Ma as she recovered.

I did notice how Pa had aged after Ma's attack this time. He also came home from work more tired. I became alarmed and asked Tony if he'd noticed it as well. We both agreed that Tommy should examine Pa one day when no one was around. He liked Tommy and would let him examine him as long as Ma or the rest of us were not informed. One day after Sunday lunch, Tommy and Pa disappeared. An hour or so later, we heard both of them laughing. The sounds were coming from the wine cellar. Tony and I approached cautiously and found the two of them enjoying themselves in the wine cellar. Apparently, Pa had convinced Tommy to try a new fruit wine he was experimenting with. Both of them were obviously tipsy from the wine tasting. I asked,

"What is all the celebrating about?"

"Tommy say I good and healthy. You two no worry. I only drink, maybe, too much, he say. That's all."

We agreed that Pa should slow down on the wine a little, but we were pleased that Tommy had found nothing wrong with the fifty-two year old man. Tommy then turned to Pa and said,

"You will have to let me know anytime you think Ma is developing a problem. I mean if she slows her walk, if she is out of breath easy, if she keeps to herself, if she becomes irritable with you, her children or grandchildren and acts strange in any way, you must call me. Do you understand, Pa?"

Tony and I didn't say anything.

Pa responded, "I know. I watch her."

What Tommy did relay to us later was that Pa was worried to death that Ma could die on him any day due to her heart condition. Tommy assured him, and us, that as long as Ma obeyed his instructions and he and the family checked on her regularly, she would be just fine.

On Easter morning, Ma attended mass for the first time since her attack. She enjoyed the fairly mild April day and wanted to walk home from church after mass. We all agreed that it would be much better if she waited a few more weeks before taking that big step in her recovery schedule. But Pa had accompanied Ma on her first attendance at Mass. He went more regularly to mass we noticed. We never asked him why, but we all understood and left it at that. He instructed us that he would walk slowly with her and that they would be fine. We all left the church in our respective automobiles. Tony and I made arrangements for me to take his wife and kids back to the big house while he drove up ahead and waited at two locations in case Ma and Pa changed their minds during their walk.

Ma did very well and both of them had time to relax and converse on their stroll home. As they turned from Broad Street to Boswell Avenue, they noticed all of us outside the house waiting for them to return. Ma called out as soon as she realized that all of us were waiting and said,
"There is no need for all of you to be outside. Go inside and prepare lunch."
We all stepped aside and let Giuseppe step in front and smile at the couple. He was dressed in his Marine Dress Uniform and looked as handsome as ever. He never said a word as Ma and Pa stared at him. Needless to say, it was a very emotional meeting between them and we were all concerned that it had been a little too much of a surprise. Pa knew better and said this was the best medicine Josephine needed. We were fortunate that Giuseppe had almost thirty days leave with us before he shipped out on the Cruiser USS Raleigh.

He brought back some very ornate Oriental Jewelry for Ma and smaller pieces for each one of his sisters. Pa, Tony, Danny and I each received a bottle of Jiu. The Chinese liquor didn't taste like anything Pa would have made. We drank several bottles of it that day and it gave us one hell of a wallop. Each of us also made time to talk with Giuseppe who had explained to us that he went by Joe in the Marines. He liked the sound of Corporal Joe Cedrone and he insisted that, like Donato had

137

been called Danny, he wanted to be called Joe. He was specific about being called Joe because he never wanted anyone to call him Joey. He wouldn't have to worry about that because there had only been one Joey in our family and little Joe Cugini, Tony's son, was the other namesake. We did as Joe Cedrone requested. The only exception was Ma and Pa. He would always be Giuseppe to them just like Danny was Donato when they called or talked about him. Maria and I invited him to our house as many time as we could. He got to know all our children very well. The twins really rough housed with him and Joe enjoyed that the most. He became Uncle Joe, the Marine to them, which became a title that would play a big role for Larry and Lenny years later. Joe adored Christine and commented regularly that he would someday love to have a little girl just like her. He had become a well fit and rugged man. Tony and I both felt that the Marines suited him. We thought that he would make a career of it. He did, and it would span more than thirty years. Within a year, he would land with the Marines in a place called Nicaragua.

Danny completed his first year at the University of Connecticut with distinction. He applied and was hired for a summer job at the Backus Hospital Pharmacy, stocking shelves, ordering supplies and anything requested by the pharmacist during the day. It was also a chance to see Lucia on a regular basis. Their relationship grew stronger and Lucia had a great influence on Danny to keep him focused on his pharmacy school objective. Tommy supported Danny and his goals, but occasionally he would mention that he should never dismiss considering medical school. Lucia and Tommy had Danny's best interest in mind, but I informed them to let Danny decide what was best for him. I figured that Danny would decide what field of medicine he would pursue. In the evenings when he was not working at the pharmacy, he continued his maintenance duties at the big house assisting Pa. The kid was

138

busy eighteen hours a day, from the time he left college for his summer break, to several days before he returned to his studies in the fall. He worked harder than I did at his age.

The year 1927 brought in a new prosperity for Joe and me. We expanded The Three C's and added a lumber business. The name also changed to just Cohen and Corcoran, Inc. As new owners, we immediately expanded our buildings to include lumber storage in Norwich and New London. Joe oversaw the specialty and furniture building shop. I concentrated on scheduling forestry surveys, wood cutting, sawmill schedules and timber shipping. Our workforce expanded threefold and our business plan for the next several years looked very promising. Joe and I had arranged for several of the local banks to finance our plan and we anticipated a profit to be realized in a relatively short time.

Tony was offered a job in the new company as work production foreman for timber shipments. We backed Kippy to take over the auto garage he'd been working at and gave him a maintenance contract of all the company vehicles we possessed. Maria became the chief accountant for the business which required her to be at the office five days a week. She handled the entire payroll as well. We made arrangements for Harriet to watch over the twins during the day and Christine when she returned from school. We also made sure Maria was home no later than an hour after Christine returned home. Harriet was paid by our business to perform her daycare services and it worked out well for both families.

It was also very nice seeing my wife for a few hours each day as our paths crossed. Maria also used Harriet for audits and as a second pair of eyes to assure good accounting practices. When Harriet did the audits, we paid for a professional nanny to watch all the kids. By mid July of 1927, Harriet predicted that

139

we would realize a profit by the end of the year. That was one year sooner than our bankers had predicted. Life and the business were good.

On a warm Saturday July morning, I received a phone call from Danny. He informed me that a telegram had been delivered to the house informing Ma and Pa that Marine Corporal Giuseppe Cedrone was reported missing in action in Nicaragua on July 7, 1927. Danny stated that Ma and Pa were distraught and taking it as hard as they did when the Navy representatives had come to the house to report that Joey had been lost at sea. When I arrived at the house, I found both of them very depressed and quiet. I immediately told Danny to call Tommy to come over immediately and check on the two of them. I worried that Ma would have another heart attack and that Pa would put himself into a drunken stupor. Despite Tommy's busy hospital schedule, he was at the house with Lucia within the hour.

I went to the telegraph office and sent a message to the Department of the Navy asking if there was any more information available on our Marine. The standard reply that more information would be forwarded once it was available. In other words, we'd have to wait and worry until some information filtered down through the system and to us. Needless to say, the following Sunday lunch, which was attended by all, was somber and not enjoyable. It was hard on the children, ranging from one to seven years old, who were constantly picked on by the adults to be quiet and find something to do.

I made it a point to talk with Pa who stayed pretty much by himself that day. I found him in the wine cellar. He hadn't been drinking. He just sat there and looked at the bottle he had wrapped the ribbons around just before Joe had left for

Nicaragua. I took the bottle from the rack and handed it to him and said,

"Pa, take the bottle and put it out for everyone to see to remind them that Giuseppe is only missing and that he is a fine Marine who can find his way back to his unit."

Pa only grunted in acknowledgement. I took the bottle and walked upstairs. He followed. I made my announcement which seemed to lighten the somber mood. It helped to ease the tension and even put a smile on Ma's face.

One week later, Danny called the house just before we were leaving for Mass. I couldn't understand what he was trying to relay as I listened intently. I thought the worst because it involved Joe. I finally calmed him enough and he informed me that Joe had surfaced from the jungle, but had been wounded. The extent of his wounds weren't described in the telegram, but it did indicate more information would be coming. I remember the tears of joy that streamed down my cheeks as I relayed the information to Maria who heard the one way conversation and thought the worst herself. It was a great day to worship at St. Patrick's and we all thanked God for the return of our family member.

At Sunday lunch, everyone became concerned at the extent of Joe's wounds. Pa ended the controversy when he stated,

"He walk out of the jungle. How bad could it be?"

That made a lot of sense to everyone. We would all have to wait and see. But our brother was alive and that's all that counted. We received a letter from him three weeks later in which he apologized for the worry he caused. He informed us that he'd been wounded in the arm and had evaded capture from a group of guerillas that had ambushed the Marines he was with. He said that they were on patrol looking for Guerilla General Augusto Sandino when they ran into the group who were protecting him. I would learn more details of Joe's

141

experiences in Nicaragua while we toasted him in Pa's wine cellar a year later. We opened that bottle of wine with the ribbons still on it in celebration. His experience was one I could relate to from when I was in the Argonne Forest ten years earlier.

The Living Center

"Mr. Corcoran. Mr. Corcoran. Liam, wake up. Come on. Wake up or you will miss breakfast," one of the aides said as she shook me.

I woke up and realized that I had overslept by almost an hour. It was almost eight o'clock in the morning as I glanced at the big numbered clock Mary had hung up for me in the room.

"Damn pills," I said as I rubbed the sleep from my eyes.

"What was that Mr. Corcoran?" the aide asked.

"It's those damned pills I take at night. They knocked me out and caused me to over sleep again," I said.

The aide smiled and informed me that the pills were to keep my arteries open, my blood pressure regulated and my heart pumping smoothly.

"The pills didn't make you sleepy, she said. "It's the hours you keep here at the assisted living home. Go to bed on time and stop watching Leno or Letterman and you'll wake up on schedule, Liam."

I couldn't argue with that because I did remember the one o'clock news starting after I finished watching Letterman.

"Come on and wash, because you still have time to get to the dining hall to eat breakfast," she said as she handed me a face cloth.

Ten minutes later, I arrived at the dining hall. As I wheeled myself in, I saw the residents all stop talking and begin to clap. I stopped the wheelchair because I was a little startled. I thought, *Did they do this for all the new members?* I looked at my aide who was smiling at me.

"What's this all about?" I asked.

"It's Veteran's Day and you are the oldest veteran in this place as well as in this State for that matter. They are just paying respect and showing some appreciation," she explained.

I nodded in appreciation and pushed myself to one of the tables to eat my breakfast. A local reporter with a cameraman approached my table and asked if he could interview me. I agreed to the interview, but only after I finished my breakfast. I spent an hour with the two of them and received about thirty seconds on the evening news that night. The local papers published a picture and a small piece in the newspaper the next day. I didn't realize how old and frail I looked. *Where had the real Liam Corcoran gone?* I thought. Then I realized that I was looking at someone who was one hundred and six years old. Maybe I didn't look so bad after all.

My convalescence at the assisted living center was working. I began to walk to and from the dining area with the use of a cane. The wheelchair was kept in reserve in case someone wanted to take me somewhere, but that didn't happen very much. Mary was the only one that volunteered to take me places, but I declined. How would a petite young woman like her muscle an old coot like me if something went wrong? She would always offer, but she knew, and I knew, that I was better off staying in the assisted living center especially for bathroom needs. I didn't need my great-granddaughter trying to help me change my underpants in case I had an accident. Even at one hundred and six, I still had some pride and modesty, so each week as I grew stronger, Mary would offer and I would still decline. Christmas was coming and maybe I would be ready to visit my great-granddaughter at her parent's house. Dick and Linda hadn't offered yet, but I'd let Mary handle the negotiations with them to put up with me for one day.

143

Mary showed up three days later with a young gentleman. I wondered where my sweetheart had been. She usually never went more than two days without visiting me. It had snowed that early week in December so I figured that kept her away. From the look in her deep blue eyes when she introduced this young man, I could see that there was a little more involvement than just a boy-friend.

"Great-granddad, this is Dennis," she said as the young man smiled and extended his hand.

"Well, I am pleased to make your acquaintance, Dennis. I didn't catch your last name though," I said.

"It's Cohen, Mr. Corcoran, and I am pleased to meet you at last."

"Cohen you say. Are you any relation to the Joseph Cohen family that lived on Division Street many years ago?"

"The one and the same, Sir. My great-grandfather was Joe Cohen of Cohen and Corcoran, Inc.," he said.

"I'll be damned. So which one of Joe's boys did you come from, son?"

"My grandfather was Alex Cohen."

"That was Joe's first son. He was quite the hero during World War II as I remember. B-17 pilot if I recall. What ever happened to him, son?"

"I'm sorry to say that he passed away last year at eighty-five."

"Oh," was all I could bring myself to say at first. There was a little uncomfortable feeling in the room until I said,

"Well, that's what happens when you live too long like I have. I should have died at eighty-five like he did. I missed that opportunity over twenty years ago. It's a curse outliving people you see born into this world. He was a good kid, man I should say. You should be very proud of him, Dennis."

"Thank you, sir. We were very proud of him and I really miss him."

Mary cut in and changed the conversation before Dennis or I became upset.

"Great-granddad, I brought Dennis to meet you so that you could meet the mysterious man in my life. I hadn't seen him in a while, but I did tell you about him."

"What else are you going to tell me my little lady?" I asked.

Mary turned a little pink in the cheeks and I grinned.

"Mr. Corcoran, I have asked Mary to marry me. We have come for your blessing, Sir," Dennis said.

"You want my blessing?"

Both of them looked at each other a little perplexed. I kept the charade up just a little longer and said,

"Well let me see. Do you like her Dennis?"

"Of course I do sir. I love her," he responded.

"That's not what I asked you, son. Do you like her?"

Both Dennis and Mary looked at each other. They probably figured this old man had lost it.

"Yes, I like her, Mr. Corcoran. I have liked her since our college days," he said as he looked me straight into my eyes.

"That's good, because you have to like her for the rest of your life. She's going to be your buddy. You probably think you love her now. Well, you don't. Your eyes are looking at a beautiful woman. Your brain thinks about the many ways you will or have made love to her. Your loins ache every time she moves in a certain way. All those things will eventually wear off over the years because nature is cruel. But being your buddy never does. So if you can stand here and tell that me you have thought about fifty, sixty or more years from now that she will still be your buddy because you like her, then you have my blessing."

"Yes sir, I have thought it through and she is my buddy now that you say it that way," he said as he reached to shake my hand.

"Have you told your parents, Mary?" I asked.

"No great-granddad. You were the first," she smiled and said.

"Well, I'm honored," I said as I stood up and hugged Mary and shook Dennis's hand again.

"Okay, off with the both of you. Go tell your parents and keep me informed of the plans," I said as I motioned with my hand.

"We thought I could visit for a little bit, great-granddad while Dennis does some errands," Mary stated.

"That's fine young lady, but don't stay too long because you need to tell the rest of the family. You made my day already so keep that in mind. You have many things to do."

Mary said that she would be right back because she planned to take more notes for our story. I watched her kiss her young man and then pinch his butt as he turned to leave the home. She surely had my blood in her genes to do something like that in the hallway of the home. I enjoyed it. I waited for her to return some several minutes later.

"Mary, what does Dennis do for a living?" I asked. "

"He's a short story writer, great-granddad, but he is interested in our story and he's thinking about writing a book using information that I've been compiling over the time we've spent together."

"Oh, so that's why you come and see me. It's a business deal," I jokingly said.

That wasn't the thing to say because her face turned and she looked hurt. Before I could make another joke to get out of an uncomfortable position because of my so called quick wit and loose mouth she said,

"Great-granddad, don't ever say that again. I love you more than you will ever know. You have always been my sounding board for anything important in my life. More than my parents even," she said in a low, but serious tone.

"I know honey and I am sorry for being an old smart ass. Of all my children, you are special."

"How long will Dennis be doing his errands?"

"Not long, why do you ask?"

"Well, a lot of what I will be telling you involves the Cohen

146

family. They were an extension of my family back in my day."
"I know you've mentioned Joe and Harriet Cohen and I didn't realize it until now how connected the families were. Maybe I'll just visit until he returns."
"No, that won't be necessary. There is a lot more to the story before I tell you about Joe Cohen's three boys, but I want him here for that. Now, where did we leave off?"
"You mentioned to your aide that you were dreaming about Giuseppe when he returned from Nicaragua."
"Right, let's continue that part of the story.

The Story

He stayed until his leave was up and then reported to Parris Island. His assignment was to train to become a drill instructor. He explained that after he worked with the non-commissioned officers there, he would have a good chance of being promoted to Sergeant. He was right. After eighteen months of training with the drill instructors, he became one of them and was promoted to Sergeant.

Sergeant Joe Cedrone spent five more years from 1928 until 1933 at Parris Island and trained many Marines. His specialty was jungle warfare because of the experience he had while fighting in Nicaragua. That experience would pay off years later in the jungles of the south pacific islands.

Ma and Pa finally relaxed knowing that Giuseppe was stationed in South Carolina. He made a point to visit the big house on Christmas and Easter every year while he was stationed there. We looked forward to seeing him during those times and he enjoyed spending two weeks during each holiday with the family. All the kids loved having him around for the holidays. He was very handsome in his dress blues as I

147

remembered. He made a point to wear them to church on Christmas Eve and Easter Sunday morning masses for the benefit of Ma and Pa.

It was on Joe's Easter leave of 1928 that Maria and I showed him the piece of land we had purchased in the country. Maria and I hoped to build our own home in Norwichtown. It was only four miles from the big house and near enough to the city to drive there in ten minutes or so. We figured that in several years, we would have enough money to get financial backing to build our dream house. I think about how cheap it was back then as compared to what it would cost today. I can't quite remember how much it cost us in 1928, but five hundred dollars comes to mind. We had another fifty dollars tied up with an architect that Joe and Harriet Cohen used for developing plans for their new house. We both thought that by 1929, or no later than 1930, we would have made enough profit from our business to afford the new homes and move from the Division Street house that we paid little rent to Pa and Ma for. Tony and Rose had already left the place and bought themselves a nice home on Williams Street next to the Norwich Free Academy. The rest of the family was on the move as well in 1928 and early 1929. Kippy and Loretta built their new home on the Lafayette Street land and Tommy and Lucia bought a large home on Washington Street. The greatest news of 1929 was Lucia announcing, during Easter Sunday lunch, that she was going to have a baby in October of 1929.

It was a hard pregnancy for Lucia because she spent too much time working long hours in the operating room which eventually took its toll on her. It seemed that physicians and nurses are their own worst enemies when it comes to taking advice from other people concerning health issues.

One afternoon during a surgery, Lucia collapsed and was

rushed to the emergency room. Tommy Parks had to watch as another physician checked on Lucia. The diagnosis was exhaustion. The doctor said that she needed several weeks of rest to regain her strength and put some pounds on her and her unborn baby. It was a wakeup call for Tommy Parks who took some time off himself and nursed his wife back to good health. He would only let her teach several days a week at the hospital until her eighth month. After that, she stayed in her home on Washington Street until the day came. Visiting her every day during the eighth and ninth months was Ma with Miss Gagnon or Ma with Miss Fortin. They set up a schedule where either Miss Gagnon or Miss Fortin would drive Ma to see Lucia. When Lucia delivered in the hospital that October, she was in top shape and delivered a baby girl that they named Julie Ann Parks.

The Living Center

"Honey, I'm a little tired. Can we pick this up tomorrow sometime?" I asked Mary. "Sure great-granddad. Dennis should be back momentarily now anyway."
Several minutes later, her fiancé returned. As he entered the room, I remarked that I expected him to make the book funny. He looked at me strangely and said,
"What do you mean, Sir?"
He then realized that Mary had told me about his profession.
"Well for one thing, you can call me Liam or great-granddad, but sir is not my name. Secondly, books about families must be interesting and funny. There is too much tragedy and bad times associated with family histories. You must concentrate on the good and funny things. Do you understand what I mean, Dennis?"
"Yes, Liam, I do. We will make it funny and interesting and thank you so much for sharing your life experiences with Mary and me," he said.

"The pleasure is mine, son. I will drag this on for as long as I can so that both of you will have to come and see me regularly," I jokingly said.

I received a glare from Mary again as she said,

"Great-granddad, we have already had this conversation. I visit you because I love you, remember?"

"I know, I know. It's time for you two to go, but I look forward to both of you returning to get going on this book," I said.

I watched them leave the home. They were a handsome couple. Then it hit me. He's Jewish. She's Catholic. I wonder if my nincompoop grandson and his wife would bring that fact up. I didn't think too much about that. Neither one went to church much. But then there was Dennis' brother, my Cardinal grandson. What would His Excellency say about his niece marrying a Jew? I pondered the thought some more. Or maybe over the years Dennis was brought up Christian. I remember how hard it was when Lucia and Tommy Parks were married and all the bullshit they went through because he was Episcopal and she was Catholic. I realized I was worrying about something that wasn't any of my concern, the kid's parents or anyone else. They were in love and like Antonio Cugini use to say, "God in my church is the same God in your church" or something like that. *This would be interesting*, I thought.

I felt a little tired now and decided to nap. It didn't take much to tire me out these days. I wondered if I would be able to finish my story telling to Dennis and Mary. It would be one of my many goals to stay alive long enough to accomplish that task. I hoped that maybe the Good Lord would see to it that he kept me alive to read the book. I thought about the month that little Julie Ann came into the world as I drifted off for my short nap.

Chapter Eight – The Depression Begins

The Story

Nobody remembers how mild October, 1929 was except for me. They only remember the financial crisis that started in New York and spread to the financial world within a few months. I do remember that we experienced Indian summer for better than several weeks. The day Julie Ann was born the temperature had reached nearly seventy degrees. By the time her Christening was held at the start of November, we had experienced some frost at night, but mild weather still continued.

After a late Sunday Mass and a noon christening, we returned to the big house for Sunday lunch. Miss Fortin and Miss Gagnon had prepared a festive spread with the approval of Ma. The three course meal consisted of soup and salad, followed by roasted chicken and potatoes and finished with pasta, meatballs and spicy sausage which were almost a standard lunch foods at the big house. Peaches and cream for the children and peaches in wine for the adults was served for dessert. Pa specialized in his peaches soaked in a special wine for special events such as weddings and christenings. The topic of conversation was the hiring of a nanny to watch over Julie Ann while Lucia worked a reduced schedule in the operating room while still teaching a few nursing classes. Miss Gagnon and Miss Fortin played a very important role for Lucia during that time in finding a suitable nanny for her baby daughter. It pleased everyone that the two ladies had taken an interest to assist in searching for the right nanny which eased both Lucia's and Ma's concerns.

Tony, Pa and I retired to the wine cellar to do some serious talking about the Wall Street crisis that had developed the previous month. With us was Joe Cohen who had been invited to the Christening that November day. We discussed the business loans that were currently on file with the local banks that financed our lumber business. Joe Cohen was particularly concerned that the banks would call in the loans we had on record. My brother Tony was more concerned with the savings accounts that the family had in the local banks. He surmised that a percentage of the monies had probably been invested into some of the areas where the market was in trouble. Pa sat and listened to all the concerns and speculations that were brought up in the conversations. He questioned all of us as to what our plans were in case the financial situation became worse and directly affected our homes and livelihoods. We stopped and stared at him for a few seconds when I asked,

"Do you think it will become bad enough to affect people's homes?"

"I see this before in old country. I leave to come here. It could get worse," he said as we all stood quietly contemplating what he just said. Pa knew he had gotten our attention.

"My house is paid for. I have money in safe. This house is big for all to live in."

We stood quiet until Tony spoke up.

"Pa, what would you do without the boarders and the income you receive from them if anyone of us had to return to the big house?"

"No need when family concerned. We all live here until things better. Houses I own will be open for rent if you all live here. We make ends meet here. Ma and me already talk," he said as he looked around and poured some more wine in each of our glasses. He looked at Joe Cohen and said,

"For you too, Joe."

Joe never said a word, but only smiled and nodded in respect for what the old man had just implied.

152

"We speak no more about this. Things be alright. This is good country. Things be alright."

Maria and I discussed what Pa had said about his and Ma's plan. We decided to remove some of our savings from the bank and keep it in the big house safe just in case. That following morning, I arrived at the bank and removed one thousand dollars from our twenty five hundred dollar account. I had intended to remove half of the money, but was instructed that the bank would only allow a limit of one thousand dollars. I was alarmed, but complied and returned home with the cash. Maria immediately took the money to Ma and deposited it in the safe in the wine cellar the next day. My other brothers and sisters followed suit and deposited money in the safe the following weeks. By Christmas, Maria and I had managed to withdraw the rest of our money and safely store it in the safe in the Cugini wine cellar. I never knew how much cash had been stored there. Only Ma and Pa knew and both of them kept duplicate records and instructions in case of their demise. Tony would know where to find Pa's records and Maria would know where to find Ma's. As traditional Italians, they designated their oldest son and daughter to the task.

At Christmas, we tried to make the gift giving enjoyable for the children, but specific goods were not available for purchase due to manufacturing cut backs. I can remember that buying additional trains for the twins was very difficult, so I made up for it by buying more track and expanding the set. The kids weren't too overjoyed at opening packages of tracks, but within a month, with the expansion of the set in the basement, they forgot about not having a new locomotive or several sleeping cars added to the set. Joe helped and made several scale houses and buildings to accompany the tin bridges and plaster tunnels I made. Maria made more clothes for the children from the material we were still fortunate to get from Mrs. Mahoney

153

and some cloth merchants in Harriet's family. We gave Christine her first new twenty-six inch bicycle that Christmas.

In January of 1930, the backlog of customer orders for the furniture business ended. Selling of the specialty items in the Franklin Square store slowed considerably. Not very many people in Norwich needed grandfather clocks or reception tables. Furniture orders for the schools declined as well. The State Hospital furniture orders remained constant for the first half of the year until the State budgets were adjusted based on the economy. The lumber business slowed. Shipments for out of state customers stopped not by demand, but by the cutbacks in rail transportation and increased costs to the lumber yards. Maria and Harriet redid the books to find costs cuts which ended in Joe and me letting go forty percent of our employees. Those that we did keep on were lucky to get nine hours a day work based on lumber orders. We closed on Saturdays to keep operating costs down. In March, Torrance Construction let Pa go. The construction company had no need for any stone or brick masons for the foreseeable future. No construction projects were available to bid on as the economy worsened. It didn't faze Pa. He immediately increased his wine cellar capabilities and worked on making more wine. No one in the family said anything about his increased wine production. We all waited to see what his plan for the excess would be.

Sunday lunches continued, but we all found it more difficult to purchase food. Food items shipped to New England slowed due to transportation shipment cutbacks. Fresh fruit and vegetable shipments slowed and prices increased. Pa began to increase his bartering with some of the local merchants and farmers for better selections of meats and produce in exchange for the fruits of his wine cellar. We figured out what the increased production of wine was for very quickly. He'd been increasing his purchasing of grapes and items he needed to make his wine and in doing so, expanded his communication and bartering skills with the merchants and farmers. Selling wine was still illegal. Pa kept a fine line to ensure that the Revenuers would not be calling at the big house. Tony and I took turns driving Kippy's modified 1927 Ford Sedan to make deliveries and pickup merchandise Pa had arranged with the merchants and farmers. We never had to outrun any Revenuers like we saw in the movies because Chief Mahoney made it his business to keep Pa informed if anything was said about Antonio Cugini's wine cellar. Usually, like clockwork, every other Sunday morning after the ten o'clock Mass, Chief and Mrs. Mahoney would visit Pa and Ma for less than a half hour and leave with enough of Pa's best table wine to last them until their next visit. That schedule continued for many years even after Prohibition was lifted in December of 1933.

After finishing Sunday lunch, blowing out her candles for her fifty-fifth birthday and thanking all of us who were able to attend, for the gifts she had received, Ma announced a plan for her children. We all kept quiet as she began talking. My first impression was that she was going to make some announcement concerning her health. We all worried that Ma would be stricken at any time with another cardiac episode, especially with all the changes that were taking place in the city, state and country. I was relieved when she started detailing her plan as to when our individual families should begin moving back into the big house before conditions deteriorated more as the depression worsened.

She explained her schedule in detail. First to move back into the big house immediately would be Tony, Rose and their twins Mary Beth and Joey. They had sold their house on Williams Street at a loss, but had gotten out of the mortgage before things became worse. Maria, me, Christine and our twins Larry and Lenny would move in a week later. Ma detailed that the cousins would share rooms by gender and age.

155

It worked out for Mary Beth and Christine because they would share the same room I had shared with my mother and sister sixteen years ago. My twins and little Joey would share the room Tony, Joey and I did until Tony got married and Joey and I left for the service. Ma seemed relaxed knowing that her family would be under her roof again. A month later Kippy, Loretta and Patrick moved into the big house from their home on Lafayette Street. Ma and Pa knew they were having difficulty meeting the mortgage payments. The couple was forced to let the property become foreclosed by the bank. Their son, Patrick was put in the same room with Joey, Lenny, and Larry which made it the loudest room in the house. It was a daily occurrence for one of the adults to remind the little rascals to be quiet after hours and to keep some type of order within the room. Despite all the quarrels, occasional fights and the chaos of having four youths in one room fostered a kinship that would last a lifetime amongst these youngsters.

Lucia and Tommy Parks remained on Washington Street and welcomed Danny into their home when he graduated from Pharmacy School in June. They were as proud of Danny as Ma and Pa were. The younger couple felt particularly responsible for guiding him into the world of medicine. Tommy Parks continued to remind Danny that medical school was another avenue for him to consider now that he had finished pharmacy school. Danny could have been accepted into medical school, in my opinion, but he was eager to start his career and spending four more years to complete medical school probably didn't seem appealing then. His room was relinquished to Joe and Harriet Cohen who moved in with their three boys in May of that year. The three boys, Alex, Aaron and Andrew stayed in Giuseppe's room. When the U.S. Marine came home, Ma had arranged for him to stay in Lucia and Tommy's house with Danny. Ma was pleased that everyone had a place to weather the depression.

156

Danny's graduation from the University of Connecticut, School of Pharmacy was a very high point for the family. We all drove to Storrs, Connecticut, to attend the graduation. We planned that trip several months in advance to make sure everyone could attend and we had enough vehicles to transport everyone there. It was important to all our children, we thought, to have the opportunity to see the University and cheer for their uncle as he received his degree. Danny was also fortunate to have a position waiting for him at the Norwich State Hospital. That meant employment close to home under the guidance of the new State Hospital pharmacist, a friend he met at the Backus Hospital pharmacy years earlier, who now needed help. Danny had kept a very high grade point average in pharmacy school and the State Hospital pharmacist had been kept informed of it. I'm sure Tommy Parks had something to do with it, but we all thought Danny was the right person for the job anyway.

The properties on Division Street were rented before the Depression worsened and the Cugini's worked out rental payments with their tenants when cash was not available to be paid at times. Ma's plan to have most of her family living under one roof enabled Cohen and Corcoran to exist with Tony and Kippy still on the payroll. Needless to say, it was an adjustment for all the parents, aunts, uncles, friends and grandparents of the children living in this home. Somehow Ma and Pa's plan worked and it was influential in keeping the family fed, warm and together during a most difficult time. The only drawback was that the train sets that Joe and I had built up for the kids remained in boxes for a while. Eventually, we found room at the shop to set up both train sets for the kids to play with after school and on weekends. We all figured it would be only a short time before we could reassemble the train sets in our own homes again. We didn't realize it would be many more years.

By the summer of 1930, the Depression deepened. Unemployment soared, goods became more difficult to get, prices increased one week and dropped the next. Life at the big house continued as normal as Ma and Pa could make it. Sunday lunches continued on schedule, but the selection of foods slightly differed from previous lunches. Spicy sausages that Ma usually purchased from the local meat cutter were now made at home from pork, beef and spices bartered from the local farmers. Ma planted her own herb garden in a small patch directly behind the big house where she had always grown flowers. She made sure the granddaughters became more interested in the herb gardening so that they could nurture and harvest the spices to add to the family meals. The Grandsons were tasked with chores around the big house. Gone were the days when we all had to feed the boarders before our own meals. We were expected to help with the meal preparations and the cleanup. I can remember as the Depression deepened, the family strengthened and adjusted.

The Living Center

"Good afternoon, Mr. Corcoran. Did you have a good nap?" one of the caretakers asked as she straightened up my living quarters and I cleared the sleep from my head.
"How long have I've been in la la land?" I asked.
"Well, your great granddaughter and her friend left about three hours ago. They said that they would be back in about three hours so that's why I came in. Plus, I don't want you staying up half the night watching TV like you tend to do when you sleep during the day."
I looked at her and asked,
"What is your name again?"
"It's Daisy."
"Like the flower?"

"Yep, one and the same."

"It's not your real name though, is it? Your parents must have named you something else, but you use it as a nick name, don't you?"

Daisy stopped working and looked directly at me. Her brown face pinked a little.

"How did you know that Daisy wasn't my given name?"

"Just a hunch, but what is your real name?"

She smiled and said, "Desire."

"Yeah, I guess that could cause some problems growing up," I said.

"Well Daisy, it's nice to meet you and your secret is safe with me."

She smiled and said, "Thank you Mr. Corcoran."

"Please, call me Liam. I like that a lot better than Mr. Corcoran, okay?"

She nodded and pointed for me to look out the picture window. I could see Mary and Dennis just getting out of his car in the parking lot.

"That was good timing Daisy,"

She smiled and left to go about her duties with the rest of the residents in the assisted living center. I thought about the relocation of the family into the big house and began to organize my thoughts. I thought about 1930 and any other occurrences during that time that I could remember as the kids came into the room.

"High Liam, You're awake." Dennis said as he walked in.

"I sure am and hi yourself."

Mary came over and bent down to kiss me on the cheek. She smelled so good and for a second, I thought it was my Maria. Reality set in and she asked,

"You set for another round of storytelling, great-granddad?"

"Yep. I was thinking about the relocation of the family back into the big house just before you came."

159

"Go with it Liam. Tell us what comes to mind about that time," Dennis said.
We spent thirty or so minutes of me going through the set up in the rooms and I joked about all the kids running around.

The Story

Pa expanded wine production to use to barter. We worried that the living conditions would affect Ma's health. Eventually we all realized that it was the best medicine for her to have her family around her so she didn't have to worry about them. If a problem developed, she was there to assist in solving it.

By summer, we had settled down to a routine in the big house. We actually worked like a military unit with each individual responsible for some task in the house to benefit the family. That was what Joe Cedrone said the first hours he was home on leave that Easter. I can remember him laughing about how the family was functioning like the Marine Corp he had just taken leave from a few days earlier. Joe was great with all the kids, but especially the boys. He would have one or two of them with him the entire time he was visiting the big house. When he would walk from Boswell Avenue to Lucia's home on Washington Street, he would have at least one of the boys trailing him on their bicycles. They must have asked him one hundred questions about military life and the places he'd seen. Joe was good. He never talked about the combat situations he'd been involved in. He only talked about the customs and people of the countries he had visited.

Joe Cohen's three sons tagged along as well with the other kids and always asked the Marine when he would be visiting Europe. Their grandfather Cohen had emigrated from Germany in the eighteen-seventies before their father was born. Even in his eighties, old man Cohen still talked to the boys about the streets of Berlin. The old man must have been a big influence on his grandsons because they constantly asked Joe Cedrone, during their walks, many questions about Europe and Germany. The Marine couldn't answer any of their questions, but he told them that he hoped he would have a chance to see Europe during one of the Mediterranean trips the Marines had planned for him after he finished training men at Parris Island. Joe didn't know then that after Parris Island, he would be shipped to the Philippine Islands. The Cohen boys would see Europe before Joe Cedrone finished his career in the Marine Corp. They also would return to Europe in the nineteen-sixties and seventies.

The Living Center

I stopped talking and looked at Mary and asked,
"What did Dick say about the train set I asked you to ask him about?"
"I'm sorry. I completely forgot to tell you what he said."
"And," I said.
"He said he'd come up some time and set up part of the set."
"Okay, when is *some time*?"
"Well, I guess in the next week or so. You know dad, he isn't too good on scheduling."
"Yeah, that's why I asked you what *some time* meant." I looked at Dennis.
"My grandson is not too fast at accomplishing tasks."
"Liam, how about Mary and I go by Dick's house tomorrow and ask for the set. I'll set it up with your help. How's that sound?"
I liked this kid more every minute I was exposed to him. I could see why Mary adored him.
"Okay, mister, that's a great idea. I'll look forward to it. Okay, where was I in the story?" Dennis smiled, paused, looked at his

notes and said,

"You were talking about my grandfather and my great uncles asking Joe Cedrone questions about Europe."

"Oh, that's where I was." I continued with the story.

The Story

The summer of 1930 was uneventful except for one incident that will remain in my mind until the day I die. It was a late Saturday afternoon in July. Maria and I had taken the kids to Mohegan Park for a swim to cool everyone. We planned to stay until dusk, but the threatening thunder and lightning storm that approached changed our plans and we left a little earlier to get home before it hit. Tony and Rose had followed us up to the park with the twins. On the way home, the kids wanted to ride all together in Tony's Sedan while Maria, Rose and I followed in my car. Several times while we were packing up the two cars, we instructed the kids to calm down. I don't know if it was the approaching storm or just the energy stored up in all of them, but they seemed uncontrollable.

Tony started off in the lead with the five kids in the car as we followed. He maintained a normal speed as the rain started picking up as we exited the park onto Boswell Avenue. It was at the right turn onto Boswell when the left rear door of Tony's sedan opened and Mary Beth fell out in front of my car. I can still see the puzzled look on her face before she hit the pavement. I thank God everyday that the traffic was light that Saturday afternoon and we were going at a reduced speed. I stopped my car just in time to miss the youth. She lay lifeless in the street as I exited my car with my heart in my mouth. I assumed the worse as I approached her.

There was only a little blood from her forehead being scraped

162

and her left ear canal was bleeding. She was unconscious and seemed lifeless. I was frozen until I heard her moan.

"Thank you God," I can remember saying out loud.

Tony hadn't noticed what had occurred until he was a block down the street and realized by the crying and chatter from the kids that something had happened. I remember him running up the street yelling and saying, oh my God, over and over again until he reached me handing Mary Beth over to her mother in the middle of the street.

By the time Tony reached us, Mary Beth had opened up her eyes and had started crying and complaining that her head hurt. I sent Maria down to Tony's car to drive all the kids back to the big house while we took Mary Beth to the hospital. We were there very quickly as I remember driving a little too fast as it poured cats and dogs. Upon reaching the hospital, we were a little more relaxed as Mary Beth had stopped crying, but still complained of a headache. When we arrived, we requested Tommy Parks, who luckily for us, was on duty that day.

As always, he took complete control. After x-rays, an exam, and an old fashion hug for Mary Beth and a few for her parents, he assured them that she would be alright. He stated that she had suffered a mild concussion. He instructed us to take her home and watch her for the next twenty-four hours for dizziness, vomiting and other signs that would indicate she had developed some swelling in her head.

When I think about it today, Mary Beth would have not left the hospital with today's advances in medicine. An MRI or some other special test would have been performed. Within a week, Mary Beth seemed herself again. We would learn twenty years later, after she had seen a specialist for occasional migraine headaches, that she was practically deaf in that ear from the fall from the sedan. How lucky that child had been to escape serious injury or worse because in 1930, things were handled very differently.

That night, after we all knew Mary Beth would be alright; I lay in bed and cried like I had when I heard news that the Armistice had been signed. Maria cuddled me until I told her that I thought that the child was dead and what would we have done if that had happened. Maria never answered me, but she knew how much love there was in this family. She looked into my swollen eyes and I can remember her saying,
"Liam, it didn't happen and she will be alright. Let's move on. It can drive you crazy if you continue to dwell on it."

The next morning, I removed the inside door handles from the rear doors of Tony's sedan. If someone needed out, then an adult would have to let them out. I realize now how dumb that was to do because what would have happened if they needed to get out in a hurry due to an emergency. Eventually, Tony re-installed the handles as the kids grew and became a little more disciplined when riding in the car.

Business continued to be slow, but Cohen and Corcoran managed to obtain small furniture orders from the State Hospital and the Norwich School Board. The lumber portion of our business actually started to pick up as rail transportation adjusted to the Depression. One particular day in the office, I found Joe Cohen sitting and reading a letter. I casually asked about it only because the expression on his face bothered me. He handed it to me. I handed it back to him once I glanced at it and laughed,
"Joe, it's in German. The only German I remember was Hande nach oben."
"Hands up? Is that all the German you know?"
"Yep. That's all I needed to know when we took prisoners," I said as he smiled and took the letter back.

164

"I didn't know you spoke and read German. I'm surprised you didn't end up translating German for the Army or Navy instead of riding out on a Destroyer in the Atlantic,"

"I never told them I could speak German. I just wanted to be another sailor doing his duty."

I didn't say another word as he changed the subject and began to explain what his Uncle, who was still living in Berlin, Germany, had written.

The letter was asking if Joe would sponsor his only son and family to leave Germany and come to the United States. Joe's father had just recently died and he knew that his father would have made every attempt to get his nephew and family here. I listened to some more of the details the old man had concerns with. The German government was heavily influenced by the Fascists who were now singling out Jews and Jewish businesses with acts of hate crimes. He was concerned not only for his son and daughter-in-law, but mainly for his two grandsons who were eleven and nine. Joe never met his first cousin, but had seen pictures of him that his father had received over the years.

I told Joe to sponsor them and see if he could get them over here. I asked what the cousin did for a profession. He explained that he was a butcher by trade and was running the family butcher shop in the city. He stated that his uncle was afraid that the shop would be damaged again and that his family could be injured. I asked if the old man was coming too. Joe just shook his head and stated that he was ill and a widower. His uncle had explained that he could live with some other relatives in the countryside after he sold the shop and used the money to get the son and his family to America.

"So what's the problem?" I asked.

"Where would they stay? I live in the big house with you until things get better," he said while pacing in the office.

"Look, we'll talk to Pa and see if he knows of some rentals opening up or even if he has something coming up soon that he can hold until they get here," I explained.

Joe seemed to relax a bit and then said,

"There is something else." I looked, and waited for his explanation.

"He's a former German soldier. He was a cook in the war, but served on the front according to what my father told me after the war. I'm sure he shot some French and British soldiers. He could have even been shooting at Americans."

Joe stood motionless and waited for my reaction. I smiled and said,

"The war is over. He did what he had to do and we did the same. He's a veteran who is now being kicked out of the same country that he risked his life for. That's got to be a kick in the ass. What would you do if all Jewish American Veterans were treated like that?"

"So you have no problem with it?" he asked.

"Hell no. I don't have a problem with it. As far as I am concerned, he is another guy, Jew or otherwise, who's looking for a clean start. It's no expense to you so what's holding you up?"

Joe smiled, shook my hand and said, "Nothing."

As usual, Pa knew someone who had a rental becoming available in the city. He also asked around if anyone was in need of an experienced butcher, not only at the markets in the area, but for the farmers who raised live stock for butchering. Pa figured that the German butcher could pick up needed cash or barter from the locals who needed butchery services. The ideas and help Pa gave reduced Joe's anxiety. Pa was good at that as always. Six weeks later, Joe received a letter from his uncle that Wolfgang Cohen, his wife Elsa, and their two sons,

Ernst and Erwin, would be arriving by ship in New York City on October 12th. It was ironic, I thought, that Wolfgang and his family would arrive in the new world the same day Columbus had over four hundred and forty odd years earlier.

During the wait for Wolfgang and his family, our family faced another health crisis. One Sunday afternoon in the wine cellar, Pa mentioned to Tony and I that he was having pain in his legs when he walked long distances. Of course, our first response was to explain that as he got older, he would have more aches and pains so he should slow down when he took long walks. The old man looked a little irritated and responded with,

"No, walk not a problem, pain happens a lot when I sit."

Tony and I looked at each other until I suggested that Tommy check on Pa when he came to the house later in the day. Tommy and Lucia would sometimes miss Sunday lunch, but they made it a point to drop by on that day with Julie Ann and visit for coffee and a snack of some sort Ma always had available.

I informed Tommy of Pa's concern when he arrived and he immediately examined him in his bedroom. Tommy informed Tony and I that he needed to have Pa see an internist to evaluate the blood flow in his legs. He surmised from his exam that this may be the problem. We made the appointment for Pa a week later and Tommy's diagnosis was confirmed. The internist informed Ma and Pa that he would need an operation to open up the arteries in his upper thighs. He did as the doctor suggested and had the operation. It did relieve the problem, but the doctor informed Pa that he had advanced arteriolosclerosis and other areas in his body could be affected. The fifty-seven year old man took the news well and went about his life as usual. Little did he know that the wine he consumed would aid in keeping him alive another twenty

167

years. The operation took its toll on Pa because he slowed down physically after it. Mentally, the condition never affected him as far as we could observe. Pa was still Pa.

The day came for the arrival of Wolfgang and his family in Norwich. The family of four departed the train on October 14th. They had spent one day getting through Ellis Island and another traveling by rail to Southeastern Connecticut. Joe, Harriet, Maria and I waited at the train station for the immigrants to arrive. When they stepped off the train, it was obvious who they were amongst the other departing passengers. The black fedora hat and black wool overcoat Wolfgang wore stood out in the warm autumn weather we were experiencing that day. Joe called out to Wolfgang in German. The man immediately smiled and relaxed seeing Joe and hearing his native language being spoken directly to him. His wife and children seemed uneasy until Harriet and Maria used their charm to relax them. Harriet's German was fair and she was able to reassure the family that they were in a safe city. Wolfgang spoke a little English and tried to communicate with us. Joe immediately explained to him that he would have plenty of time to learn to speak English, but for now, he wanted him to understand everything that was being said so he continued to speak to him in German.

Wolfgang and his family settled into a two bedroom apartment on Lake Street. The location served both Wolfgang and Joe well because both streets ran almost parallel to each other. It would be several months before I had a chance to talk to Wolfgang personally and get to know him better. He was a polite man and a very good butcher as I immediately observed. His knowledge of his trade became evident as more shops and farmers requested his services as the months went on. Pa especially liked the sausage packing techniques he showed him as well as his ability to perfectly spice meats and poultry. It was in Pa's wine cellar when I did have that chance to talk with Wolfgang as Pa poured him one of his gallon jugs of wine for services he had performed for him.

As the three of us consumed several glasses of Pa's best, the subject of the Jewish situation in Germany under the new Nazi fascists came up. Wolfgang described as best he could in his broken English, what had transpired after the war in Berlin and the surrounding communities. He detailed the shop business they tried to maintain during runaway inflation, lack of meat and vegetables and unrest. He explained the change of the German people in their views of the Jews in the country. He didn't understand, and couldn't explain, how the fascists used the Jews as one of the reasons the Germans had lost the war. Pa and I just listened as the man slowly, and sometimes emotionally, detailed his experience.

His emotions were only heightened as Pa poured him another glass of wine. It was evident that he was mad that the German people blamed the German Jews for the loss of the war. He explained that the Jews were not treated any different in the German Army during the war. It was years later that the prejudice began, he explained. He was visibly upset as he described the hurt he felt being an army veteran who was eventually spat upon for being Jewish. He emphasized that no German soldier asked him if he was Jewish when they were in the trenches. It was during that part of the conversation that I learned that Wolfgang had been in France during the war. I explained that I had been there also. We never discussed where or when we were there. It was just understood we knew what each had gone through. We left it at that. Years later, I would find out that he had been transferred to Belgium during the latter part of the war and that we never belonged to units that faced each other.

Later in 1931, Joe attempted to bring his uncle to America. Before he could arrange anything, his uncle died at the farm he had gone to live at when Wolfgang left. We realized that even if Joe had succeeded in convincing the elder man to come to this country, his health would have prevented it. Years later Wolfgang would mention that his father had served during the Franco-Prussian War at twenty years old. No one cared then that he was Jewish.

It didn't take long for Larry and Lenny to Americanize Ernst and Erwin. Ernst became Ernie to the kids on the street. It reminded me how I nicknamed Donato - Danny. Erwin remained Erwin. It blended in and didn't seem too German. The boys fit in well and were soon playing baseball on the Lake Street playground. Despite the Depression, life was good for the Cohen family in America. Nineteen-thirty closed and the Cohen family celebrated Hanukkah. They rededicated Judaism of the Temple of Jerusalem in America for the first time. The eight candles of the season were lit and glowed brightly in the Wolfgang Cohen home.

Chapter Nine – Hard Times

The Story

During the first winter months of 1931, Wolfgang and his family adjusted to American life. One of the niceties that still existed that was affordable was the movies. Maria and Harriet convinced Joe and I to see the movie 'Romance'. I wasn't too excited about seeing it, but the women were constantly organizing a time to see the movie. I can remember that it starred Greta Garbo who Joe and I didn't mind going to see. We invited Wolfgang and Elsa to accompany us. We made it a night. I don't remember too much about that movie, but I do remember seeing attractions for the war movie '*All Quiet on the Western Front*'. After the movie, Joe suggested that we go to see it. None of the women were overjoyed about seeing it so he asked me if I would go with him. Although it looked interesting, I wasn't convinced that it would be something I wanted to see: Hollywood's interpretation of what war was like on the front.

Wolfgang surprised me when he stated that he would be interested in seeing the movie. I can remember Joe looking at me and waiting for me to change my mind. I was steadfast for another week until it was brought up again. I relinquished and the three of us attended a Saturday Matinee. About an hour into the movie, I had enough. Too many thoughts, rekindled images, and sounds were released from my subconscious until I had to get up and leave. I stayed outside the theatre until several minutes later Wolfgang appeared sweating profusely despite the cool temperature in the theatre. He lit up a cigarette and drew in deeply. He exhaled and repeated the act several more times until he seemed to recompose himself.

He smiled at me and never said a word for several more minutes. He broke his silence with only a few words that I can remember to this day.

"Nobody knows what war is. I know you know. You know I know,"

he said as he finished his cigarette and lit another before crushing the first out on the pavement. Thirty or so minutes later, Joe joined us. His only comment was,

"Thanks guys for coming with me."

We walked home and never discussed the movie. I can't remember what we talked about, but it wasn't the movie we had just seen. We found out years later that the Nazis forbid the movie to be shown in Germany because it depicted the German defeat. Without speaking another word about the movie, a common bond began to develop between Wolfgang and me.

The Depression deepened in 1931. It didn't stop the effects it continued to have on us despite most of us being consolidated in the big house. Ma and Pa had to notify Miss Fortin and Miss Gagnon that their services could not be paid for anymore. Ma organized all of us to take on parts of the specific duties both these great women performed in the big house. An arrangement was made for the two of them to live at the big house until they found a job first, and then an apartment, before they would have to leave. The two women were like family and had been valuable assets especially to Ma and Lucia in their times of need. Pa worried that Ma would resume her old ways and become ill. But Ma assured him that the children and grandchildren would be organized to keep the house running smoothly.

Within a month of Ma and Pa informing the two women that they would have to seek other employment, a family member came to the rescue and helped them get it. Fortunately for the two women, Tommy Parks practiced part-time at the Norwich

State Hospital examining and treating the mental patients. He was influential in getting them employment at the Hospital as ward aides. He kept abreast of staff needs and openings when they became available. With the new employment, they found themselves an apartment on Stonington Road in Preston which was walking distance to their new job. They would remain in that location for many years until they retired from the State Hospital with a pension. They remained relatively close to the family for many years.

That Easter, Joe Cedrone came to visit for two weeks as planned. The family looked forward every Easter and Christmas for the Marine's two week visits. The boys were even more ecstatic knowing he would be home to tell them all about his experiences at Parris Island and the Far East. But this visit would be different, at least for the kids. Unannounced, he brought his fiancée with him. Tony and I had taken an hour off early from the shop to meet him at the train. We spotted him first in his green and tan uniform as he stepped off the train. To our surprise, he turned and helped a very attractive, petite, woman down the steps. We knew something was different because the red headed young lady just beamed at him as he helped her down the train car steps.

Tony looked at me and said,
"The marine doesn't seem bashful with women anymore does he?"
I just continued to look at the two of them as they turned and Joe spotted us.
"Hey there brothers, it's good to see you again," he said as he extended his hand to me first and then to Tony. Before we could say a word, he turned and took the hand of the young woman who stood there smiling and said,
"My brothers, this is my fiancée, Suzanne Le Francois. Suzanne, these are two of my bothers, Liam and Tony."

173

Our mouths were probably still open as Suzanne, in a very distinct, but soft southern accent told us how happy she was to meet us.

"I have heard many nice things about you all and your families. I just can't wait to meet everyone," she said as she grabbed Joe's arm.

Tony was still tongue tied when I got out the first words.

"It's nice to meet you as well, Suzanne. This is a very pleasant surprise to us. Joe had not mentioned that he had a girlfriend never mind a very pretty fiancée," I said while I looked at Joe.

"Giuseppe, did you tell Ma?" I asked looking directly at him.

"No. Unfortunately, I haven't said a word, but I'm sure she will like her. Isn't she a beauty?"

By then, Tony had found that he could only smile and nod. Suzanne spoke up. "Giuseppe? Joe, I didn't know you still used that name."

"I don't sweetie, but my brothers occasionally use it when they are concerned," he said. Joe looked at the two of us.

"When we get to the big house, I will see Ma and Pa first so I don't shock anyone. Suzanne and I love each other very much and things have progressed very rapidly. Suzanne is the daughter of my Gunnery Sergeant, Simon Le Francois. I met her at a dinner almost a year ago and ....well things have progressed. I assured Gunny that his daughter was staying with a very strict Italian family and her honor and virtue was safe." Suzanne just smiled as we continued to walk to Tony's sedan.

We arrived at the big house and the kids immediately mobbed Joe. As always, he had small gifts for each one of them that he pulled out from his duffle bag. Suzanne stood by his side and smiled. She commented that she had never seen so many kids in one family. I asked her how many children were in Gunny's family.

"Oh, my father only had me. My mother died in childbirth

174

when I was born. But I have two half-brothers though which are about these children's ages. My dad married my stepmother when I was ten."

As we conversed, Ma appeared at the front door. She smiled as soon as she saw Giuseppe. Her expression didn't change when she spied Suzanne. She exited the door and walked to Giuseppe as he was preoccupied with the children. He stood up as soon as he saw her approaching. She hugged him and whispered something in Italian. He laughed, whispered back, and kissed her on the forehead. He turned to Suzanne and said,

"This is my mother, honey." Suzanne smiled and first extended her hand, but Ma passed by the hand and hugged the petite woman.

"Giuseppe has very good taste. You are a beautiful child," she said in almost a whisper, hiding what seemed to be her choking up a just a little.

"Ma, this is Suzanne."

Before Giuseppe could say another word, Ma was talking to Suzanne and escorting her into the house as the entourage followed. When Pa saw her, he rose up from the kitchen table and exclaimed,

"Ma, Che I bei capelli rossi."

"My husband said what beautiful red hair."

"Oh thank you, Mr. Cugini. It is so nice to meet you at last. I have heard so many wonderful stories about you two," she said as she turned back to Ma.

It was done. Suzanne had won over Ma and Pa. Joe sat there for almost forty minutes before he was invited into the conversation. As he was about to say something, another member of the family entered the kitchen and was introduced to Suzanne. Each one stayed around and listened to her talk. The South Carolinian drawl hypnotized every one of them as they began to draw up chairs and sit around the large kitchen table.

Pa exited slowly and headed for the wine cellar. Within a few minutes, he set a half gallon of his best wine on the table.

"Do you like to taste?" he asked.

Suzanne must have been filled in on the customs and she responded with,

"Joe has told me so much about the exquisite wine you make, Mr. Cugini."

"You call me Pa. I like you to do that, okay?" he asked.

"Okay Pa, and yes, I would like to taste it. I must tell you that I haven't had any alcohol in my life you know with prohibition and all," she said.

That was probably the wrong thing to tell Pa. His goal now would be to make sure Suzanne acquired a taste for his wine. Ma made sure that Pa didn't feed the pretty thing another glass after she tasted and finished the first. I was pleased that Ma took control halfway through the first glass because Suzanne's cheeks were becoming the same color as her hair. It was several hours later that Pa actually struck up a conversation with Giuseppe. That was okay with him because he hoped that the family would accept his southern girl. Everyone did, hook, line and sinker.

Joe and Suzanne stayed at Lucia and Tommy's home for their stay in Norwich. Both guests were assigned their own rooms as instructed by Ma to Lucia. No one ever asked or knew if Joe paid a visit to Suzanne's room during their stay. I told Maria, "The first night I would have paid a visit."

Maria rolled over in bed and said, "Yes I know Liam. We have firsthand experience on that."

Their visit came and went so quickly it seemed. We were all invited to attend their wedding in South Carolina later that year, but we all knew it would be literally impossible for anyone of us to attend. On the day before they returned to Parris Island, Ma and Pa held an engagement party for them at the big house and invited the guests they would have invited if the couple had been getting married in Norwich. They appreciated it and actually received some nice gifts and money. I guess the most important facts that eased Ma's concerns were that Suzanne was Catholic and very much in love with her great nephew. Pa could have cared less about her religious affiliation; he was just pleased with Giuseppe's choice for a wife and happy that she came from a very patriotic family. Maria and I were pleased that he now had a companion who was use to the military life he had chosen for a career.

In September of that year, Sergeant Giuseppe Cedrone was married to Suzanne Le Francois at the Marine Base chapel at Parris Island. To our delight, Tommy and Lucia were able to travel by train and attend the small wedding. Ma and Pa took care of little Julie Anne for the week that they were in South Carolina. Tommy took some nice pictures of the event which included pictures of Gunnery Sergeant Simon Le Francois, his wife and two young sons. Giuseppe made an enlargement of his wedding picture for Ma and Pa which came in the mail several weeks later.

The Living Center

"I still have that picture somewhere in the boxes of albums and picture frames stored in the basement of Dick and Linda's home."
I stopped my story telling and looked up at Dennis and said,
"Are you sure you don't mind getting that train set for me?"
"No problem Liam. I'll check with your grandson, but I'm sure Dick will get the set up to you as soon as he can," Dennis said as he looked at me curiously.
"Yeah, you figured me out son. I need another favor while I have you on the hook."

Mary interrupted the conversations and said,

"Great-granddad it is no bother."

"Listen to what I have to say before you go committing to anything more," I said.

"What else do you need, Liam?" Dennis asked while looking at Mary.

"I would like you to go through the albums and loose pictures and pull out ones of Ma and Pa, my brothers and sisters and the Cohens. Could you do that for me?"

The couple looked at each other and said yes in unison.

"Good. Now I am tired. We will do this again tomorrow and I am sure you two have better things to do this evening with each other. I'm going to have dinner and then turn in early," I said.

"Are you feeling alright, Liam?" Dennis asked.

"I feel great son. I'm just tired and hungry. I'll see you tomorrow so off with you both," I said as I smiled and motioned for them to leave as I would do to little children. They obliged and left.

The next day while sitting in the sun room of the assisted living center, I noticed a pickup truck park directly in front of the center. I recognized the driver of the truck as my grandson Dick. To my delight, Dennis, and then Mary, exited the truck from the passenger side. I knew then that Mary and Dennis had convinced my grandson to help them bring the train set. I quickly, as quickly can be described for an old man like me, returned to my living area and awaited for the arrival of the three of them. Mary glowed as she approached with that mischievous grin she always had when she was pleased with herself.

"Hi great-granddad, we brought the train set and some pictures you wanted." I smiled, nodded and watched as Dennis and Dick brought in quite a few boxes.

"Okay Gramps, where do want it set up?"

I hated the name Gramps, but Dick had called me that since the late sixties when he was going through his semi-hippie bullshit phase of his life. Dick was sixty now and he hadn't changed his social skills. It stuck with his younger brother as well, the Cardinal. They both called me Gramps.

I paused and looked around the room and asked,
"How much track did you bring?"
"Enough to go around the goddamned room twice," Dick commented with a little irritation in his voice.
"Well then, let's go around one time and see what we have left over,"
I responded with a soft smile. I did that on purpose because if I had snapped back it would have given him an excuse to leave and leave all the setup work to Dennis. Within an hour, the train tracks were placed around the room. A few tweaks here and there were required, but Dennis made them as Dick watched. Mary pulled out the first of the two locomotives they had brought. It was the 1860's replica of the 'General' used during the Civil War.
"How about this one, Liam? It looks to be in good shape." Dennis said.
By then, Mary had pulled out the second one. It was the 1930's high speed locomotive I had bought on a deal during the Depression for the twins. Just based on my facial expressions, Mary said,
"I guess this one is your choice."
"Yeah, it's my favorite."

We assembled the locomotive with a dozen or so cars and started it around the room. It took about thirty seconds to circle the room at high speed. It was fun to see it working again. Dick said that he would take the rest of the tracks and trains back into the truck when I stopped him and asked,
"Are there more at home?" He nodded and was about to speak when I interrupted him. "Good. Bring the rest and leave what

you have here in the boxes." Dick looked at me perplexed and asked,

"Where in hell are you going to put them?"

I looked and paused for a few seconds before I answered.

"Are you going to set them up again, Dick?" I asked.

"No. Not at my house."

"Then I will set them up here at the living center. It will be good therapy for me and something to keep me busy."

"Gramps, you don't have enough friggen room here. What are you thinking?" he exclaimed.

"Dick, I have a few bucks and I will get some plywood and hire some guys to build me some tables in the basement. I'll put them there. I still have enough mental capability to design and build the set again."

There was silence for a few seconds when Mary spoke up.

"I'll help. It will be fun," she said as she looked at Dennis.

"Count me in too. I have a few tracks and trains left from my grandfather's set that was split up years ago. I'll add it to the set," he said while smiling at Mary.

"That stuff is probably pieces from Joe Cohen's set he built for your grandfather and great uncles when they were kids," I said.

Dick looked at all of us and said,

"I'll bring the rest over in a few days. Maybe it's a good idea to get the trains out of storage and run them again. Don't hire any carpenters; I still have most of the train tables. Dennis, maybe you can help me set them up?"

That was the best thing Dick had said in years. I thanked him for his generosity. It was a good moment.

After I got permission from the administration, it took Dick, Dennis, Mary and me one week to reassemble the train tables. Dick set them even higher than had originally been designed so that I could use a wheelchair to move under the tables to get to various sections to monitor the trains. We began placing some of the old buildings and houses that were in decent shape on

180

the set. Dick brought some plaster so that I could make new landscaping items and try to reconstruct the city and countryside that I had developed when I first retired.

We worked several hours a day on the train set until it was ready for me to begin my slow process of building and adding the new houses and extending the landscape. I could only work on the set for two to three hours a day. I usually did as much as I could in the early morning hours after breakfast. That made the aides happy because I was up early, ate breakfast and did my work. The most pleasing point was that I didn't stay up late and watch TV. I was in a routine now because after lunch, I napped until Mary and Dennis came to continue on with the story. Sometimes if I had the strength, I would go down to the basement and work while I talked. At the rate I was telling the story, and the rate I was building the train set landscaping, I would have to live a lot longer to get both done. Staying alive was a good goal and working on the train set was something to look forward to each day. Occasionally, Dick and Linda would show up to see how I was progressing. Dick would actually help sometimes for an hour or so. The damned train set was bringing us a little closer after all these years. I should have thought about that a few years ago when his father died. My son, Lenny, had kept the set at Dick's house and often visited to run it in the cellar. When Lenny died of heart disease at eighty two, a part of Dick died with him. I should have seen that, but….well that's another story.

As I began finishing one house at a time, Mary commented that the houses and buildings represented old fashion America. I told her she was correct and that I was going to create a city and surrounding countryside that represented a much slower and peaceful time in America that I remembered.
Mary asked, "Great-granddad, aren't you describing the prewar years? That was still during the Depression and not the

greatest time of your life."

I looked at her and smiled.

"It was hard times, but life was still simple. People worked together to survive. The pictures you found and set up for me in my living room of our family during those years is inspiring me to keep telling their story."

The Story

By late 1932, we had elected a new President. Franklin Roosevelt won and was busy telling us all that we didn't have to fear anything. His quote that says "...all we had to fear was fear itself," was well documented in the history books. That was the usual political bullshit. What Maria and I were afraid of was that our children wouldn't get a proper education and the opportunity to compete with other children to get into higher education. Christine had to transfer from St. Patrick's Parochial School to the Norwich Public School system when she turned ten years old in 1930. Maria and I couldn't afford to send her to parochial school anymore. She adjusted, and the religious instructions she had received up to that time stayed with her the rest of her adult life. I couldn't say that for Larry and Lenny because they finished their religious instructions during catechism classes held after Mass every Sunday morning through 1933. It was a chore to make them attend, especially on Sundays when they were free to play ball and do other things. Maria and I persevered and made sure they continued until they were all confirmed by 1934. Education in Norwich was maintained and we were fortunate enough to have a strong city government and school board that tried to keep the educational standard current. Christine would eventually attend the Norwich Free Academy in the fall of 1934. She became a graduate of the class of 1938.

We received correspondence from Joe and Suzanne informing us that she was expecting a baby in June of 1933. We were all very excited at hearing the news and we discussed it many times at dinner. A concern was noted on Ma's face when she pointed out to all of us that Suzanne would be in the Philippine Islands when she delivered. Joe's term at Parris Island had come to a close and he had been informed that he would be stationed in the islands. We contemplated having Suzanne stay in Connecticut until the baby was born, but through discussions with Tommy and Lucia, they saw no reason why Suzanne couldn't travel in her seventh month to the Philippines and deliver her baby at the Army hospital there. Tommy explained that the facilities at the Army hospital equaled or exceeded what was available anywhere else in the country. It sounded very convincing and put everyone's concerns temporarily at ease. Joe and Suzanne were very good about keeping Ma and Pa up to date on her condition and their plans for moving to the Philippines.

All went well for the time being. We received a letter that they had arrived at the islands by steamship in early May. Everything seemed in order as we received another letter at the end of May. The letter contained mostly the description of the area where they were living, the customs of the natives, and the warm and sometimes violent weather that occurred there. We all waited for more letters, but none came throughout June. Ma waited almost everyday for word of the birth of their child. No word came. Several letters were sent off during that time frame as I could remember, but they went unanswered.

On July 1st, an event took place that shook the foundation of our family again. Recently promoted Staff Sergeant Joe Cedrone entered the big house alone with a small duffle bag strung over his shoulder. The majority of the children had just finished breakfast as the adults were straightening up. Ma was the first to see the Marine standing there looking dejected and scruff. Joe had a two or three day growth on his face and his usual military bearing wasn't visible. He put down his bag as Ma approached him. He broke down and hugged her for several minutes. We all knew that something had happened. Once Joe composed himself, Loretta handed him a cup of coffee. He explained that Suzanne had complications during the birth of their daughter. Joe cried as he explained that he had to make a decision to save his wife because the baby's chances of survival were minimal according to the Army doctors. Suzanne survived the childbirth, but later died due to internal hemorrhaging that occurred from the delivery.

He explained that the Army had shipped his wife and daughter back to South Carolina to be buried close to where her father, stepmother and brothers were living. He went on to say that Suzanne's death affected her father enough that he retired from the Marine Corp a few days before Joe departed for Connecticut. Ma asked why Joe had not informed us so that his family could have been there for him. He had no answer and just sat at the kitchen table in silence. We did find out that he had two weeks of emergency leave left so he planned to stay in Norwich until he had to depart on a westbound cross country train and then a troop ship that was scheduled to leave San Diego for the Philippine Islands. Needless to say, the Fourth of July was not a very festive event in the big house that year. Before Joe departed for the Philippines, we found out that he had made sure the baby was baptized and given a name. Just as he was about to enter the train in downtown Norwich, he mentioned the baptism, then turned to Ma and told her that he had named her Josephine. There wasn't a dry eye at the station when he left.

We didn't see Joe again until his tour of the Philippines was completed in 1938. I remember that he did keep in contact with

184

Ma. She received a letter three or four times a year while he was away. She wrote to him monthly for at least the first year. As the years wore on, when the hurt of losing Suzanne and baby Josephine began to subside, Joe stated that Ma was like a therapist for him. Her letters helped him get through the hurt. He told me how Ma had opened up to him on how she felt when she was informed that Joey had been killed during the war and when little Michelle had died in front of her. I never knew Ma's inner feelings on those subjects and Joe never revealed them to any of us. All he knew was that they helped heal the hurt he felt.

In December of 1933 Prohibition ended. With the end, the need for bars, night clubs, and liquor stores began to increase. One member of our family saw the need and approached Pa to help finance him in his endeavor to open up an establishment to sell wine, beer and liquor. Kippy Sullivan saw the need for one such place in the neighborhood. He had experience in business ownership and operation. His garage business was booming before the Depression and when Joe and I offered him the maintenance of our carpentry and lumber trucks, he made out very well. As the lumberyard business declined and people spent less on vehicle repairs, Kippy was forced to close down his garage. Pa liked the idea of backing Kippy's Pub. It opened up on Boswell Avenue on Valentine's Day, 1934. By St. Patrick's Day, the following month, the Pub had become a good place for the locals to get a good drink and sandwich at a fair price. Loretta made sandwiches, soups and snacks for the patrons. I tended bar there a few nights a week and the pay and tips I received helped out with the family budget. Despite Prohibition ending, the Depression continued to cut into our profits at the lumberyard until Joe and I had to entertain selling it.

We sold it at a price that allowed us to pay off the liens and
185

mortgage on the business. The new owner kept on some of our original employees. Tony remained to help run the lumberyard. Joe and I left for a new job that Tommy Parks had found for us at the Norwich State Hospital. Tommy had arranged for Joe and me to interview for the maintenance carpentry position that was opening on the Hospital grounds. Joe got the job based on his finished carpentry experience and interviewing skills. There were no hard feelings that he got the job and I hadn't. Six weeks later, I was working for Joe in the Carpentry Shop at the Hospital after he convinced the Hospital Engineer that he needed more help to handle the needs of the multiple buildings on the property. The other coincidence was that Hospital Engineer, Norman Angel, was a college friend of Danny Cugini, Pharmacist at the State Hospital. Need I say more of the coincidences?

Joe and I managed to keep the Cohen and Corcoran Carpentry shop open long enough for a new owner to take it over. As with the lumber business we sold earlier, we sold the carpentry business with just enough profit to pay off the mortgage with a few thousand dollars left over. We did steer the new owner to contact the State Hospital for possible furniture contracts in the future. Working maintenance at the hospital was not my choice of profession, but the steady income and benefits outweighed anything else that had become available to me or Joe for that matter.

The Living Center

I looked at Mary as I was finishing up a model building I had been working on.
"Honey, do you think you've gotten enough information for one day. We have been at this for the entire time I have been down here making this model," I said.

186

"Great-granddad, you have been kind of in a mood ever since you described what great uncle Giuseppe endured when his wife and baby died. Maybe I have gotten enough information for today. You seemed upset telling me about it," she said.

"I guess I was. That death affected the entire family for years after that. By the time we got over it, the Second World War started and changed everyone's lives. We'll talk more about that tomorrow. There are some good times to talk about before we go through those years. How about helping me out of this basement in a few minutes? I want to run the trains around a few times before we go. It's four o'clock and a few of my friends will want to come down and watch the trains for a few minutes."

Mary nodded as I turned on the switch for the four trains to begin moving through the model city and countryside we were building in the living center's basement. Everyday at four o'clock, several members of the living center would come down to the basement and watch the daily changes in the set. They enjoyed watching the trains move about the landscape. I guess they were all little boys and girls at heart. I would keep the set on for a half an hour before I shut it down for the day. It was good therapy for them as well as for me. I was also very proud of what my family had done for me in helping to set up the train set that I remembered as a source of relaxation for me for over seventy years.

That night, as I was sitting in my living room watching television, I looked around again at the pictures Mary and Dennis had placed for me. As I gazed at a picture of Wolfgang and his family, I thought of the many talks I had with him concerning some of the relatives that were still in Germany.

187

The Story

I can remember his concern because the letters he sent never were responded to. After many tries to contact some of his cousins, he took the initiative to write to a non-Jewish friend who lived close enough to his cousins to inquire about them. Almost a month to the day after sending a detailed letter identifying his concerns for his cousins to this friend, Wolfgang received a two sentence reply. He brought the reply over to the big house and let Joe read it. I remember Joe reading the words,

"Jude, schreibt an uns nicht. Ihr inquieries ist in Lagern," and handing it to me.

I asked Joe what he said. He looked at me and translated,

"Jew, do not write here. Your inquiries are in a camp."

I couldn't believe that they didn't want him writing them, but the information they supplied in the second sentence about the camps only alarmed us more as to what was going on in Germany in those days.

"What kind of camps?" I asked.

"It must be some kind of detention camp. I know the Germans were shutting down Jewish businesses, but I didn't realize that they were moving people to detention camps," Joe said.

"We don't know that for sure, Joe," I said. Wolfgang spoke up, "I think Joe's right. I remember the hate they had for us before we left to come here. It must be worse now."

Neither Joe nor Wolfgang mentioned any of this to their children. They both felt that they were too young to experience the prejudice that was festering in Germany in the 1930's, but the kids suspected the prejudice by what they read in the newspapers or saw on the news reels in the theatres. The Cohen cousins, all five boys, would experience firsthand the horror the European Jews experienced at the hands of Nazi Germany.

As I looked at the pictures of the youths that night sitting in my living room, I remembered how handsome they were. I could see the resemblance Dennis had now, at his age, for his grandfather and great uncles. I was getting tired and the night aide had made sure I had taken my medications. I looked over to my bedroom and could see that the bed had been drawn down as if to summon me. I glanced at the clock. It was almost nine o'clock. I thought to myself, *Why fight it. Go to bed.*
I made some mental notes about things I wanted to tell Mary and Dennis when they came over tomorrow.

Chapter Ten – Happier Days

The Living Center

I awoke the next morning feeling rested. I was pleased that I took my own advice and went to bed early. I didn't realize that talking about events in my past would affect me as much as they had. Talking about the deaths of Suzanne and baby Josephine and the concern for Joe and Wolfgang's apprehension of not knowing where their relatives were in Germany, unlocked forgotten sadness and anger that I had not experienced in seventy years. I spent the rest of the morning in the basement working on the train set landscaping. Dennis and Mary arrived with Dick and had lunch with me. That was a welcomed surprise, but I had to inquire why Dick had come. I shouldn't have because it almost ruined the visit and lunch. Dick sarcastically said,

"Damn Gramps, I didn't have to work today, it's Monday, Memorial Day."

I had completely forgotten because I lost track of calendar days, never mind holidays. I guess Christmas and the Fourth of July were the only holidays that gave me sufficient warning that they were approaching so I would remember. I answered, "Oh, I forgot about that."

No one said a word until I spoke up and asked,

"Maybe we should go to a parade or memorial ceremony. I think I'd like to get out of here today."

All three of them looked at each other. Dick spoke up and said,

"Gramps, do you really want to be in crowds trying to hear some politician blabbering about our lost generations of veterans?"

I didn't answer at first because he always irritated me when he talked like that even though he had the right to say so.

"Dick, Vietnam was a long time ago. World War one and two are even longer, but I still remember family and friends who were lost or are gone now that served. I want to go if you would take me. The train set will wait. The story telling will wait."

Mary spoke up and said, "Come on Dad, let's all go. I haven't been to a Memorial Day parade in years."

Dennis nodded in agreement and Dick made a nonchalant gesture of approval. We missed most of the parade, but managed to hear the speakers and see the ceremony to honor our servicemen and women.

As the festivities were going on I thought immediately of my brother Joey still at the bottom of the Atlantic Ocean. I became chilled as I remembered the eyes of the young German runner I had killed in the trenches in France in 1918. The others that I knew I had killed or wounded in combat were a blur now, but the eyes of that German kid still haunted me. I realized I had tears streaming down my eyes as I thought about all those soldiers I saw fall around me on those ridiculous advances we were ordered to make. By the time I began to think about the Sea Bees I had joined years later, I felt the tears on my cheeks being patted by Mary. I regained my composure long enough to see Dick blinking and trying to keep his composure as the taps finished playing. I guess the memories of his tour in Vietnam came back to haunt him. Not many people in our family knew what Dick experienced in Vietnam. I don't think even his father ever knew what his son had seen. Lenny was a World War II veteran and I knew what he'd gone through during the war in Europe because we talked about it in Pa's wine cellar years ago. I knew Lenny's relationship with his son wasn't as close as I had made with mine. Dick never experienced the serious talks a father and son could have in the wine cellar as Pa poured his best for those who participated. I

191

made a mental note to someday try to draw out Dick's story.

To break up the silence on the drive back to the living center, I began talking about the benefits that the Norwich State Hospital had on the family. I mentioned how I thought it was a crime that the State Hospital had been shut down by the State of Connecticut and that the property was deteriorating before our very eyes. It didn't spark any conversation so I dropped the subject and concentrated on remembering what opportunities the place offered to our family and began to tell the story.

The Story

About a year after Joe Cohen and I started working at the Norwich State Hospital, Norman Angel informed Joe that he was considering hiring a mason to perform repairs to the buildings. He was in need of someone with experience who could repair plaster walls, do brick work and pour concrete. We asked if there were any age restrictions and he immediately replied that he expected that the experienced mason would be of a mature nature.

About three weeks later, Pa and several other individuals interviewed for the job. We waited for the results of Pa's interview. I returned from Mass with Maria and the children and heard the good news for the first time at Sunday lunch. Pa announced to all who attended that he had been hired, with one other mason, for the position of mason repair technician at the State Hospital. He also told us that he would report to work in a week after completing a physical. Pa was approaching sixty, but his physical appearance made him look like a man in his early fifties. The operation he had for arteriosclerosis had allowed him to maintain his vigor. It was a concern in the back of his mind that the record of having that operation would

192

hinder his new employment opportunity.

The next week, Pa was informed that he'd passed the physical and would start on the job the following week. We celebrated again at the next Sunday lunch. Pa would work for the State Hospital ten years until he retired at seventy-years old in 1944. In that time span, he became one of the most liked and respected individuals that had ever worked in the maintenance department. His time there resulted in a small pension and survivor benefits for Ma. It also expanded his wine cellar activities from the State Hospital employees he worked with who added to the demand for his quality wine.

After the celebration for Pa's new job, Ma handed me two yellow roses before we left for home and said, "Lam, it has been twenty years today."
During all the celebrating, I completely forgot about my mother and sister's anniversary. I took the roses, kissed Ma and asked Maria to accompany me to the cemetery while the kids stayed at the big house. To my surprise, Christine, Larry and Lenny asked in unison, if they could accompany us. Needless to say, it was a touching moment for all. I'm sure my mother and sister enjoyed seeing how big my children had grown. We spent about an hour at the cemetery. I tried to answer all the questions the kids had about their grandmother and aunt. It was difficult to do because I only knew them for a short time, but it was a nice time reminiscing.
The year 1934 was a turning point for our family and friend's in terms of income. With Pa, Joe Cohen and me employed at the hospital, Kippy owning a very successful pub, Tony still employed at the lumber yard and Danny's Pharmacist income, life at the big house greatly improved. We discussed a plan to branch out again. We talked about building or purchasing new homes. We all agreed to wait and plan for one more year at the big house before implementing anything.

Danny approached Pa one day while both of them sat in the cafeteria at the hospital having lunch. It was almost a daily schedule to have one of us who worked there find another one sitting and having lunch. Such was the case this time when I found Danny in deep conversation with Pa. Both of them stopped talking as soon as I sat down. I sensed their uncomfortable feeling as I sat there. I was about to say something when Danny asked me,

"Liam, what would you think about me opening up my own pharmacy in the city?"

"I think that would be a wonderful idea, but would there be enough demand from the Norwich public for two pharmacies in the city limits?"

"I've done some investigation and put together a business plan that indicates that if I position my pharmacy closer to Backus hospital and away from the center of the city where the other pharmacy is, I could draw on those that need prescriptions filled immediately as they left the hospital. I can also draw on people who are moving out of the city limits to Norwichtown and the surrounding towns on that side of the city."

"So you have already worked this out, have you?" I asked.

"Yes; but I would need a building right now and the only thing available in the immediate vicinity is houses."

"So what's wrong with buying one of the houses, remodeling the lower floor and living in or renting the upper floor?"

"Nothing, but it would add to the cost of setting up the pharmacy to have that work performed," he stated.

I remember looking at him and Pa and saying,

"Danny, your family has enough experience to remodel a home into a pharmacy for hardly any cost at all. Between Tony, Kippy, Joe Cohen, Pa and me, we could remodel the lower floor into a pharmacy with very little problems. The cost would be in the material."

194

I can still see the grin on Danny's face as he looked at Pa for the last nod of approval. He got it. Four months later, Danny purchased a home on Lafayette Street. We remodeled the street floor into a pharmacy, the basement for storage and the second story for Danny to live in. One bedroom upstairs became his kitchen, the second bedroom his new living room, and the third bedroom, his. I can't remember the initial investment Pa made, but Danny paid Pa for the remodeling costs in less than two years. The Family Pharmacy opened its doors in May of 1935.

One of Danny's advertisements before he opened the doors of the pharmacy was that he offered home delivery of prescriptions. Danny hired sixteen year old Ernie Cohen part time after high school classes to drive Danny's Model A Coupe to deliver prescriptions to patrons in the afternoon and early evening hours. It was a unique idea for a pharmacy to deliver prescriptions in those days. It was soon after that Danny's crosstown competition did the same. Within a month, Danny had to hire a fulltime store clerk to handle the patrons while he filled prescriptions. The new store clerk was the youngest sister of Rose Ronaldi Cugini. Lilly Ronaldi was a few years younger than Danny as I remember, but quite a pretty youth in her day. She was the complete opposite of opinionated Rose and she kept to herself.

I remember the girl vaguely when Tony and Rose were married years earlier and I also remember that the three girls of the six children in the Ronaldi family were named for flowers. I will never forget the names of Rose, Violet and Lilly. I do remember joking to Joey in those years that Mr. and Mrs. Ronaldi had a funny sense of humor to name all their daughters after flowers. I also remember that Violet took a liking to Joey before he went off to the Navy. Violet was too young for Joey to have any interest in at that time, but I wonder what would

195

have become of those two if Joey had lived to return to Norwich. I lost track of Violet until a few years later when Joe Cedrone came home on leave again.

Danny worked ten hours a day, six days a week in the pharmacy. He spent several hours in the evening checking his stock and preparing his store for the next business day. It was also not uncommon for him to open the store on a Sunday to fill an emergency prescription for one of his patrons. It was during those days working in the pharmacy that a romance developed between Lilly and Danny. Rumors began when Lilly would be seen leaving the upstairs apartment at hours not associated with social behavior of that time. Tommy Parks, who sent a multitude of business his way, got wind of the gossip that floated in the hospital. When Lucia heard it, she instructed Tommy to have a man to man talk with Danny. She also clued Rose in on what was being said about her younger sister. I guess Tommy and Rose did their job well. The rumors began to subside especially when Danny proposed to Lilly several months later and set a wedding date for August of 1935. Life had become good for Danny Cugini and it only became better with Lilly in his life. The only negative comment came from Tommy Parks. He realized that Danny's success in the pharmacy business had prohibited his interest in ever pursuing medical school and becoming a doctor.

Joe and Harriet Cohen began building a home on the land they had purchased six years earlier. With Joe's steady employment and the banks loosening up with money for home loans, they ventured out first. I spent as much time as I could to work with Joe on weekends and summer evenings on the house. The three bedroom Federal home on Harland Road, took us almost a year to complete, but Joe, Harriet and the boys moved in the following spring and continued to work on it until it was completed the summer of 1936. By then, Maria and I had started construction on our piece of land in Norwichtown at the end of West Towne Street. The two-story Cape Cod house with three bedrooms, took us the whole next year to build. Joe reciprocated, and in September of 1937, we entered a completed house. The completion was due to three important factors. One was that Joe and I had gained considerable experience on his home. The second was Maria's observance of what Harriet went through trying to set up housekeeping while construction was going on. Third, was that number two was not under consideration. There would be, under no circumstances, any conditions upon which Maria would move into the house until it had been completely finished. We moved in when our house was completed.

Our family and our personal lives were better now that we had our own home. We continued to meet at the big house for Sunday lunch, but we began to change our Sunday schedules around lunch or dinner at our home. Christine was entering her senior year at NFA and the twins were sophomores now, playing junior varsity football, basketball and baseball. Pa and Ma understood our family needs and we made it a point to still have several Sunday lunches at the big house a month. We visited as often as we could on those other Sundays when we didn't have lunch.

The Cohens stayed close to us despite our living apart now. The kids would see each other at the high school and after classes on the different playing fields. An interesting point in the relocation of Joe and his family was their re-association with the local Synagogue. Joe had been influenced by his cousin Wolfgang and his family who were very devout in their religion. It wasn't too long after Wolfgang and his family arrived in Norwich that they influenced Joe and Harriet to revisit their faith. It wasn't long before all of us were attending Bar Mitzvahs for Joe's boys as they each reached thirteen. We

197

were probably seen as a little out of the ordinary as Roman Catholics to be attending Jewish religious events. We didn't see it like that because Joe and his family were our extended family and Bar Mitzvahs, Christenings and Holy Communion ceremonies only added to the uniqueness of everyone's ties to the big house and all its occupants.

The Living Center

Dick worked on the train set while I talked to the kids. Eventually, when he finished and joined us, I could see him becoming inpatient while I told more of the story the kids wanted to hear. He lasted another half hour until he interrupted and said,

"Hey guys, I'd like to head out for Dodge City in a few. Would that be alright?"

Friggen Dodge City, I thought. *Couldn't he have just said that he wanted to go?* But I refrained from snapping at him because we had a nice day so far despite the little emotion we experienced at the Memorial Day ceremony on Chelsea Parade. I stopped the story and paused. Dennis and Mary waited patiently until they probably became uncomfortable while I sat there not saying a word, but reacting to Dick's request.

"Great-granddad, are you alright?" Mary asked.

"Yeah, Liam, everything okay?" Dennis inquired immediately after her.

"Yes, I'm just fine.

"Don't you all see how unique it was to accept religious differences?" I said.

"Liam, that happens all the time. Jew, Catholic, Protestant, Hindu, and Islamic religions live mostly together in countries without any prejudice. There are exceptions, but....."

I stopped him mid-sentence.

198

"Dennis, I'm talking the nineteen thirties. For God's sake, people were getting killed for being of a particular race or creed in our country never mind Germany and other the countries of Europe and Asia. The big house was unique. Ma and Pa Cugini were unique. Think about it. They took in an Irish orphan like me, treated me like a son, approved my marriage to their oldest daughter, took in a Jewish friend and his entire family, and gave them a home until they got back on their feet. They accepted their religious beliefs, and accepted inter-faith marriages. Should I go on?"

The two of them realized what I had said, but both were a little concerned because I had turned a little rosy in my facial color.

"Great-granddad, relax. We understand your point and I'm sure Dennis will make note of that when he begins writing," Mary said.

"That's another thing Dennis; I want to see something in the next few weeks. I think you must have enough information to start writing. I don't expect the final draft, but I would like to see a chapter or two or even a little bit of what you plan to do with all this information. I don't have forever and I would like to live long enough to read what we have discussed over the past months. Can you do that for me?" I asked.

Dennis smiled and looked at Mary and said,

"I have something already and I will be happy to let you read it soon."

"Good. And while I have your attention and I am on a roll, are there any problems with either of your families with the two of you having an interfaith marriage?"

"No. There are none, and nothing had been said by either family," Mary responded.

"Liam, we have agreed to have a civil ceremony for all who attend our marriage. A family rabbi and Mary's uncle Donald will bless the marriage after the ceremony and before we have the reception. We are planning it that way even though we haven't asked them just yet," Dennis said as he and Mary looked at Dick who stood near the door.

"No problems with me and Linda, Gramps," Dick said.

Both kids smiled and laughed at that. We called it a day. The three of them departed as I started the train set in anticipation of the residents coming to watch the trains move about and see how much we had completed on the landscaping that day.

The next day I got up very early. For some reason, I had too many dreams that night. I guess the events of the Memorial Day ceremony rekindled some hidden memories about the wars I fought in. TV also contributed to my unrest that night. CNN had round-the- clock coverage of the kids in Iraq and Afghanistan. It upset me to see and hear those young soldiers reciting messages to their loved ones at home. It was nice though to see that there was some appreciation of our young men and women internationally. I skipped breakfast and began working on the train set landscaping. I lost track of time as I worked on the set. I realized I must have fainted while I was working because when I woke up, I was looking at Mary's face.

"Are you alright, Liam?" she asked.

I knew I was in trouble because she never calls me Liam unless there was concern. There was.

"You fainted and fell. The train set table lessened your fall. Daisy found you," Mary said.

I glanced over and saw Daisy holding some food on a tray and one of the living center nurses standing by. Before I could say a word Daisy said,

"Your Glucose level dropped and you fainted. That's because you didn't eat breakfast like I have told you to do one hundred times before. Please drink this orange juice and eat this muffin."

I knew better than to say a word. They were right and it had been a dumb thing for me to do. I looked at my watch. It was almost noon. I must have been here a while. I was glad Daisy was on days this week and looked for and found me. I stood up with their assistance and sat by the train set and ate the food they put in front of me. Dennis came in without saying a word, but looked at Mary.

"I know I screwed up. I'll be just fine. Now where did we leave off from yesterday?" "We'll do this tomorrow," Dennis replied.

"No we won't. I don't know how many more tomorrows there are, what our Creator has in store for me or worst yet, what I have in store for myself when I pull stunts like this."

"OK, let's try to finish lunch before we continue," Mary said.

No more was said about my skipping breakfast and fainting, but I made a very large mental note not to do something that stupid again. I began to collect my thoughts to remember events and started to tell more of the family story while being watched under the watchful eyes of the kids.

The Panay Incident came to mind. Both kids looked at me strangely when I mentioned it. I could see there confusion until I started with Joe Cedrone's return to Norwich in the summer of 1938.

The Story

I recall that the event actually took place around Christmas of 1937, but we knew very little about the Japanese attack on the Panay while she was anchored in the Yangtze River. Joe knew more than what I wanted to hear. He warned us that the Japanese were the next military adversary for the United States. We weren't very interested in his political opinions when he returned. We were interested in how he had been since the

201

death of Suzanne and Josephine. He didn't talk much about that except that he missed them every day. Joe was cold compared to the man we knew and loved the day he and Suzanne left for Parris Island with their bright future ahead of them. None of that came to fruition. His interface with the grandkids was more guidance now than that of a fun and loving uncle. We thought that maybe it was because the kids were older now so he treated them as young adults, but we all noticed that change in him. Ma and Pa didn't care how he had changed. He was home for Easter and on leave for a month. His next assignment was the Quantico Marine Base in Virginia. He was excited about going there because he would have the chance to learn new tactics and teach there as well. In fourteen years, Joe Cedrone had exceeded in all aspects of military life.

He pulled out an envelope which contained orders and a multitude of chevrons he would need to have sewn onto his various uniforms. He announced that he had been promoted to Gunnery Sergeant and that he would be able to sew on the chevrons before he reported for duty at Quantico. Ma immediately volunteered to assume the duties of lead seamstress. We all couldn't have been prouder.

It was during a play that Mary Beth and Christine were in at the high school that changed Joe's life again. The two NFA seniors were part of a glee club production in Slater Hall on the NFA campus. They'd been in the glee club together since their sophomore year. Of course, most of the family was there to see the two potential Broadway stars sing and act. I can't remember for the life of me what the play was about, but I do remember we enjoyed it very much. At intermission, we were given refreshments while the stage was being reconfigured for the second half of the show. Danny and Lilly had come and brought along Violet Ronaldi who I had not seen in many years. She was introduced to all of us including Joe. We learned, from the brief conversation we had while we waited for the play to resume, that she was single and was starting a new job at the Norwich State Hospital as a secretary to the business manager. I could see that Violet had an eye for Joe in his green and tan Marine uniform. Joe was polite, but uninterested in her I thought at first. We didn't know it yet, but things were changing between the two of them.

After the play, we all decided to get some ice cream at Bee Bee's Dairy. As we descended upon the popular establishment, we split off into groups of six to sit in the booths that were available. Some of us sat at the counter. It was at the counter that Violet had managed, I thought, to maneuver to be the only person sitting next to the handsome Marine. It wasn't long before Violet had Joe laughing. He seemed to come out of his protective shell that night and I hoped that Violet had crushed that shell for good. Several days later, we learned from Lilly, in front of Joe, that he asked Violet out to dinner and a movie. Needless to say, Joe had to endure some bantering from the kids as well as the adults until Ma put an end to it.
"You all stop this. Giuseppe do nice thing."
We all obeyed and Joe was very appreciative.

There were more movies and by the third week of Joe's leave, nobody saw very much of either of them. He invited Violet to Sunday lunch to the pleasure of Ma and Pa. They too noticed a difference in him.

Joe and Violet corresponded during the months that he was away at Quantico as she involved herself in her new career at the State Hospital. We would see her occasionally at the Family Pharmacy, at Sunday lunch when Ma invited her to come with Danny and Lilly, and at Mass. We all just hoped silently that something would come of it. I wasn't sure, but Maria and Christine had no reservations. Christine, all of eighteen and working at the Dime Bank by now, predicted that Joe would propose to her on his Christmas leave. He did and she said no. Joe was gone before we all knew what the hell had happened. Several days later when the story came out through Rose and Lilly, we learned that Violet had turned him down because she was afraid of military life and being away from home. Needless to say, within a week, the two very forceful sisters had her on a bus for Virginia unbeknownst to Joe.

Years later, we heard the story as to what had happened. He was in the NCO club on the base when he was summoned by the evening duty officer that a woman was requesting his presence at the front gate. Joe thought it was a stunt by some of the other Gunnery Sergeants in the club until a very frustrated Lieutenant came into the club with two MPs and physically escorted him to the front gate. He was ordered that under no circumstance was he to return to the club, or even the base, until he resolved the matter with the very persistent woman the duty officer had failed to reason with. When they finally came face to face, she apparently apologized and explained her reasons for turning him down. Whatever she said convinced Joe to accept her apology. They were married three days later. She quit her job by making a phone call to Norwich. She found a job working at the Base Exchange.

My work at the State Hospital and Maria's work at the Dime Bank enabled us to maintain the new house. My daughter, on the other hand, chose not to enter college that fall like Joe's son Alex had. Christine applied for a job at the bank as soon as she graduated from NFA that June. We must have spent many hours and spent countless nights encouraging her to go to college, but she stated to us that she did not want to waste money going to college trying to figure out what she wanted to do in life. I explained that Alex Cohen wasn't sure what he

204

wanted to do in engineering, but he still was going to college. That didn't work for her. She quickly pointed out that he, at least, knew that he wanted to be an engineer.

She had grown up watching her mother work at Cohen and Corcoran part-time, as well as the Dime Bank on and off, and she must have been impressed with the type of work her mother performed. I knew I wouldn't give up on her attending college. I hoped, and bet, that she would change her mind after she realized that she would need a formal education in banking to move ahead in the profession. Christine entered the bank work force at the entry pay level. Like her mother, it wasn't long before she moved up in position and responsibilities. It also wasn't for long that a young man appeared on the scene. This young gentleman was a sailor assigned to the U. S. Submarine Base at New London. Jim Dermody was a young third class machinist mate from Detroit, Michigan. He met Christine through one of the girls that worked at the bank who was married to a sailor and was a buddy to Jim.
"You know how that goes don't you Mary,"
I said while I sat exhausted from the day's work I had done on the train set landscape. Mary asked, "Are you able to continue great-granddad or are you too tired?"
"No let's continue if it's okay with Dennis?" He just nodded.

Jim seemed like a nice kid, but he was only twenty and Christine was eighteen. I explained to my wife that they were much too young to be dating pretty regularly. That was probably the dumbest thing that I had said to Maria in the nineteen years I had been married to her. She quickly brought it to my attention, as most loving wives do, that I was out of touch with reality. That upset me as I explained that as Christine's father, it was my duty to point out my concerns and one concern I had was that she was too young to get seriously involved with a sailor. With that said, Maria quickly pointed out not only was I out of touch with reality, but how absurd I was. She also pointed out that I was a soldier of nineteen and not a mature sailor of twenty when we got married. She was eighteen and the same age as Christine, never mind just dating. She drove the nail home with the last statement. The more I opened up my mouth, the more uneducated I sounded. Needless to say, I shut up and let the courting process begin, which pleased everyone except me.

That fall, the boys made the NFA varsity football team. Larry made defensive end while Lenny played linebacker. They both played the right side of the defense for the team and it was evident that many team's offense would concentrate on the opposite side where the twins weren't.

By working at the State Hospital, it afforded me the time to attend most of the home scrimmages and games in which, even today, I am grateful that I was able to attend. During one scrimmage I attended, a large storm caused it to be cancelled. The Great New England Hurricane of 1938 hit Norwich in the late afternoon of September 21st. It rained on and off that day and I wondered if the coach would cancel the contest. The scrimmage consisted of the varsity splitting up into two groups with other positions filled by the better VJ players. It was instructional for the kids and fun for the parents and other bystanders to watch.

The winds and rain increased as the two groups assembled on the football field. It wasn't long before the winds and rain made it too difficult to play so the coach called it off. Of course, all the players hit the showers and locker rooms in the 'Wildcat Den' as we called it in those days, and the power went off. It took some time before the kids dressed and left the Den. By this time, trees were falling and things were getting dangerous. I was able to fit two other boys in my car to take them home. They usually walked, but the weather conditions prohibited that. It took over a half-hour to drive three or four blocks as we had to stop and remove branches from the road to pass or detour through other streets to deliver the kids to their homes.

We arrived home in time to watch several small trees uproot, fall and just miss the house as we drove into our driveway. Maria and Christine were home already and I thanked God that we were all together. The power had been out by that time. Maria attempted to call, but the phone lines were also affected. I was very thankful that our new home withstood the blasting of sand, water, flying branches and debris that we heard hitting the house during the evening and night hours. We lost a few shutters and a shingle or two on the house, but the damage was minor and we were unscathed.

The next day, it continued to rain off and on in the morning, but we were able to get out of the house and begin to check on, and assist, other family members and friends. We left Christine home to maintain the house while the rest of us attempted to drive to the big house only to find that we were better off walking because for most of Washington Street, by Chelsea Parade, down McKinley, and over Broad Street were blocked by numerous downed trees. Some of the areas reminded me of France in 1918. It was a mess everywhere. We checked on the Parks and their home was in good shape. Lucia was concerned that Tommy had not returned during the previous evening hours, but he had stayed at the hospital to assist with the growing number of patients coming into the emergency room. Lucia and Julie were fine. Lucia urged us on to check on the Ma and Pa at the big house.

We found Pa on a ladder fixing a section of shingles he had lost on a portion of the hip roof. The house was in relatively good shape except for some water damage on the second and third floors. The Wilson house next door had a large elm tree on it and the Farragher home on the opposite side was heavily damaged from rain on the third floor from a torn off section of the roof.

I left Maria and Lenny to assist Pa and Ma as I ventured back with Larry to check on the Sullivans and other Cugini family members. Larry and I met Joe Cohen and two of his boys who were checking on people. Wolfgang's store, which included his home above, was damaged. With no power, Wolfgang worried about the large meat locker he had bought only a few months earlier that was full of assorted meats. There was nothing we could do to save his meats and produce so Wolfgang cut up his meat supply and offered it to the fire department and Red Cross. They fed many people that had become homeless that week.

The fall of 1938 had two good things that came directly from the storm. The first was the news that the family would be blessed with another baby. Danny and Lilly announced that they were expecting their first child in May of 1939. The second was that after Pa fixed the roof, he decided to remodel the house on the second and third floors due to water damage.

The individual rooms that housed the boarders and children over the years were combined to make larger rooms so that their tenants, who were constantly changing as they came and went following job openings and layoffs respectively, were able to cook and live independently in the big house. Cleaning was handled by local cleaning women that Ma hired. The cost for these services had been absorbed by the tenants in their rental agreements. My adoptive parents made good money on these arrangements and with the women on board, it also kept Ma from having to do physical work. She ran the big house like an office manager while Pa continued to work at the State

208

Hospital and make his best wine in the cellar. Life continued to be good at the big house as we cleaned up from the storm and the Depression loosened its death grip on the Norwich community.

The Living Center

"Okay Liam, let's call it a day," Dennis said as he closed his laptop. I looked at the clock on the wall and it had only been several hours that the three of us had gotten together.
"What's up with you leaving early today?" I asked.
"Well, I have this meeting at six o'clock this evening. I'm a member of the Connecticut National Guard and we are being mustered to listen to the unit's readiness need for service, possibly in Afghanistan."
"I didn't know you were in the reserves."
"Yeah, I joined to get some college assistance and have been with this unit for six years now."

We finished up and the two of them left so Dennis could spend the rest of the evening at the unit. I was going to switch on the train set, but I was tired from the incident and activities I had gone through today. It also bothered me that Dennis could possibly be called off to Afghanistan in the next few months. It was an all too familiar feeling I had felt myself and I know my brothers and friends had when there was the possibility of going off into harm's way. My kids and grandkids felt it too years earlier as they were called to duty. It sickened me, but it also made me excited that another generation was answering the call. Then I thought about what I just felt and realized that people, even me, never changed. We like the thrill of the unknown and then pay for it the rest of our lives thinking about the carnage and death we experienced while in the service. Maybe I was thinking too much. The Connecticut National

209

Guard was probably just being notified that they were being reviewed. Maybe it was nothing at all. I went to dinner and put the thought out of my mind. I figured I'd wait to hear what Dennis and Mary had to say the next day when we met again.

I turned in and almost immediately fell asleep. I slept soundly. No dreams, pee calls, no anything. The no pee calls were the most rewarding because I had a chance to have a very sound sleep. I washed, dressed and walked to the dining area. I made sure to eat a poached egg, toast and some coffee. I felt good. I shouldn't have, but I did. At my age, you aren't supposed to feel good. Except for this past stroke that I miraculously recovered from, I had maintained good health in my life. I realized I was better than twenty six years past when most of my family and friends had departed this world. I was still here and couldn't, for the life of me, figure out why the good Lord had been so generous. They say the good die young. Well, I thought I was good, but I guess not. I was still here at one hundred and six and realized that seven was approaching. It wasn't right to outlive your children. I assured myself that I would not have to endure the loss of a grandchild or great grandchild. Even God wouldn't be that cruel. I hoped and prayed anyway.

Mary appeared a little earlier than usual. Dennis was not with her. By the look on her face I knew that the news from his meeting probably wasn't very good.
"Well, how'd he make out last night? What's the story with his unit?" I asked.
Mary smiled a little and said,
"It isn't sounding good. Dennis had to do some more work for the unit and is still there. He told me over the phone that they would probably be called up in three to four months. The unit would have to report to Texas for some training before they were shipped to Afghanistan. That's what he knows right

210

now."

"Well honey, the military is a strange lot and things can change in a heartbeat. Keep your emotions in check because it will truly help him while he adjusts to the possibility of being sent overseas."

"I understand great-granddad, but it isn't easy to do," she said and sat down at the train table.

"I know Mary, I know."

"Now where did we leave off, great-granddad?" she said.

"Ironically Mary, we are going to talk about the same subject we just talked about, but it happened many years ago," I said and smiled.

Chapter Eleven – The Gathering Storm
The Story

Christine continued to date Jim Dermody throughout 1939 while his submarine, the USS Seal, was being overhauled at the Electric Boat Shipyard and then tested at the Sub Base. We knew Jim would remain in Connecticut until the end of the year, but then he told us that he would be assigned to San Diego at his sub's home port. I waited with bated breath hoping that he would not ask Christine to marry him during his stay in Connecticut. I didn't want him to take her away to the west coast. They continued to date on weekends when he got passes. She continued her career in the bank that year until the sub's overhaul had finished just before Thanksgiving. He left never asking for her hand in marriage. They wrote to each other after that and that's where it stayed to my delight.

Alex Cohen entered aeronautical engineering at college that year. He was very interested in flight and the design of airplanes. Joe Cohen was very proud of his oldest boy because he had not only entered the aeronautical engineering field, but he started pilot instructions in the summer of 1939. According to Joe, the kid was a natural. He stated that Alex had looked into applying to the Grumman, Boeing, and Martin companies after college. This was the most interesting educational plan we had seen since Lucia finished nursing school and Danny became a pharmacist.

Joe's nephews Ernie and Erwin worked in their father's grocery and butcher store on Franklin Street that Wolfgang had started several years after arriving in Norwich. Pa had financed him and Wolfgang did well specializing in kosher foods. The boys handled all the phases of the grocery store under the watchful eyes of their father. By 1940, the store expanded to employ six or seven employees and was one of the main grocery stores and only butchery in the area. Wolfgang often wondered what his and his family's life would have been like if he had stayed in Germany. None of us knew then just how incomprehensible that thought was for a Jew in Germany.

My sons Larry and Lenny continued to play sports at the Academy through the fall of 1939 and spring of 1940. They played hard and maintained good grades, but neither of them made any attempt to research colleges or technical institutes. As many times as Maria and I preached about how well Alex was doing at college, I think we drove them further away from higher education. We were also very concerned about the war in Europe. In just twenty years, war had returned for a second time. Germany, England, France and Poland were now at war. It wouldn't be long before more countries, like Russia, would be involved. We were even more concerned now that Larry had mentioned he was interested in joining the Marine Corp. I think Joe put us at ease in one of his letters that explained that the United States would not get involved in a European war. We became apprehensive again when he did mention how he felt about the possibility of an Asian war when he was on Christmas leave in 1939.

Lenny excelled in wood working at school and he spent many evenings and weekends with Joe Cohen who was still making special ordered grandfather clocks and specialty furniture for some of the affluent citizens in the immediate vicinity and as far away as New York. Joe's second son Andrew was also interested in wood working. Although he was several years younger, the boy was a natural finished carpenter. When time permitted, I would visit the wood shop and watch Lenny and Andrew make many of the cabinets, tables and mantle clocks

Joe had orders for.

Tony's boy Joey had enlisted in the Navy after high school graduation. He was stationed onboard the USS Enterprise aircraft carrier as an aircraft mechanic. He loved it based on the letters he sent Tony and Rose. He explained that they were doing practice maneuvers in the Pacific for several weeks at a time and then returning to Pearl Harbor, Hawaii for resupply and shore leave. Their daughter, Mary Beth, entered her second year at the Backus Hospital Nursing School where Lucia still enjoyed teaching part-time.

The birth of Danny and Lilly's son Donato, Jr. was a silver lining in the cloud of the gathering storm. The boy was delivered by Lucia and Harriet very early one January morning before Tommy Parks could free himself from an emergency he was attending at the hospital. Tommy arrived after the fact only to be kidded that he wasn't needed anymore. Lilly had a difficult delivery because the boy had been breach, but Lucia persevered and delivered the healthy little tyke just as Tommy had entered the room. Absent from the delivery was Ma. We found out later that she had another cardiac episode which prohibited her from going to Lilly's to assist Lucia and Harriet in the delivery.

After Christmas of 1939, or sometime in January 1940, Tommy Parks suggested that Ma visit a heart specialist in Boston who was known for his work treating heart disease. She declined because she was sure that if she had any more incidents, Tommy could take care of them. She never realized how much pressure she put on him to try to keep her in relatively good health, all the while his knowing that one major attack could kill her.

214

"I think about all the progress medicine has made in treating hideous diseases like heart disease, but back during that time, there wasn't much help besides prayer and luck," I said when Mary stopped her notes.

"Great-granddad, I know what you are thinking about."

I looked at her and paused before I said,

"Yeah, that disease has hindered this family and all our generations one way or another for decades."

"Do you want to talk about it and how it affected the family?" she asked.

"No. It will raise its ugly head as I talk to you and Dennis more. Hand me that model house in that box over there would you, dear?" I asked to change help my mood.

"This one?" I nodded and she handed it over to me.

"It's in pretty good shape. I can use it the way it is. You know your grandfather made this model in Joe Cohen's shop while he was in high school. Lenny did a good job, don't you think?" I asked.

Mary just smiled and made some more notes.

"I guess I'm getting off the subject aren't I?" I said as I placed the model house on the landscape.

"You were talking about Ma Cugini and her discussion with great-great Uncle Tommy Parks about her condition,"

Mary read back to me from her notes while she checked the small recorder she was using.

I began to organize my thoughts and then continued.

The Story

The Norwich Bulletin ran daily stories about the war in Europe. It became one of the main topics of discussion at the

State Hospital during lunch and break conversations. For those employees at the hospital who had relatives in the warring countries, the letters they received described worsening conditions. Some uncomfortable situations developed at the hospital between German, English, French and Polish Americans because of those letters. On several occasions, some yelling and pushing did occur in the cafeteria.

Joe Cohen was a German Jew descendent and the carpentry department foreman. He worked directly for Hospital Engineer Norman Angel of Scottish-English heritage. They worked very well together since Joe was hired. They were concerned for family and friends in those countries whenever they heard the news. The third party to this story was Hoyt Wilhelm who had immigrated to this country right after the First World War. Hoyt was a cobbler by trade and worked at the State Hospital several years before Joe and I did. He had served in the German Army during the closing months of the war. He was a nice guy and usually kept to himself. He made and repaired shoes for the patients. He knew Joe and I were veterans through casual talks.

As veterans, we never discussed the war, especially with Hoyt having served in the German Army. It wasn't important to us by then because Hoyt was an American citizen, the father of several high school kids and seemed to have struggled like the rest of us had during the worst Depression years. One day, Hoyt entered the carpentry shop and asked if we could make several shoe forms. He explained he used them to mold leather to make shoes. Joe immediately looked at the cobbler's tool and was thinking how he would make new ones when Hoyt struck up a conversation concerning the war in Europe.

Immediately, Joe and I didn't like his tone and his thoughts about the blitzkrieg. We didn't comment, but felt

216

uncomfortable with Hoyt's continued conversation. He went too far when he stated that Hitler was making the Jews pay for helping the French and English defeat the German Army. When he said that, Joe Cohen exploded. He didn't let it pass by with just shaking his head after the comment was made as he usually would do when he didn't like what someone said. Whether Hoyt knew Joe was German Jew or not, it wouldn't have mattered because Joe grabbed him, pushed him up against one of the table saws in the shop and threatened to cut his head off if he muttered another word. While Joe had Hoyt pinned and had his attention, he explained very softly and slowly through clenched teeth that he had firsthand experience of Chancellor Hitler because his cousins hadn't been heard from in two or three years. Joe mentioned that the Jews he was talking about fought in the same army that Hoyt had.

Needless to say, the Hospital Administrator never heard about what happened in the carpentry shop because we kept it to ourselves. Hoyt Wilhelm never said a word either. He remained distant from us throughout the beginning of the war. I know that his younger brother who had stayed in Germany served in the navy. We found out that he was on a U-Boat in the Atlantic. The brother was killed at sea during the early years of the war. Hoyt never acknowledged the condolences Joe relayed. We never knew if it was because he was preoccupied with grief for the brother or if it was his hatred of Jews that prevented him from acknowledging them. Hoyt Wilhelm committed suicide at home several months after the death of his younger brother.

The Living Center

"Great-granddad, were there stories like that in our family? I mean, there had to be cousins or some type of relative that

217

served in Mussolini's services." Mary asked.

"Oh yes, my brother Joe Cedrone had first cousins that served in Italy's army and navy. Years later, we found out that a few relatives had been killed in North Africa while in the Italian army. Several had been in the Navy and were killed in the Mediterranean Sea. Can you imagine if the Italian Americans had been treated like the Japanese Americans had been, how our lives, as we knew it now, would have changed?" I asked. Mary never said a word.

I do remember that after the war, it was still unacceptable for Americans of Jewish and Italian heritage to buy beach property at Groton Long Point. I knew that for fact when I bought the beach cottage in my name for Tony and Rose. After a few years, I turned the deed over to them for one dollar. I could never understand prejudice, but I did have firsthand experience with it. I wish they still had that cottage, but that is another story we'll get into after the war years. As I finished up on this point to Mary, Dennis appeared in the basement smiling.

"Oh there you are," I said as he came over and kissed Mary. "You seem in a good mood. What's happening with the Guard?"

"Well Liam, it looks like I won't be going to Afghanistan anytime soon. We found out that it will be eighteen months before our unit might be requested for training in Texas. It would be, at least, two years before we would be going over there. My six years are up in one month and I can muster out."

"Are you going to muster out?" I asked.

"I don't know. I'm a first lieutenant now and I could be a captain in another two years. It's good money as a supplement to my writing career. I'll have to think on it more."

I dropped the questions and just let him and Mary sort out what they wanted to do. Personally, I wanted him out of the Guard as soon as possible. Afghanistan had Vietnam written all over it and this family had firsthand experience with that war.

The Story

We continued to hear more bad news from Europe. First, we heard the news of the war in France. Based on my experience, I assumed that the Germans would attack the same way they had in the First World War. I expected the trenches to be dug up and used all over again. Nobody expected the quick defeat of the modern French Army. It was over in less than two months. Several weeks later, the British Army had been pushed back to England and we listened to the firsthand reports of the evacuation of the Army from Dunkirk. Hitler seemed unstoppable. It was during 1940 that the War Department called for two year service for young men. My son Larry joined the Marine Corp and left for Parris Island that summer. He wrote many letters describing his training in the Corp and the Marines he met. Some of his letters were sent to Gunnery Sergeant Joe Cedrone. I know Joe thought a lot about Larry and years later, we found out that he mentored him on the do's and don'ts in the Corp. Joe was actually called back to Parris Island from Quantico, Virginia to train more Marines for combat. He attended Larry's graduation from Parris Island. There was no one else in the family, including me, that could have better represented the family.

Larry's letters had no effect on Lenny. He had no desire to be in the military and he enjoyed carpentry work, both in construction and part-time work in Joe's carpentry shop. Maria and I were pleased that Larry had joined and was enjoying his career in the Marines, but we were also pleased that our second son was home performing a trade he liked and was good at. Mainly though, we were just pleased that he was home. With the world situation as it was then, we never knew day to day what our armed forces, with our other son a part of it, would be commanded to do. Every day, that thought resided in the back of my mind. I knew it was in Maria's as well, even though we tried to keep from thinking or talking about it. Pa made a statement that further bothered us. He said that there were too many grandsons and friend's sons that were the right age to be called up if there was a war. We all listened to the President when he assured us that he would keep us out of the war. I never bought that message. It was a matter of time before we would be drawn into the war. I was right. It came a year later.

Good news came that year on Christmas of 1940 when Joe and Violet visited us. She announced that she was going to have a baby in July of 1941. Ma and Pa were pleased that Giuseppe was going to be a father and that his life had turned around. He was happy with Violet and looked happier now that his family was growing. Larry came home as well and the young Lance Corporal and the seasoned Gunnery Sergeant had time to bond and banter to the amusement of us all. I couldn't have been prouder of my son and brother as I was that Christmas. That would be the last Christmas that I would see them together.

We also saw Jim Dermody again that holiday. He had returned from the USS Seal to the Submarine Base to teach. The lad was now a Second Class petty Officer and lived off base. Christine and he dated, but then decided to remain friends for the time being. I had to rely on Maria's intuition and assessment of the relationship because I constantly thought that there was more to it than they let on to everyone. That approach also relieved me from some stress that fathers usually put on themselves when a young and good looking stud is around his daughter. I noticed a smirk on Mary's face and a glance at Dennis while I was talking.

220

The New Year brought in more bad news about the many merchant ships that were sunk by the German submarines in the North Atlantic. I also feared for the people I worked with who had sons on some of those U.S. Navy ships that accompanied the convoys. I relaxed a little knowing my nephew Tony, Jr. was on the USS Enterprise in the Pacific. He was playing war, but wasn't in one. Tony and I talked a lot about this in the wine cellar on the Sundays when we did get together at the big house.

We got news that Joe had received orders to report to the Marine barracks at Pearl Harbor in April. He was able to make bring Violet over in May. When I heard that, I thought of Suzanne dying during childbirth just when she had arrived in the Philippines. I kept my thoughts to myself until one night I confessed to Maria about my concerns. She said that it was the first thing she thought about when she heard the news that Violet would have to follow Joe by leaving for a cross country trip to San Diego and then a steam ship to the Hawaiian Islands all alone.

The family had another nurse in the family by then. In June we watched Mary Beth receive her nursing degree from Backus Hospital. One of the presenters of the diplomas was Lucia Cugini Parks. Mary Beth graduated with distinction and was immediately employed at the Backus Hospital Surgical ward where she would regularly see her aunt and uncle.

Six weeks later, we were all relieved when Joe actually called Ma at the big house from Hawaii to inform us that Violet had delivered a healthy baby boy. Those were the best words we ever heard as Ma passed the information from one member of the family to another. She said that 'mother and baby were doing just fine.' I'll never forget that Dominic Joseph Cedrone was seven pounds, seven ounces and born on July 7, 1941. I

221

don't remember the time he was born, but Joe made reference that little Dominic was his lucky sevens. Joe had to point out and explain to Ma during the phone call that 7-7-7 was a lucky payoff at the gambling machines that he had played. Once Ma understood that she began to ask questions concerning his gambling habit. He convinced her that he only occasionally played slots during his single years in the Marine Corp. Ma had difficulty explaining what Joe had said as she passed the information about what lucky sevens meant. Some of us knew what it meant. We didn't bother correcting her and let it pass. We did notice that Ma looked better now that little Dominic had arrived safely. Any sort of stress directly affected her and that still worried us.

Larry, by now, had shipped off to San Diego for advanced Marine training. He wrote home almost weekly and he seemed happy with his career choice. Maria and I talked at night about the news coming from Europe and Maria felt that Larry was out of harm's way and the country seemed to be keeping out of the European conflict. I knew better and figured it would be just a matter of time before some idiot bombed somewhere that included US troops or ships and we would be in the thick of it. Franklin Roosevelt had no more power to keep us out of war in the upcoming year than Woodrow Wilson had in 1917.

The nights of that summer were very hot as I remember. The humidity was relentless and it took its toll on Ma. We received a late night phone call from Tommy Parks that Ma had been admitted to the hospital. She had sustained another cardiac episode and was being kept cool in the intensive care ward at the hospital.

We rushed up to find her in relatively good spirits, but thoroughly exhausted. She was stable, but Tommy warned us that if she was stricken another time, it could be fatal. Tommy was always the bearer of bad news when it concerned Ma. He could not understand what kept her alive with only forty percent of her heart working. It would be even less now that she suffered another attack. She persevered and returned home several weeks later to the big house. The now sixty five year old woman had slowed considerably and looked frailer than I had ever seen her. By Thanksgiving, she looked more like herself despite her thin appearance.

The second Sunday after Thanksgiving, Maria and I stopped off at the big house after Mass and visited Ma and Pa. I remember this day because it was the twenty-fourth anniversary of Joey's death. I remember distinctly that Christine and Lenny were not with us after Mass, but had promised to be in time for Sunday lunch. Ma, of course, questioned why they were not at the big house for lunch. I explained that they had some things to do, but I assured her that they would appear momentarily. All seemed fine until we sat down at two o'clock for lunch and the two were still not present for the meal. Ma never said a word, but I could hear a little irritation in her tone as we began to eat and she kept glancing at the two empty seats. I made an attempt to apologize for their tardiness. Ma just nodded, but I knew her thoughts of Joey had affected her mood. Pa laughed and said that they could eat anytime. They were kids and had more important things to do. It was at that time when I heard Lenny's car squeal as it quickly pull up in front of the dining room window that faced the front steps. I was relived and irritated at the same time.

I could hear him talking loud, but it was inaudible until he entered the house with Christine following him. As a father, I figured that my daughter was arguing with my son. That was not the case because as I attempted to quiet the two and put some order back to the lunch at the big house, Lenny motioned

223

for me to be quiet as he went over to Pa's radio and turned it on. Before I could get irritated from his be quiet gesture I heard that the Naval Base at Pearl Harbor had been bombed by the Imperial Naval Forces of the Empire of Japan. We all stopped eating, rose from the table and sat around the radio in the living room listening to the latest news of the bombing.

We immediately thought about Joe, Violet and little Dominic. *Damn,* I thought, *did they survive the bombing?* We kept hearing news of the base, air field, hospital, barracks and even civilian homes and buildings being strafed and bombed. I couldn't picture, for the life of me, where Joe's house was in proximity to the naval base or air field. No one said a word for ten or fifteen minutes until we had almost memorized the same report as it was repeated over and over again. Maria sat near me as her eyes swelled and an occasional tear would flow down a cheek. She tried to wipe each one that appeared nonchalantly. Rose and Tony looked terrorized as they realized that Joey was on the USS Enterprise that was home ported at Pearl Harbor. Ma cried as she listened and occasionally blessed herself. Her melancholy mood from Joey's anniversary turned worse as more bad news was reported. There were no reports or any mentioning of any carriers in the news broadcasts. Only the names of battleships and others types of ships that were damaged or sunk were given. Pa disappeared during the repetitive broadcasts. I eventually found him downstairs acting very solemn and tying ribbons on three bottles of his best wine. I didn't have to ask what he was doing because he looked up and said, "One for Tony's Joey and one for your Larry and one for my Giuseppe. There will be more."
He then turned and hugged me and said,
"It will be easier for me this time." I looked perplexed until he said,
"You here now with you brothers to worry. I not alone down

here this war."

His statement haunted me that night while I lay in bed. It must have been very difficult for Pa during the first war when he was worrying about, Joey, Tony and me. It was unconscionable to me what he must have felt when the news of his son's death was given to Ma and him the day the Navy representatives showed up at the front door. Now I would have to endure the possibility of that happening to me. I pushed it out of my mind, but it continually returned. Neither Maria nor I slept that night. The next morning we got out of bed early to get a copy of the Norwich Bulletin and listen to any new reports that had been released by the Navy from Pearl Harbor. One positive aspect of the entire bleak news was that there was no mention of any damaged or sunk aircraft carriers. I called Tony and Harriet to inform them of what I had heard and read, all of which they already knew. They confessed that they hadn't slept either.

I met Joe Cohen at work early that Monday. His first concern was Joe Cedrone and his family. I told him we would have to wait to see if he could get a message to us. We both couldn't believe what had occurred. Norman Angel saw both of us in the shop and stopped by to talk about the news. One interesting thing that Norman mentioned was that he was considering joining up. Joe Cohen asked,
"Norman, you're thirty-five years old. You have never been in any service. You were too young for the last war and too old for this one."
I'll never forget Norman's look when he said,
"Think Joe, the country will need all types of professions to win this war. It will take time for them to realize it, but they will need more than just young men as fodder for combat."
The thought of young men becoming fodder again sickened me. I saw that firsthand in the Argonne Forest in 1918. Joe and

I looked at each other. Norman knew he had not made his statement clear.

"Look, the services will need engineers, construction workers, tradesmen and all sorts of professions in support of the combat troops and ships at sea. That's where I'm going if they will have me." he said as he headed towards his office.

We never gave it another thought as we went to work everyday and read and listened to the dim reports we were receiving from the Pacific theatre.

Several days went by and we still hadn't heard anything about the aircraft carriers. Tony and Rose relaxed a little as we all convinced them the no news was good news. In the weeks after Pearl Harbor, and until she received a letter from Joey, Harriet aged before our very eyes. In late January, she received a short and censored letter from him in which he stated that he was fine. Anything that remotely talked of the ship's condition or where they had been had been darkened out. The letter didn't make too much sense with the strike-outs, but it was the best letter Tony and Rose ever received.

It was only a week or so later that we received a brief telegram from Joe. I'll never, to this day, forget what the telegram said.

"To Cugini Household. Stop. We are alright. Stop. God bless America. Stop. Love, J V and D. Stop."

We waited another three weeks and received a nice letter from Violet that did not mention anything that happened. She concentrated her letter on the baby, herself and Joe. There were no blackened sections as I can remember. It greatly relieved Ma, and for that matter, the rest of us.

Larry wrote us several weeks after the attack. He had been promoted to Sergeant and was assisting drill instructors in training the new recruits that were pouring into a new camp near San Diego called Camp Pendleton. Larry explained that

226

he would be there training Marines in weapons handling. We didn't love it, but for now, our oldest twin son was safe.

Christmas of 1941 came and went. The news we heard that new year wasn't very encouraging either. Every day we heard about another kid in the neighborhood had joined one branch or another of the armed services. In late January, Alex did not return to college. He came home one day and informed Joe and Harriet that he had signed up for the Army Air Corp. Within a month, he would be reporting to Maxwell Field, Alabama where he would receive advanced pilot training seeing he had already soloed while he was a sophomore in college. Alex was going to be a First Lieutenant in the AAC upon graduation. He would later pilot a B-17 bomber in Europe with the Eighth Air Force.

Enlistments continued one by one in the family until all our youth that were of age were consumed. Lenny joined the Army in March and by July; he was at Fort Knox learning to drive a tank. I had seen a few tanks in France and had a vague understanding of the advantages and disadvantages of being in one. He wrote home and explained more about the people he had met from all over the country than what he had learned in the armor school he was assigned to. The letters made his mother feel better. I wondered every day what it would be like for him to be in a tank during combat. Norman Angel was a pretty good source of information about tanks. He had considered working for a company as a mechanical engineer that designed tanks for the Army. He kept an eye on mechanical articles that were published on the subject and he was aware of the advanced tanks that the Nazis had developed. His comparisons of American to the German tanks alarmed me especially with a son in the tank corp.

Joe informed me one day in May that his nephews, Ernie and

Erwin, had finished basic training and were being assigned to Army Intelligence as translators. We were pleased to see that the two boys would spend most of their time in the Army listening and reading German information. It was during that conversation that Norman Angel came into the carpentry shop and announced that he was leaving the State Hospital and joining the U.S. Navy Seabees as an engineer. We couldn't believe what he was saying. We asked if he was sure that he wanted to leave his wife and son.

"I have never been surer in my life. I have a chance to serve my country and do what I love most, engineering," he said. He continued on telling us that the Navy was looking for tradesmen of all types and we should consider joining the Seabees.

The Living Center

I paused for a few moments to sip on some ice tea that Daisy had brought in. I smiled at her with acknowledgement. She didn't have to do that, but Daisy had become more of a family member than just a caretaker. She enjoyed seeing the kids who took the time to give me a purpose in life by allowing me to tell my story. I turned to Dennis and said,

"I remember your great-grandfather Joe sitting with me in the carpentry shop contemplating what Norman Angel had said."

"What do you mean, Liam?"

I'll never forget what he said. He asked if I thought the Navy would take him or me for that matter, at forty-one years old. I told him I didn't have any idea, but if I went home and told Maria that I wanted to go into the sea bugs or whatever Norman called them, that he had another thing coming and he better stop worrying the shit out of his wife talking like that. He never said another word and went back to work looking at the list we had for jobs we needed to complete at the hospital."

The kids laughed at what I said to Joe, but knew the outcome was different. I got back to the story.

The Story

Several days went by and Joe and I never mentioned what Norman had said. I did think about it at nights and it caused me a considerable amount of lost sleep wondering what it would be like serving in, what I later learned to remember, the Seabees. Norman informed us that he had been selected to be an officer in the US Navy Seabees. He announced that he was resigning his position as hospital engineer and would be leaving for his new career within a month. When Norman finished his announcement, we clapped for him and expressed our appreciation that he was going off to serve his country. The happy mood quieted when Joe asked him,
"Are there age restrictions for the Seabees?"
Norman looked at him and said that the age requirements were eighteen to fifty. No more questions were asked until I talked to Joe on our way home.

I asked him how serious he was in joining the Seabees. His only answer was that he would let me know in the morning. I remember returning home that night, eating little of the dinner Maria had prepared and contemplating what Joe had said. By bedtime, Maria had enough and began to question me on the gloomy mood I was in. It took her all of about two minutes to get me to fess up. She listened and never said a word until I explained what had been said and what I understood Norman would be doing. I told her that Joe seemed very serious about joining. Maria looked worried as I finished telling her what had been said. Her only comment was that Harriet would not want Joe going off to be in a construction unit. I didn't ask Joe about his decision until we attended a party in honor of

229

Norman's departure.

The engineering and maintenance departments put on a nice send off for Normal Angel. The event took place after-hours for the day shift in the cafeteria. The hospital administrator praised Norman for all he had accomplished at the hospital and he received the usual accolades that accompanied events of this nature. It was just after Norman's farewell speech and his encouragement for all of the other tradesmen to consider the Seabees that I asked Joe what he had decided. He didn't immediately answer my question because he was more amused watching the Hospital Administrator cringe as Norman went on and on about the Seabees. I'm sure the Administrator was more concerned about losing more technicians to the service then he was concerned about replacing just one engineer.

I waited a little more for Joe's response to my question, but he only commented about the Administrator's uncomfortable posture and expressions as Norman continued his farewell speech. I can remember nudging him and asking him again. He told me we would discuss it as soon as the event was over. About an hour later he informed me that he was going to join up. He said he had made arrangements for Wolfgang to assist Harriet with the house and his youngest son Aaron who was only sixteen and too young for any service. He also stated that he had borrowed money to cover his mortgage on the new house from family. I looked at him strangely as he gave this information and asked,
"What happens if you get killed doing this?"
He smiled and said that he had made arrangements for the beneficiary of his insurance policy to be the person who lent him the money. He also said and smiled, "If I make it back, I'll pay back the money with interest."

The arrangements Norman made for Joe Cohen would be that

he entered the Seabees as an enlisted Petty Officer reporting under him. I asked when he would be shipping out. He smiled and said,
"I'm heading to Davisville, RI in about a month where they are setting up a Seabee's camp there."
He paused and looked me in the eyes and smiled and said,
"You interested? I know Maria has been talking to Harriet."
I smiled and told him I would talk to him about it in a few days. We left it at that. The ride home was a long one. I passed the house several times and I realized that I had some financial items that needed to be settled and Joe had given me some ideas. I realized that I would make my decision known after we attended Sunday lunch at Ma and Pa's. I planned to talk to Pa that day in the wine cellar where we had done a lot of planning over the years. There was no need to rush into this, so I decided to wait until I spoke with Pa before I even attempted to talk to Maria.

The Living Center

"So you didn't even mention that you were planning to leave for the Seabees to great-grandma, did you?"
Mary asked while Dennis looked at her a little annoyed and said,
"Mary, let him finish the thought before you go asking questions that will divert his attention. I want to capture this information while it is fresh in his mind."
I sat there and stopped the story for two reasons. One was they were talking about me and not to me while I was sitting there. Secondly, I was one hundred and six, but I still could organize my thoughts and they pissed me off a little so I said,
"Hey, you two hold your horses. I still can talk and change thoughts and come back to them. No Mary, I did not tell your great-grandmother of my original intentions because I didn't

231

want to upset her until I had all my facts in order. I also wanted to talk to Pa to see if he would spot me the money to keep my mortgage current while I was away. The idea that Joe gave me of using insurance money seemed like a good idea. I also thought about Ma. I didn't want her upset with my decision which could possibly affect her heath."

I paused a few moments and collected my thoughts.

"With my leaving, as well as all her grandchildren and friend's children, maybe that would be the straw that breaks the camel's back, " I continued.

"I didn't want to be the cause of a fatal heart attack. It was very upsetting to her to think about all those young men who were joining every branch of the service to fight the Japanese, Germans and Italians. The Italians brought even more stress to Ma thinking of her relatives in Mussolini's services. So I had a lot of stuff on my plate, if you know what I mean."

There was silence in the room for a few uncomfortable moments. Dennis even shut off the recorder and doodled on his note pad. Mary looked a little flush either from embarrassment or irritation from Dennis. I looked at both of them, smiled and said, "Now, if I can continue?" Neither one said a word, but Dennis did put on the recorder. Before I began, I looked at the clock. We still had another hour or so. I asked for some plaster to be mixed so I could finish a tunnel I had started for the train set. While Mary mixed, I continued.

The Story

For several days, Maria and I avoided the topic of what Joe Cohen was going to do. I knew she knew what Joe was going to do, but I kept quiet on the subject. Sunday afternoon at the big house came and before lunch, I motioned for Pa to follow me down to the wine cellar. I opened one of his better bottles and poured two stiff glasses. By the look on his face he knew he was in for a serious discussion. I began. I explained how Joe Cohen had been approached by Norman Angel to join the Seabees. I had to digress to explain what the Seabees were about before Pa relaxed and listened. With that cleared up, I informed him of Joe's intentions to join and his arrangements with his cousin to insure his home would be maintained.

Pa stopped me after that and said,
"You want to join?" I nodded positively.
"You wife not know yet?" I went to answer and he put his hand up to stop me and said, "Talk to Maria. You no worry about home and money. I tell Josephine tonight."
The old man didn't fart around. He got to the point and embarrassed me a little on the way. He had forced my hand to tell Maria and eased my decision concerning the home and her welfare. I knew I'd better let Maria know before Ma called her to get more details. I drank another glass of wine and took a third one with me upstairs while I had lunch. Maria never said a word even on the drive home. We listened to the radio and the news of the war. Everything was still bleak and bad. We prepared for bed when she approached and hugged me. She always felt good when she did that and I relished the attention. She held me for a little longer than I expected until I said,
"You know, don't you?"
I could feel her head move affirmatively under my chin and against my chest.
"Why didn't you say something?" I asked her.
She gently pushed me away with tears beginning to stream down her cheeks and said, "Because I know you, love you and waited until you were comfortable telling me. You had to work it out in your mind and I'm sure Pa helped you finalize your decision. Am I correct?" she asked.

I explained in detail what had transpired from the time

233

Norman Angel announced his resignation from the hospital engineering position. Maria confessed that she had kept communications open with Harriet and that she knew before I did that Joe had committed to the Seabees. I asked her,

"Maria why didn't you say anything if you knew?"

She smiled and wiped away some tears and said,

"You had to make sure all was right in your mind before you would say anything. You have been that way all your life, Liam."

She continued to explain that she didn't like me going in the Seabees, but she would have liked herself less if she were the cause of me not joining. She also stated that Davisville, RI wasn't very far away. She knew I would have to stay there for quite a while to complete training. I agreed with her. She told me to call Joe Cohen and inform him of my decision. Joe took care of my arrangements and was influential enough in getting Norman to add me onto his list for immediate duty. I left for Davisville, RI on February 1, 1942. I didn't know that I would be in harm's way by that August.

Ma took the news very well. I guess Pa explained that I would be doing my part to build things for the Navy and Marines. He explained that there would be travel for me, but that I was in a construction battalion and would be in the rear until areas were free from the enemy. I don't know if she bought all that, but she wasn't too upset the day I left with Joe. The one that was most upset was my daughter Christine. Years later I would find out that Jim Dermody had detailed what the Seabees were all about and what he knew from other sailors that had connections in the Rhode Island group. Christine never said a word to her mother or grandmother during the first months that I shipped out with the Seabees. When my letters began to come home and I described the places I had worked at, they all understood how involved the Seabees were supporting the Marine and Army landings in the Pacific

Islands.

Chapter Twelve – 6th Naval Construction Battalion

The Story

Joe and I arrived in Davisville, RI and were soon transported, by rail to Camp Allen, near Norfolk, Virginia. We were assigned to the 6th Naval Construction Battalion known as the 6th NCB. We found Lieutenant, J.G. Angel in the officer's mess the second day we were assigned to a barracks. Joe had been rated as a Chief Petty Officer by then as planned and somehow I was made a First Class Carpenter Mate with their help. I thought that was a pretty good rate for a guy that was rusty after being discharged from the Army twenty-two years ago. I guess Norman convinced the Navy that we were two guys that knew something about construction. I expected a pleasant reunion, but Norman made it very clear that he was an officer now and that in the future he would summon us if he needed to speak to us about anything of importance. That was a quick realization that we were in the military now and officers and enlisted ranks did not fraternize. We settled with that reality and began to meet the men that had been assigned to our battalion. We would spend the next four months learning weapons handling from the marine instructors assigned to us. Joe lead me and six other first class men in instructing us to read, implement and perform to the Naval Construction Battalion handbook on temporary building construction. This training consisted of us learning basic welding, fitting, electrical and piping construction from other instructors assigned to our NCB. We also took a hand at driving equipment as back up to the machinery drivers and mechanics assigned in the battalion.

None us could have known in such a short time, that the 6th

NCB would depart Norfolk by rail to Gulfport, Mississippi in June. We eventually arrived in San Francisco, California and were immediately loaded onboard two steamships in early July. The USS Wharton and the USS President Polk would carry the 6th NCB to the Pacific theatre. When we left San Francisco we had the light cruiser USS Helena to accompany us. By the end of July, we arrived in Samoa. Almost thirty days at sea took a toll on many of us. In Samoa we anchored, but were not allowed off the ship for a week. We ended up at a place that was becoming very familiar to the US Marines. It was called Guadalcanal and our job would be to build an airfield that the Japanese had started. The United States wanted it rebuilt to specifications that could accommodate both fighters and bombers.

We worked every day non-stop until October to complete the airfield. For many days, we repaired what the Japanese destroyed daily with artillery and mortar shells. We worked hard so that Navy, Marine and Army planes could land continuously as we repaired and built more runways. We built wood buildings and then surrounded them with sandbags for protection. I was thankful that the Marines kept the Japanese from overrunning the airfield while we worked. A lot of people were killed on that island because of its strategic location. I know because I witnessed the many burial sites as the Seabees assisted in burying the Japanese dead. We also observed too many markers where U.S. Servicemen had been buried on the island.

I noticed that my feelings were becoming numb. It was like the way I felt years ago when I first experienced combat and saw all the carnage it produced. It was no different than the First World War. Only the location and the uniforms were different. It was on this remote piece of island jungle that I experienced one of the most thrilling coincidences in my entire

237

life. I had just finished supervising the building of some temporary showering stations for the Marines on the island when I heard a voice yell out to me.

"Hey sailor, do these showers have hot water?"

I turned, expecting to tell whoever had yelled, that the water was cold and remind him that he was in the tropics. I looked to find the wise-ass that had made the joke when, there he stood, dirty as I had ever seen a marine, smiling a shit eating grin and pointing at me. It was Joe Cedrone, Gunnery Sergeant in the flesh. I immediately yelled when I saw him. My God! It was so good to see him. We embraced in front of quite a few Marines that were lining up to get their chance to take a shower. They were covered in grime and most of them hadn't, in lord knows how long, taken a shower. We slapped each other on the back. When Joe attempted to let go, I continued to hold him close. I remember him saying,

"Hey man, you alright?"

He found out a few more seconds later when I looked at him through my misty eyes. He then understood why I had held him a little longer than expected. Some Marines were watching our reunion and a few of Joe's boys whistled. Joe turned around to those gawking and immediately told them specifically, in gunnery sergeant language, what they should be doing or else they would be missing their showering privileges. The very mad marine gunnery sergeant's action put everything back in perspective. After he was done, he turned and winked at me. We talked for several hours while the marines went in and out of the showers. When he took his turn, I waited and brought him back to my Seabees hut.

Joe Cedrone enjoyed the hospitality we offered, but not for too long. He felt he needed to be back with his men as soon as possible. He did take the canned fruit, cigarettes and chocolate we gave him back to his unit to spread amongst his troops. I snuck him a quart of brandy which he gladly took a swig of

238

before he capped it and put it in the bag I gave him. He did mention that the brandy was for him alone. He told me he'd think of the wine cellar whenever he took a swig. It made both of us mist up a little. I didn't see him until he returned to Norwich four years later with his family. I tried to keep in touch by letters about every two or three months. They were brief, and it seemed to take forever for them to get to him.

The Living Center

"Great-granddad, what were the chances of you meeting Joe Cedrone on Guadalcanal?" Mary asked.
"Well honey, I don't know what the chances were, but it happened. We'll talk more tomorrow, okay?" I said.
"I guess you have had enough for the day," she said.
"Yeah, I'm a little more tired today for some reason so I'm not going to push it. You know, I have to live long enough to finish this story."
I could see by Mary's expression that bringing up that subject again, my longevity, really bothered her. I smiled and patted her on the cheek and gave her one of my funny faces. For a second or two she didn't seem amused and then, the slightest bit of a smile could be seen registering on the corners of her mouth.
"Aw come on. I'm only kidding around with you," I said.
"I still don't think it's funny when you say things like that," she said. The frown she exhibited was a fake one. She knew it and I did as well.
"We'll see you tomorrow, Liam. Come on sweetheart, it's time to run," Dennis said while he gathered his recorder and notepad.

I was very restless that night. I didn't stay up late either. I kept getting weird dreams of people and places that I hadn't

239

thought about in seventy years. I guess going over the events that took place while we were building Henderson Field had been released from my subconscious. At breakfast the following morning, Daisy kept asking me if I was feeling alright until I had to ask the dear lady to stop asking me. I explained that I was alright. I guess my tone was a little on the sharp side because I could see the hurt in her expression as she listened to me vent. She quickly backed away. I felt worse after that. I called her over after I had eaten a little. She approached with a little caution. I smiled and then apologized. I explained that I knew she was always looking out for me, but this morning, I just needed to be left alone. She smiled and nodded. I needed Daisy on my side all the time and I didn't need to screw that up. I could see that she was still watching me so I made a good attempt to smile and finish most of my breakfast.

I returned to my living quarters and dialed Mary. She didn't answer, so I left her a message to come early today because I wouldn't be spending any time in the basement on the train set. I sat down to relax a bit.
"Good morning great-granddad, its Mary and Dennis. Come on sleepy head, wake up. We're here early like you requested. We have a surprise. Come on, wake up,"
I heard Mary saying and could feel her gentle hand on my shoulder.
"Wow, I must have nodded off. I'm sorry about that," I said and noticed, to my surprise, that Dick and Linda had come to say hello.
"Hi Gramps, you okay? I mean, do you feel alright?" Dick asked showing some concern. "Dick, I'm just fine. I'm just very old and I nod off more than I would like to. Hi Linda, how are you doing honey?"
I asked as I stretched and rose up from the chair and kissed her on the cheek. That was to ensure everyone that I wasn't dying

240

for the moment. My granddaughter-in-law smelt very good. I missed that. I missed the smell of a lightly perfumed woman. Even though I was old, I wasn't dead in that sense. I could still appreciate a good smelling woman.

"Gramps, I checked out the train set and it looks like you have almost finished it. It looks great," Dick said with his hands in his blue jean pockets.
"Thanks, but maybe you could spend a little more time helping me. I'm getting tired more these days and I would like to finish it sooner than later. The residents here enjoy it and it makes their day if you know what I mean?"
I said and looked directly at Dick.
"Sure, I'll come a couple times a week and help you finish it up. It doesn't look like there is much more to complete. I checked and you have all the sets and more landscape stuff than we ever had," he said while looking at Linda. Linda actually said that she thought it was a good idea.

"There's one thing that I want to add to the landscape," I said.
"What's that?" Dennis and Mary asked in unison.
"We need a cemetery and a church. I mean we have a town with all the major businesses in it. We've covered police, fire, and ambulance. We even have a windmill, a tunnel, a school and a freight terminal dock. We don't have a cemetery and a church," I said and smiled.
"That will be easy enough to make," Dick said. "I'll work on it in a few days."
"Good. Surprise me. I'll stay away for a little while. I need a break anyway and it will be nice to see and speak with you when you come here and before you go down stairs."
Now, where did I leave off in the story?" I asked as Dick and Linda disappeared.
"Oh yeah, Mary you asked if I had ever had a similar coincidence like I had with Joe Cedrone. Besides meeting Joe

241

on Guadalcanal and your great uncle Tony Cugini aboard ship on my way back from France, I met his son Joey a month later. But that's another story and a good one, I might say, but not ready to be told yet."

The Story

Henderson Field was probably the busiest airfield I had ever seen. It took several more months to finish because combat was still taking place. Eventually, the Japanese were pushed back to the other side of the island and things quieted down. Of course, when things quiet down, we were quickly able to finish things up there. We prepared to pack up and head out to our next assignment. One day, Joe Cohen informed me that I had been promoted to carpenter Chief Petty Officer effective immediately. Besides the crew of twenty I already supervised, I now had about one hundred or so to supervise. I later found out that the Chief I had worked for and was replacing had a heart attack and had just been shipped back to the Navy freighter off the coast of the island. So now I had responsibility that I really didn't want. The good thing was that I still was working with Joe and occasionally we saw Norman who was now a full Navy Lieutenant and engineering officer for the 6th NCB.

A month or so later, we had a small reunion and Norman even acted pleased to see the two of us this time. He informed us that we had done a great job according to the reports he received from several of the young officers we worked under while we performed under dangerous and exhausting time tables to get the air field structures up and functional for the pilots and plane mechanics while the field was being built. He even mentioned that our service jackets would be so noted and he was sure that some decorations were in order. He also said that when he reviewed my records, he noted that it listed the

decorations I had received in France years earlier. I could not have cared less. Everyone around me was doing their job and I wasn't any different. How foolish Norman sounded as he hinted about decorations. I wanted to say,
'Norman, give everyone a decoration and let's get the hell out of here.'

It was during this brief reunion that the ammunition dump at the far end of the field exploded. The sound was deafening and knocked the three of us to the ground. We later found out that the dynamite that the Seabees had been storing in the ammunition dump had not been monitored like it was supposed to be. We found out the hard way. We had forgotten about how dynamite sweats nitro glycerin when it reaches certain temperatures. Needless to say it was hot there. The explosion caused the .50 caliber aircraft ammunition to light off which in turn set off grenades and so on. It was one hell of a mess for about two days. While we all scrambled to get under cover, some of those stray bullets from the .50 calibers killed several Seabees and Marines near Joe, Norman and me. One of those rounds hit me in the left thigh. When it hit me, I can remember being pushed five of six feet sideways and away from where Joe and Norman had been lying and feeling one hell of a pain in my leg. I must have passed out because I woke up on a stretcher and there was a Navy Corpsman attending to my wound. It didn't hurt as much as it did when I was first hit. That corpsman must have injected me with some morphine which eased the pain. I remember Joe Cohen standing over me telling me that my leg would be alright as soon as they got me to one of the ships. I believed him only after they propped me up and I could still see that I had my foot and could still move my toes despite the pain. I puked several times as the landing craft hauled me and some other casualties to a Navy freighter. The corpsmen took one look at my wound and immediately headed me into the operating room. I was amazed how they stripped and prepped me in a few minutes. I made a point to say that I wanted my leg to still be on when I woke up. After that statement, all I remember was bright lights and people talking loudly and incoherently as I tried to listen, but failed.

It was during the night hours when I woke up from the anesthesia. I looked down and tried to focus on my feet. The light was poor and my vision was blurred, but I made enough noise that a corpsman heard me and came to my assistance. I had to repeat my question three or four times until he understood what I had asked. The effects of the morphine and anesthesia affected my ability to speak coherently. When he finally understood me he smiled and said,
"Take a look for yourself Chief. It's there."
He propped my head up enough so I could look and see that I had two feet and something on the left side covered in a cast and bandages was connected to one foot so I knew my leg was still there. I fell back to sleep and woke up the next morning. By then, I was informed that the ship had just started its voyage back to Pearl Harbor with the three hundred or so casualties it had on board, including me.

When I arrived at Pearl Harbor I remained on the freighter for a few weeks until room at the hospital barracks was made available to handle the constant influx of casualties coming in from the various combat areas. By this time, I had a good sense of what had happened to my upper thigh. I wrote to Maria and the family and explained what had happened. I assured them that I was alright because I know the telegram they sent to Maria scared everyone to death. In my first letter I wrote that my femur had been cracked where a .50 caliber round had grazed it. I explained my muscles had taken the full brunt of the force of the round. I didn't relay to her that the surgeon had explained to me that if the round had hit my femur it would have shattered the main bone and could have caused me to

244

possibly lose my leg. It didn't, and I didn't want to dwell on it and surely to hell not tell Maria and the family about it. The wound was a clean one. The surgeon left two open areas in my cast so that it could be watched for infection and dressed daily. About two weeks after I had been assigned to the hospital barracks, I made my first attempt to walk around on crutches. It took a while to get use to them and the pain and soreness associated with the healing of the wound.

Several weeks later, I had mastered the art of crutches. I was glad to get the cast off. My skin itched and the skin was dry and could be peeled away in sheets. It didn't smell the best either. Within a few days, the hospital staff surgeon allowed me to go to the Chief's Club for my first beer since I had left Guadalcanal. It was on my return a few hours later in the afternoon, completely exhausted, that I was informed by one of the corpsman that a visitor was waiting for me outside my hospital barracks. I grabbed a wheelchair and wheeled myself to the area. I was too tired to use the crutches. Waiting with little Dominic in her arms was Violet Cedrone. I couldn't believe my eyes, but there she was, tanned, pretty and someone to hug. We hugged each other while little Dominic cried. Apparently, I wasn't the most appealing sight for the little tyke, but it wasn't long before she had him calmed down, sitting on her knee as we sat and talked.

She filled me in on the latest news she had received from Joe. He was still writing from Guadalcanal based on the last letter he wrote several weeks ago. She also informed me that she knew about the ammo dump explosion on the air field and he managed to find out that I had been wounded. He didn't know where I would be going for medical treatment. Violet had received a letter from Maria only a few days prior that the Navy had informed her that I was at Pearl Harbor. She also stated that Maria had received my letter explaining the wound.

245

I wondered why Maria's return letter hadn't arrived. It eventually did almost a week later and I was sure that the government postal system had screwed that up.

Violet updated me on all that Maria had written to her about Joey on the Enterprise and Larry meeting up with Joe Cedrone on Guadalcanal. I had missed my son's arrival by two days, but he knew I was alright through Joe. She explained that Lenny was still in training in the tank corps and that Mary Beth was now a second lieutenant nurse in the Army. Violet explained that Mary Beth had been home when the wounded in action telegram came. She was instrumental in calming everyone down after the brief explanation the Navy had given of my condition. I thanked God that she was able to keep everyone's mind at ease.

I asked if she heard from any of the Cohen boys. She knew that Alex was an Army Air Corp pilot, but could not tell me anything about Andrew who had enlisted in the Army and was in basic training. She had no news on Wolfgang's sons except they were in Army Intelligence. I asked if Harriet had mentioned to Maria where Joe Cohen was now. She had no answer. We parted after an hour of conversation. She promised to return in a week or so when she had more information. I hugged her and little Dominic when she left. The boy could be heard crying as she departed. He didn't like me too much at that age, I guess. Violet didn't return because I was ordered back to San Diego three days later by request of NCB headquarters.

As I gathered what few belongings I had, I observed an aircraft carrier docking. The giant ship could be easily seen from my hospital barracks. I asked which carrier had docked and was informed that the markings indicated she was the Enterprise. The thought of seeing Joey Cugini for a brief time

246

was the only thing I could think about. Despite being a distance, I used my crutches to walk the half mile to the dock to get some information about when liberty was being granted. I also hoped that I could get a message to Joey Cugini.

A few officers and lines crew were busy on the dock when I slowly approached. I saluted one Lieutenant and asked if I could get a message to one of the crew. The young Lieutenant looked me up and down and then stared at the ribbons I was wearing and he must have been impressed. He asked the name and as soon as I said Petty Officer Joey Cugini his eyes lit up. He corrected me and said that he could get a message to Chief Petty Officer Cugini as soon as he was off duty. He asked who I was and I explained and where I could be found because I couldn't stay out in the hot sun and wait for him. The Lieutenant was a good guy because he quickly told me that he would send a runner to the Chief and give him my message as soon as possible.

I returned to the hospital barracks completely exhausted. I must have fallen asleep because of the long day that I had. I awoke to find the chief's ambulatory barracks pretty much empty. I hoped that the Lieutenant had given Joey the message. I ate alone in the hospital mess that evening and decided to turn in early. I had just showered for bed when I heard a noise coming from the adjacent barracks. I assumed it was a few sailors who got tanked a little and were on their return to their barracks. The group didn't stay in their barracks because they crossed over into the Chief's quarters. I was the only chief and it was going to be my duty to quiet these guys down when they came blasting through the door.

I prepared to reprimand them when I realized they were all young chiefs. At the head of the small group was Joey Cugini, who yelled at me and said,

247

"Hi Uncle Liam. God, it's great to see you."
Well, it was a very emotional reunion for both of us. The young chiefs respected our display of emotions. I'm sure they all had a brother or uncle or friend somewhere that they would have liked to embrace like we did. We talked for several minutes when one of the men told me to get dressed because they were all going out to celebrate. I obliged and spent the entire night and half way through the next day with my nephew and his friends off the Enterprise. I didn't get to see Joey again before he shipped out because the carrier was in for only a short time.

Ten days later I arrived in San Diego, called Maria and told her that I had been ordered to report to Davisville, RI for administrative duty. It was probably the best news that she had heard with the exception of the fact that I could have been discharged. The second best news was that I was going home on a thirty day leave which meant I would be home for the upcoming holidays. It took five days by rail for me to arrive in Norwich to a waiting wife, daughter and mother at the train station.

They didn't recognize me at first when I stepped off the train. I must have looked a little gaunt because of the months I spent in the hospital. I'm sure my new Chief's uniform was unfamiliar to all of them as well. I guessed the cane I was using threw them off. Christine yelled and ran towards me. The reception was overwhelming. Maria hugged me forever as Ma looked on pleased and poised to wait her turn. When I hugged Ma, I immediately felt her slimness. She had always been a full figured woman, but she had become too slim to my liking. As I hugged her slim frame, I felt that I could have broken her. It was an uncomfortable feeling.

Maria, on the other hand, looked more voluptuous than she

ever did. You have to realize that I had been away from my soulmate for almost a year. Christine, standing before me, had grown into a beautiful young woman. I held off asking about Jim Dermody. There would be time for that later. We arrived at the big house to drop off Ma and for me to stop in and greet my stepfather. When I entered the kitchen expecting to see him he wasn't there. I yelled and he answered. Of course, I should have known he was in the wine cellar. I slowly descended the steep stairs and found the aged gentleman smiling with two empty glasses for his best wine, placed on his work bench. He hugged me for just a little too long, but I understood why. After he cleared his throat several times and wiped one eye, he grabbed the two glasses and handed me one. He poured slowly as he regained his composure enough to say that he was pleased that I was home and safe. He saluted me with his glass and said,

"You home now safe. This is to those who follow you."

He pointed to the bottles of wine that still had ribbons on them. The one he had just poured from had its ribbon placed next to it. We brought the bottle upstairs and finished it in a very short time with the help of Christine, Maria and Ma. We opened more bottles as Tony, Lucia, Loretta and Danny and their families arrived later in the evening. Needless to say, a lot of Pa's wine was consumed. I felt entirely relaxed when I left the big house that evening for home.

As we turned into my driveway later, the house looked more majestic than ever, even being illuminated only by the lights of the car. I hadn't realized how a home could look so inviting. I guess spending a year in tents and under the stars had a little to do with influencing me. Maria had kept the home in excellent condition. I also found out that she had help from my brother Tony and, occasionally, Jim Dermody when he was at the Sub Base. Jim was now on a new boat that he had taken out of the Electric Boat Shipyard and was in the Pacific according to the few letters that Christine had received.

I learned during the next few days that Jim had been assigned to the USS Amberjack which had departed for the Pacific the previous July. Christine talked about him a little, but I wasn't sure if she was in love with the guy or not. During pillow talk I found out from Maria that she liked him, but that she wasn't ready for a more serious relationship. That was fine with me, but I did respect what the kid had done and where he was going. I learned that he was patrolling off the Solomon Islands the same time I was building the runway on Guadalcanal. Christine received a letter in October that informed her that he had visited Brisbane, Australia. She didn't receive any more letters during the holidays of 1942.

The holidays came and went and I reported to Davisville, RI for my new assignment. I was put in charge of several Seabee Petty Officers to interview and select new recruits for the Seabees. It was a good job and allowed me to be home almost every weekend. My routine was to bus from the base to New London, switch over and take the Norwich bus home. It was a great way to fight a war and I was in a position to keep track of wherever Norman and Joe were in the Pacific. January and February flew by as I worked and organized new recruits for the Seabees. Harriet was very appreciative of knowing where her husband was even before he had a chance to write and tell her. This helped her cope with the constant fear of Joe being in harm's way.

My leg completely healed and had regained all its former strength. The recruiting was going very well and occasionally, I had a chance to talk with the senior trade school classes to educate them on the need for Seabees in the Navy. I stressed the fact that they could join the U.S. Navy and serve their country while using the trade skills they learned. The prospect of new recruits for June looked good based on the interest we received at the classes we presented to in the surrounding schools.

I returned home on a weekend pass in late February to find Maria and Christine sitting in the living room very somber. I observed that both of them had been crying and could see an opened letter on the coffee table. My heart was in my throat as I asked why they were upset. Christine handed the letter to me. It had been sent by Mrs. Marge Dermody who was unfamiliar to me at first. As I read, I realized that she was the mother of Petty Officer First Class Jim Dermody. The letter stated that she was notifying Christine that the USS Amberjack was reported lost at sea with all hands. It had taken the grieving mother a week to write Christine and inform her of the tragedy.

My heart sank as I continued to read how the woman was actually consoling Christine on the loss of Jim. Needless to say, I hugged my daughter for a long time while the emotions of World War I and Joey's loss, the carnage I witness in France in 1918 and on Guadalcanal six months ago were all unleashed at the same time. I think I scared both of them to death as I released those emotions that dreadful day. I followed up with a few of my contacts at the New London Naval Base to inquire about the USS Amberjack and Jim Dermody to see if I could get more information on the boat. I didn't really know why I did it, but I wanted to know the official report on the boat. I never got one. I always felt guilty about my cool feelings for Jim. He seemed to be a nice kid and I knew he loved my daughter. I guess if he had lived and returned to Christine, things could have been different. None of us will ever know how that would have turned out.

No one in the room said anything as I finished this part of my story. Mary broke the ice and asked,

"Great-granddad, what did happen to the USS Amberjack?"

"Well honey, it was months after the war that the Navy discovered during questioning of some Japanese Naval officers, that the USS Amberjack was sunk by Japanese sub chasers using depth charges. Somewhere in my papers you'll find the exact coordinates of where the sub was lost. I saved the report I received from a friend about the USS Amberjack and kept it all these years. I don't know why. I like to think it's a tribute to that young sailor or maybe all of those men that died in those subs. Your great Aunt Christine has never talked very much about Jim Dermody. I haven't either until just now."

"Great-granddad, do you think great-aunt Christine would be able to tell me more about Jim Dermody if I went to see her?" Mary asked.

I smiled, shook my head negatively and said,

"Mary, she has trouble remembering her name never mind remembering a beau she had many years ago. The last time I visited her was when you took me to see her before I had the stroke. If you remember, she wasn't too responsive to either of us then."

Dennis said that it wouldn't be necessary to obtain details because Jim would just be a mention in the book as a young sailor that crossed paths with a member of the big house. I looked at him and nodded. He understood that it didn't matter if she remembered or not. The fact that I had mentioned him only added to the story and paid tribute to the men that were lost in the war. I paused to say some more, but felt it was time to move on. I continued when Dennis turned the recorder back on.

The Story

By the summer of 1943, all the kids in the neighborhood were in the service. One of the last was seventeen year old Aaron Cohen who had just graduated from NFA in the class of 1943. I felt terrible for Harriet because she was now all alone. She had two of her boys already in the service as well as her husband and her third son had joined the Army and had just left for training. The Cohen home was empty and Maria worried about Harriet who became a recluse and never ventured from the house, not even to go to synagogue.

Recruiting duty continued to be good, but I also began to feel guilty. I was soliciting young men to join the Seabees and risk their lives building things the troops needed. It was an honorable task, but I also had two to three weekends a month at home, good food, a warm bed with my beautiful wife and a lot of amenities that the average service person overseas couldn't even imagine having. But I was doing what the service wanted me to do and feeling guilty didn't last long.

My recruiting duty came to an end. I received new orders that I was to report to NCB debarkation office at the San Diego Naval Base by September 1, 1943. I didn't tell Maria until two weeks prior to my departure. I just couldn't bring myself to tell her until she figured it out all on her own as always. She knew my mannerisms when something was bothering me and it took her about a week to pin me down. She did, she cried, she was mad at me, but she loved me and accepted the fact that I had kept the news from her only to delay the agony it would bring to her.

Once in San Diego, I was placed on a transport ship to Pearl Harbor the very next day and arrived at Pearl the following week. Then I was put on another ship until I reached a fleet of ships going to some classified location. The destination was finally revealed to us forty-eight hours before we landed. The place was called New Britain. Upon my arrival in the hottest, buggiest, dirtiest place you could imagine, I was instructed to go to the makeshift headquarters of the NCB. I found a familiar face, a little gaunt from recovering from malaria, but still a good sight for sore eyes, was, Joe Cohen. It didn't take us long to catch up and I found my assignment was exactly the same one that I had just before I was wounded. I'd be working for Joe and I was to immediately find my group and get it organized because we were going to build airfields and facilities for the support troops. I asked Joe what the layout would be and he said he wouldn't know until our troops secured the place. He instructed me, in the meantime, to try to get as many workers healthy. Within a few days, I contracted dysentery which led to malaria. I was sick for another week in which I never helped Joe at all. I recovered in time to make a good effort recalling who I was to supervise. I received my first letter from Maria on the first day I was feeling better.

She updated me on Ma's health. I was alarmed to hear that her health was failing. She had been reduced to a frail old lady according to Maria's description. She said that Tommy Parks diagnoses was that she was stressing herself with all the worries of the sons, grandsons, nephews and friend's sons that were in harm's way. Maria said that she prayed everyday that Ma would be able to see all of the men she worried about return home safely. I thought to myself as I read the letter that maybe, just maybe, she would fight to recover from the stress she induced on herself when everyone came home safely. I should have prayed like Maria, but I never found the time. We waited weeks while our troops secured the island. We used our bulldozers to make open areas in the jungle for the Marines to flank the Japanese with. We lost several operators to sniper fire doing that time. It wasn't until New Year's Day that the area was secured. I was happy to leave there in March of 1944. I could never get use to the smells and sights of the thousands of Japanese soldiers that we buried in mass graves there. The sight of our bulldozers burying them became etched in my mind. Our battalion didn't go far from New Britain because we ended up building more airfields on another set of islands called the Admiralties. I stayed on one called Emirau Island building airfields, storage and fuel dumps and miles of roads around the island connecting those places through the summer of 1944.

The Living Center

"Great-granddad, do you want to call it a day?" Mary asked. I paused and said,
"Yes, I guess we should stop now because the story to come becomes a little morbid. I have been dreading talking about it, but it is the story and I will try my best to accurately describe."
"Liam, we can skip that part of the story because we don't want you getting upset and possibly making yourself sick," Dennis said.
He sparked a little anger in me and I lashed out.
"Dennis, for Christ's sake, I have lived with what happened during the war and other wars before and after. It's part of the story and must be told accurately for the memory of those involved. I'll be fine."
I stared at him for a few uncomfortable moments until he smiled and said,
"You're right, and my comment was inappropriate. Please continue."
"My apologies are needed here son, not yours, for my lashing

255

out at you. I guess I'm old and cranky at times. That's a good excuse, I think. We will take this up tomorrow. It will give me time to put it all into perspective so you can hear it as accurately as I can remember it."

Both Mary and Dennis left quickly. I know I had upset them and they knew that the next part of the story would upset me. We needed to get through it like I had over sixty years ago. I guess you never really get over it, but you just live with it. I skipped dinner that night, but my trusty guardian angel, Daisy, made sure the evening shift brought me a sandwich and a glass of milk. I ate it and retired. I didn't sleep much thinking about all the facts I needed to unlock from my subconscious and bring out for Dennis and Mary to hear and record.

Chapter Thirteen – Seven Letters

The Living Center

The next morning I went down stairs before I ate breakfast. I was curious as to what Dick had started to construct for a church and cemetery on the train set. What I found was more than I had expected. My grandson had built a handsome church that looked similar to St Patrick's. Behind the building was a small cemetery with an American flag and several crisscrossing roads through it. I couldn't have done a better job myself. The set was now officially completed. All that was left to be made was a small sign with all the names of the family members that helped build the set. That would be Dick's last task.

Dennis and Mary showed up an hour later that I expected. I didn't fall asleep waiting for them as I would usually do because my mind raced with all the details and facts I needed to give to the kids for this part of the story. I was a little upset that they weren't punctual, but I didn't mention my irritation because I needed to stay focused. After the usual niceties, Mary asked if I had slept well. I lied and told her I slept fine. I don't think she bought my statement because as she looked at Dennis she maintained a look of concern on her face. She didn't know it, but her expression looked exactly like my Maria had exhibited many years earlier. I began.

The Story

While I was on Emirau Island, I received the first letter from Maria that had been dated two weeks earlier. The letter informed me that Ma had died from heart failure and had been buried at St. Mary's Cemetery in the family plot next to my mother and sister. My heart sank as I read the letter several times to make sure I completely understood what Maria had conveyed to me. Her letter also stated that Pa was having difficulty accepting her passing. She updated me on the letters she had received from our sons, but the news of Ma overshadowed the news that my sons were fine. More letters arrived in the next several weeks telling me that Pa was getting worse. The family, and his co-workers, encouraged him to retire from the hospital before he ended up being fired and losing his pension. Apparently, he had gone to work under the influence and was escorted home by some of the men in the maintenance shop. The hospital engineer had insisted that he retire based on this last episode. He was given a few weeks of medical leave and then retired the month he turned seventy.

Maria's letters expressed her concern that he spent several hours a day walking back and forth to the cemetery and staying by the grave hours on end. During inclement weather, Maria had to drive to the cemetery and retrieve him before he caught a cold or worse yet, pneumonia. She described him as just sitting on the ground next to the grave which was becoming an alarming situation for the family to go through. I had more guilt because if I had not volunteered for the Seabees I would have been home to assist my wife and family in their time of need. I made it a point to write a note every day to Maria suggesting different ideas to get Pa back into a stable mental condition. I remember our letters and notes passed each other where sometimes my suggestions and Maria's responses didn't make sense when we read the outdated responses we received from each other.

I suggested that Tommy Parks medicate and work with Pa because he had a good relationship with him during all those years when Ma had bouts with her heart. I was shocked to find out that Tommy was in the Army Medical Corp and had just left for England a few days after the funeral. It seemed that the big house Sunday lunches were becoming emptier every month that this war continued. Joe Cohen wrote home to find just about the same information from Harriet that Maria had been writing about to me. The Cohens had just as much to worry about as we did because their youngest son Aaron was on his way to England. Joe now had all three boys in the service of their country. Joe convinced Harriet, through his letters, that she needed company and not to stay home alone all the time. Maria's letters to me alerted Joe to Harriet's isolation. It was a good thing to do because Harriet began to come around and spend many evenings with Christine and Maria at my house. It eased Joe's mind knowing that.

The letters continued to be exchanged regarding Pa. Maria sent me the second letter informing me that my nephew, Joey Cugini, had been injured on the USS Enterprise. The letter stated that a telegram had been delivered to Tony and Rose's home informing them that he had been wounded in action. Within a week, I received updated information that he had been wounded by Japanese air attacks on the Enterprise. More letters indicated that he would survive the wounds, but he had been transferred off the carrier to another ship to return to the States for rehabilitation. I would learn many months later that Joey would undergo several surgeries to repair the wounds he received to his legs. Maria's letters stated that she hoped Tony and Rose would fair well until their son was shipped closer to home and assigned to a rehabilitation hospital.

Joey would eventually return home from the Navy after almost a year of rehabilitation at the San Diego Naval Base Hospital. Upon his return, he informed his parents that he had been medically, but honorably discharged because he would not be able to return to active duty and a career in the Navy due to the injuries to his legs. He would eventually recover, but his

Navy career days were over to the relief of his parents. Tony and Rose still worried about their daughter, Mary Beth, who had left for England just after the Normandy invasion.

One unusually peaceful night I was instructed that I would give the assignments for the following day. I received the list from the duty officer and quickly passed out the assignments. Joe Cohen had not reported to the NCB headquarters like he always did to update his chiefs on the business at hand for the next day's tasks. I inquired where the senior chief was. I found him sitting alone in his tent and the look on his face alerted me to what had taken place. In an envelope with Harriet's letter to Joe, was a telegram that Harriet had received from the Department of the Army. I read it. Private Aaron Cohen was KIA two days after the invasion of Normandy. That was the third letter. My heart sank as I stood there and reread the telegram. Joe said nothing as he handed me Harriet's letter informing him that Aaron had been buried in France, but that they, as the parents, could request his body be returned to Connecticut. I remember asking Joe what he had planned to instruct Harriet to do. His reply was,
"Liam, does it really matter? He's gone forever. I'll tell her to wait until I return when we can sit down and discuss where will be the proper place for an eighteen year old to rest in peace for eternity."
I couldn't say anything to lessen his grief. We sat there until the early morning hours when sleep and exhaustion overcame us and we slept for a short while. Joe was a different man after that night. He never acted like himself again on the islands. He had a difficult time sleeping and it took its toll on him over the next month.

"Great-granddad, can I get you a cup of tea or something," Mary asked.

"No, I'm okay. That's what happened, Mary. I can remember it like it was yesterday."

I paused and recollected my thoughts and continued on with the dismal facts of this part of the family history. Mary and Dennis sat quietly as I began.

The Story

Joe Cohen received another letter with a telegram in it from Harriet almost exactly a month later. I found him sitting in his tent motionless and staring into apparent space. The look was evident that he had received more bad news. He looked at me after I had asked several times what did the letter say. Without saying a word, he handed the envelope and letter to me. In the envelope was the telegram that said that Alex's bomber was shot down over Holland in route to Germany. This was the fourth letter. He was listed as missing in action. The letter was a little more encouraging because Harriet indicated that the Red Cross had received information from the Germans in Holland that he was a prisoner of war. I remember saying to him that Alex was an officer and the Germans would treat him with respect under the rules of war. Joe never acknowledged what I said. When I attempted to repeat it, he held up his hand and said,

"He's a Jew, and if they find out, he'll be treated a lot differently."

For several days Joe didn't say much and his mood affected the NCB. Norman Angel found out about Joe's two boys and immediately had orders for Joe drawn up for him to return

home. By August, I had received news that Joe was home
dealing with the loss of Aaron and had found out Alex was still
a POW. We found out later that the senior officer of the POW
camp hid the fact that Joe was a third descendent German Jew,
but made known the fact that Alex could read and write
German. These abilities kept Alex constantly at the right side
of the senior Officer and out of the scrutiny of the SS assigned
to the POW camp. Joe was assigned to Davisville for a short
time, but then honorably discharged by recommendations from
the commanding officer of the 6th NCB.

I found myself very busy with Joe Cohen gone. His
administrative and construction skills were truly missed, but I
slept a little better at night knowing he was home taking care of
his family business. By September, I was functioning as the
senior Chief when my whole life changed. The fifth letter
came. I opened the letter from Maria and found a telegram
stating that Larry had been killed on an Island called Peleliu.
The date of his death was listed as September 21st. I had
received a letter from Maria the night before informing me that
Lenny had landed in Normandy and his tank corp. was in route
across France under General Patton. I was devastated and I
don't even remember what I did for those few days. I must
have been useless because Lt. Commander Norman Angel had
me shipped home the same way he had Joe sent. It was
unusual for anyone to get sent home for a war casualty, but I
figure Norman owed us that for getting us involved in the
Seabees. As with Joe, I had orders for Davisville, but it
wouldn't take more than a month for me to be honorably
discharged from the Seabees, right before Christmas.

I don't remember my trip back to the States. I found myself
calling Maria only one time from San Francisco informing her
that I would be home in less than a week by train. She never
answered any of my questions. I was forced to hang up when

the operator interrupted the call because Maria had hung up on her side. I drank pretty heavily on my return. The steward never questioned my calls for more rounds as I stared out the dining car window at the ever changing landscape of the country my son had given his life for.

I stepped off the train in Norwich and immediately took a cab to my home. The door was locked and it seemed that nobody was home. I managed to jimmy the back kitchen window and I crawled through it like a thief would have. The house hadn't changed. All the pictures of my sons and daughter, my nephews and nieces, Ma, Pa and siblings were all displayed like I had remembered seeing them. I checked every room to make sure it was empty. I looked at myself and realized I looked a sight. I washed quickly, shaved and straightened my Navy Blues. I poured myself another drink and waited for someone to return. I thought about calling the big house, but realized Ma would not be answering. I thought about getting in touch with Joe Cohen, but he had enough to deal with. I realized it was Sunday morning. Everyone was at church. I realized that I should be there when I heard, and then saw, the car enter the driveway. Christine and Maria slowly departed without saying a word. Both women looked visibly upset. I knew they must have been in a serious conversation.

I waited for them to open the rear door of the house and enter the kitchen. I stood directly in front of them which startled both of them for a brief moment. I didn't know how my wife would react seeing me there. She surprised me. She smiled and walked to me quickly. She held me for several minutes without saying a word. The more I hugged her and tried to console her, the more she tightened her grip and sobbed loudly. Christine attempted to assist me with her, but I motioned for her to let her mother continue. We both needed to cry and I don't remember to this day how long we stood there, but we

263

cried for a long time. I eventually saw the expression on my daughter's face and hugged her and repeated the emotions all over again. We went to the cemetery that afternoon. I visited my mother, sister and saw, for the first time, where Pa had Ma interned. It was a somber moment and I decided then that I wanted my son to rest next to his grandmothers. The idea was well received by Maria and seemed to give a little closure.

I waited until the next morning to visit Pa with Maria. We found him at the kitchen table all alone sipping a hot cup of coffee. He didn't look up when we entered because I'm sure he knew it was Maria checking on him. She normally did that every morning. It took a moment before it registered that I was with her. He began to cry and said,
"I so sorry."
He never finished his condolences as we hugged in the middle of the kitchen floor. I tried to console him, but failed miserably, as we both sobbed and patted each other on the back. Maria finally broke the engagement and told us that she would make breakfast so that we could celebrate my return. I remember her saying we had something good to talk about. That seemed to change the mood for a short while.

After a few days at home, I ventured down to the basement and turned on the train set. I sat there for who knows how long until Maria came downstairs. We reminisced about the twins running the train sets for hours at either house. I remember that Larry had bought a special dining car just before he shipped out for the Marines. We never had one for the set and that car completed it. I realized then that I had spent a considerable amount of time in a real car just like that on my second return home from the west coast. There was one thing that disturbed me about the train set. It was the cemetery that the twins had made on the corner of the set. It was a simple landscape, but I removed the headstones and church and turned it into a pasture. I didn't need to be reminded of the tragedy when I was trying to relax playing with the set of trains. That status remained for over seventy years until just recently.

The Living Center

"That's why you asked dad to make the church and cemetery to complete the set. That's what you meant. He knew the story, didn't he great-granddad?" Mary asked. I smiled, nodded and continued on.

The Story

Just before Christmas of 1944, we were continually reminded of the battle that was taking place in Belgium. I prayed every night that Lenny was out of harm's way during the German offensive. We didn't know for weeks after Christmas where or how he was until we received a letter that he was part of the relief troops that freed up the surrounded soldiers at Bastogne just after Christmas. He never gave any details except to say that he was fine and that Patton's tanks were driving east into Germany as fast as they could go. I always thought that being in a tank was better than being in the infantry until years later when Lenny told me how a German Panzer tank could easily stop any American or British tank.

Tony and Rose continued to get letters from Mary Beth who was now in France tending to American and British wounded. She assured her parents that she was safe from harm. Years later, she talked about the shelling from the Germans they occasionally experienced despite being several miles from the front. Mary Beth continually asked about the rehabilitation of her twin brother. She was very influential months later after her return to help Joey recover almost completely from his injuries.

265

Joe and Harriet began to come over and visit on weekends. I must say that the first few months when they visited, it was very hard not to talk about Larry or Aaron. It was during that time that we influenced Joe and Harriet to request that Aaron's body be shipped home. We had requested the same for our son and we awaited the government's response to schedule the event. Neither of us would know that it would take another year before the government committed to a timeframe.

Andrew Cohen remained in England. He was assigned as an aircraft mechanic repairing B-17's for the entire time he was there. Joe and Harriet relaxed knowing that he was out of harm's way and not flying in the planes that he fixed.

When we stopped by Wolfgang's store, we always inquired how his boys were doing. He could never tell us because they didn't write and the Army would only say that they were in the theatre of operations and could not be reached due to national security. We never knew what the boys did for Army Intelligence until many years later. Neither boy returned immediately after the war because they were assigned to remain in Germany during the trials of the Nazi war criminals. Joe and I thought they could have been mixed up in spying, but we found out we couldn't have been more wrong. They both remained as interpreters listening to German radio traffic until the holocaust camps were discovered. They spent months recording the horror stories the incarcerated gave them and using that information to help the Allies prosecute the Nazi war criminals. That's when Joe received a detailed account in a letter Erwin sent to him on what he and his brother had found in the camps. They were assigned to record what the survivors had to endure while in the concentration camps. When Joe let me read the letter, its contents sickened me. The horrors he described were unbelievable if it had not been written by a man I considered truly trustworthy. That was the sixth of the seven letters that changed our family and friends.

Lucia kept us informed about Tommy Parks. He'd been assigned to the Third Army and followed it into Germany as the chief trauma surgeon. His skills at the Backus Hospital Emergency Room were greatly utilized in the Army, and the experience he obtained in a combat environment served the community of Norwich for another thirty plus years upon his return.

Kippy and Loretta worried continually about Patrick. He joined the Army in time to arrive in Belgium just after Christmas and got wounded in the leg after one week in combat. That was the seventh letter. I remember seeing Loretta bringing it into the big house just before Sunday lunch. We all froze until she explained that he was wounded and was returning to England for recuperation. We all cried with relief and drank much wine to relax. Patrick returned to Germany during the last few weeks of the war in Europe. He remained in Germany until 1946 when he was finally sent home in the spring.

The Living Center

"Great-granddad, so that's what you meant by the seven letters." Mary asked as I sipped a cup of tea she had prepared for me.
"Yes. Those seven letters changed the lives of our family forever. It's easier to talk about it now, some sixty or so years later, and I'm pleased that it will be remembered in your book as it happened. I'll sleep better tonight now knowing that I have moved past it."
Mary looked at me and I knew I had been caught in a lie when I told her I had slept well. "Before you go off on me, just be

267

happy this old fool can still remember what really happened," I said as I looked at the young beauty.

"I just didn't want you to be upset trying to remember all the gloomy details of all that death and tragedy," Mary said and poured herself a cup of tea.

"It will always be upsetting, but it was easier to tell the story after all these years had passed."

I looked at both of them, smiled and continued on with the story.

The Story

Life became better as everyone began to return home during the fall of 1945. The first to arrive was Captain Alex Cohen, a B-17 pilot and former prisoner of war. He was liberated by American and British troops in late May in Germany. Besides looking a little thin and peppered with gray throughout his black hair, he was one of the handsomest officers you would ever put your eyes on. Next to come home was Lt. Colonel Tommy Parks who was released from the Army Medical Corp to resume practice at the Backus Hospital. He cried when he saw how grown up and beautiful his daughter Julie Ann had become. I remembered even then, as a high school teenager, she was the spitting image of her mother Lucia. Third to come home was Lenny. He wanted to surprise us so he showed up at home on a Friday night. The funny thing was that no one was home. Even Christine was out with her friends when the Army Tank Corp Staff Sergeant entered the house hell bent on surprising us. He got his chance though. When Maria and I returned, we found the front door unlocked and the lights turned on in half the house. We heard the train set moving down in the cellar. Maria immediately began to cry as she shoved me to go downstairs to see who had started the trains. There he was, a little older, a little thinner, but alive. It was a great reunion is all I want to say. The three of us remained in the cellar and relived Larry's death and talked about our experiences until we were joined by Christine a few hours later. We stayed up all night and talked, hugged, cried, laughed and ate. We were a family again despite Larry's absence. We all agreed that we would be a whole family when Larry was returned to us.

Mary Beth returned in November. The young First Lieutenant immediately applied for a nursing position at Backus. She started a few weeks later. Lucia Parks, now the head of the Nursing School and Chief Anesthetist, made sure that the very experienced nurse was put on the hospital payroll. Andrew Cohen came home alone on the train to Norwich. He coincidently met several high school friends in Grand Central Station in New York City. He couldn't believe it. The chances of meeting high school friends, that had also been discharged, was probably one in a million, but it happened, and they all returned to Norwich just before Christmas.

Joe, Violet and Dominic returned to Norwich for several weeks during the holiday season of 1945. It was a very emotional meeting when I saw my brother and his family on my doorstep that year. I immediately saw the ribbon on his uniform when I looked him up and down. He was a good sight for my eyes despite looking through the mist. Joe had received the Navy Cross for heroism on Iwo Jima. It took many years for him to tell me what he did to receive that medal.

The Living Center

"Mary, the Navy Cross and citation are in the chest. Read the citation when you have a chance,"
I said and continued the story.

269

The Story

They stayed at the big house because there was more than enough room. The only room in the big house that we found to be too small was the wine cellar. All of us who partook drinking with Pa didn't mind the crowded conditions we experienced during those weeks after the holidays of 1945. All the bottles with ribbons on them, except four, were drunk. Two remained for Wolfgang's two boys who would return later in 1946 and two for Larry and Aaron. We drank them both after two military, and very emotional funerals.

The Living Center

"There were two more letters that were sent by the Government that caused mixed emotions for our family and friends,"
I said as Mary looked at Dennis.
"What two letters are you referring to, Liam?" Dennis asked.
"The day we received notification that the body of Larry would be sent from Peleliu in January of 1947 was the first," I said and paused as I looked at both of them. I swallowed, cleared my throat and said,
"Your great uncle was sent home with full military honors. Along with and guarding his casket, was a Marine Sergeant not much older than Larry would have been. I can't remember his name for the life of me, but he accompanied Larry's casket from San Diego to Norwich. He brought along official documents including the citations and medals my son had earned. They included the Bronze Star with an oak leaf cluster and the Purple Heart. Those and the other decorations are all in the trunk I maintain at your father's house, Mary. I'm sure the name of that young sergeant can be found there as well."

I said that to make sure she knew where to find them when she wanted more details. I didn't tell her that I didn't want to look at all that memorabilia again. I knew it would be too emotional. I thought, maybe after I read the book, I'd open that trunk again and look at its contents. For now, it would remain closed in Dick's house.

"We buried him with full military honors at St. Mary's cemetery in between Ma and my mother Christine. My wife, I should say, your great-grandmother and I felt much better knowing he was home and at peace next to both of his grandmothers," I said and continued.

The Story

It was a very proud moment for me despite all the pain it rekindled in the family and our friends when we buried Larry in the family plot. The other letter I refer to is when Joe and Harriet received the notification for Aaron a month later. We did it all over again across town at the Maplewood cemetery when they had Aaron brought home from Normandy, France. He too was awarded the Bronze Star and Purple Heart. Each time we laid each son to rest, Lenny Corcoran, Joey Cugini, Patrick Sullivan, Joe Cedrone and Alex and Andrew Cohen volunteered as pall bearers. They all dressed in their uniforms and displayed the ribbons they earned in respect for their fallen family member. Tommy Parks and Mary Beth dressed in their Medical Corp dress uniforms out of respect. Joe Cohen and I dressed in our Chief's Dress Blues as well. It couldn't have been a more fitting tribute for those two boys.

The Living Center

I sat and didn't say a word for a minute or so while Dennis and Mary collected their notes and recorder and prepared to

271

leave. I looked at the clock on the wall. It was a little after four o'clock in the afternoon. I reminded Mary to tell her father to make the sign for the train set so that all the residents would know who helped to complete it. Daisy came into my living room while the couple prepared to leave and asked whether I would be eating with the residents or taking dinner alone. Mary suggested that I come with her and have dinner at her parent's house. I declined because it would have been a bother to get me up and about and I wanted to turn in early. I thanked Mary for the suggestion and told Daisy that a light dinner in my bedroom would be fine. Within an hour, I had eaten and prepared for bed. I was exhausted and don't recall if I finished the Discovery Channel which was to end at nine o'clock. I slept sound. No dreams. No nightmares. I didn't even have to get up and pee during the night. It was just welcomed sleep.

The next morning I woke very early. Early for me was 6 o'clock these days. I dressed and walked to the dining room. The attendants were just making coffee and were a little surprised to see me waiting for something to eat. One of them even asked if I was alright. Sounding appreciative, I expressed that I was just up a little early because I had gone to bed early and had a restful sleep. By then, the chief cook asked if I wanted toast or something while he prepared the usual breakfast items. I told him I'd read the paper and wait.
"For you Mr. Corcoran, I'll fix you a nice breakfast. You can eat it and get down to the train set and start your work a little early," he said and stood waiting for my order.
"Well thank you very much, but I'm done. The set is finished. My grandson put the final touches to it yesterday. But I will go down and run the trains for any of the early risers,"
I said and then paused to order my breakfast.
"I'll take three fried eggs. Make them sunny side up and four or five strips of bacon and two, no three, pieces of the white

toasted bread. Oh yeah, and some orange juice, the pulpy kind would be preferred, okay?"

He looked at me, smiled and said,

"How about I make you two scrambled eggs, a small piece of Virginia ham and some wheat toast? I can give you the pulpy orange juice, though. We want to keep those arteries open, don't we?"

I smiled and just nodded because he had to serve food from the healthy menu the living center boasted about for its residents. I wanted to say, but kept it to myself, that the son-of-a-bitch could have broken the rules because no one was around. As I stood there I thought, *who gives a shit about arteries when you are one hundred and six years old?*
I was, at least, twenty years over when I should have gone. Then I thought about the book. *The bastard was right. I needed to keep these arteries open long enough to read what Mary and Dennis write. Then, damn it, I'd change my diet and eat what the hell I wanted.*

I went down stairs and turned on the lights and started the trains. No one came and then I realized it was only seven-thirty in the morning. Everyone was eating. It wasn't long before a few of the regulars came down to see the set. Nobody really noticed the church and the cemetery. It was just as well. It might have upset some of them. They were kids to me. Not one of the four that did stay and watch, were older than eighty-five. Hell, I was a legal man of twenty-one when they were born and old enough to be their father. But it didn't matter. Old is old when you are in your thirties and forties. When you are in your fifties you begin to think about old and by the time you reach sixty you live telling yourself that you are not old yet. The slogan of sixty is the new fifty makes me laugh. Anything after that is luck, God's choice or just plain good genes.

273

I was concentrating on the train set when Dick came into the basement. He had finished the sign. He stood and watched the five trains as they moved along the tracks through the stockyard, Main Street, tunnels and over the five bridges we had set up. He called over and asked me to turn the wall switch off as he stood on the opposite side of the train set and said,

"Gramps, I got a surprise for you."

I flipped the switch. It was a great surprise when he flipped a switch he had mounted under a section of the set and the street lights, bridge lights and quite a few building lights went on illuminating the entire train set in the dark of the basement. He never told me he had been working to illuminate the set. It was superb. We had never done that in the many years we had trains set up in. When I turned on the lights he said,

"Well gramps, what do you think?"

I didn't answer right away because the look on my face and on the faces of the few residents that had ventured down to the set was evident. We were all pleased. I looked around and said,

"This is my grandson, Dick. He did all this for you and me."

Dick never liked attention and he diverted it to the sign he began to place on the wall in back of me as I sat near the train set switches. The sign read, *'This model train set is a tribute to all grown men who are still little boys at heart and in memory of the Corcoran family members who played with it.' Liam Corcoran 2006.*

I wanted to get up and hug the man, but I knew better. We didn't say a word to each other for probably ten or fifteen minutes until Mary and Dennis came down to fetch me for another session of storytelling. Our eyes, glancing at each other and gleaming, were enough for both of us to understand what had just transpired. When Mary read the freshly varnished pine sign with the most eloquent words painted in black, she

274

turned and hugged her father. It was the beginning of a good day for all of us.

Chapter Fourteen – Better Days

The Living Center

"Liam, are you ready for another round of storytelling today?" Dennis asked while I began to shut down the train.

"Sure, let's get started," I said and noticed a few more people had come down to the train set to see the lights that Dick had engineered.

"Dick, you mind running the set a little longer for our friends here that have just come down?" I asked.

He obliged and I left with Mary and Dennis for my living room to continue telling the story.

"Liam, maybe you want to step back a little and tell Mary and me what you did after you got out of the service. I mean, all of you guys were coming home during 1945 and 46, so what did you do to readjust to civilian life?" Dennis asked.

I sat there for a few minutes, literally, to gather my thoughts. I think Dennis and Mary became just a little concerned as I sat there thinking over what to say. It was funny to watch the cute couple exchange concerned glances at each other. I let it go on for a few more minutes just to see the different expressions they were making until I finally spoke up, almost laughing and said,

"What, you think that this old man has really lost it? I'm just thinking, relax. When I decide to go senile, I'll give both of you a better clue."

Mary started laughing and said,

"We deserved that. We were a little concerned, you know. Yesterday was a very stressing day and we..." I stopped her and said,

"Mary, that was yesterday and, yes, it was stressful, but it's over. I'm fine and let's get on with the story."

That was the signal for Dennis to switch on the recorder and open up his steno pad. I began.

The Story

The Servicemen's Readjustment Act better known as the G.I. Bill provided college or vocational education for returning veterans. We actually picked up some unemployment compensation as well. It came in handy because it gave me time to decide if I wanted to use it. Maria made that decision for me. She convinced me to go to college and take up business administration so that I would have the knowledge to run my own company. It would only enhance my ability to get contracts and run a successful contracting business. We had talked about me going back to the State Hospital and doing the maintenance work I had done until the war started and I joined the Seabees. She inflated my ego and told me that people worked better for me than I did for them. It was true. I was much happier as a partner in Cohen and Corcoran than I was working for Norman Angel and the State Hospital. I went back to school in the fall of 1945 while Maria and Christine worked at the bank. Liam Corcoran was now a 45 year old freshman at the University of Connecticut, class of 1949.

I guess I was a poster child for the rest of the family. I worked on Lenny and finally convinced him to quit working carpentry construction and enroll at Brown University for civil engineering. Another fact that helped convince him was that Alex Cohen had returned to college at UCONN and was finishing his degree in aeronautical engineering. He already had an offer from Boeing's Plant in Kansas to begin work on new jet designs once he graduated. Lenny then realized what opportunities were out there for a young man with an engineering degree. Lenny lived on campus for the four years

277

while he attended Brown. I stopped for a minute and sipped the fresh cup of tea Mary had set in front of me.

The Living Center

"You know Mary, that's where he met your grandmother, Olivia Oldfield. Yep, double oh, as your grandfather would call her when he had crossed her,"
I said for Mary's sake and laughed out loud. I thought about the impeccable mannerisms she had.

She was very cool under stressful situations and it would take a lot to light a fire under her. I wonder today if holding in stressful situations was a contributing factor in cutting her life short. She kept everything inside. I never saw the woman mad. I didn't want to get ahead of myself in the story. I wanted Mary to really get to know the lady that died when she was only four years old. Anyway, I gathered my thoughts while Mary and Dennis watched me again glancing at each other as I continued.

The Story

She was a sophomore history major when he met her. She was about twenty and he must have looked like an old man at twenty-six to her. She was the upper classman as she always kidded him while they dated in school and she graduated before him. She was a first generation American of an English couple that came to this country just after the First World War. Olivia's father, Tom Oldfield, was a stretcher bearer in the British Army. He could tell you some very interesting stories about France during the early years of the war. He worked most of his life in a hospital as an orderly while Olivia's mother taught school. Her mother was a grammar school

278

teacher, if I remember correctly, named Clara.

The Living Center

I stopped and said,
"Mary, if you go into that chest some time you'll find some pictures of them standing with Lenny and Olivia during her college graduation ceremony. Your great-grandmother and I went to the event. We knew that your grandfather was pretty stuck on her by then. I don't have very much memorabilia on the Oldfields. Your father has all that stuff. You might ask Linda to help you to find it." I re-gathered my thoughts and continued.

The Story

Occasionally they would come home and visit with us, but they spent most of their time on campus until she graduated and landed a job in Warwick, Rhode Island while she lived at home with her parents. We thought that, but she spent a lot of time on campus with your grandfather. We soon found out that we were right. When your grandfather graduated, she was five months pregnant with Dick.

The Living Center

I stopped because I could feel something wasn't quite right. I saw Mary smiling at Dennis and I asked,
"Are you pregnant young lady?" She must have turned three shades of red and quickly stated that she wasn't and almost scolded me for asking. She did say,
"I am surprised to hear that my father was conceived before they were married."
I responded, "Mary, if you do the math for a quarter of the

279

children born in this family that were considered premature you might be in for a shock. Do I need say any more?" I left it at that. I continued.

The Story

Lenny landed a job as an engineer in the Connecticut Highway Department two weeks after he married your grandmother Olivia. By that time, I had found a few backers and had started my small construction company with my old partner Joe Cohen. Joe elected to use his G.I. Bill to go to a heavy equipment school in Hartford and learned as much as he could about the latest equipment that had been developed during and after the war. We used Lenny in a very discreet way to keep us informed on the new highway contracts that were going out for bid in the State. That perk allowed us to make some serious bids on some of the road construction jobs that became available when the new Eisenhower Administration came into office in 1953. By 1954 our new construction company, named Corcoran-Cohen, was becoming competitive. The name was in honor of Larry and Aaron, not their fathers. Joe had 'Larry' painted on the first bulldozer we purchased with a USMC emblem next to it. Our large grader had 'Aaron' painted on it with a US Army emblem next to that. Our site truck had a Seabee emblem and a set of chief stripes painted on it. They were big hits with the crews we hired and they attracted good quality ex-G.I's who had Army engineering or Navy Seabee experience.

Lenny only worked for the Connecticut Highway Department a short while. He came to work for Corcoran-Cohen in 1952. He was a great asset to the family business and it was nice seeing him day after day as our company grew. Joe waited patiently as Alex spent his time in the mid-west working for Boeing. I'm sure that deep inside he wanted his son to be the other engineer in the office. A nice surprise came when Andrew Cohen joined the business. He had earned a mechanical technicians certificate to repair and maintain heavy equipment through the G.I. Bill. His days in the Army Air Corp patching up B-17s, P-47s and P-51s and keeping them airborne was more than enough experience to master the bulldozers and other heavy equipment we had. He also became our company representative and manager for all purchases of any type of equipment. If we needed to buy equipment, we went through Andrew. If we needed someone to survey the construction site and inform us what equipment we needed to do the quickest and best job, we relied on him.

Maria and Christine both resigned from the bank. They came on full-time to maintain the books and employee payrolls. It wasn't long before the books and payroll were in need of another office person. Maria convinced Harriet to come back and work with her and Christine. It was during this time that Christine and Andrew became attracted to each other, we thought. Maria and I never interfered with Christine's personal life, but she was approaching thirty years old and never had a serious relationship with a man. There was Jim Dermody who worshipped her, but that never developed into anything. When he was killed in the Pacific, she didn't date anyone for months after the letter came. As the boys returned as men by the hundreds to Norwich after the war, she maintained her occasional date once or twice a month or so. Maria and I watched a turn of events right before our eyes when Andrew began working for the family company.

At first, only pleasantries were observed between the two of them, but we soon noticed Christine changing her mannerisms when Andrew would be about in the office. He usually was sweating and smeared with mechanics grease. He occasionally smelt of diesel fuel when he entered the office, just wearing a tee shirt and shorts when it was warm outside. The boy was a picture of manhood. We all noticed it while Christine pretended not to. Andrew was oblivious to her glances because he was constantly busy checking orders for parts and keeping within the equipment budget he was given. He always approached her in a businesslike manner. She actually made the first move when we took delivery of a new bulldozer to add to our inventory.

Andrew was pleased with his purchase for the company and he had come into the office to show Joe and me what we had invested our money in. As we departed the office, Christine asked Andrew if he would show her it as well. We all listened as Andrew explained the new machine and its latest technology to us. I can remember Joe saying, after the two of them had departed in their separate ways, "Wow, even a bulldozer couldn't get them to notice each other." In defense of my daughter, I responded with,
"She noticed him a while back. He still doesn't see it."
Christine returned to the office and never said a word. Harriet and Maria remained silent, but the glances between the two of them couldn't have been missed by anyone else who came into the office that day. A few days later, Christine made a comment to Maria about her being two years older than Andrew. Maria told me later that she informed Christine that Andrew's age was not a factor to be concerned about. She made sure to remind her that Andrew was more than enough man for any woman to want.

The relationship became more friendly than romantic. Andrew and Christine were just good friends as it turned out. They dated a few times, but it was Andrew who introduced Christine to one of the newest mechanics that he had solicited to help him with the equipment maintenance. Randal Cranston was a thirty-two year old veteran who had been stationed with

Andrew in England. The two men hooked up with each other when they both attended a Caterpillar Corporation equipment exhibition we had sent Andrew to for the company. Within weeks, after a few letters and numerous phone calls, Andrew convinced Randal to visit our company. Andrew pitched to get him to join our small, but growing company. He was relentless in his attempts to get him to come and work for us. The convincing point came when he introduced Randal to the office personnel and he saw Christine. It was obvious from the body language from both of them that there was some chemistry. He joined our company and his relationship with Christine began. When Maria and I were invited to celebrate our grandson Dick's second birthday at Lenny and Olivia's home in 1952, Randal asked me for Christine's hand at the party. It was a great day for Maria and I. Our family was growing with a bright future of more grandchildren to come.

We were pleased that Joe, Violet and Dominic had been visiting with us and they had a chance to meet Randy, as he insisted that everyone called him. Joe also announced that he had orders for Korea and that he was leaving Violet and his son with Danny and Lilly for the one year deployment. Tony suggested that Violet and Dominic stay at the beach cottage at Groton Long Point that they bought several years ago. I thought it was a good idea and thought that Violet would have more privacy. Joe thanked Tony, but thought that being around the family would be better for the two of them because he was concerned that Violet would be too anxious being alone with her son with no adults to talk to when she sometimes became depressed. I should have listened more when Joe released that information that day.

Mary looked a little perplexed when I said that.

"Honey, we'll talk more about that. I just wish that I had delved into that more when I first heard it. I will explain more as the story continues.

The Story

The Sunday before he left us, we all met at the big house where Rose, Lilly and Violet prepared a nice dinner for the family and guests. Most of the men retired to the wine cellar where Pa performed his ribbon ceremony again. This time it was for Joe. Pa had saved every ribbon he had untied from a bottle. He pinned them to a cellar beam with a small tag indicating who it had been saved for. There were almost too many to count, but one caught my eye. It was Larry's ribbon and I remembered becoming melancholy until we drank some of Pa's best in honor of Joe. Joe departed the following week.

One person that was pleasing to see at Joe's farewell lunch was Miss Fortin. She had retired from the State Hospital and lived alone after Miss Gagnon had died of cancer. Pa convinced her to come back and work part-time at the big house to oversee the running of the apartment houses he still owned. She did a good job for him and was good company for him during the day. Nighttime was the problem we had with Pa as the months and years passed. The wine cellar was sometimes his bedroom when he couldn't make the steps at night, too unsteady to climb them. Miss Fortin found him more than once asleep in the wine cellar. Despite Lucia's and Maria's counseling, Pa did what Pa wanted to do until prostate problems began to force him to quickly reduce his daily consumption of wine. When Tommy Parks informed him of the seriousness of his problem he behaved himself. His condition continued to worsen and more tests were suggested by Tommy. He sent him to a specialist in New Haven to perform the tests and give recommendations.   The specialist recommended surgery. Pa agreed. When the specialist opened him up, he found that the cancer in his prostate had also spread to his bladder and intestines. The specialist informed Tommy and Lucia first so that they could talk with Pa and then inform the rest of the family of Pa's prognosis. It wasn't very good. We never told Pa that he was dying, but within four months of the operation he did.

Even if he knew he was dying, he never said a word about it. He remained in bed the last few weeks of his life, except for one day. How he managed to sneak out of bed with Miss Fortin in the house and Lucia visiting until the early evening hours, we never knew. But he managed to descend two flights of stairs to the wine cellar. Miss Fortin found him in the wine cellar, hunched over on the small table he kept with two chairs for any guest he invited down. On the table was a picture of Ma he had taken off one of the living room end tables on his way there. There was two glasses of wine on the table as well. One was partially empty. The one near Ma's picture was still full. He was seventy-eight years old.

We buried our father three days later and interned him next to the love of his life for almost fifty-five years. For almost fifty of those years, they were married. It was a sad day when we buried him, but there was a silver lining of good in the grief that we all shared. Everyday that he lived, for almost eight years after her death, he wasn't the same man. There was always the stare in his eyes of a man who had his mind somewhere else. That was gone now. He was with his maker and companion, and that thought pleased us all. As I waited for the funeral guests to leave and watch the cemetery caretakers lower his coffin, I looked around. I prayed for the first time in many years that he was wrong about the afterlife when he always said,

"Dead is dead."

I wanted him in heaven and spiritually alive with all those that we had interned in this cemetery plot over the years. That family plot that I first observed back in 1914 was almost full now. Seven of the eight plots were now eternal resting places. I prayed that my mother and sister, Joey, Michelle, Ma, Larry and now Pa rested peacefully. I also prayed they were all in heaven. They should be. They were all good people.

The Living Center

"Great-granddad, do you want to stop for a break now?"
Mary asked with concern on her face. I looked at her and smiled and said,
"You are a good lass, but I'm just fine. It's the story and I'm pleased that I am still able to tell it. I'm fine and don't be concerned. I am a little hungry now, though. Maybe you could ask Daisy to get me a sandwich from the kitchen like a good girl. Could you?"
"No, I'll just get it for you. What would you like?" she asked so sweetly.
"Anything, but tuna fish, okay?"
"You got it," she said and immediately disappeared.
"You know Dennis, you are a lucky man. She reminds me of my wife at that age. God, you are a lucky man," I said and waited for a response.
"Liam, the more you tell me about your Maria and the women in this family, if Mary turns out half as devoted as they were during their lifetimes, I'll be a very lucky man," he said and then smiled at me.
"It wasn't all devotion Dennis, it was companionship, team

work, understanding your partner and liking each other. Remember when I asked you if you liked her?" I said and looked in his eyes.

He nodded, smiled and said,

"Yes, I do and I will always remember that."

"Good," I said as Mary returned and said,

"Daisy will bring it in a few minutes. All she can do for now is a peanut butter sandwich until the kitchen opens up in an hour." I rolled my eyes at Dennis and said,

"Thanks honey, I guess peanut butter it will be for now."

"Liam, whatever happened to the other nephew and nieces and family friends after the war? You know, Patrick, Ernie, and Erwin. We haven't covered them,"

Dennis said trying to keep some order to the story. I paused and was about to talk when Daisy came into the living room with the sandwich and a glass of milk.

"I'm glad you asked for the sandwich. It will keep your blood sugar normal until lunch time," she said and set it in front of me.

"I wasn't thinking about blood sugar. I was just hungry. Thanks anyway," I said and bit into it. As I chewed, the information came to me and I continued.

The Story

Patrick went back to the pub and helped his father expand it. They added on a larger kitchen and expanded the eating area. On Friday nights and weekends, they had a small band come in and play. It worked out well until it became too popular and too noisy for the neighborhood. The pub moved to the Greenville section of Norwich in 1955. It was a good spot for some good food and music, and was popular well into the nineteen sixties. Patrick met a singer from one of the bands that frequented the pub and he married her.

The Living Center

"For the life of me I can't remember her name, but she was a firecracker," I said and paused. Both kids looked at me until I explained.
"She had the reddest hair I had ever seen. It was natural and she had a temper to go along as well. They fought all the time as far as I could remember. Kippy and Loretta could never understand what either of them saw in each other."
Her name clicked in my memory,
"Maureen, that was her name. Maureen O'Keefe. She came from New London, I think."
I continued eating and explained.

The Story

Maureen was several months pregnant and the couple decided to marry despite their abusive attitudes toward each other. I remember that Kippy closed the pub for two days to have a Jack and Jill shower there, followed a few weeks later with a nice, simple and small wedding. They lived over the pub until it moved to Greenville. Maureen had a baby girl that year. Pa never got a chance to meet little Samantha Sullivan. She was born with the same red hair as her mother. Kippy and Loretta were very happy to be grandparents, but Kippy didn't have very long to enjoy his new grandchild. He became ill a few weeks after the christening of little Samantha. He began to miss time at the pub and Loretta finally convinced him to make an appointment with Tommy. Tommy did some tests on him and immediately referred him to a pulmonary specialist. Upon further examinations and tests, Kippy was diagnosed with lung cancer.

We were all devastated because the specialist gave him about six months to live. Back in those days, there wasn't too much you could do for someone with an advanced lung cancer case. I always told Maria that I thought all the smoke he breathed in the pub never helped him, plus he smoked pretty heavy like most people did then. He died in January of 1953. He had just turned fifty six-years old. We were all devastated, but Loretta and Patrick took his demise even harder. Loretta did manage to overcome her grief and concentrate on raising Samantha because Maureen and Patrick continued to quarrel as they managed the pub for her.

Loretta became a full time babysitter because there were times when neither Patrick nor Maureen came home from the pub. We later found out that Patrick was always too drunk and Maureen began to have an eye for some of the steady patrons of the pub. There was one instance when Lenny stopped at the pub one late evening and noticed Maureen entering a parked car with a gentleman. He then entered the pub to find Patrick slightly intoxicated behind the bar as the crowd waited for the band to finish its break. Lenny knew, but asked where Maureen was. He was quickly told that she was taking a break outside. Lenny put two and two together and left the pub and went to where he had last seen Maureen entering the car. His hunch played true because he found her and the band's drummer in the back seat of his car. The scene ended with me having to go down to the Norwich Police Station and bailing out my son for grabbing Maureen half clothed out of the car and beating the ever living daylights out of the drummer. Maureen pressed charges against Lenny, but Patrick had her drop them once he found out the circumstances of the altercation. The drummer never pressed charges and that band never played there again as far as I knew.

This relationship continued for a while longer until Patrick stopped drinking and started paying more attention to his wife. They managed to salvage their marriage and produce a second child. Patrick Sean Sullivan the fourth was born in 1955. By then, Maureen stayed home to raise her son and get reacquainted with her three year old daughter. Loretta went back to running the pub with her son. It worked out better for all concerned.

Erwin Cohen returned to Norwich for only a short time in 1947. He stayed and worked in the grocery store for about a year as most of us were off to college or technical school. He left for Palestine in 1948 and became involved with the new State of Israel. His involvement with seeing the holocaust, his reaction he had to the interviews with the survivors of the concentration camps and his disgust with his German heritage pushed him to identify himself as an Israeli. He found himself in combat for the newly formed Israeli Army and by 1950 he was a citizen of the newly recognized country. His brother, Ernst, returned to the Army and stayed with Army Intelligence until he retired as a full colonel in 1972. Ernst and Erwin's career paths would cross several times in later years as the United States and Israel become closer allies in Middle Eastern affairs. Wolfgang and Elsa closed the store in 1975 because it was too much for Wolfgang to maintain the store and care for his wife. Elsa died of Alzheimer's disease the followed year and he followed a year later. That was one of the few times I ever saw their two boys. They returned after the war and then, only for the funerals of their parents thirty years later.

The Living Center

I finished my sandwich and glass of milk and said,
"I think that covers all I can say about the Cohen's of Wolfgang's family for now. We'll talk some more about the

two boys later. They had interesting careers and we'll get back to them. For now, I need to get back to my family."
Mary and Dennis continued to listen as I began.

The Story

With Pa gone, the family waited until Probate Court settled Pa's estate. We all decided that we would have Tony lead the remodeling of the house into six apartments. We converted the wine cellar and the attic into two additional apartments. The cost to renovate the place was $25,000 in those days. We borrowed against the house and completed the renovations. We also voted to pay Rose to maintain the books and divide the profits equally. Tony and Rose's salaries would be taken before the profits were distributed monthly. Tony's employment at the State Hospital allowed him the time to maintain the place and he did a good job. Maria audited the books yearly and Rose did a fine job maintaining them. The sad part about this family business was that we never met for Sunday lunch nor attempted to meet at anyone's house, even on a monthly basis, after Pa's death. Everyone was too busy or couldn't have been bothered. Kippy's wake, funeral and funeral reception set precedence because we didn't meet any more except when someone died, was married, or a new baby was christened in the family.

We did have a new baby born in the family. Lenny and Olivia had another son born in 1956 who they named Donald. It was the first time in almost a year that we gathered at Lenny and Olivia's house after the christening at St. Patrick's. He was a beautiful baby and six years junior to my other grandson Dick. The attention to Donald caused some resentment from Dick which carried on until they both reached adulthood.

291

The Living Center

"What resentment did my father have for Uncle Donald?" Mary asked looking a little upset.

"Mary, your father hardly ever spoke to your uncle while they lived in your grandfather's house. It wasn't until after your father had joined the army in 1967 and went away did their brotherhood improve. We'll talk about that some more later. I'm sorry to upset you, but let's continue on with the story, shall we?"

The Story

It was during that christening get-together that Joe Cedrone had returned from the west coast with his family. He had just retired from the Marine Corp and was considering working in security at Electric Boat Shipyard and a few other defense plants in Connecticut. Joe and Lilly told us that they wanted to keep their roots in Connecticut and were considering their options based on employment. It was very nice to see Joe, Lilly and Dom, which was what Dominic insisted we call him at fifteen. Also Danny Cugini, Jr. was sixteen now and at the party with his parents. I don't know what happened, but while the family celebrated, Dom and Danny, Jr. got into a fist fight. By the time we realized what was happening, the two boys were really going at each other. Enough damage was done during the fight that both of them needed to be cleaned up from bloody noses and some minor facial cuts by Lucia and Mary Beth. Joe Cedrone was beside himself and it took me and Tony all our strength holding him back from beating Dominic to within an inch of his life while Danny and Lilly made it worse by defending Danny, Jr. and saying it was all Dominic's fault. I remember Violet and Rose taking Lilly aside and threatening her to either shut up or they would do bodily harm to her. Danny finally calmed down when he realized that Danny, Jr. was only bruised and was calmed further by Lilly's attitude readjustment.

That fight ended, the two kids were made to shake hands and it was considered ended as far as everyone was concerned. Danny and Lilly didn't see it that way. They kept a cool relationship with Joe and Violet because of the stupid kid's fight for many years afterward. If Pa and Ma had been alive, that would have never been able to continue. But it did and festered until another incident pulled those families further apart.

The Living Center

I looked at Mary who looked perplexed by what I had just told them. She was about to ask questions when Dennis put up his hand with his index finger extended indicating that she should wait a minute until I finished my train of thought. I agreed and said,
"Mary, hold off. I'll give you more details on what went on further between the two families. Needless to say, the christening was the only bright side of that episode when the family got together that year."

The Story

The year 1956 was good for Corcoran-Cohen because we landed a portion of the road construction contract for Route 52. This new interstate roadway addition, when built, would connect Interstate 95 with Interstate 90. The road went north-south through Connecticut. Today, we call it Interstate 395, but in those days it was Route 52. Our area of construction was from Niantic to Norwich and couldn't have been a better

293

project to keep our business growing. There was another family get together for a christening when Christine gave birth to my third grandson, Michael Randal Cranston, that same year.

Christine had a very difficult time having her only child. The results of that labor and birth caused a considerable amount of medical problems for Christine. She was forced to agree to have a complete hysterectomy when she was thirty-seven years old. I never knew why they both didn't consider adopting a child when they knew she would not be able to conceive any more children. But they never did. They concentrated on raising Michael who they made sure, attended the best schools and colleges.

Joey Cugini was in and out of the Veteran's Hospital with recurring leg problems. He walked well, but always with a slight limp. The internal scar tissue and nerve damage from the injuries to his legs from the multiple operations he had endured in the Navy, had to be re-operated on again several times in the 1950's. It was while he was recovering from one of those operations that he met a nurse named Bonnie Lawrence. She had changed her name back to Lawrence since becoming a widow when she was twenty-one and her Marine Corp husband was killed in action in the Pacific. I do remember she told me he was killed on Iwo Jima. I don't remember his name. She had no children and probably wouldn't have remarried until she met Joey who charmed her. She eventually moved in with Joey in a Laurel Hill apartment when he returned to Norwich from the veteran's hospital. She left her job there and followed him here. She found a job at Backus with Lucia's help.

The greatest thing that ever happened to Bonnie was that she was impregnated with twins. Then, the two of them decided to get married. Tony and Rose were thrilled and I wonder today what Ma and Pa would have said about the living arrangements and the pregnancy before marriage. Things were changing, I guess, and in 1958, she delivered twin boys. Twins still ran in the family. We all met for the christening and nobody had a fight. Danny Cugini, Jr. and Dominic Cedrone were very friendly with each other by then. The kids were fine, but Danny and Lilly were still cool towards Joe and Violet even after the two boys showed no signs of hostility for one another during the christening of Anthony and Allen. The twins were named for their grandfathers, Antonio Cugini and Allen Lawrence.

I did dig further into the cool feelings between Danny and Lilly and Joe and Violet. It bothered me, but Maria didn't think it was a good idea for me to get involved. I explained to Maria that blood sisters and cousins, who were like brothers, shouldn't be carrying on the way they were. I dug and found the reason for the cool attitudes.

Apparently when Violet and Dominic stayed with Danny, Lilly and Danny, Jr. there was an incident just before Joe returned home from Korea. Violet had been taking prescription drugs for anxiety. Her anxiety stemmed from Joe's career in the Marine Corp. All the time Joe was in the Pacific, Violet became addicted to medication for her anxiety. Even after Joe's safe return, she needed the drugs. She got help to get off them, but then Joe received orders for Korea. She was put back on the drugs by the Navy Doctor at the Submarine Base Violet went to. She also received another prescription from Tommy Parks who she saw in the Backus emergency room when she had an anxiety attack. So between the Sub Base doctor and Tommy Parks, she had two active prescriptions. Her mistake came when she filled the Sub Base prescription at Danny's drug store. Danny found out that she had two active prescriptions and he informed both physicians that there was a substance abuse issue. Needless to say, the shit hit the fan.

I realized that I had used a little vulgarity.
"Sorry kids," I blurted out after I realized it. I paused and gave them my opinion.

"Danny should have approached Violet directly as a pharmacist should have done. He didn't. First he informed his wife, Lilly. Then he informed Lucia and Tommy Parks. And then he called the Sub Base doctor who immediately contacted Violet. Violet was asked to come to the Sub Base and undergo treatment for substance abuse. It was a good thing for her to be treated for the abuse and her anxiety, but the way Danny went about it complicated the need for Violet to seek help."

"Great-granddad, how did you find that out?" Mary asked.
"I asked Violet straight away one day in front of Joe, why there were some strained feelings between her and her sister and Danny and Joe. By then Violet had been getting treatment for her addiction and she explained the details. I was grateful for the information and let it go. I looked at Mary and Dennis and smiled and said,
"There was no need to stir the shit as they say because I know the more you stir it the more it stinks." Mary rolled her eyes and Dennis laughed.
"I'm serious. I never really forgave Danny for the way he handled the situation because it only made things worse."

I did get a chance a few years later to talk with Danny about his unprofessionalism. It was at Lilly's surprise fiftieth birthday party that another incident occurred that had to be rectified in Danny's family. Danny, Jr. attempted to have Dominic try some prescription pills. My ten year old grandson Dick saw the exchange and asked me innocently if Danny, Jr.

was a pharmacist like his father. I asked why and figured out what was going on from the few details the kid could give me. I told Maria and then cornered Danny, Jr. alone.

I paused and looked away and said,

"He started to make a scene and even used some foul language at his aunt so I slapped the ever living shit out of him."

"Oh great-granddad, you didn't," Mary exclaimed. I looked at her and continued.

The Story

That immediately got everyone's attention because Danny, Jr. screamed at me and began calling me a lot of names. By now Joe, Danny, Tony and a few other men came to the scene. Danny, Jr. had to fess up that he had been stealing pills from certain prescription deliveries and selling them to kids in college. He made a mistake when he approached Dominic and Dick observed the exchange. That set off a big exchange of words between Danny, Joe and the rest of the family where the whole Violet addiction problem came to light. Joe attempted to grab Danny, Sr., but we held him off. Lilly slapped Danny, Jr. for what he had been doing, Dominic was severely punished by his mother Violet for his attempt to try prescription drugs illegally and every one of them hated Dick for snitching to me about the drug exchange. Needless to say, Danny, Jr. really ruined his mother's surprise fiftieth birthday party.

The Living Center

"What happened to Danny, Jr.?" Dennis asked.

"Nothing except some lame minor punishment his parents gave him." I continued on.

The Story

Danny, Sr. let it slide because he didn't want his son to be labeled as a drug dealer. He didn't want an incident like that to hurt him in any way or interfere with the applications Danny, Jr. had into various Pharmacy schools he was applying to. Dominic joined the Marine Corp like his father had done when civilian jobs couldn't fulfill his need to find something he liked. That pleased Joe and set Violet down the path to more anxiety now that her son was in the service. The three sisters, Rose, Violet and Lilly, were never the same after that. Rose became the go between concerning any matters that arose for the Ronaldi family. Tony remained friendly with Joe and Danny, Sr. Violet and Lilly hardly ever talked to each other again.

Julie Ann Parks graduated from Harvard Medical School in 1956. She immediately married a medical doctor, who was also a professor that she had met while at Harvard. His name was Benjamin Blum. He was a native New Yorker who specialized in genetics at Harvard. He was ten years her senior, but that didn't sway her from marrying him despite some comments made by Tommy and Lucia that he was a little old for her. She quickly pointed out to her parents that only eight years separated them. The minor discrepancy was overlooked by her parents after that dose of reality. I think the real problem was that Lucia and Tommy wanted Julie Ann to practice close to home and they didn't want her in the research field. The other item that bothered Tommy and Lucia was that Benjamin constantly talked about going to Israel. He took Julie Ann and went there in 1966.

298

Chapter Fifteen – The Quick Years

The Living Center

"I'm going to eat lunch in a few minutes. You two are welcome to sit and eat with me. I'll put it on my tab," I said and laughed.

"Thanks, but Mary and I have to run some errands and I would like to take her to the Sun Casino. They have a new sandwich shop that has just opened. I hear it's real good so we're going to try it. We'll see you at, let's say, 2:30 p.m. How's that sound?"

Dennis asked. I glanced at the clock on the wall. That gave me two and a half hours.

"Sure, that would be great. See you then," I said and began to walk to the dining area. The kids were out the door in a jiffy. I watched them leave and thought how nice it was to be young and in love. Within a half hour I had finished my lunch and returned to my quarters. I was always sleepy after lunch and the kids knew it. They gave me the extra time to catch a few winks before we started on the story again. Within minutes, I was napping.

"Liam, Liam, we're back," Dennis said and gently touched my shoulder. I woke up and he handed me a tissue. Apparently I had drooled and I needed to clean up a little. I cursed to myself for being a pathetic old man.

"Sorry about that. It's one of the perks of being a dirty old man," I said to ward off the little embarrassment I had.

"Okay, are we ready for the tumultuous sixties?" I asked and looked around the room.

"What are you looking for, great-granddad?" Mary asked.

"I'm just making sure your father is not here. A lot of this information will deal with him."

She looked over at Dennis who started the tape recorder.

The Story

By 1960, I was a sixty year old man. I felt like I did in my mid-forties. I had kept the weight off and I hadn't smoked in forty years except for an occasional cigar with some brandy. Maria didn't like cigars or cigarettes and it was mainly for her that I never smoked much except for my Army days in France. Cigarettes were taking their toll on our family members by then. Kippy had died from lung cancer and Tony had his first heart attack that year. One of the things he was told to do was cut back on his two packs a day habit. I don't think he really listened until he had his second attack a year later. Rose put her foot down and began to watch him like a hawk. He medically retired from the State Hospital and concentrated on running the apartments we had in the big house and on Division Street. Pa had a few more in the city, but we sold them and pocketed most of the money. Checking on the apartments was good therapy for Tony for the next five years. It kept him busy, but wasn't too demanding on him.

We heard regularly from Dominic and saw him, maybe twice a year, when he was on leave. He did well and had attained the rank of corporal within the first two years he'd been in the Corp. We did have a small concern when the Cuban Missile crisis occurred, but it was almost a year later that we found out that Dom was on one of the auxiliary carriers and waiting for deployment into Cuba, if ordered. Joe had a little trouble with Violet during that time. She worried constantly about her son to a point where Joe was forced to get her psychological help at the Sub Base hospital. She didn't respond well to the therapy and Joe had to commit her to the Norwich State hospital for almost a year until she became more stable and returned home.

During that time, Tony and Rose would make the effort to see her. Maria and I did as well and we worked out a schedule where someone from the family would see her once a week. Danny and Lilly declined saying that their presence would only upset Violet. While we dealt with Violet's psychological problems, another event happened that overshadowed that.

Mary Beth was still single and in her mid-forties. She had moved up the nursing ladder at Backus and was then the supervising nurse for the Emergency Room. She also maintained her commission in the Army Reserves and once a month, she was a weekend warrior as we teased her about. For two weeks a year, she went off to Mobile Army Surgical Hospital duty.

It was during Mary Beth's drive home to Connecticut in her 1962 Corvair that she was involved in an automobile accident just outside Fort Meade. She was severely injured by a drunk driver who hit her on the driver's side of her car when he ran a red light at an intersection. The impact crushed her left hip and she was hospitalized at the Walter Reed Medical Center in Maryland for six months. The accident shocked the entire family and landed Tony in the hospital with chest pains for a short while. Mary Beth never recovered fully from the accident and spent the rest of her life undergoing hip, back and neck surgeries due to the undiagnosed trauma she received to those areas from the accident. She had to quit working at the Backus Hospital and she finally received a settlement from the insurance company that represented the guy that hit her and from Chevrolet for the Corvair not being a safe car. That money provided support, but her handicap forced her to move in with Tony and Rose by the time she was fifty

I paused and shook my head. The kids looked at me, but waited for a little while to comment on my gesture. Realizing that I had made a gesture, I said,
"There were a couple of incidents in Norwich that were probably the two most freakish events that I had ever seen in civilian life."
I continued slowly as I recalled what had happened.

The Story

The first was an explosion that happened in April of 1962 when the Van Tassell Storage Company Warehouse blew up. The incident killed four firefighters and blew out windows in many of the houses within a half mile radius. I remember that one of the firefighters was a cousin to the Ronaldi family. It was a terrible accident and we spent several days attending very emotional wakes and heart breaking funerals. Tony Cugini had a contractor come and repair multiple windows that were damaged in the big house from the explosion. It took several days to complete. The second incident happened a year later. It was more bizarre than the first and directly affected our family.

It was just after Patrick and Maureen had set up housekeeping at a house they bought on East Baltic Street. The two story structure had just been renovated when disaster struck. They were not home on that night. Lucky for them they had attended a birthday party for Maureen's mother in New London and were in route home when the Spaulding Pond earthen dam broke in Mohegan Park The water rushed down from the park, cascaded across and down numerous streets until it reached the center of Franklin Square. One of the streets affected was East Baltic Street. Almost exactly where the water crossed the street was Patrick and Maureen's home. It was hit by the full force of the water which flooded the first floor and knocked the house partially off its stone foundation.

They returned to their home a day later to find most of their first floor belongings either missing or heavily damaged from water and ice. The assistant fire chief told them that if they and their two children had been in the first floor of the house at the time of the flood, they would have not lived to tell of their experience. They stayed with Loretta until the damage was repaired several months later. Six people lost their lives in that freak incident. Most of them were mill workers of the old Turner Stanton Mill. Several years later, they moved from that house to a three bedroom cape on Canterbury Turnpike which was well away from Spaulding Pond and any future freak chance of the dam breaking.

Danny, Jr. graduated from the UCONN Pharmacy School in 1963. It was a great event that most of the family attended. Within a few weeks of graduation, he was working at his father's pharmacy. The Family Pharmacy had a new owner when Danny made Danny, Jr. a full partner in the business. Danny expanded the Pharmacy and added an optometry center, on recommendation from his son, for patrons to be examined and purchase prescription glasses from an Optometrist that Danny, Jr. had met at college and highly recommended to his father. Dr. Joe Hillman was a good addition to the business and it began to grow as they purchased the building next door to expand the eye center and lunch counter that became very populated during the lunch hour. Life and prosperity were good for Danny and Danny, Jr.

Alex Cohen returned in 1958 to stand up for his brother Andrew. Andrew had finally met a nice woman through his brother-in-law and best friend Randy Cranston. Candice Bergman was the daughter of a Rabbi who had remained at home caring for her invalid mother and very devout father. The only connection I could make between Candice and Randy was that they lived next to each other when he was a teenager and before he went off to war. When Mrs. Bergman died and Randy and Christine attended the funeral to pay their respects, they struck up a conversation and the couple rekindled a friendship with Randy's old friend Candice. It was at Michael Cranston's sixth birthday party that Andrew attended and met Candice. I was sure it was planned because each of them was quickly heading towards bachelorhood. The two of them hit it off and within a year they were married. Rabbi Bergman performed the wedding ceremony.

When Alex stood up for his brother he brought along his fiancée Elizabeth Wagner. Beth, as she liked everyone to call her, was a banker's daughter. Her father was the bank president of the Wichita, Kansas Savings Bank.

The Living Center

I stopped the story and looked at Dennis and said.
"You realize that I am talking about your grandmother, Dennis, don't you?" He smiled and said,
"I forgot that she went by Beth. I never knew her because she died before I was born. My mother's mother was the only grandmother I have ever known," he said and looked at Mary.
"Yeah, I know, but just to let you know something, she was probably the prettiest woman I had ever laid my eyes on. At your Uncle Andrew's wedding she got more looks than the bride herself. She was a knockout and very much in love with your grandfather. They married a few months later in Wichita. I couldn't attend the wedding because someone had to run the

304

business while your grandparents and uncle and aunt went west to the wedding. Your father was born eight months later. Your great-grandmother Harriet explained in detail how premature your seven pound father was."

I smiled at Dennis and winked at Mary and said,

"Get your calculator out sweetheart and figure that out." She replied,

"Dennis and I get it great-granddad."

The Story

Joseph Andrew Cohen was born in 1959. He lived in Wichita until his mother died of breast cancer in 1978. A year or so after Elizabeth died, Alex sent his son to the University of Connecticut to attend the school of engineering. Joe and Harriet loved having their grandson visit periodically from campus the four years he was going to school there. Joseph met a nice girl at UCONN named Martha Ward. We actually met her a few times when Maria and I visited with Joe and Harriet.

Alex never remarried and retired from Boeing Corporation after almost thirty-five years of service in 1982. It was a year later that Joe graduated from UCONN with his engineering degree, a bride and a two year old baby boy.

The Living Center

I looked at Dennis, who stood there perplexed and then said,

"Son-of-a bitch, my parents weren't married when I was born?"

"Nope, but everything turned out alright. Joe and Martha married in your grandparent's living room in 1983. You were almost three by then and a few years later your brother Joshua was born."

Dennis looked bothered.

"Look Dennis, your family helped out your mom and dad to complete their education and to assure that they were meant for each other. Your parents turned out to have a very strong marriage in which you benefited very well from. Get over it. They were young, in love and not careful. Look at what they have today."

Dennis turned off the recorder on the coffee table.

"I think that is enough for one day, Liam," he said and rose up from the couch.

Mary seemed surprised, but she followed his lead and stood up as well. I glanced at the clock and realized we still could have another hour or so, but Dennis made it clear he had had enough. He said he would see me tomorrow and left. Mary followed. She glanced at me and put her right hand to her ear with her thumb and pinky finger extended. She mouthed the words,

"I'll call you later."

I didn't receive a call that night from my great-granddaughter. She must have either forgot or Dennis was still upset a little about finding out his parents conceived him out of wedlock. I sat in my living room trying to watch TV, but my mind wondered to thinking about Dennis. I couldn't quite comprehend why he would be concerned about something that happened over twenty years ago. I let it go and I figured tomorrow during our story telling session I'd inquire. I went to bed.

The next day it was a stormy and rainy. The thunder and lightning woke me up about five in the morning and it continued through breakfast. The lights dimmed a few times and I surely thought we'd lose power. I didn't like thunder and lightning very much since my experiences in the trenches in 1918 and on Guadalcanal in 1942. I guess my subconscious was brought out of submission and I thought of all that carnage I had seen and tried to forget. The kids showed up at nine just as the storm subsided. Mary could see that I was a little on edge and she inquired,

"What's wrong great-granddad?" I smiled as I looked at the genuine concern on her pretty face,

"Nothing really. It's just that thunder and lightning set off things in my mind that I thought I could forget. The storm's going away and I'll be just fine,"

"Are you okay now young man?" I asked Dennis.

He never looked at me, but answered,

"Yeah, I'm okay. I just don't know why I never put the dates together to figure it out, that's all. I guess I was a little embarrassed, but my future bride here straightened me out." He then looked at Mary and I could see that she must have been a good talker because it looked like she had eliminated any embarrassment he might have felt.

"Dennis, when people are in love or think they are, they do natural things like make love and sometimes babies come a little earlier than they planned. It's been going on for thousands of years and hopefully, it will continue. The greatest thing about most conceptions in this world is that they are made with love. You can rest assure that yours was. Now let's continue with the story before I croak,"

I said and remembered that words like that usually offended Mary. She just looked at me and frowned for only few seconds this time.

The Story

In early 1967 my grandson Dick was considering joining the U.S. Army. Vietnam was becoming a household word and Walter Cronkite brought it into our living rooms every night. It

307

was during a Sunday evening at Lenny's house that Dick announced that he was going to join the Army as soon as he graduated. He explained that he had gone to the Army recruiter in Norwich and was told that a three year hitch in the Army was a good deal especially if you wanted to travel. The recruiter promised that Dick would most likely be sent to Germany for most of the time he was in the Army. So, like most kids his age in their pre-twenties, the story the recruiter was telling him made sense. He signed up for three years with the title of volunteer. After boot camp and advanced infantry training, Dick found himself in Germany in September of that year.

In 1966, Dominic Cedrone received orders for Vietnam. The twenty-five year old Marine Staff Sergeant came home for several weeks before he shipped out to Southeast Asia. Maria and I had dinner with the young Marine and his parents at their house. To keep with tradition, Maria brought two bottles of Pa's best that we had saved for special occasions. During the dinner, we drank one bottle, but the second was never opened. Maria stood up and toasted the young Marine and told him that she looked forward to cracking open the other bottle when he returned home. She tied an old ribbon on it and explained that it was one of the ribbons she found nailed to the cellar rafters in the old house just before we renovated it into an apartment. She didn't know which soldier, marine, airman or sailor Pa had used it for, but there was enough tradition in this family that it didn't make a difference who the ribbon had been for. Dominic was family and it was just right to tie it on a bottle and wait for his return. She tied it, placed it on a shelf of Joe and Violet's hutch. There wasn't a dry eye at the dinner table when my beautiful wife finished her toast. Those occasions were always done by the men with Pa in the wine cellar, but she was the one who kept the tradition going. It made us all feel good and actually reduced some of the anxiety that Violet was exhibiting just before Dom went off to Vietnam.

Maria did the same toast for her grandson when he left for Germany eight months later. It was at that dinner that some differences of opinions were exchanged after Maria's toast. My other grandson, Donald, who was a whole eleven years old at the time, expressed his negativity on the war in Vietnam during the dinner conversation where he was expected to listen and not participate. But that was not Donald's personality. Even back then, he made his opinions known. It really irritated Dick because his younger brother and he did not get along very well and his age didn't really give him any credibility about the things he had read about or had heard. It ended with me calming Dick down from physically hurting his younger brother who was probably right, but way out of line to bring up a topic at a family get together that was splitting a nation, never mind a family. Dick left for Germany. A few days later, the lives in our family changed again with tragedy.

Joe and Violet returned from Mass one Sunday morning to find two representatives from the United States Marine Corp standing at the beginning of their sidewalk leading to their house. The two officers stood there and waited for Joe and Violet to exit my car. Maria and I had driven the two of them to Mass that day as we occasionally did, especially if we had visited with them the night before for dinner or some occasion. It was a good way to keep communications and family ties open. I thank God that we were there that day to help Joe and Violet. It was the commencement of another tragedy that Joe would have to endure more than anyone of us.

The Marine officers immediately informed Joe and Violet that Dominic had been killed in action in Vietnam at a place called Dong Ha. They explained that his remains would be home within the week and that a Marine Corp representative would be coming to their home to work with the local funeral director of their choosing. It was good we were there because Violet completely collapsed uttering incoherent words. I did manage to make sense of a few sentences she said. In essence, it was what she expected to hear ever since Dominic left for the Corp. We had to call the ambulance service to get Violet to the hospital. She was kept there for several days while Joe made all the arrangements with our help.

Dominic's body was sent home within a week. It was a closed coffin wake. Violet requested that she be allowed to see her son before he was buried, but Joe was informed by Mr. Krodel, the funeral director, that in his professional opinion, Joe should not allow his wife to view her son. The extent of Dominic's injuries was to the upper torso due to an explosion. In essence, the man was unrecognizable which would have been too much for any parent to endure. We placed a nice framed picture of Dominic that was taken when he was promoted to Corporal, on the metal casket. Next to that picture were several medals. One was the Bronze Star and another was the Purple Heart. Our family was very familiar with both. We stood in the rain as Dominic was laid to rest with full military honors in the last Cugini plot that was open. Joe Cedrone wore his Marine dress blues with all his medals in tribute to his fallen son. It was an impressive sight to see him again in his uniform that still fit like a glove. Violet, on the other hand, sat motionless in a chair at the cemetery. She couldn't bring herself to even accept the flag that was presented to her by the honor guard that folded it. Joe moved over and accepted the flag and saluted the officer that presented it. It brought back too many bad memories for me and I knew exactly what Joe and Violet Cedrone were going through. Only a few yards away were two flat stones near the family headstone that I almost stepped on while carefully walking to the burial site. One read; Lawrence Corcoran, 1922-1944

Sergeant, USMC, WWII. The other one read; Joseph Cugini, 1900 – 1917, Petty Officer 1st Class, USN, WWI. I wept uncontrollably looking at those stones while listening to Dominic's Taps. It was one of the worse days of my life.

It was worse for Joe Cedrone because within a month of losing his son, Violet overdosed on the prescription anxiety pills she had been using and died. Joe woke up one morning to find her sitting in a living room chair with a picture of Dominic in her hand. At first, he told the police, that he thought she was sleeping from being up half of the nights since Dominic's death. When he approached to wake her he could tell by her pallor and the coolness of her skin that something was wrong. He tried to revive her. He called for ambulance assistance, but the technicians that arrived immediately knew she had expired. Ironically, Tommy Parks was the physician that pronounced her dead in the emergency room at Backus.

The autopsy revealed that she had died of an overdose of anxiety pills. The police investigated the case and surmised that she had been saving one or two pills from reach refill and accumulating them for just the right occasion to end her life. Nobody knew what she was doing over the past year or so except her. Nobody could take any blame because Violet planned her own death by overdose. Joe buried her in the Ronaldi family plot. He stayed in Norwich for several months and decided to visit Italy and the Cedrone families still over in the small town of Santa Lucia where he originally came from. He stayed in Italy for several years by extending his visa every six months until he returned to sell his home and household items. He returned to Italy, but began traveling to other European countries as the mood fit him. He did that for ten more years until 1978 when he died from a heart attack in Malta and was shipped back home in an urn. He made Maria and I the executors of his estate. There wasn't any estate left

311

except the money he had saved from his Marine Corp retirement. We arranged to have his ashes buried in a shallow hole on top of Violet's at the Ronaldi cemetery plot. His name was etched under hers on the stone. We didn't have a military funeral for the Navy Cross recipient because in his last will and testimony, he had forbidden us to do so. His will stated that his funeral were the days he buried his two wives, infant daughter and Marine son.

The Living Center

I stopped the story for a moment and said to Mary,
"In my chest at your father's house are two boxes. In the red oak box are the medals that Joe and Dominic earned while in the Marine Corp. I didn't know what to do with them so I kept them next to the pine box that holds my medals from the two wars I was in and those from Larry"
Mary just nodded and wrote it down in her note book.

I looked around the room and then back at both of them and said,
"I think there are some letters I received from Joe Cedrone while he traveled about after the funerals. Use the information contained in them to add to the story if I failed to mention something."
Neither of them said a word, but only nodded. I continued, knowing I had made the point.

The Story

By early June of 1967, I had retired and turned over my responsibilities to Lenny. Joe Cohen stayed on for several more months, but soon tired of being in the way of our sons and turned over his responsibilities to Andrew. But that was not the highlight of 1967 by any means. We awoke to find out on the news that a state of war existed between Israel and the neighboring states of Egypt, Jordan and Syria. The Israelis launched a preemptive attack on Egypt based on what the other countries had been planning to do first. The war started and ended in six days. It was weeks later that Ernie Cohen told Joe, Alex and Andrew Cohen that he had been informed by the Israeli Government that Erwin had been killed in the hostilities in the Sinai Desert. Ernie was now a full Colonel in the US Army Intelligence and he had been contacted as the next of kin for Erwin. From what I remember, Erwin was killed in an early morning attack on an Egyptian position. The forty-six year old Colonel was killed leading his brigade into action. Ernie was informed that Erwin was buried in the Mount Herzi Military Cemetery in Jerusalem, Israel. Joe and Harriet Cohen would eventually visit the cemetery when they traveled to Europe and the Middle East in the 1970s.

Ernie eventually retired from US Army Intelligence the following year with twenty- eight years of service to his country. Ernie went to Israel and visited the cemetery plot of his brother. Within a year, Ernie, was asked to join the staff of the American Embassy to Israel. He accepted, and spent another fifteen years between Israel and the United States heavily involved in the American Embassy in Israel. Ernie continued, in a different way, to add to his brother's military career in Israel. Ernie always stated that Erwin was a good kid who served two countries well in his lifetime. Ernie retired for the second time in 1983 from the American Embassy in Israel. He spent his remaining years traveling until he returned to attend the funeral of my ninety-four year old friend and partner Joe Cohen. Ernie died the next year and was buried near his mother and father.

Dick didn't write very much from Germany. Lenny would

occasionally mention that Dick had traveled in Germany and France when he took some leave. I know Lenny offered to pay Dick's plane fare home to come and visit for Christmas, but he made an excuse that he was too busy. It was evident he wanted to be away from home. It changed when he received new orders while he was in Germany. Dick's supposedly thirty six month tour in Germany was reduced to fifteen months. He received orders to report to Saigon, South Vietnam for security duty. The good thing was that he would now be home for Christmas, but would have to leave the day after. It was a bittersweet announcement when Dick wrote home informing Lenny and Olivia of his new orders.

In the meantime, Lenny and Olivia had their hands full with Donald. He was a brilliant kid and lot smarter than most kids his age. But he was constantly getting into trouble for bucking the system as he always found something wrong with it. The complaints about Donald that Lenny and Olivia had to endure were that he was disrespectful to his teachers and even the clergy at his school. Already, at twelve years old, he was anti-war, anti-establishment, anti-Vietnam, anti-Catholic and probably anti-Corcoran for all we knew.

If he wasn't in detention every night, he was locked in his room for being disrespectful or doing something to enrage his parents enough to want to kill him. One thing that Donald could do was pass tests. Because of his attitude, the principal dragged his parents before a board to report that the boy had been cheating on his midyear tests at school.

It was obvious to the teaching staff that Donald, with his attitude, was not capable of the marks he had received. I'm sure the principal's office couldn't accept that he had aced all his subjects despite being one of the worse kids in school.

The teaching staff was trying to convince Lenny and Olivia

that they should consider some type of reform school for this kid before he became a criminal. When I got wind of the impending board inquiry, I asked Lenny if Maria and I could attend with them. Olivia and Lenny welcomed us. Any outside help or even opinions might ease their concern for their son. We attended the board meeting at the principal's office and watched the inquiry begin. Several of Donald's teachers asked him questions on certain tests he had taken and his normal answer was that the tests were too easy. The response from most of them was that he probably had cheated because the best students were only obtaining ninety-five percentile on the same tests. Of course, Donald's smart ass response was that they were just stupid or just teacher's pets. Now this is coming from a twelve year old as his parents and grandparents are listening with some embarrassment. This show and tell went on for another twenty minutes or so as different teachers asked questions. Finally, I stood up and requested that the same teachers that had just asked questions go back to their respective classrooms and draw up new tests on the same subject matter and give him the tests in front of us right here and now.

The principal and some of his staff agreed, but the teachers complained that they couldn't issue a new test until the next day. It was agreed that Donald would take the tests in the principal's office with several proctors in attendance to make sure he was not cheating in any way. Just to make sure the playing field was fair; I came along to observe as well. Plus, I needed Lenny at the office and away from this irritation and distraction because he was running the business now that I was in retirement. I drove Donald to school that morning. All the way there he never said a word until we pulled up into the school parking lot.

"Gramps, this is all bullshit! You know that don't you?"

I was about to scold him for his language and calling me gramps, but I realized this kid was a lot further ahead in intelligence than some of the men I dealt with in the service or business.

"Yeah it is Donald, but you brought it on yourself by being a wise ass. If you act like a twelve year old, but continue to think like an adult, you'll really have the best of both worlds. People don't like a smart ass, especially a twelve year old that makes them feel inferior. Play the game kid and you'll have a lot more going for you."

He looked at me and said,

"I guess I really pushed it this time, but I am so bored here at this school. I just wished that they would let me study high school level subjects. You know Gramps; I read most of dad's college books. Not the engineering ones, but the other subjects he took. Did you know that?"

I smiled and said that I hadn't known that, but I told him that if he did well and showed the principal and the other teachers that he was as smart as I thought he was, I would do all in my power to get him in the grade that would challenge his intelligence.

We entered the office to have Donald begin the tests. I had to stand there while they asked him to turn his pant pockets inside out, remove his jacket and sit at a desk placed in the middle of the room as two proctors sat on either side and the principal observed from his desk. They checked his hands and arms to make sure he didn't have anything written in ink on them. That really pissed me off when they subjected the kid to that bullshit. I realized that the incident still made me mad. I managed to get my anger under control. I was asked to leave the room, but I refused and said that if I was not allowed to be in the room with my grandson, then the tests would not be allowed to be given to him. Of course Donald had to make the comment,

"Go get them Gramps," which didn't help in the negotiations. They granted my stay and the tests were administered.

As Donald finished one exam, another was given until all five subject tests had been administered. Each exam was checked by the Principal while the two proctors continued their observations of Donald as he took the next test. We were in that room for a little over two hours. When Donald finished the last test he handed it to one of the proctors and said,
"Okay Gramps, lets get out of here." I first stared at him with a look that could kill and politely said,
"Don't you think we deserve the results, seeing that we had to spend so much time here because they said you were a cheater?"
Donald sat back down, crossed his arms and waited.

Within a few minutes, the Principal finished his reviews and informed the two proctors, Donald and I, that he had aced four of the exams and scored a 97 percentile on the fifth. He also thanked both of us for coming in, apologized for the accusations, and dismissed us politely. On the way out Donald asked,
"Which one did I get wrong?"
The principal only stared at me and I quickly escorted Donald out of the room. Within a month, Donald was advanced from the seventh grade to the eighth grade midyear. Within a year he finished eighth and ninth grade and prepared to enter his sophomore year of high school at thirteen in the upcoming fall of 1969. We had to interact a lot differently with him from that point on. We all realized now that he was a very brilliant kid. It wasn't easy, but we all managed to get use to it.

Dick returned home from Germany to everyone's pleasure. It didn't take long for Donald and Dick to begin the sibling confrontations. Donald constantly reminded Dick that the U.S.

317

Armed Forces shouldn't be in Vietnam and the whole war was a travesty. He said that the government of this country was using its forces to make a lot of money for big business. He tortured Dick every moment they were together. Donald's knowledge of the history of Southeast Asia and his disgust for the Nixon policies only added more gasoline to the fire Dick was building up inside.

The Living Center

"Your Uncle Donald could be such a little bastard when he wanted to be,"
I said and then realized I had been thinking out loud. Mary and Dennis never said a word as I continued the story.

The Story

He upset his parents almost every day Dick was home on leave. There was one instance when Lenny had to literally keep Dick from choking the life out of the lad. The situation was bad enough to have Lenny ask Maria and me to take Donald and keep him with us while Dick was at home. It wasn't a very nice Christmas, to say the least, with those two siblings confronting each other on almost every subject of conversation.

Lenny, Olivia, Maria and I took Dick to Bradley International Airport for his flight to California. He reported to Fort Ord in Monterey, California and departed from there, several days later, for Saigon. We kept Donald with Christine, Randy and Michael until his parents could return to claim him. It worked out well because Donald liked his aunt and Michael was a pretty smart kid who could relate to Donald. They would become close cousins as the years passed.

Dick arrived in Vietnam ten days after New Years 1969 and was assigned to the 7th Infantry. He ended up performing Military Police duty in Saigon. Five months into his tour in the country, he found himself in the thick of things. He was rushed to a fire fight on a mountain called Ap Bia Mountain. I found out later that he saw some of the fiercest fighting of the war within those ten days. Dick was one of the four hundred wounded in the fight that was later called 'Hamburger Hill' by the men who fought there. He never spoke too much about that time he spent in combat. A few times, he compared notes with his father on what it was like fighting in Vietnam to what World War II was like. The experience affected Dick for a long time after he returned home in 1970. Some of those horrible experiences still affect him today.

The Living Center

I looked at Mary who sat scribbling notes on her steno pad.
"One detail you should note. He had bad luck. Hamburger Hill was the last major action of its type in Vietnam and he got caught right in the middle of it. What details did you note?" I asked.
She looked up a little startled and then said,
"I made some notes to read about Ap Bia Mountain and what actually happened on Hamburger Hill at that time. I know my father won't give me any information so I want to get a feel of what he could have experienced during that time," she said and continued to jot down a few more notes.

I stopped her jotting as I reached over and gently touched her writing hand. I needed to make a point.
"If you talk to him about his experiences in Vietnam you will need to approach the subject cautiously. I have never gotten all the details of what your father went through and neither had

319

your grandfather before he died. Despite both of us being combat veterans and understanding the carnage of war, he never opened up to us. He hasn't opened up to anyone, not even at the sessions he attended at the VA hospital that your mother told me about. Mary, it has been thirty something years since he returned home scarred for life."

Mary looked at me slightly alarmed, but understood the seriousness of the subject if she chose to address it with her father in the future.

The Story

I began to shake my head and smile a little before I began to speak. For the first two weeks or so, while Dick was home from Vietnam, Lenny and Olivia kept Donald away from him as much as possible. Even though Donald was in high school now, he still was very opinionated and it was thought best to keep him from spending time with his older brother. There was one incident when Lenny and Olivia had invited Maria and me over for Sunday lunch. Also in attendance was Linda Collin who had rekindled a relationship with Dick that started in high school. Of course, Donald was there as well. To my surprise, Olivia had also invited Christine, Randy and Michael for lunch too. It was nice to have our two children, their spouses and our grandchildren all together at the same table on a Sunday. It brought back memories of how it used to be when we all met at the big house many years ago.

We almost finished the meal like civilized people do on a typical Sunday afternoon until one subject that should have not been brought up, was. It was Michael who asked Dick how much more time he had to serve in the Army. Dick explained to Michael, and those that heard the question, that he had less than three months to serve at Fort Meade and then he would be discharged. Donald made the point to ask if his discharge would be honorable. No one said a word for several very uncomfortable seconds until Dick challenged his younger brother and asked him what he meant by that comment. Lenny or I should have intervened, but for some reason, in which I kick myself in the ass, I didn't react quickly enough. After Dick had asked for an explanation, Donald sarcastically said that in his opinion, and the opinions of a lot of other people, the war was a dishonorable one.

I'll never forget the next line he blurted out, "Anyone who fought in a dishonorable war was dishonorable and should receive a dishonorable discharge." Dick became enraged and snapped. He almost came across the table as he immediately grabbed for Donald. The look on his face scared me. I hadn't seen that rage of anger in a man in a long time. Donald avoided the assault. Dick only succeeded in knocking over plates of food and breaking some of Olivia's best china. Needless to say, it ruined the meal, disbanded the company and upset the entire family. Maria and I took Donald home with us and kept him at our house until Dick left for Fort Meade a few days later. The problem we thought about then would be when Dick was discharged and returned home. Lucky for the family, brilliant Donald was accepted into the Canterbury School in New Milford, CT.

The Catholic school was founded in 1915 and offered dormitory life and a chance for Lenny and Olivia to get Donald away from his brother. They also thought that the school would challenge their thirteen year old son who entered the school as a sophomore because of his high placement exam results. Donald would only spend two years at the Canterbury School because he finished his three year studies in less than two years. One subject that did get his interest was theology.

The subject fascinated Donald to the point that he almost became obsessed with finding out as much as he could about the great theology figures St. Augustine, Thomas Aquinas, Karl Barth and others. Lenny showed me the books the kid was reading when he was at home on break which completely baffled both of us. But he was a changed boy. At fifteen, he chose to accept admission into the University of Notre Dame in Indiana. Whichever the case, he excelled there as well and completed his four years of studies in three years. His calling to the priesthood followed and he entered the seminary at eighteen years old in 1974.

The Living Center

I stopped the story and paused for a few minutes while Mary and Dennis stood there waiting for me to continue. I guess the minutes became uncomfortable for the couple and Mary asked, "Would you like to stop for the day?" I looked at her for several seconds until I could see her glancing at Dennis with a little concern on her face. I responded,
"No, we'll continue. I just want to get my facts straight and try to keep my opinion out of the story, that's all."
Mary and Dennis looked at each other. Dennis shut off the recorder. I put my hand down on his and told him to keep it playing because I was ready.

The Story

The very religious members of our family which included Maria, Lucia, and Loretta were ecstatic that Donald was studying for the priesthood. Olivia and Lenny were astonished that their younger son had chosen the life of the clergy. The rest of the family were simply polite and waited to see how the youth would turn out. I'm sure there were some that doubted that he would ever finish his studies.

The Living Center

Mary stopped me and asked, "Who wondered? I mean, that was a great profession for him to choose and look at him today, great-granddad." I looked at her and said,
"Well, the cousins made comments. Their grandparents, Tony and Rose chastised them for their comments in front of me. There was probably some jealousy there as well because the twins were off to UCONN as freshmen in 1974 when Donald was through college and into the seminary. He was already four years ahead of them. Michael Cranston had just started Yale and never commented as far as I know. Samantha and Patrick Sullivan never even addressed the subject because Patrick started working in the Pub with his grandmother and parents and Samantha went off that fall to Suffolk University in Boston for Accounting. I don't know if that generation had matured enough to understand the commitment Donald was making to his Maker and the Church or they just didn't care." Mary and Dennis never said a word as the tape recorder was turned on again.

The Story

The year 1976 brought the family tragedy. Tony Cugini was diagnosed with prostate cancer. The illness that killed our father struck his name sake. Tony tried hard as hell to fight the disease as he participated in several experimental procedures that were being tested for prostate cancer patients. He underwent surgery, experimental chemo therapy, and sustained many radiation sessions until he had withered into a one hundred pound walking skeleton. In those days, cancer treatments were being tested and adjusted and life expectancy

323

was very short. He died a miserable death and I prayed that he would die much sooner than he did. My nephew Joey and niece Mary Beth made all the arrangements. They arranged for his body to be buried within a few yards of the Cugini Family cemetery plot. .

Donald returned from the seminary and personally asked Joey, Bonnie and the twins, if he could write and deliver the eulogy for his great uncle. He approached the podium at St. Patrick's Cathedral in his plain black frock and Roman Collar and knelt, for what seemed an eternity. I felt uncomfortable until I began to listen to the words that Donald was saying about his great-uncle. Donald described his great-uncle's religious faith, family values, being a life long partner to his great-aunt, and an American veteran who served on ships during the Great War. He touched on his bravery to face the dangers at sea while he grieved for a little girl he tragically lost and barely knew. Needless to say the tears flowed and the hearts saddened as Donald culminated the life of Antonio Cugini, Jr. in the presence of God, his family and friends.

The Living Center

I stopped for a few seconds and looked at Mary and said, "That's why I held off on my opinion of Donald when I first mentioned that he was going to enter into the seminary."
I gathered my thoughts and continued.

The Story

Most of us thought a young man like him, especially being only eighteen, had not experienced enough in the real world to make a decision to be a priest and wouldn't last more than a year. After hearing the delivery of the eulogy that he'd written for his great- uncle Tony, it was enough for me to realize that the snotty kid I knew in grammar school had developed into a very holy man. I was very proud of my grandson and I was a little ashamed that I did not see the potential he possessed. He also impressed the twins on his ability to communicate with their grandmother who was in the early stages of Alzheimer's. Even though Rose had been slightly confused over the last several years, the death of Tony caused considerable added stress and confusion for the woman that her children could not help her deal with. But Donald was able to make her calm and eased her anxiety and confusion as to what was happening during the wake and funeral. The twins even commented that he had a natural calling.

Donald was not back in the seminary for more than several months when he was called back by the family again and requested to write a eulogy for Rose who died from the hideous disease she only had for less than five years. Both twins went to the seminary to pick up their cousin this time. A bond between the three of them was cemented from that time on. In St. Patrick's Cathedral Donald delivered a simple eulogy for his great-aunt that pleased the family and paid tribute to the faithful wife of Tony for almost sixty years. Rose was buried next to Tony in a simple ceremony as requested by Joey, Bonnie, Mary Beth and the twins.

With the deaths of Tony and Rose, Mary Beth tried to maintain the homestead. With her handicap, she found it more and more difficult. She had to rely completely on contractors for any repairs and soon found she was becoming frustrated and strapped financially to continue maintaining the place. Joey and Bonnie advised her to sell the homestead and invited her to live with them. She declined until the winter came. She realized then that she needed to bury her pride and move in with them as it got colder and she was alone in the house. She put the house on the market and told them she would move in once the house was sold.

It was during a snowy winter weekend in February of 1977 that Mary Beth slipped outside while dusting off some snow from the front sidewalk. She fell backwards and struck the back of her neck on the front entrance steps. The fall caused her to crack and dislocate one of her already delicate vertebrates that caused paralysis from the neck down. She laid in the snow and cold for several hours until the neighborhood mail carrier found her. She was immediately rushed to the hospital and admitted into the intensive care unit. Joey and Bonnie were beside themselves with guilt and sorrow for what had happened to their sister.

We consoled the two of them because it was a freak accident and there was no need for her to be out and about dusting off snow from her sidewalks to begin with. Joey had a contractor on retainer for snow removal and he would have come if there had been any accumulation. There hadn't been up to the time when she fell. I know it didn't help Joey much, but consoling Bonnie did help. They were told by the doctors that Mary Beth would not be able to breathe on her own without the assistance of a machine. She was completely paralyzed from the neck down, but the doctors hoped that they could relieve pressure on her spinal cord enough so she could breathe on her own and have feelings in her upper torso. The problem that her doctor's feared was that she had developed congestion in her lungs due to her exposure to the elements while she lay on the sidewalk. They hoped that she would not develop pneumonia which could prolong her operation to relieve the pressure. We all waited and hoped that she would be able to have the operation. Despite treating her with antibiotics in advance for the possibility of contracting pneumonia, she developed it almost immediately. It worsened until it strained her heart and she went into cardiac arrest. She died within three days after developing it. She was only fifty-seven years old. Her family buried her next to her mother and father in a simple funeral ceremony. Donald was brought home by the twins again from the seminary to eulogize their aunt. He was nearing his studies to be a priest. Most people that attended the funeral addressed him as Father. He quickly corrected them that he was a seminarian and not a priest. The title 'Father Donald' was with him now despite his attempts to correct individuals that addressed him as that.

By the summer of 1978 our family witnessed four graduations. Anthony and Allen were the first two who both graduated from UCONN. Anthony had participated in Army ROTC while at UCONN and he accepted a commission into the US Army commencing immediately. Allen on the other hand, had applied and was accepted to a graduate degree at UCONN in Education. Despite being identical twins, each man couldn't have been more opposite from the other. Michael Cranston had finished his pre-law degree from Yale and had been accepted into the Yale Law School the following fall. It took Michael a little longer to complete his studies. During his first year at Yale, he almost failed out until he stopped partying and paid more attention. He spent a year on probation and an extra year retaking subjects he needed to have better grades in order to get accepted into Yale Law School. He managed to do it to the credit of the constant pushing by Randy and Christine. I credit them for their extreme patience. I thought, and occasionally said to Maria, that I would have kicked his ass and shut off the money, especially with him being at Yale. As usual, my brilliant wife ignored my comments and when he did graduate, as he walked across the stage to receive his degree and we watched with his proud parents, she whispered into my ear and reminded me that an ass kicking was never needed.

The most spectacular graduation was the day Donald was ordained to the priesthood. He took his vow with eleven other seminarians from Terence Cardinal Cooke of New York. It was an emotional day for our family as we watched Donald, lying prostrate, with his thumb and index finger tied together with linen strips in front of the Cardinal, several bishops and a multitude of monsignors and priests as well as hundreds of family members and friends of the twelve. I sat in awe as I realized two thousand years of church tradition for ordination was happening right before my eyes. I had never been a very religious man, but witnessing the experience my wife and her sister's were experiencing as they watched their grandson and great-nephew respectively, receive his holy orders was the holiest moment in my life that I had ever felt.

The Living Center

I stopped and looked at Mary who seemed absorbed in the moment of the story. Realizing I had stopped, she asked,
"Are you alright?" I smiled and said,
"I'm fine, but I wanted to break your spell on visualizing what that ordination was like." She looked confused until I said,
"Your mother and father didn't attend the ordination. Your father wasn't interested in anything to do with your Uncle Donald. I guess the animosity that developed between the two of them carried over to that time. It would be five more years before my grandsons would reconcile their differences."

Mary didn't say a word until Dennis suggested that we call it a day. I was tired by now and agreed. Within a few minutes both kids had left the living center while I casually walked down to the dining hall and prepared for dinner. Daisy was still on duty as I entered the dining hall and she asked me why I was there so early. I realized that it would be almost another

328

hour before dinner was served. I spent the next hour watching the trains run in the basement with a few other residents while I thought about my grandson.

I realized that it had been almost a year since I had seen him. I really didn't have the time to say anything to him because he was only at the hospital two times. Once to perform the last rites on me when they thought I was buying the farm and then again probably several weeks later when the family was informed that they had no hope of me coming out of the coma I was in. When I did start to recover, Donald had been called away to Rome and then Palestine to do some work for the Vatican there. I did hear about his comments about me in his letters when he did write Dick and Linda.

While I sat and ate my dinner, I made notes on a napkin about the events that I knew of in Donald's early life as a priest that most members in our family did not know about. I planned to take the notes back to my living room and make an outline for the kids that would spur details from me as I told the story. A few residents and staff casually asked me what was I writing down that now had consumed quite a few napkins. I remarked that it was personal until one resident kept breaking my thought process, asking me the same question over again until I screamed at him and told him that it was a hit list and he was the first one to go. Daisy quietly escorted me out of the dining hall and back to my room.

She never said a word until we reached the privacy of my room and said,
"What the hell is wrong with you, Liam? You don't say things like that unless you want to be evaluated by the center's shrink and possibly shipped off to some low budget home. What was on the napkins anyway?"
I realized that she was right and I simply said that it was notes

329

on specific incidents concerning Donald in his early days in the priesthood.

"So what is happening with His Eminence, these days by the way?" she asked.

"He's between Rome and Palestine. I don't hear much from him. I'm compiling notes for tomorrow's session with Mary and Dennis and I just wanted to have my facts in order as I remembered them," I said.

"Well, please behave yourself. You can't go around yelling at people when they ask you questions."

"Mary, the son of a bitch is nuts. He repeats himself constantly and if you don't answer him he's nuts enough to drive you friggen crazy until you answer him," I said while trying not to raise my voice. She shook her head and said,

"Please, have more patience with the patients here. It will make everyone's life a lot easier."

Chapter Sixteen – Decades of Good Byes

The Living Center

By the time Mary and Dennis arrived at nine o'clock, I had rewritten the information I had captured on the napkins the night before and transferred them in an outlined form on three pieces of letter paper.

"What's all this?" Mary asked when she noticed napkins and crumbled up pieces of paper in and around the waste paper basket.

"My original notes, that's all," I said and motioned to Dennis to start the tape recorder. Mary began to clean up for me.

"You need to have better aim great-granddad," she said.

I paused while I watched her take off her coat and get ready for the next session.

"I want you both to be aware that this is another one of those times in my life where it will not be easy for me to remember all the details that occurred, but there are eulogies that I saved on the relatives and friends that we are going to talk about. In the upper dresser drawer, in my bedroom, there is a large manila envelope that contains some of those eulogies which were written and delivered by close family members. One is very special to me. It is the eulogy that was co-written by Dick and Donald for my Maria."

I felt myself choking up a little even after all these years she'd been gone. I looked at Mary and Dennis who just stared at me until Mary nodded that she understood. I took a deep breath and exhaled. I looked out at the rain falling on the sidewalk and parking lot of the center. A few visitors were quickly walking into the entrance way with umbrellas. I thought about Tommy Parks. I began.

331

The Story

February 1983 was like any other February with cold, windy and continually unsettling weather. Tommy Parks celebrated his 86th birthday. It was a small party with Lucia, Maria, Loretta, Danny, Lilly and me in attendance. Julie Ann and Benjamin had been home the previous year for Tommy's 85th birthday and told him that they would be back from Israel when he turned 90. They did arrange to coordinate a phone call from Israel as I remember, with Lucia saying a few words to him and his guests during the party. It was a good time. Tommy, even at 86, was very active and still consulted on matters at the Backus Hospital. By 1983, time had taken its toll on my family. It was obvious with the missing siblings. Danny and Lilly were the youngest and they were both in their mid-seventies; but we were family no matter who was able to be there.

The party began to wind down as the attendees noticed the snow that was accumulating outside. Most of them didn't like driving in inclement weather, especially snow. Loretta was alone and Tommy offered to take her the five miles to her house so she wouldn't have to drive in the snow. She accepted, but told Tommy that she would have Patrick come by the next day and pick up the car. With that being known, we all left within a few minutes. During Tommy's return home he misjudged his car when it went into a slide while traveling down a hill and around a corner. The car landed on the side of the road and became stuck.

According to the police report that we all saw later, Tommy exited the car and attempted to assess the situation. He tried to rock the car by accelerating and decelerating to get some traction to exit the ditch which apparently didn't work according to the tire marks. They figured he decided to exit the car for the second time and walk back up the hill. We realized he was heading to Loretta's home. We guess that he figured he could walk the mile and a half. No one knows why he just didn't walk to the nearest home and use the phone. Almost everyone in Norwich knew Dr. Parks.

Lucia called Loretta after an hour wondering why he was taking so long. Loretta informed her of the time he had left. The police found Tommy lying on the sidewalk next to several parked cars, heavily dusted with snow, half way up the hill to Loretta's home. Lucia was informed that he had expired from a heart attack and hypothermia. What the most common sense man I knew was thinking, still remains a mystery.

His wake took two days and two sessions each day. Lucia was exhausted. Several times, she had to leave the funeral parlor while Julie Ann and Benjamin received the hundreds of guests. Father Donald returned for his uncle's funeral and said the eulogy at the Christ Episcopal Church. Tommy maintained his religious affiliation all those years. It didn't seem a problem for each spouse to attend different Sunday services for all those years. Julie Ann and Benjamin, at the time, continued the same practice.

The Living Center

I stopped and looked at Mary and Dennis and said,
"I am assuming that you two will continue down that path when you are married. Am I correct?" I asked.
Dennis immediately commented, "We've talked about it, Liam."
"We'll talk some more before you marry. I don't care what you decide, but decide. My stepfather use to say that the God

333

in my church is the same God in yours, or something like that," I said and continued.

The Story

As usual, Donald eulogized Tommy to the fullest and made us all proud of the contributions Tommy had given to the hospital, community, country, charity organizations, and most of all our family.

It was at the funeral reception that I noticed Dick and Linda with Donald in pleasant conversation. Linda was seven months pregnant with Billy at that time and it was especially moving for me to see Donald bless the swollen belly of my granddaughter-in-law before he departed from the reception a little early. I tried several times, weeks later to delve into what took place only to hear from Linda that her husband and brother-in-law had a nice conversation and that she was pleased that they were getting along. That was it.

The Living Center

I looked at Mary and said,
"Maybe someday your father or uncle will tell you what made them reconcile with each other. Or maybe it's not important the more I think about it." She didn't comment.

The Story

Billy was born in April. He was a big kid even then. Nine pounds something as I remember. His poor mother had to have a caesarean after a day of labor. But everything turned out alright. Linda has always stated that Donald's blessing helped her through the ordeal. If anything, it strengthened her bond with Donald. That flowed over to Dick one way or the other I thought.

A year later, Danny, Jr. finally announced that he was engaged. He was forty-four years old and had found himself a thirty year old medical drug saleswoman that he met through the Connecticut Pharmacist Association he was an active member in. The June wedding was probably the biggest that Norwich had seen in years. Danny and Lilly spared no expenses for their son. Neither did Dr. Richard Mellow and his wife June, for their daughter Christina Mellow when it came to expenses. Danny, Jr. and Christina contributed as well and the gala turned into a thirty thousand dollar event I was told. That was a hell of a lot of money for a wedding even then.

Not only was it a big wedding, but Bishop Daniel Patrick Reilly married them. I guess Dr. Mellow had one up on Danny Cugini. The Mellow family and the Reilly family had known each other for many years. But not to be outdone, my son, Monsignor Appointee to the Diocese of Albany, New York, was also present and assisted Bishop Reilly. Of course each man brought along their assistants and St. Patrick's alter looked as if a Queen and King were getting married. A simple ceremony would have been appropriate for Danny and Christina, but the women in the family enjoyed all the pomp and ceremony the clergy exhibited for the four hundred or so guests.

The reception lasted well into the evening in which we were fortunate to have Donald stay at Lenny's house. His assistants slept at Dick's house and the following morning we attended an early morning Mass and then went out to breakfast which was my treat. It was the first time in years that almost all of my immediate family was together and happy. I sat amongst my oldest and youngest grandsons and their father. We laughed until I cried as Dick and Donald talked about their childhood altercations and pranks that their father had to deal with. No one was more pleased than the three women that sat opposite us at the long table. Maria, Olivia and Linda beamed as they watched Mary and infant Billy and the grown men laughing and acting like foolish boys. I'm sure it was amusing to the two priests that had accompanied Donald as well. I can't remember why Christine, Randy and Michael didn't attend the breakfast because they surely would have enjoyed it as I had.

We attended another wedding that summer when Patrick Sullivan, III's daughter Samantha, married Ryan Maguire. Ryan was an immigrant from Ireland who came to the United States during the late sixties. He joined the Army and served in Vietnam. His reward was earning his citizenship. The Army became his career. He seemed a good kid and we enjoyed having Donald back from Albany to perform the ceremony. It was at the reception that Maria became ill. She had felt a little faint the morning of the wedding and had managed to sit through the ceremony. I drove her home to freshen up before we attended the reception. While at home, she vomited and had to lie down to gather her strength. I suggested that we skip the reception, but she countermanded me and explicitly stated that it would be very rude for us not to attend our grandniece's celebration.

We attended, and managed to stay for most of the reception until Maria's pallor exceeded gray and turned to white. She was weak and felt nauseated until she realized that we better leave before she made a scene at the wedding reception. She felt cold and clammy and I couldn't get her out of the place soon enough. As we left, our children and grandchildren looked concerned. Maria, as always, assured them that she had only picked up a bug or something and that she would be fine once she had time to rest. She promised to call all of them in the morning because she surely knew she would feel better then.

By early evening, Maria had been laying down for more than several hours when she called out to me in a faint, but concerned tone in her voice. I entered the bedroom to find her clutching her chest and having difficulty breathing. I immediately called an ambulance and we transported her to Backus. I followed directly behind, praying that she would endure what seemed to be the beginning of a heart attack. Pictures and thoughts of my stepmother raced through my mind as I sped down the road following the ambulance. I convinced myself, after I had said multiple prayers to every saint I could think of, that she would be okay after treatment and rest. I could have never been more wrong because my wife, my soulmate, the mother of my children and best friend, died in the ambulance on the way for treatment.

I wasn't given any information until I had been waiting in the emergency waiting room for over an hour while they waited for my family to arrive. One of the attending physicians knew our family and was kind enough to get in touch with my son and daughter. When I saw Lenny and Christine come through the emergency room entrance, I knew by the expressions on their faces that the love of my life, their mother was with my son and their brother Larry. Not a word was exchanged while we all hugged and stood in the center of the waiting room trying to console each other.

The Living Center

"It has been twenty-two years since that day and it feels like it was yesterday," I said and stopped my story. Dennis turned off the recorder. Mary wiped back tears and I tried to regain my composure. I realized that I was teary eyed and needed to freshen up a little. Mary found and dampened a wash cloth and I used it to apply some cold to my face. I motioned to Dennis to turn on the recorder as I forced myself to continue and describe the following events.

The Story

We had a wake several days later. I don't remember too much except many people passing by me in the reception line. I was grateful that Christine planned for the family to view Maria several hours before the scheduled time for the wake. We had time to cry, talk, laugh, re-bond as a family and pray together. Our grandson led us in prayer and said the most uplifting prayers that I had never heard up to that time or since. I never realized the bond he had developed with his grandmother once he became a priest. But he was truly sorrowful when he said Mass at St. Patrick's that day. Dick and he had co-written the eulogy, but Donald delivered it without ever referring to the script. I was very proud of both of my grandsons who had written this eulogy from the heart. Donald delivered it while he walked amongst the family and funeral attendees. He always paused at different parts and looked back at his brother to assure his approval. It was truly a sight to behold and listen to.

I buried my eighty-three year old wife and partner of sixty-five years in a duel plot in St. Mary's far at the end of the cemetery where she, and eventually I, could lie in peace together for eternity. We decided years before, when we had purchased the plot, that it would only be for the two of us. We both were superstitious that if we had plots in reserve we would end up using them. We rested assured that Larry was accompanied by enough relatives at the Cugini family plot that

338

he would lie peacefully. We did not want to bury another child or grandchild in a new Corcoran plot. We both assured ourselves that we would all meet spiritually someday. Maria convinced me that cemetery plots were only receptors for bones.

I had second thoughts though after several days when I realized that my wife would be all alone in the far end of the cemetery until I calmed myself by remembering what she called cemetery plots. I found myself visiting the plot several times a day until Christine began to worry and follow me daily. I realized what my stepfather had gone through when he lost Ma and I determined then that I would grieve with dignity and not become a problem for my family. I realized that in a few years I could lie peacefully next to her so it wouldn't be too long of a wait. I couldn't have been more wrong.

The Living Center

I looked over at Mary and Dennis and said,
"It has been twenty-two years since that day and I'm still here. I should have gone many times, but..."
Mary sat next to me on the arm of the chair I was in. She bent down, hugged me and softly spoke and said,
"You're here because we still need you. When it is time, God will take you. But for now, you need to be here for us."
We hugged for a few minutes until I sat up and cleared my throat and said,
"It's almost lunch time. How about I treat, but you fly, and get us a large pizza or two? Pepperoni and mushrooms would be nice. I don't care what the second one is." An hour and one and a half eaten pizzas later, we continued with the story.

The Story

339

Death was still an uninvited guest. We were stricken in grief when we heard the news from Lenny that Olivia had developed breast cancer several months later. The treatment and time Lenny spent with Olivia made him take a leave of absence from running the company. Andrew and Candy Cohen were forced to maintain the entire business. Joe Cohen came out of retirement and forced me to help him. He called me one day and chewed my ass out for not helping his son and my son keep the business running smoothly. It had been only several months since Maria's death, but Olivia's sickness was a wakeup call to get me out and about. I realized I was old now, but my brain could still operate a construction business. My old senior chief got me away from my pity party and back to reality. I needed to help my kid and this was a good way to do it.

We labored at first, but within a few weeks, we were up to speed and directing the staff in the day-to-day operations of the company. Andrew handled the new business while we all waited for the return of Lenny, praying for a good report on Olivia. Months passed as Lenny continuously postponed his return as he relayed the worsening reports he received. She underwent two single mastectomies six months apart hoping to rid her body of the hideous disease. Upon completion of the second, they found more cancer developing in her reproductive organs. To continue the fight, she agreed to undergo a complete hysterectomy only to relapse several months later when the surgeons informed Lenny that they had found cancer in her liver and pancreas. Lenny never told his wife just to spare her from the agonizing truth.

My grandsons were wonderful with their mother in her last weeks. Donald returned from Albany and stayed at his brother's house and visited with Olivia every day while she slipped in and out of drug induced sleep. Donald prayed with her. Dick read to her. Each one doing what he could to ease her mind from the pain she endured. Lenny slept every night in a cot beside her hospital bed. When she returned home in her final days, I found him sleeping in her bed when I visited their house on an early morning visit. I thanked God that he had been merciful to me because my lovely wife died within hours of her affliction and I was spared the horrific conditions my son and grandsons had to endure watching that beloved woman agonize. She died one year after her initial diagnosis. She was only fifty-nine years old.

We buried her in St. Joseph's cemetery across the road from St. Mary's in a corner plot that Lenny had picked out on his own several weeks before her death. He went alone so no one would know that he was preparing for her death. He stopped by my home after he finished with the undertaker and informed me what he had done. He cried and asked me if he would need forgiveness for what he had done. I remember that I didn't answer him for a few minutes while he sat in my living room looking at all the family pictures I still had displayed. When I knew I could talk without a trembling in my speech, I said,
"Is the cemetery plot that you purchased peaceful?" He looked at me strangely, but didn't speak.
"Can you go there and talk and not be disturbed by others visiting their deceased relatives?" I asked.
He paused and answered, "Well, yes. I mean. I guess so."
"Good, because you will be there many times when the end comes for Olivia. You will speak to her every day and you won't want anyone disturbing your conversations you will be having with her," I said.
I also reaffirmed that his sacrifice to go alone to pick out a cemetery plot relieved his sons from having to do so during a time when emotions were high which made common decisions difficult.

When Olivia died, Donald delivered a very emotional eulogy for his mother. His older brother had to relieve him at the podium when his emotions overcame his usual brilliant delivery. Dick began to read the eulogy until he realized that he could glance at Donald's notes and still speak from the heart. When Dick finished, he turned to his brother and embraced him. They descended the podium together and embraced their father sitting in the front pew. An ovation from the attendees began until Donald returned to the Alter to finish the Mass. I was proud of those two boys that day and I'm sure their father remembered that scene until the day he died.

The Living Center

"Do you want to rest now, Liam?" Dennis asked.
"No, I'm fine and need to continue while it is fresh in my mind,"
I said and smiled at Dennis and Mary to reassure them. I continued.

The Story

Several months went by and I would occasionally call or stop by Lenny's house to look in on him. A few times, we went to dinner and chatted. Dick and Linda kept a better watch on him and made sure he was eating and adjusting to life in his home without Olivia. On one specific visit, while I was talking to Lenny, the subject of France came up. I don't know why we ended up talking about France, but the conversation expanded as we compared stories of our experiences in the country. Lenny had seen more of France than I had due to the nature of the campaign he participated in, but, nevertheless, we had some similar stories to tell about the culture, customs and people we observed during war time.

The idea hit me while we talked. It could have been the few glasses of wine we drank, but the idea came to me and I said, "Why don't we go there?"

Lenny looked at me strangely and began to make up some lame excuses concerning the house, kids, cost and time needed to undertake such a trip. I waited until he finished his logic and responded,

"Dick and Linda can watch the house. You own it so you don't have to pay a monthly mortgage. Your kids are fully grown, you have more than enough money, and I am sure that the business can run without you for, let's say, two weeks and maybe a few days added on. Don't you agree?"

My son didn't say a word as he looked around the kitchen we were sitting in. I said another sentence before he could reject what I had already brought to his attention,

"Plus, you are sixty-three and it's been forty years since you left that tank you rode in through France. Wouldn't you like to see the place again? Now tell me why you can't?"

He smiled and looked around again. His eyes swelled a little and I knew what he was thinking about. He looked at me and said,

"Sure, let's do it. It will be just you and me for a couple of weeks. You can make all the arrangements seeing it was your idea. We can split everything,"

he said and then poured us both another glass of wine.

"Whoa, slow down cowboy. I have to drive home sometime. This reminds me of some of the days when Uncles Joe and Tony with Pa and me would sit and talk in the wine cellar while you kids played upstairs and Ma bitched at Pa for keeping us down there too long. I miss those days."

That was it. Two weeks later, we drove to Bradley International Airport and caught a redeye flight to Paris.

We spent several days visiting some of the museums and we

343

even ventured out to see the Versailles Palace. We visited several of the battlefields and cemeteries from both World Wars, but we tried to keep from revisiting too many stored memories we both had from each war. We hit every cultural place we could fit in during the trip, but the highlight of it all was the visit to the Cathedral of Notre Dame where we attended mass and lit candles for the deceased loved ones of our family. We felt at peace upon leaving the Cathedral. I did want to see two more places after the Cathedral visit. I convinced Lenny to rent a car. I wanted to see the cities of Verdun and Forges, and I wanted to walk the river bank there where the Meuse River passes them. He obliged me and I spent several days tracing my footsteps when I was there in 1918. I was actually able to see some familiar sites as Lenny walked with me. He honored my silence and never asked any questions, only when I spoke. When we were through, we ate dinner at some restaurant in Verdun and I remembered what he distinctly said to me,

"Dad, I want to drive to the hedge country outside of Normandy. I watched you for the last several days and I want to do what you just did and feel what you felt. Was it closure?"

I smiled, continued eating my dinner and only nodded as I controlled my emotions. We spent the next three days in that part of France and delayed our return home a couple more days. We both walked the beach at Normandy as Lenny described the landing. I described my arrival up the coast several hundred miles, twenty five-years earlier. That was the closest I had ever been to Lenny and I cherished that trip even to this day. One thing that we did notice was that the English Channel looked more picturesque than it did in the summer of 1918 and the late spring of 1944.

"Do you have any pictures of the two of you in France during the trip, great-granddad?" Mary asked. I nodded, but paused for a few moments and said,

"There is a photo scrapbook in which I have kept them. You will also find the pictures of Donald when he became Bishop of Albany in 1986. I have kept those pictures together because they were very bright moments in my life just after Maria and Olivia had passed away."

Dennis looked and made a motion to Mary and then said,

"Liam, how about we talk about the Bishop after lunch? It's already lunch time." Without saying another word, we broke up our session and the kids left. As I walked to the dining area, Daisy was waiting for me.

"Taking a break, Liam?" she asked and smiled.

"Yep, I need some nourishment," I said as I rolled my eyes and passed by her.

"Don't roll your eyes because today the chef has made a nice chicken soup and you have a choice of several different types of sandwiches. Look at the menu."

I didn't answer her because I was thinking of a juicy hamburger on a roll with lettuce, tomato and mayo with some French fries. No such luck because all there was to select from was friggen tuna fish, turkey and egg salad. I ate several bowls of the soup and returned to my living room to sleep a while until the kids returned. I awoke when Mary gently touched my shoulder. They had already set up, waiting for me to stir. I didn't. She nudged me to awake me. I took the cool and damp face cloth she handed me and washed my face to alert my senses.

"Okay, you revived the old man. I'm ready," I said and smiled at both of them.

"On our way here, we were talking about Uncle Donald, great-granddad and when you and dad and the rest of us went to Albany to see him appointed the Bishop of Albany," Mary said. "Do you remember the ceremony? You were only five years old and Billy was just three," I said.

"Yes, I remember some of it," she responded. I began.

The Story

Donald was appointed Bishop with the retirement of his predecessor. It wasn't a very difficult decision for the Vatican to make because Donald just about ran the Diocese because his predecessor had been ill for several years prior to his forced retirement. We attended a rather simple ceremony. That was what Donald had requested from the Cardinal. Newly appointed John Cardinal O'Connor performed the ceremony. It still remained a very high point in our family in 1986 when only thirty years old, Donald was elevated to a Bishop.

Donald only lasted four years as the Bishop of Albany. In 1990 he was replaced by an Auxiliary Bishop when the Vatican recalled him to work in the office of the Roman Curia. When Donald was received in an audience with Pope John Paul II, he was informed that he would be the assistant to the new Secretariat of State for Relations which was also in charge of the Public Affairs of the Church. That function would take him to the four corners of the world with the Secretariat Giovanni Cardinal Batistanni. Donald assisted him in that function until Donald was appointed to it in 2001 and elevated to Cardinal the following year. My grandson, Bishop Corcoran, did manage, in his busy schedule, to pay a visit to me in Norwich on my one hundredth birthday in 2000. I was unable to visit Rome and see him become Donald Cardinal Corcoran. By that time, my son had convinced me that it would have been too

346

tiring for me to travel to Rome and see him made a Cardinal by Pope John Paul II. Lenny, Dick, and Linda were the only three that attended and I couldn't blame them for not wanting to take me along.

The Living Center

I looked at Mary, who quickly defended her grandfather and parents and said,
"Great-granddad you had just moved into the first senior center that year because you had fallen twice. Don't you remember that?"
"Yes, I remember. It was the right decision, but I was irritated with myself that I was unable to attend. That's all," I said.
I commented that I hadn't seen my grandson since his father died.
"Despite him being a world traveler, he only came to Connecticut to see me and his brother when his father died."
Mary defended her Uncle.
"Great-granddad, Father Donald is a very important Cardinal in the Church. His job is like our Secretary of State for God's sake. I don't expect to see him unless we know when he will be in New York or Washington. If you like, I will have Mom or Dad write him and get his schedule. I'll take you to see him. Would that be alright? We plan to write him anyway because we would like him to be here for our wedding."

I didn't pursue an argument because she was right. I thought to myself, *The kid was busy.*
"Okay, you write him and tell him I would like to see him when he is back in the States." Mary and Dennis looked at each other and both nodded in agreement that they would. I collected my thoughts and continued on with the story.
"2004 was a shitty year kids," I said and realized that I hadn't

347

used the nicest language. Neither kid paid attention to my vulgarity.

The Story

We had three deaths that year. First was my son Lenny who reached eighty-five years and died in his sleep. Dick found him in his bed several hours after he failed to answer his morning check call that Linda or Dick always made. They informed me several days later after they had found out what had caused his death. It was listed as natural causes.

The Living Center

I stopped the story and looked at the two of them and said, "It should have been me kids. I was almost one hundred and five when we buried him next to Olivia on that cold February day. No man should outlive his children," I said and stopped trying to control my emotions.
"My son should have been allowed to see his grandchildren marry. Your wedding would have been his first. I truly think he would have enjoyed watching your wedding," I said to Mary and looked over and smiled at Dennis.
"Great-granddad, you will take his place and watch us take our vows in front of God, Uncle Donald and our parents," Mary said and hugged me.

The Story

We no sooner buried Lenny when Lucia expired at one hundred and one. She had spent five years in Israel with Julie Ann after Benjamin died. The visit to Israel was good for both of them and they had a chance to see Donald on one of his visits to the Holy Land. That was probably the biggest thrill for Lucia because she also received special Rosary Beads that had been given to her by Donald from the Pope. She was buried with those beads in her hands when we laid her to rest next to Tommy Parks twenty-one years later.

Lucia lived a good life. The only thing that would have been better would have been her having grandchildren. That's something she would have enjoyed.

Loretta never knew that Lucia had died. She had developed Alzheimer's in her last five years and died just before her one hundredth birthday. She had outlived her son and daughter-in-law who were killed in a car crash and never knew that as well. Samantha had been in charge of her affairs and health issues and when Loretta showed signs of the disease, she immediately committed her to a convalescent home. Her brother, Patrick IV, never attended the funerals of his parents, but did show up for his grandmother's. He never returned to Norwich after he had a falling out with his parents due to his life style. I guess that his parents, Patrick III and Maureen, could not accept his male companion and words were said. It was a sad situation for a father and son to have a falling out for that reason. I didn't see Patrick IV until he showed up for his grandmother's funeral. Loretta had always favored Patrick IV despite realizing he was gay at an early age. I remember joking with Patrick IV and his friend Roger when they attended the funeral. They were two good kids and seemed happy. They were happy and that was all that counted.

I looked at Mary and said,

"I haven't seen him since then."

"He's in Denver, great-granddad, Dad writes to him occasionally."

"It's a shame because Samantha and Ryan never had children and, well, Patrick ain't going to have any." Mary looked at me and said,

"Great-granddad, Dad says that they tried to adopt and they were turned down in the 1980's when gay couples found it almost impossible to adopt kids. Now that adoption agencies accept that, they figured that they are too old. They are both in their fifties now"

"Oh, I didn't know that. Yeah, being fifty and having a baby could be a problem. But they can do that now?" I asked. They both nodded.

I thought to myself how things had changed. I thought some more about what she had told me and figured it was for the better. I wondered to myself what the Cardinal's views were on that subject. I made a note, if I ever saw him again and had time to have a personal conversation with him; I'd ask what his views were on gay couples. I knew the church's position, but I wondered what my grandson thought.

"I guess we can call it a day, Liam," Dennis said.

I looked at the clock on the wall and said,

"If you two don't mind, and you don't have anything important to do in the next hour or so, would you mind sticking around?"

Both kids just smiled and Mary said,

"As long as we stop at five o'clock so that you won't miss dinner. What's going through your mind great-granddad?"

"I was thinking about Harriet Weis," I said.

"Who?" Mary exclaimed.

350

"Sorry honey. I'm talking about Dennis's great-grandmother," I said and looked at Dennis.

"You know, Joe Cohen's wife, my Maria's best friend."

Dennis smiled as he moved the recorder closer to me.

"Harriet died last year and I was unable to attend the funeral for several reasons. One, I was having those headaches that almost killed me. Eventually, when I had the stroke, no one would tell me until many weeks later that she had died. I guess like all old people, once you get into assisted living or a full convalescent home, they forget to tell you things like that." I stopped and looked at both of them.

"Everyone feels that it is in your best interest not to inform you of things like that because it might upset you or worse yet, cause you to get sick and die. Well, sometimes they should stop and think that old people are more mature and can accept events like that. We have seen more of it than any of you have." Both kids just listened.

"Harriet died a peaceful death I was informed a few months later when Danny Jr. stopped by to see me after I had the stroke." I looked at Dennis,

"He went to the funeral your father arranged for your great-grandmother, Dennis. I haven't seen your father Joe in many years. I hope you tell him what we have been doing here." Dennis replied and said,

"Liam, he is looking forward to seeing you soon. We are planning a little get together in a few weeks so that my family and Mary's can meet and get to know each other before the wedding. We call it a Jack and Jill Party and you will be there to meet and see everyone that comes."

I sat back and contemplated what he had just said and responded,

"A Jack and Jill Party? That sounds much better than a stag or bridal shower." Dennis laughed and pointed out,

"Well Liam, we are still going to have both, but we'll use the

Jack and Jill to have everyone meet and get over any inhibitions they might have because I am Jewish and Mary is Roman Catholic."

"Good, you kids are smarter than I gave you credit for," I said and continued.

The Story

Harriet lived a good life. She was one I should have taken lessons on how to die gracefully. She had all her faculties at one hundred and three and uttered Joe Cohen's name when she expired, I was told. I often thought I should have married that woman after Joe and Maria were both gone. Even though we would have been an ancient couple, we could have been good company for each other. We sure had a lot in common. We had babies together, lost sons together, kept the same friends for many years and we loved each other and the mates we were married to. I know when Danny, Jr. told me that she had died it upset me greatly.

The Living Center

I looked at both of them and said,
"The friggen stroke should have done me in. It didn't and here I am talking about that beautiful woman, my best friend's wife, dying."
Nobody said a word as I vented until Mary spoke up,
"Maybe we should stop now?"
"No, I need to talk about this."
I remained silent for a few moments.
"I think of how she cared for Joe while he laid in bed for five or six months after he stroked back in 1994. I went to see him and all he could do was stare into space like I had a few months ago. I could never converse with him once he had the stroke

and I remember sitting with Harriet next to his bed and just talking for hours about the events that we shared over the many years we had been friends. We both hoped that it would bring him back to us, but all he did was stare out with no expression on his face. It was horrible for both of us to watch him just lay there. We laughed and told funny stories so that he would maybe react and indicate that he was still in that shell somewhere as he lay there expressionless. Nothing changed in the five months that we sat next to him daily. Well, Harriet went daily; I came several times a week because I couldn't stand it every day. Plus, Lenny complained that my driving wasn't that good by that time and he kept me from going as much as I wanted."

I felt better getting my feelings out in the open.

The Story

Joe closed his eyes forever one night a few hours after I had left him and Harriet.

She was with him to the end. She was a very dignified woman, but she wept uncontrollably when I arrived at the cemetery in my Navy Chief Dress Blues. I did it in tribute to my best and lifelong friend, fellow Sea Bee and business partner for over seventy years. I held her and apologized for wearing my uniform that hung on me, but she couldn't have thanked me more for the tribute I paid to her husband and my best friend. When the Navy Commander handed Harriet the folded American Flag and told her that on behalf of the President of the United States for Joe's faithful service to his country in two wars, she accepted it and then turned to me and handed the flag for me to hold. I held it for a brief moment and handed it to his son Alex.

The Living Center

I looked at Dennis and said,
"Your great-grandfather."
Dennis remarked,
"Yes, I remember. I was fourteen when my great-grandfather died. I remember now that you were the old man in the Navy uniform."

The Story

Needless to say, I could barely keep my composure, but I did. I held one of her arms while Alex held the other as they lowered his coffin into the ground. I remembered that as the sun began to set in the west, the light from the red ball reflected off some of the headstones. One flat stone that caught my eye was the one that read, Aaron Cohen, Private First Class, US Army, 1925-1944, WW II. I thought then, Joe Cohen has finally met up with his youngest son. I felt at peace when I left the Maplewood Cemetery. I relayed my experience to Harriet just before she entered the car to take her away. She just smiled, nodded, squeezed my hand and turned to enter the car with Alex. I never saw him again and only just heard that he died.

The Living Center

I looked at Dennis and said,
"I guess you informed me." He smiled and nodded.
I looked at the kids somberly, got up, and headed for the dining room. I never said a word until I reached the door on my way out and turned and struggled to say,
"We'll pick this up tomorrow. I love you both."

Chapter Seventeen – Jack and Jill Party

The Living Center

We continued on meeting every day for the next several weeks until I finished filling in the two kids on every detail I could remember. Dennis had me going back and forth though the years trying to fill in as many blank areas or those that needed more explanation. It was good for me. He was able to pull out of me the things that I missed or actually forgot about the relatives and friends I had described to him since we started this story. It was good because he made a story board every night when he went home and eventually bought it to my living center for my review when we were close to the finish. It was a great tool because it allowed me to organize my thoughts even better and inspired me to mention tidbits of facts that he made me expound on to further enhance the story. The kid was good at it and I couldn't wait to read what Mary and he would eventually put together.

Once we got the storyboard in relatively good shape, we met every day for afternoon sessions where we concentrated on those missing people's stories. I remember a few days before the Jack and Jill Party we concentrated on one area that needed detailing. Dennis left the storyboard in my living room on many nights so that I could look at it and jot down notes on things, places, people and events that came to my mind. The next day, I would present them to Mary and Dennis only to be shown that I had already mentioned it, gone into more detail than they wanted or needed, or it was insufficient information that really didn't add to the family story in their opinion. As on previous days, they came just after lunch and always caught me napping as I waited for them.

"Okay sleepyhead, it's time to awaken," Mary said.

It was almost regularly said to me every day. I was happy she woke me because I was embarrassed that I probably drooled onto myself as I usually did. I was also thankful she always had a damp face cloth available for me to use. I was ready now and we began. One area that I realized I had forgotten to talk about was Danny and Lilly.

The Story

Danny and Lilly did the damndest thing. They separated after being married for forty years. We think it centered on Danny, Jr. and his marriage to Christina. Things seemed normal until their grandson; Christopher began to have convulsions when he was about three years old. Eventually, by the time Christopher was six years old, the specialists that Danny, Jr. and Christina brought Christopher to eventually made a diagnosis of Autism. Danny and Lilly could not accept that their grandson would need special attention and care. Danny, Jr. and Christina were devastated, but coped with the problem and made progress at understanding the affliction and helping Christopher make great strides in overcoming some of the conditions he had. He eventually finished high school and was only several years behind the kids his age.

I personally think that Danny could not cope with the fact that his grandson would not be a pharmacist and take over the Family Pharmacy from his father like Danny, Jr. had done when Danny retired in his sixties. Danny always inferred that his son and daughter-in-law were not doing enough to get Christopher the care he needed to overcome his handicap. Lilly, on the other hand, supported her son and his wife in everything they did. It eventually boiled up to some heated

356

arguments between Danny and Danny, Jr. in which Lilly sided with her son and his wife. One day Danny came home and found Lilly's personal items and clothes were gone. She had moved in with her son, daughter-in-law and grandson. There was never mention of any divorce, but they were separated until the day Danny died in 1988 when Christopher was eight years old. Lilly stayed with her son and family and spent twelve more years helping them with raising Christopher until she died at ninety years old.

The Living Center

"I believe that Lilly was very influential in making life more normal for Danny, Jr. and Christina while raising Christopher," I said.
I was about to move on to other areas I had made notes on when Mary said,
"We invited Christopher to the Jack and Jill Party, great-granddad. He lives by himself in Hartford. I understand that he has become quite an artist and some of his work is getting some attention in New York and Boston."

I smiled when I heard what she had told me.
"I'm happy to hear that and I am even happier that I will be able to see the young man when we have the party. Will his parents be there?" I asked.
She nodded and we continued on to the other areas I needed to be able to cross off my note pad. I read off Andrew Cohen's name and was about to give some details when Dennis stopped me.
"Liam, great Uncle Aaron died last month while vacationing in Spain with my great Aunt Candice. His funeral was several days later. I did not have the heart to tell you because I know it would have upset you and postponed the story. I am sorry. I

guess I was selfish."

I stopped and contemplated what he had just informed me of
and said,
"My God. How did it happen?"
"Rabbi Aaron said to Dad that his heart gave out. I guess that
the heat he experienced in Spain was too much and it affected
him,"
Dennis said and kept his head down as if I was going to be
upset with him for not telling me. I shook my head and only
remarked,
"Is his wife, Candice, doing alright?" Dennis took a few more
moments and began to give some details of the funeral when I
stopped him and asked,
"Was he given a military funeral?" Dennis looked at me
perplexed and then regained his thoughts and said,
"No Liam, he did not want a military funeral according to
Rabbi Aaron."
I explained that Andrew had been a mechanic fixing aircraft in
Europe during the war when Dennis stopped me mid-sentence.
"Liam, his will was specific and his wife fulfilled it exactly as
he wanted it to be."
He knew I was perplexed and he further explained and said,
"Andrew felt that the true warriors and veterans in his family
were his brothers Aaron who was killed in Europe and Alex
who was the decorated and POW pilot and his father who
fought in two wars. He just wanted it that way."
I sat and let all that he had said sink in.
"I have one last question. Have they marked his grave with a
veteran marker?" I asked. Dennis nodded and assured me that
there was.

I was about to commence going over my notes when Mary
interrupted me and said, "Great-granddad, I have something to
tell you too."

The look on her face indicated that someone else had died.

"Okay, now you're going to tell me that somebody else has died. I can see it in your face. Who died?" She hesitated.

"Last night, great Aunt Christine died in her sleep at the rest home she had been in for the last few years. Michael called me and wanted me to tell you that he and his father wanted you to know right away. The arrangements are being made and they both want you to attend the services."

I was numb, but I was relieved. I didn't want the kids to think I was a monster of some type, but I was relieved that my beautiful little daughter was the way I envisioned her again in my memories. Not the fetal positioned old woman that could not recognize any of her family or even remember who she was. Deep in my soul I was thanking God that he had sent her to see Maria, Larry and Lenny. I regained my composure and looked at the two of them sitting with me with very concerned looks on their faces,

"Will you take me to the funeral?" I asked. They nodded in unison.

"Will there be a wake?" I asked. Mary moved her head negatively without saying a word. I was about to ask why when Dennis, sensing my next question said,

"It is a closed casket, Liam. It's the way Randy and Michael wanted it."

I thought about it and remembered that she did not look good when Mary had taken me to see her and she didn't recognized either of us. Alzheimer's was a terrible affliction for anyone to endure and I reasoned that the husband and son wanted everyone to remember her the way she had been before the sickness.

God, I thought, *I should have been dead long before my wife and children were gone.*

I searched my soul as to why my Maker had tortured me to

359

have to witness all my loved ones die before me. Was I being punished for something I did that upset my God and he relished his ability to punish me in my hell on Earth? I could hear voices in my head, but I ignored them.

My Christ in heaven, was it the revenge of that young blue eyed German soldier that I killed with my bayonet in France? I thought.

I could see his eyes staring into the lightning as the rain poured down on us.

Was it the sin for the orders I gave my bulldozer operators to cover the bodies of all those Japanese soldiers we buried? Could it be all those souls had gathered together to make my life a hell in my old age? Why was I still alive?

I realized that there were several attendants around me as Mary and Dennis stood by looking horrified. I came to my senses and looked at them and heard Daisy say,

"Liam, talk to me. Come on, talk to me."

I must have scared the hell out of all of them, but I didn't know what I had done.

"I'm talking Daisy, I'm talking. I'm fine. I can hear everyone. I know where I am. I was just upset. I'm fine. Please leave me. I will be fine."

I jerked my arm away from one of the technicians who was trying to take my blood pressure. I repeated myself.

"I'm fine. Let me be."

Daisy spoke up and said,

"We need to calm you down so that we can see if we need to medicate you. We don't want you getting sick on us."

I had to laugh and couldn't hold it in.

"For God's sake woman, my daughter just died, I'm older than dirt and you are worried that I might get sick. All of you get out now before you make me sick."

Everyone backed away. Daisy was about to start her calming

speech when I looked at her with the look she always said I had when I looked really mad. She backed off and told the others to follow her out. Dennis and Mary began to leave when I asked again, "Please make sure you come by for me when all the arrangements have been made. I want to attend her funeral."

They both nodded and left.

I stayed in my living room and thought about my little girl. I wondered where the dollhouse went that Maria and I had Joe Cohen make many years ago. I made a mental note to ask Randy and Michael if they knew. Daisy came into my living room with some tea and a sandwich.

"I thought that maybe you should eat something, okay? I am very sorry about Christine." "Thank you," I whispered.

I was going to apologize for my act when she said,

"Just eat, okay, just eat."

I took a bite without realizing that she had made me a thick roast beef sandwich with some melted cheese with plenty of pepper. I smiled and said,

"You know how to take care of a man, don't you Daisy." She smiled and said,

"Yes, especially a crazy old one like you."

I had many thoughts about Christine and my boys while I ate. I thought about the happy times that there were in the 1920's and 30's. It all changed in the next decade when the war came. But then there were good years when we went back to school, started our business and awaited our grandchildren's arrival. The empty feeling that always hung around, especially on holidays and special events, when Ma and Pa were gone was replaced by those new arrivals. I also thought about how simple life was then and I longed to go back to it. I got the coldest feeling. I realized that I was all alone. There was no one left until I forced myself out of my pity party as Joe Cohen

361

use to call it and realized that I couldn't blame myself for living more than anyone in my immediate family had. God only knows why He had kept me alive all these years. Mary informed the staff that they would pick me up in the morning to attend the funeral.

I looked at the clock on the wall. It was 2:43 a.m. I was wide awake and in nine hours or so, I would be standing in the cemetery as we paid our last respects to my daughter. I tried to get some sleep. I must have succeeded because I was awakened at 7:00 a.m. by one of the attendants that Daisy had instructed to wake me and help me prepare for the funeral. Mary and Dennis picked me up in an unfamiliar sedan. As I slowly walked to the car I recognized that Billy was behind the wheel. He smiled and waved as I got closer. He rolled down the window and said,

"Hi great-granddad, I'm your chauffer today."

I smiled and slowly got into the sedan with Dennis's help. Once I was seated and buckled in, I remarked to him,

"How long has it been son?"

"Since 2003 great-granddad when I went off to college. I finished several months ago. I graduated from UCONN, just like you. I'm going to UCONN Med in the fall."

"Why didn't you tell me Mary?" I asked as I turned to her sitting in the rear passenger seat.

"Great-granddad, you were sick and just getting back on your feet and it just slipped our minds about Billy's graduation and acceptance to medical school."

I just shook my head in disbelief that it was just another thing that they had failed to tell me about my great-grandson. We drove to the cathedral and attended the funeral mass. I hadn't been to the cathedral since Lenny's funeral. Now, I was going again to attend Christine's. We arrived and some young boy came to the side of the car and opened the door for me. He had

362

a wheelchair waiting. That's how I entered St. Patrick's. I didn't argue because I did not want to have the embarrassment of falling or doing anything else that would embarrass me or my family. I didn't remember anything except for when my youngest great-granddaughter Christine ascended the podium to eulogize her grandmother and namesake.

She said all the right things and delivered the eulogy almost as well as Father Donald would have if he had been there. She was amazing and only seventeen years old. My mind wondered all during the eulogy until little Christine kissed me on the cheek as she passed me sitting in the front pew of the cathedral. I came back to reality when she did that. The cemetery ceremony and the funeral reception at Dick and Linda's house were respectful and traditional. I didn't say much because most people quickly gave me their condolences and moved on for more detailed conversations with Randy, Michael and his wife Nicole and praised Christine for her eulogy of her grandmother.

Nicole actually spent some time with me. I thought at first that maybe she just felt sorry for me sitting there all alone sipping on a brandy that Michael had given me, but then I thought that maybe she felt uncomfortable receiving all of Michael and Randy's friends and relatives. We spent some quality time together during the funeral reception and I was happy that she spent that time with me so that I could get to know her better. I complemented her that she and Michael had done a great job raising Christine who would be entering Boston College in the fall. I was informed that she was leaning towards teaching, but hadn't made up her mind as to what age level of teaching she would pursue. I didn't know Christine very well, but maybe in time I would get the chance to spend some time with her. Then I realized that would never happen. She was probably way too busy and I hadn't spent time with her parents, so why would she ever even consider spending time with me.

As I looked around the room while Nicole and I conversed, a few of the great- grandchildren approached me. In most cases they had to introduce themselves because I didn't recognize who they were. I managed to get a few correct, but most of the time I had to ask who their parents were or what was their last name. I'm sure they thought I was this doddering old man who had lived passed his usefulness. I was smart enough though not to embarrass myself when one of Joey's twins, Anthony, introduced me to his daughters Kimberly and Crystal. They were spitting images of their mother Dorothy. We talked for a little while. I asked him what ever happened to the Groton Long Point Cottage. He explained that his sister-in-law was presently living there while his brother and she worked out their problems. Anthony's brother, Allen, was the next to come by and sit a spell. I had learned through his twin that he was separated, but he told me himself that he was. He then introduced his son Carmine. The kid was only fourteen and a freshman at New London High School, but he looked like a linebacker for Notre Dame. I think the boy was fascinated that he could look at a relative that was almost one hundred and seven years old. I never asked to see the cottage. That would have to wait until they settled their differences or she got it in the divorce settlement, I pondered while he talked to me. I also wondered what Tony and Rose would think about that if they were alive. When he excused himself and his son, I thought about all the fun we had at the cottage during the fifties and sixties. Rose and Tony put on some good clam bakes and parties in those days.

Billy came over after I had finished talking with Allen and Carmine and asked if I needed anything. I asked,
"Take me to the men's room if you don't mind." He looked a

little confused and then I realized that he probably thought he was going to have to change my diaper or something.

"Billy, I can pee on my own so don't worry. Get the thought of you having to assist in some embarrassing task with some old man out of your head."

"Oh, sure great-granddad, I'll show you where it is. Do you want me to push you over there?"

I nodded. I figured it was best to stay in the chair and not cause any scene if I tripped or peed myself. I returned after I had finished my business, but quickly lost Billy to the bar. I wheeled myself over there and asked him to get me a gin and tonic. I returned to my table and was approached by Danny, Jr. and Christina.

I recognized him right away, but Christina had aged considerably since I had seen her several years ago. With them was Christopher. The twenty-seven year old was a handsome young man. We were introduced, and he seemed polite, but a little distant. I ignored it knowing what they had gone through with him in his early childhood. It looked like they had made considerable progress with him. I was informed that his art was to be shown in an exhibit in Hartford in a few months. His parents were thrilled and continued to give me details of the art he had completed and even sold in the region.

"Christopher, what do you like to paint?" It was the first time he actually looked at me. He paused for a few moments. It was long enough for Christina to intercede, but I cut her off with a wave of my hand. I waited.

"Well great Uncle Liam, I like to paint landscapes with lots of light and colors in them. I like everything bright." I smiled and said,

"Would you paint me a landscape?"

He looked away and I thought that maybe I had either offended him or had done something to turn him away when he turned back and looked directly at me and said, "Would you like a seashore painting? Not a New England one, but a tropical island. They are bright and colorful."

"Sure, I was on islands like that during the war and they were very picturesque. I'd like that."

He just nodded and walked away while his parents were about to make excuses for him when I motioned that it was okay and told them that he was a very handsome and bright young man. I also told them I looked forward to getting that painting.

It started to get late in the afternoon and I asked Billy to drive me back to the assisted living center. As I was about to leave, I was approached by Patrick Sullivan, IV and his friend Roger Stuart. They were tanned and in fine shape for men in their early fifties. Patrick looked generally happy to see me and Roger was quiet and polite. We talked only for a few minutes where they both relayed their condolences. I never did get any further information from them as to what they had been doing since I last saw either of them at his grandmother's funeral. If Loretta had been alive today I wondered if she would have liked how he had turned out. Now Kippy, his grandfather, would have been a different story. I smiled thinking about Kippy. I calculated his death year in my head. He had been dead fifty-four years. I shook both men's hand and excused myself with Billy in tow.

On our way out, Dick called out to his son and said, "Take good care of Gramps and be careful driving." Billy smiled and continued to push me outside in the wheelchair. I looked back at him as he pushed and said, "What did he mean by saying that dumb ass remark? You're just driving me home. I've taken care of myself for twice as long as he has been on this earth. Billy, do you plan on crashing on the way to my place?" Billy laughed, "That's typical for my father. Don't pay any attention to it."

366

I thought the kid was right. It was just Dick acting concerned, but it was just bullshit. If he was really concerned he would have stayed around me and not ignored me most of the afternoon. I got in a bad mood again thinking that I should be dead now. I was just hanging on to be a nuisance to most of them here. I realized it was a pity party again and snapped out of it.

   I told Billy to stop pushing me in the wheelchair.
"Go back in there and get one of those brandy bottles and bring it out here."
Billy hesitated until I gave him the look. Several minutes later, we were driving to my place. I took a few swigs of the brandy. It warmed my stomach and eased me. Billy asked for a swig.
"Nope, you're driving. Keep your eyes on the road, son."
The brandy was a good idea because after I had eaten at the center, I took a few more swigs of the brandy and slept very peacefully. No dreams, no pee calls and no thoughts of what had occurred that day. The next morning was a little different. I hadn't had a headache due to alcohol abuse in thirty years. I did that morning. Daisy took care of me and by the early afternoon I was almost back to normal.

   Mary and Dennis came by and we went over some more details and talked about the funeral and the people that attended. I explained to them that despite the situation, it was nice to see the great grandchildren, double great nieces and nephews. We talked about the book and did some more review and updates to the story board. We also just talked and they informed me of their latest wedding plans including the upcoming Jack and Jill Party. I realized that it would be next week, so I decided that I was going to look my best and convinced them to take me to one of the men's stores I used to shop at for my suits and jackets. I gave them several names and they told me that they were nonexistent now. I ended up at a place called the Men's Warehouse. The description did not impress me until I actually was in the establishment in one of the new malls they brought me to. They fit me well and I was able to pick up a nice blue blazer and a gray summer suit with matching vest, a new white shirt with cufflink cuffs so I could wear my seventy-five year recognition American Legion cuff links that I had received a few years ago and had never worn. I was about to purchase a new hat when Dennis and Mary convinced me not to. They explained that I would never need it. I did purchase a new pair of cordovan oxfords and a belt to match. The kids didn't know it, but if I died tomorrow, I would have a pretty good set of clothes to be buried in. At least I'd know that I was going to look good in the blazer and gray suit pants for the party and the whole suit when the wedding came. If I died anywhere in between or after, the suit was ready. I'd make sure to leave a note in my dresser drawer that I wanted to be buried in this suit. I felt pleased.

The day of the Jack and Jill Party came. I was up, dressed in my blazer and gray pants, a nice robin's egg short sleeve shirt and a bright red and blue striped tie. I sat and waited for a while and then realized it would be mid-afternoon before anyone came to pick me up. I removed the shirt and tie and laid the blazer over the chair in the living room. I knew I was beginning to slip a little. I realized I did get confused at times, especially if I was stressing a little. I guessed it was because I was going to see friends and family, some I hadn't seen in years. Daisy came by and commented on the clothes and how good I smelled. I had also purchased some cologne that Mary had picked out for me. Noon came and went. I ate a salad that Daisy had prepared. I waited until almost two o'clock and started to slowly dress in my shirt and had just tied the knot for my tie when Billy's sedan came into sight outside my window. Someone did remember me.

368

The Jack and Jill Party was to be held at the Wauregan Hotel in downtown Norwich. I hadn't been in the establishment since the mid-sixties. They had done a wonderful job renovating the building and it looked much like it did when Maria and I had thought about staying there in our early courting days. The banquet hall door opened and the place was pretty full. Billy explained that there were some two hundred family and friends present to honor Mary and Dennis. The couple immediately came over and welcomed me. They then escorted me to one of the tables very close to where they had been sitting. The first person to approach me was Father Donald. I didn't notice him at first because he was dressed in his black priest's suit and Roman Collar. The only thing that distinguished him was his cardinal cap and rope sash he wore. He looked great and came to me and we hugged. I held him a little longer that he expected, but he succumbed to my grip because he knew it was very emotional for me seeing him and just adjusting to my daughter's death. I composed myself and he sat and we began to talk.

"How have you been?" he said. Before I could answer,
"You look well. You still look fit. Do you like it at the convalescent home? Do they feed you well?"
He was about to ask another question when I said,
"Christ Donald, let me get in a word edgewise would you."
It startled him for a brief moment and then he laughed. I could see by the reaction of some of the people that were in hearing range that their eyes widened and they stiffened a little by my tone and selection of words while talking to the Cardinal. I guess his reaction even made them more perplexed.
"You haven't changed Gramps. You're still a feisty old bastard, aren't you?" He moved close to me and kissed me on the cheek.
"I'm fine, they treat me well. It's an assisted living center and I like it okay. I'd rather be at my own home, but that was sold a

long time ago as you know. If I was living at home I would be alone and I don't like being alone."

"I'm sorry about Aunt Christine. I have just been talking to Uncle Randy about it," he said. I looked him in the eyes and said,
"He probably told you that it was the best thing, right?"
The cardinal knew I was pulling him into a trap because he knew I did not like the way my daughter had been put in a home earlier than she needed to be because Randy said he could not handle her.
"What I mean is that she is with Christ now, Gramps. That's better isn't it?"
I trapped him again,
"Your Eminence, you are talking with me now. I would rather have Christine, Lenny, Larry and my Maria with me than having them with Christ. Remember the saying Pa used to say? Oh, no you couldn't have. You weren't born yet when he died. But he used to say, when you are dead, you are dead."
"I did not come over here to upset you Gramps," he said.
"Okay, let's start again. First, I am your grandfather so call me that or Granddad like everyone else does. You and Dick are the only two that call me Gramps."

"Okay, Granddad I apologize if that has always annoyed you," he said. It looked like I had hurt him the way he answered and the tone of his voice.
"Apology accepted. But I'm still pissed at you for not being around very much. The only time I see you are for damned funerals."
He was about to smile, but respected my mood and said,
"Look, I'm here now for this party and I will be officiating with Dennis's cousin, Rabbi Aaron Cohen during the ceremony."
He smiled and waited for my response.

370

"Do you have any problems with her marrying a Jewish boy?"
He smiled and looked me straight in the eye and said,
"Not one iota. Someone else might, but not me."
"Good. They haven't corrupted your common sense. I am now very happy to see you." He laughed and then hugged me again.

"I understand that you have been working with the two of them and cataloging all the people and stories of our family. That's wonderful. I can't wait to read the book when it is published," he said and smiled.
"I'm hoping that they write it as me telling it. I asked them not to write it in the third person. I want the reader to know what I thought about what happened and not someone else's interpretation," I said.
"That's what Mary and Dennis said when I was talking to them. They wanted your personal experiences told by how you saw and experienced them," he said and I was sure he was sincere.
"Good, I'm pleased to hear that coming from you. They have said this to me regularly. I figured that if the All Mighty had been cruel enough to keep me on this earth for over a hundred years then he can make sure people read what I really said. That's the least He can do for me."

The cardinal only smiled and nodded,
"Granddad, I know He has a special place for you with him. I truly believe that," he said and put his hand on my shoulder.
"Good. He owes it to me big time for leaving me alone these many years," I said and was about to say more when he stopped me.
"Granddad, He has his reasons and you must try to accept them. Look what He has done."
I looked at him a little confused.
"He has brought you together with your great-granddaughter and her fiancé to tell your story, your family's story, to as

many people that the book will reach about family values, the family nucleus that all religions strive to reinforce to their members, good times and bad times and how a family, and especially you, dealt with them. It's a guide that no clergyman or clergywoman could possible tell anyone about unless they personally experienced it."

Neither of us said a word for a few moments until he spoke again.

"Your book will be used by me long after you are gone as a guide for a lot of lost souls who hate God or members of their family for events that happened in their lives. I have read a few chapters Mary has sent to me to critique for any suggestions and things of that nature. I have only read the first few that they sent and I can assure you, I have not made any suggestions. It's a wonderful start to a great book."

I didn't answer him because he had one up on me. He had read excerpts from a few chapters. I looked at him and said,

"Thank you. I hope that it does what you have just described."

"I'm sure that it will. You'll see that when you read it. You will be very proud of it and know that it will entertain and influence many readers," he said.

"Now, let us enjoy this day. There is someone I want you to meet. I'll be right back."

While he was fetching the individual he wanted me to meet, I thought about what he had said and described on how the book would influence many readers. I never even considered that the book would do something like that. My intent was to inform the family members of their heritage. I felt very good inside. I hoped that Donald was right. I realized that I had no reason to believe that he wasn't. He approached me with a middle aged gentleman in tow.

"Liam Corcoran, I would like you to meet Rabbi Aaron Cohen. The Rabbi will be officiating with me during the wedding.

Rabbi, this is my grandfather Liam Corcoran." We shook hands and the Rabbi spoke first.

"I remember you Mr. Corcoran. My father was Andrew Cohen. He worked with you and my grandfather in Corcoran-Cohen."

I realized that he was referring to Andrew and then I remembered that he had recently died. I was unable to remember whether I attended the funeral or not. I didn't want to embarrass myself. I did remember that his mother Candice was alive and said,

"Your mother is well?"

"Yes, she is, but she has recently undergone hip surgery and she is convalescing presently. She just started walking. Her physician says her recovery is on schedule. I hope to have her attend the wedding next month."

I responded with just a look of concern, but did manage to say,

"I look forward to seeing her at the wedding."

"Rabbi, I remember your entire family very well. They were a good family."

I stopped and restated myself,

"They are still a good family. It is nice to see you again and it is a wonderful event that will take place soon when Dennis and Mary unite in marriage. Our families were very close, but over the years, they had drifted apart for many reasons. But now they will be united again in an even stronger bond. Marriage has replaced friendship."

I guess I really impressed the Rabbi because he looked at the Cardinal a little surprised that this wrinkled up old man could still talk and a make reasonably good sense. The three of us talked for quiet awhile until we all needed to concentrate on the two people we had all come together to congratulate.

When the Rabbi was called away, I looked at Donald and said,

"The Cohens are a great family."

"Yes, and he has his wife and two sons with him today. They are a nice family. His kids are interesting. His oldest son, Mark, will complete rabbinical school soon and become a Rabbi. He's the tall one talking to Mary and Dennis right now. The other son, Ben, is finishing up grad school. Finance I think, but I don't see him right now. I'll point him out to you later,"

Donald said as he sipped on his glass of wine.

"That's one good thing about the Jews; their Rabbis marry, multiply and usually have kids that follow the faith. That's why they have lasted all these thousands of years. That's what you should have done, but your church forbids it.

"That's bullshit" I said, for the lack of another word.

I said it to drive home a point about one of the rules the Catholic Church needed to change in my opinion. The Cardinal didn't take the bait.

"Granddad, I'm sure that will change in the future of the church. That's only my opinion, but I have had that discussion at the highest levels within the church. Maybe not in your lifetime or even mine, but it will change."

I looked over at him and I could see in his eyes that he didn't want to further expound on the matter. I let it lie. I did manage to smile and just say,

"Good, I'm pleased to hear that. Now please be a good boy and fetch your grandfather one of those glasses of wine. Is it dry or sweet they are serving?"

"Here, taste mine," he said and handed me his glass. I sipped and remarked,

"That will be fine. It's has a nice taste. Nothing like Pa's, but a nice taste."

"You know granddad, I have a bottle of one of Pa's best. Did you know that?"

For some unknown reason my stomach turned because it took me by surprise. I looked at him and said,

"Really, where did you get that?"

"Dad gave one to each of us before he died. Apparently you or gram had given them to him when the big house was remodeled years ago and the wine cellar was turned into an apartment."

"Well you should drink it if it's still good. It was excellent wine as I remember. Any that I had I drank on special occasions," I remarked.

"I have a little secret. Dick is going to make a toast at the wedding with Pa's wine. He is going to ask you to open it and probably say a few words before the toast. I wanted you to know so you can be prepared. I know you don't like surprises."

I laughed out loud and said,

"You know; even after all these years you are still ratting on your older brother. Cardinal or not, you haven't changed." I laughed some more. He thought I was quite amusing and said,

"Yeah, but am I right or not? You don't like surprises."

I looked at him and continued to laugh and just shook my head that he was right. I finished my chuckle and said,

"Yes, unfortunately, you are right."

It was good being with Donald again and it was a great day.

Chapter Eighteen – The Wedding

The Living Center

Several weeks went by after we finished the book. I told Dennis that I knew that he had handed Donald some of the first chapters to read and comment on. At first he seemed uncomfortable, but I reassured him that the feedback I had received from the Cardinal was good. It relaxed the boy and Mary began to explain why they had presented a few chapters to him. I cut them short and explained that I wasn't interested, but just glad that he received the book very well. Then I asked, "When will I be able to read it, Dennis?"

He hesitated and said that he still needed to finish up with his agent and book cover illustrator and that the final editing of the book was at least a week away. I accepted all that he informed me of, but I asked again.

"Dennis, once it has been edited, I would like a copy before it is put into the press. I'm not going to change anything; I just want to read it as soon as possible for obvious reasons. Look at me. Do you understand what I'm saying?"

He smiled, looked at Mary and said,

"I will make sure you have a copy of the final before it goes into press. It won't have any of the pictures we have slated to be on certain pages, but you will have the final text. It's double spaced and will be very easy for you to read, okay?"

I thanked him. I changed the subject and asked,

"How long will you be on your honeymoon?"

"We are only going on a four day honeymoon, but we'll have it ready for you as soon as we return."

"How come you are having such a short honeymoon?" I asked.

"We plan to go to Ireland, Italy, Germany and Israel in the winter to do some research on the family ancestry for another book after this one is published and that will be our long honeymoon." He smiled at me and Mary.

"You know, you never told me what you were going to title the book, I said.

"Mary and I have decided to call it 'Liam's Story'. What do you think of that?"

I swallowed very hard and held my breath for longer than I needed to keep my composure. It took me a while to regain it. I whispered,

"That sounds very nice. Thank you." The couple looked at each other and smiled because they knew that the title pleased me. I joked a little once I regained my composure.

"What's the next one going to be called? How about calling it 'Before Liam' or something like that."

They both confessed that they had not thought about a title for the next book. They informed me that they did not have a title for this one until the Cardinal suggested it. I smiled and couldn't have been more pleased.

The wedding day finally came. Daisy woke me at seven o'clock.

"Good morning Liam. It's time to get up. I have something for you."

My eyes adjusted and I realized she had a package in her hands and she set it on the base of my bed.

"What's that?" I asked.

"Well, it came a few minutes ago by a currier. Based on the writing on the delivery truck I would say that it is a tuxedo," Daisy said and smiled.

"So get up, get washed and let's get you into this thing."

"I thought I was wearing my new suit," I said as my feet hung over the edge of the bed. "Well, I guess the kids have one up on you and they figured you are such a pain in the ass they just sent it to you to put on. You know and I know you would have complained about wearing it, right?"

I smiled thinking that the two of them had pulled one over on me.

It rained on and off in the morning up until Billy came to fetch me in his sedan. When he came into my living room, he remarked how dapper, I guess was his expression, I looked in my black tuxedo.

"It fits you very good. You look wonderful," he said and handed me a red rose boutonniere. I looked at him and said,

"You got to be kidding me. I could never attach these things properly. My wife would always have to do them for me."

Daisy came in and heard the end of the conversation.

"I'll do that. I haven't met a man yet that could attach one properly," she said and took it from Billy.

She affixed it and turned me around to look at myself in the living room mirror.

"I look pretty good for an old son-of a-…." I stopped and said, "Old man."

"That's better, and you look darling, Liam," she said and winked.

"Now aren't you glad I convinced you to wear the tuxedo that they sent over to you this morning?"

I didn't answer her, but only kissed her on her cheek and left in the wheelchair with Billy pushing me to the car. She remarked, "I guess that's a yes."

I never answered her because she was right. The tuxedo looked a lot nicer than the gray suit I had bought.

The rain had diminished to a sprinkle by the time we had gone a few miles.

"Too bad it's raining, great-granddad. I hope it doesn't ruin all that my sister and Dennis have planned,"

Billy rather loudly exclaimed while he drove in the mist.

"That's good luck, son," I said and noticed the perplexed look he gave me.

"Yes, just what I said. When it rains on a wedding day, it's good luck. It's an old wives' tale. Just go with it, Billy."

I explained that the love I saw between the two of them was enough to impress me that a hurricane could have happened and it would have not made a difference for them.

We reached my grandson's home and Billy assisted me out of the sedan. By the time we had reached the large tent that had been set up in Dick and Linda's back yard, the sun began to break through the clouds and it promised to be a good day. The garden flowers glistened from the morning's rain and the smell of freshly cut grass filled my nostrils. The hanging baskets of summer flowers lined the entrance to the tent. As Billy rolled me to the front of the tent, I noticed the opposite end had a raised platform just several yards outside of it. A white trellis had been placed there with red and white roses intertwined with the lattice work of the trellis. The green of the rose leaves accented the color scheme to perfection. Around the trellis were more baskets of roses. I could actually smell them from where I was sitting in the tent.

The guests were arriving quickly and I began to see many family members as they found their seats behind me. We smiled, nodded, briefly talked as the three piece string orchestra began to play classical music the couple had picked out for our enjoyment. Rabbi Aaron was the first to ascend the raised platform. He stood before the red and white roses in his white gown with blue stripping. He stood and faced everyone and awaited the cardinal. Donald ascended the platform and shook hands with the Rabbi. He was dressed in a plain white robe similar to the Rabbi's except for his red cap and red sash. He whispered something to the Rabbi that made him laugh, but otherwise, he stood and waited. Next to appear was the Justice

379

of the Peace which surprised me at first. I asked Billy what was with him being there. Billy explained that Dennis and Mary had thought carefully about the ceremony and did not want any Hebrew or Catholic symbolism in the wedding. They just wanted the blessing from the clergy of their faith. I thought that these kids were a lot smarter than I gave them credit for. I knew that if my stepfather was looking down on this marriage, he was laughing and was very pleased. 'God is the same in my church as he is in your church' was very apropos at this cerebration. I don't know what Ma, Maria, my sisters or Harriet Cohen would have thought about this wedding, but they had nothing to say about this one. I laughed to myself heartily inside. My big grin could have given it away as Billy and Dick commented about it. I just brushed it off that I was very happy because this was a very happy day. They both bought it.

Dennis appeared looking stunning in his tuxedo. He was the only one wearing a white jacket. His brother Joshua and cousins Mark and Ben all wore black tuxedos. Each one had a red rose boutonniere except Dennis who's was white. The kids had great taste as far as I was concerned. The bridesmaids began to slowly walk to the base of the steps leading to the raised platform. Each maid wore a different pastel color. The first was in yellow with a bouquet of red roses. The second was in light green holding a bouquet of white roses and the third was the bride's maid of honor in light blue holding a red rose bouquet. The three girls were friends of Mary's that she had gone to college with and had stayed close since those days. They were all beautiful in their gowns. I noticed that they had avoided a flower girl and a ring bearer as was traditional in our family for years, but then I realized that there were currently no children at the age that could have performed the function. It was a mute point. I enjoyed the ceremony and became a little emotional when both clergy blessed the couple in their traditional Hebrew and Latin. The Justice said it all when he pronounced them husband and wife.

We sat for a while as the wedding party posed for professional pictures and the guests mingled. Wine and mixed drinks were served, but I kept with soft drinks so that I could enjoy the wine toast and maybe a few more glasses of wine later after I had eaten before I began to feel the effects. My constitution wasn't like it used to be plus I needed my wits about me when the toast came. The wedding party began to seat themselves at the head table and I noticed Dick rise and go to a special table. He motioned for Billy to come to him. They both looked at me and I knew, and thanked Donald that I knew, they were coming for me.

"Great-granddad, could you please come over here," Billy asked.

I rose up very carefully from the wheelchair and walked to the table. Sure enough, there was a corked bottle of Pa's best.

Dick pointed and asked, "Do you know what this is?"

"Yes, I do. It's unmistakable to me," I said and looked at the bottle.

"Well, please open it. I want to toast the kids with it and I want you to sip some before we toast," he smiled and put his arm around me.

He helped me with the wine bottle opener and we succeeded in opening up the vintage spirits. We both took turns smelling the cork. It brought back many memories for me in an instant.

"Taste it," he said as he poured a little in the wine glass he handed me.

"Make sure it's still good, you know." I laughed.

"Sure," I took it to my nose and smelled and then tasted it. It was very good. I just looked at Dick and nodded. He poured me a little more and then I returned to my chair.

Dick waited until the waitresses had filled the glasses of the

381

guests with the wine that had been picked out by the kids to be served at the wedding. There was only enough of Pa's wine for Mary, Dennis, Dick and Linda, Dennis' parents Andrew and Martha, Donald, and Rabbi Aaron Cohen. Dick made the toast as requested by the bride and groom. After he had gotten the attention of the guests, he rose and explained the bottle that he had opened had a little bit of the history about it. He apologized for not having enough for all the guests to have a sip. I was sure they all understood. He went on to explain that this bottle was one of many that were consumed at past weddings and special occasions that were to celebrate or pay respect to family members. Some of the guests laughed when he emphasized consumed. He became very serious when he explained the ribbons that were tied around the many bottles for the family members that left for service to their country. He lowered his voice when he mentioned that some did not return. He smiled as he knew that one person who was here would be able to remember the winemaker who provided many a glass of his best for weddings just like this one many years ago. He continued and went on to thank the Rabbi and the Cardinal for their blessings. He joked and thanked the Justice for keeping things civil which brought laughter from the guests. He mentioned how proud he was to have Dennis as a son-in-law and reminded Mary that she would always be his little girl. He raised his glass in salute to the newly wedded couple. Everyone raised their glasses. While holding his glass, he turned to me and said,

"And to you Liam Corcoran, our patriarch, thank you for living all these years and guiding us with your wisdom, temper, kindness, selfishness and love for all these years. Salute."

I had happy tears as I sipped the wine. Its taste filtered through my taste buds and to my brain. Pa's wine was even better now that it had aged. Or maybe it was the emotions I was experiencing, but is tasted exceptional. We ate and ate some more. We toasted and toasted some more. They danced and I was even able to dance briefly with the bride. By the late afternoon it had become very muggy due to the temperature increase and the dampness of the morning rain. Breathing became a little harder and I was pretty well full and a little nippy. It was time to leave. Billy obliged and I excused myself and thanked my hosts. I wished the newlyweds a great four day honeymoon and looked forward to their return so that I could begin reading the book.

I pulled Dennis aside and said,
"Remember to like your wife," I said and winked. I turned to Mary and just told her that I loved her and was very happy for her. She kissed me and said,
"We'll see you as soon as we return and give you the editor's copy." I nodded and left. As Billy drove me home, I became exhausted, but the air conditioning in the car soothed me. I remember that I asked him to turn it up so that it would make it easier for me to breathe. He obliged. By the time I arrived at the assisted living center, my joints were stiff. I had a hell of a time getting out of the car.

Daisy, of course, was waiting and remarked,
"Liam Corcoran, are you drunk?"
"Awe, for heaven's sake Daisy, I'm stiff from the air conditioning in the car, that's all," I shot back a little irritated with her remark.
"Uh huh, uh huh, sure you are," she said.
As Billy took out the wheelchair from the trunk of his sedan, she helped me up to stand near the car until I could be seated. I thanked Billy and Daisy pushed me into the assisted living center and into my living room.

I was physically whipped and she assisted me in disrobing and getting into bed. She mumbled all the time while she was helping me. I could see that she was irritated that I had overdone it physically and she wasn't sure yet whether I was unsteady due to the exhausting day or too much spirits. I assured her it was the former. She really didn't believe me. I slept until the next morning. I had slept for thirteen hours. I did notice that I had developed a cold because I could feel it in my chest. It had to be the air conditioning in Billy's sedan. Donald came to visit for a short time and informed me that he was off to Chicago to meet at a Bishop's conference and then eventually back to Rome. I joked with him that I was happy that the U.S. Taxpayers were not paying for his air flights. I told him it was good that he worked for the Vatican. They had more money. He laughed and bid me farewell. He blessed me and hugged me. It had been good to see him. He commented to Daisy to make sure she kept an eye out on me to take care of myself and especially that summer cold that I had developed. He blessed her as he departed. I'm sure she appreciated it.

The next few days I became weaker as the cold settled into my chest. Daisy summoned the center's doctor who prescribed some decongestive cough medicine and gave her and me the usual spiel to drink plenty of fluids and rest. I did as I was told except when I went down to run the train set. It was difficult to do. I used the elevator, but I was too exhausted to stay, but ten minutes to run it. I returned and slept some more on that particular day. The kids showed up as promised with the book in hand. Mary had a worried look on her face when she came into my bedroom where I had laid for several days trying to fight this thing as I called it. She had to have been talking with Daisy before she came in. Daisy was always an alarmist.

I asked about the honeymoon and joked with Dennis if he still liked his new bride. He blushed, but I ignored picking up on his embarrassment when he just nodded. I just said, "That's good."

They handed me the editor's copy of Liam's Story. It was over a four-hundred page double spaced document, typed on eight by eleven inch paper.

"Wow, this is bigger than what I thought it would be. Well, I have the time to read it. I'll start once you leave."

We talked a little more until I could barely keep my eyes open because the cough medicine and other stuff Daisy had given me made me sleepy. The kids left, but promised to return in a few days after I had read several chapters of the book. I woke up around eleven at night. I was perspiring and I noticed that my chest was a little tight. I then realized that my heart was beating a little faster than normal. I suspected that the medicine had wired me up. I did notice I was a little weaker.

The night attendant came in. It was Daisy.

"Why are you still here, girl?" I asked.

"I needed the overtime and I got stuck with you to watch," she said nonchalantly.

"You know Daisy; you are full of what the birds eat. Are you worried about me?"

"A little bit. You need to fight this cold. I don't want it turning into pneumonia," she said and fluffed up my pillow.

"Do me a favor, will you, and grab that book over there," I asked.

She looked at me strangely and said,

"Liam Corcoran, its eleven o'clock at night. This thing looks more like a document than a book"

"It's the editor's document. The book will be much smaller."

"You need your rest you know."

"I know and I assure you this will put me to sleep. It's not that it is a bad book. It's that reading always makes me sleepy at night."

She handed it to me and remarked on its weight and thickness. She laughed when she read the title.

"Don't read too long. I'll check on you in a bit. You better be asleep."

She left smiling as I nodded and smiled back. The book was heavy. I opened up it up and read what Dennis and Mary had written about me. It was a nice tribute that they paid in acknowledgement of my contribution. I turned to the first chapter and began to read.

Chapter One – Remembering. The big house stood at the top of the hill for as long as anyone could remember. It was built by one of the founding city members who had long been deceased since the mid-eighteen hundreds. The present owners had bought it with all the money they saved in the first ten years they lived in this country. They managed to save the minimum down payment for the one hundred year old home that the local Dime Bank of Norwich required for a thirty year mortgage

I stopped reading and coughed several more times and could feel the congestion in my chest that caused a tightening. I figured I read just a little more.

Antonio and Josephine Cugini had lived in the house for twelve years when I first arrived there with my mother and sister just after St. Patrick's Day in 1914. It was a cold March day when we departed the train that had taken us from Quincy, Massachusetts. My sister asked my mother if the building in front of us was our new home. I remember my mother smiling and explaining that the large building in front of us looked like a bank to her.

"We'll just follow the instructions Mr. Cugini gave us in his letter to get to his house," she said.

As we climbed a slight hill from the train station, a horse drawn trolley car had just arrived. My sister asked if we could take the trolley to our new home.

"No Mary Beth, we will walk. I'm sure it isn't very far," my mother explained.

Mary Beth complained that her suitcase was too heavy. I remember mother took it away from her. As we started up a street that I would later know as Franklin, the wind picked up and an occasional snowflake could be seen blowing around. It was getting late in the afternoon as the gray sky hindered any sun from shining through and began to darken the day. We walked about a mile through the bone chilling wind and frozen streets of Norwich until we reached Boswell Avenue. The street was mostly hill at the beginning. The three of us trudged on, counting the house numbers as we climbed. What we eventually found was a majestic house with white clapboards and a large porch.

My mother, holding the letter she received from our new landlord several weeks earlier, knocked on the door. She glanced at it one more time assuring herself it stated that he had agreed to boarder us. The letter also stated that he agreed to take three months board in advance to stay there until she could find work and a place of her own.

I struggled to focus as the next sentence became blurry. I used my index finger to guide me. I concentrated to focus and read.

It had been three months since my father… … … … … … … … ….

"He got that far child,"
Daisy said and handed the book to Mary and pointed to where he had his index finger pointing to. Mary smiled through the stream of tears as she received the book and held it to her chest. Dennis consoled her as they looked at his slightly graying skin. "He looks at peace, honey," he said and hugged her from behind as she gently looked at her great-grandfather.
"Mary and Dennis, you two were the best thing for him in the last eighteen months of his life," Daisy remarked.

"You were too Daisy. Our family can never thank you enough," Mary said. Dennis only nodded.

Epilogue

The Cardinal flew back to Norwich and said the funeral Mass. Many clergy and spectators attended the high mass and funeral ceremony at the Cathedral of St. Patrick in honor of the cardinal's grandfather. Only a few tears were shed for the old man because not very many people knew him personally. The Cardinal gave a beautiful eulogy and tribute. But it only touched a few people. Only a few relatives knew Liam's story and felt the loss. One family friend cried steady tears, but laughed to herself thinking what Liam would have thought of all the pomp and ceremony. One of her remarks that Billy heard while he stood next to her was,

"Damn, if Liam saw all these Catholic clergy sitting here for his funeral he'd have something to say that would probably embarrass us all."

The funeral procession passed by the big house on its way up Boswell Avenue to St. Mary's Cemetery. Only a few family members could have identified the old house that hardly resembled the home that Liam had described. None did. No one paid any attention to any of the passing houses in the neighborhood. The trip to the Greenville section of Norwich and his final resting place in St. Mary's Cemetery next to his waiting wife only took five more minutes. It was an hour's walk up and back when Liam went to see the graves of his sister and mother back in 1914. When the immediate family assembled at the grave site, the Cardinal blessed it and said the traditional prayers. Within minutes, the brief religious ceremony was concluded. The rifle squad made up from both the Army and Navy fired a twenty-one gun salute. Taps were played and a Commander from the Sea Bees presented Dick with Liam's flag. He immediately turned and handed it to Mary. Mary and Dennis stayed until almost everyone had left.

Mary placed Liam's copy of his story on top of the coffin. The Cardinal saw her gently place it.

"He can finish reading it now," she said looking at Dennis.

"He won't have time, honey," the Cardinal said standing behind the two.

They turned in surprise in hearing his remark. He noticed their perplexed looks.

"He's with them all now. He doesn't need the story to read anymore, but we do. Keep it to remind you that he touched and read a part of it. Daisy told me he had it clutched in his hands when he passed."

He bent over and removed it from the top of the coffin and handed it back to her. They smiled at him and left. The Cardinal looked across to the Cugini cemetery plot and thought,

It's true. There are only bones here my grandmother use to say. He's in a better place now. He looked to heaven and said,

"My dear Lord, You know what You have in store now that he is with You."

He didn't know Daisy had heard him.

"Amen to that Your Eminence."

He smiled hearing her remark and then laughed inside and thought,

Maybe that's why it took you almost one hundred and seven years to take him.

The End

About the Author

Tommy Coletti is a U.S.A.F. Medic (1968-1972) of the Vietnam War. He used the G. I. Bill after his discharge to obtain a college degree in 1976 from Eastern Connecticut State University. He has been married for almost forty years and lives in the Town of Sprague in Southeastern Connecticut with his wife, Donna. Together, they raised four children. All are college graduates and have received advanced degrees. Tommy worked at the Electric Boat Shipyard for over thirty-five years until his recent retirement. He has two publications to date; Special Delivery and Dishonorably Interred. Both are available at HWPublishing.com, Amazon.com and Barnes and Noble.com and are electronically downloadable through Kindle.

Liam's Story is his third publication based on stories he remembered being told from his mother, in-laws and close family friends that he incorporated into Centenarian Liam Corcoran's life. His passion for literature continues as he releases this book to the public.

Tommy is in the process of completing another book of a much different genre than his three previous. A Journey to the Gallows– Aaron Dwight Stevens, has been co-written with Vic Butsch over the past year. Stevens was born in Lisbon, Connecticut and moved to Norwich, Connecticut when he was nine. This book is an historical fiction based on the very little known life history of John Brown's trusted lieutenant who followed him from the battles of Kansas and Missouri to the raid on Harper's Ferry.
An autumn 2012 release is planned.

www.ingramcontent.com/pod-product-compliance
Lightning Source LLC
Chambersburg PA
CBHW030804260626
47169CB00001B/183